THE LIBRARY OF NETHERLANDIC LITERATURE

Egbert Krispyn, General Editor

Offered by Twayne as part of its world literature coverage, *The Library of Netherlandic Literature* complements the critical studies of Netherlandic writers which appear in *Twayne's World Authors Series*. Both the critical evaluations and the translations are edited by Professor Egbert Krispyn of the University of Georgia.

The Library of Netherlandic Literature, devoted to the literature of Holland and Belgium, includes translations of some of the finest fiction, drama, memoirs, and essays produced by Dutch and Flemish writers. The program consists of first translations as well as reprints of out-of-print volumes and will include both classical and modern works.

The project is directed to meet the demands of teachers and students of Netherlandic literature in American and British colleges and universities, while serving the literary appetite of the general reader as well. Cooperating with Twayne, the Foundation for the Promotion of the Translation of Dutch Literary Works will nominate titles for translation and publication by Twayne.

The first works to be published in the series are an anthology representing the new voices in Netherlandic literature and Louis Paul Boon's 1953 novel *Chapel Road.*

Egbert Krispyn, currently Professor of German Literature at the University of Georgia, has both editorial experience and an extensive knowledge of Netherlandic studies.

The critical studies of Netherlandic writers contained in *Twayne's World Authors Series* include volumes on Erasmus, Jean LeClerc, Multatuli, Spinoza, Hendrik van Veldeke, and on the contemporary scene.

THE LIBRARY OF NETHERLANDIC LITERATURE

Volume 2

Modern Stories from Holland and Flanders

Edited by Egbert Krispyn

Modern Stories

from

HOLLAND AND FLANDERS

an

Anthology

Edited by Egbert Krispyn

TWAYNE PUBLISHERS, INC. - New York

THE LIBRARY OF NETHERLANDIC LITERATURE
published with the cooperation of the
Foundation for the Promotion of the Translation
of Dutch Literary Works

Egbert Krispyn, *Editor*

Volume 2

Modern Stories from Holland and Flanders
Edited by Egbert Krispyn

Table of Contents

INTRODUCTION

This collection of short prose pieces presents fourteen contemporary writers from Flanders and Holland, whose work gives a striking indication of the stylistic and thematic range of modern Netherlandic literature. Not included is the youngest generation of authors who are at the beginning of their careers, and often seek different modes of literary expression than those represented in this volume. Neither is there an example of the writing of Willem Frederik Hermans, who by generation and significance would certainly have merited inclusion. The reason for this regrettable omission is the author's refusal to give permission for the translation and publication of his work.

The large majority of the texts appearing here are by men in their forties and fifties, established figures in the world of letters, which derives its present tone and direction from their own early, often experimental efforts. These writers, who now dominate the literary scene, have, as a consequence of their age bracket, one experience in common. As children or young men they lived through the German occupation of their country during the second World War.

The invasion by the German military forces in the spring of 1939 introduced a period in which all normal life came more and more under the shadow of foreign domination and war. Raids and razzias, the deportation of Jews and antifascists, acts of terror and violence on the part of the occupying forces and local Nazis became as much a part of life as air raids and an ever worsening shortage of food, fuel, clothing, and all other amenities of civilized life. Many of these deprivations lasted until well after the end of the occupation, which in Flanders and the southern parts of Holland came with the liberation by allied forces in the fall of 1944 and in the rest of the Netherlands with the surrender of Germany in May, 1945.

The traumatic impressions of the war and postwar years have to a greater or lesser extent contributed to the creative stance of the now middle-aged generation of Netherlandic authors. Their preoccupation with these experiences is not infrequently reflected in the subject matter of their works, as in the story "The Decline and Fall of the

Boslowits Family" by Gerard K. van het Reve, which captures the atmosphere of the occupation years with uncanny accuracy.

But the influence of the wartime experiences also pervades much writing in which it does not manifest itself in thematic details. There are frequent allusions to it, as in Heere Heeresma's "From Your Evil Ways," which show that even after more than twenty years the memories of blackouts and raids are very much alive in the characters. Moreover, the impact of the writers' exposure to terror and want in their formative years is indirectly evident in a number of characteristic stylistic traits. The apocalyptic delusions of the youthful protagonist in "The Horses' Jump and the Fresh Sea" by Harry Mulisch provide the basis for a legend which symbolizes the irrevocable and total loss of past and tradition in the pseudomythology of the Isle of Schokland, now a part of the mainland.

The horror of the war appears to have destroyed the nostalgic feelings normally attached to one's infancy. Instead of being idealized as the individual's private paradisiac state on which he looks back with tenderness, childhood and youth are seen in their chronological coincidence with or proximity to the occupation period as filled with misery, ugliness, and violence. This motif assumes prominence in quite a number of the stories collected in this volume: "A Pause in the Thunder" (Jacques Hamelink), "A Hole in the Ceiling" (Anton Koolhaas), "The Horses' Jump and the Fresh Sea" (Harry Mulisch), "Decline and Fall of the Boslowits Family" (Gerard K. van het Reve) and "Minister in a Straw Hat" (Jan Wolkers).

Even where the experience of youth is clearly set in the postwar era, as in "A Trip to Zwolle" (Remco Campert), the atmosphere is one of unhappiness. The only text in which childhood regains some of its enchantment is "The Black Emperor" by Hugo Claus, but this seeming exception actually only corroborates the evidence of the other stories about the depressing quality of that phase of existence. The children live drab and unsatisfying lives, and this normal level of existence forms the sharply contrasting background for the wonderful, exotic figure of the black man with whom they strike up an acquaintanceship. Significantly, the figure who redeems their childhood by providing an element of wonder in their otherwise gloomy lives, mysteriously and inexplicably enters into their sphere from an unknown realm outside.

In other cases, the exotic world itself provides the setting for the narrative. Since the days of youth cannot provide the kind of positive, ideal object that might be juxtaposed with the dismal state of existence

in the contemporary overcrowded, inflation-ridden, tense, systemati-
cally uglified society, some authors are apt to exploit a scenery and
environment which still retain some primitive strength and grandeur.
Herman Vos situates "The Sons of Pepe Gimenez" in the desolate
Andes Mountains, "The Madonna with the Lump" (Ward Ruyslinck)
is set in the remote Italian countryside, and Jef Geeraerts' "Indian
Summer" evokes the majestic, practically uninhabited scenery of
northern Sweden. But the scenic splendor serves only to heighten the
stark horror of the human dramas which are enacted in it. Whether
accidental or caused by base passions of greed and jealousy, or insane
rage, suffering and death provide the main themes of these works.

This links these tales with their contemporary settings, not only with
those evoking the past in the form of childhood memories, but also
with a futuristic text like "The Day of the Dead God" by Jos Vandeloo.
In this story, a grotesque vision of the third World War and its mutual
annihilation is presented, with the ironical twist that the outbreak
of hostilities was due to the misinterpretation of an attempt to achieve
the opposite purpose of disarmament.

Instead of using temporal or spatial dimensions to locate and indi-
vidualize his protagonist, Hugo Raes in "Explosion" explores the
timeless and spaceless realm of the mind as he re-creates the oppressive, menacing atmosphere of a nightmare which foreshadows another
sudden and violent death. With this psychological orientation, the
author is within a very old and strong tradition in Netherlandic
literature.

Even in the one story in this collection that displays a rising curve of
vitality and serenity, Dirk de Witte's "A Blind Cat," everything that
happens is related to, and centered on the slow and humiliating death
of an old woman, and the theme of decay is continued in the figure of
the old man and his blind pet. Their option for life, in the final para-
graph, still places them in the service of the dead and is, in any case,
scarcely more than a last, brief flaring up of the flame of life, before
it is extinguished.

Yet, in spite of the all-pervading preoccupation with the more dismal aspects of human existence, these fourteen prose pieces are very
dissimilar. This is largely due to the variety of narrative styles and
techniques employed by the authors. Within the broad framework of
a realistic, concrete presentation of characters and action, the language ranges from concise statement to elaborate word-picture, from
understatement to rhetoric.

The most interesting structural device is that of the alienating commentary appended to Jef Geeraerts' "Indian Summer," which underneath its sarcastic surface is strangely defensive, and indirectly heightens the effectiveness of the tale itself.

The original language of the collected texts is Netherlandic, which as a West Germanic tongue occupies somewhat of an intermediate position between German and English. There are, of course, dialect differences between the various parts of the area where this language is spoken. These have been accentuated and crystallized by the political separation of Holland and Belgium, but essentially Dutch and Flemish are identical. In literature, except for some dialect authors, the differences between the two are further reduced by the normal desire to reach as much as possible of the potential reading public—which is small enough in any case.

The writers, and their publishers, have a natural tendency toward a generally intelligible, standardized mode of expression based on the common denominator of the major dialects. Nevertheless, in the original many of the texts owe a peculiar flavor to the specific speech patterns and habits of the authors' origins. Unfortunately, these shadings and overtones are next to impossible to preserve in translation. But within its inevitable limits, the collection offers an accurate and entertaining cross section of Netherlandic short prose written in the fifties and sixties.

Egbert Krispyn

REMCO CAMPERT

A *Trip to Zwolle*

WHEN Peter Gimberg was almost thirteen years old, he was allowed to go to Zwolle with his father for a day. It was the last week of the summer holidays. Peter Gimberg lived with his mother in The Hague. His father, who was divorced from his mother when Peter was six, stayed in Antwerp, and Peter seldom saw him. The excursion to Zwolle didn't appeal to him very much—he'd much rather have gone to Antwerp for a few days—but he couldn't easily refuse, not only because he was too young to refuse whatever was offered to him by an adult, but also because in the letter his father had written to his mother—which Peter had surreptitiously read—it was clear that Mr. Gimberg had high hopes of this excursion, and that he was laboring under the illusion that his generous invitation would set his son's heart joyously aglow.

There were indeed several attractive sides to the invitation. The most important was that they would be staying at a hotel and that would make Peter feel excitingly grown-up, especially since his mother wouldn't be there to reduce him to his proper status of a child with her gentle criticism. The shortness of the excursion also contributed to that idea of being grown-up; after all, grown-ups never have time to stay anywhere very long, their presence is required everywhere, and if they don't hurry everything will go wrong. His father, who was the sales manager in the Netherlands for a brand of Belgian beer and had to go to Zwolle on business, owned the newest model Studebaker, and because the majority of his friends' fathers had never got further than a simple Volkswagen, this was another item on the agenda which he was eagerly

1

looking forward to. His parents might be divorced, but his father lived abroad and drove around in a very expensive car, and sometimes went to Paris and sent Peter colored picture postcards of the Eiffel Tower or the Seine and sometimes of both.

He fervently hoped that he would not go unnoticed next to his father in the Studebaker. Chance, that conjurer whose spine-chilling agility sometimes leads us to lose sight of the fact that his main aim in life is to surprise and delight children, was kind, pulled a rabbit out of the hat especially for him by seeing to it that his friend, Wim Enkelaar, whose father had never risen higher than a motor bike, was standing at the corner of Laan van Meerdervoort, less than two yards from the pale pink Studebaker which, humming almost inaudibly, was waiting for the light to turn green.

Peter tapped on the window but Wim, stupid kid, didn't hear him. It was only at the very last moment—the traffic in the other street had already come to a standstill—that Wim turned to look at the Studebaker (ten rabbits out of the hat for Peter) and Peter observed with great satisfaction that Wim's face went through all the desired stages, that of nonrecognition, that of unbelief, and finally (the light turned green, the car whizzed off), that of envy. Once they had left The Hague and were out on the open road, the trip lost much of its fascination. Both father and son were uncomfortable with each other, and could not think of anything to say. The flat green landscape with its eternal cows, grazing on both sides of the road in clean-shaven meadows, soon bored Peter. The fact that other, less conspicuous cars kept passing them because his father drove so slowly and carefully, really bothered him, but he didn't dare mention it. He once tried enticing his father to go faster by asking him what the maximum speed of a Studebaker was, but it didn't get him anywhere, because his father answered, "Faster than is good for us." They ate the sandwiches and bananas that his mother had given them for the trip. They didn't see a single accident.

As they were nearing Apeldoorn, the sky turned gray and it started raining. "Too bad," said Mr. Gimberg, "there's a nice playground here, but there's no sense in going there now." That remark certainly didn't cheer Peter up, because it made it clear that his father considered him just as much of a child as his mother did. He turned on the radio to Hilversum One. Coincidence rubbed it in: a thin male voice sang a song called *You and Me on the Slides.*

Between Apeldoorn and Zwolle, near Epe, Mr. Gimberg suddenly braked and turned into a side road. "A surprise," he said. He wanted to show Peter the house where the Gimberg family— still young and, in spite of the trying times, happily united in the last year of the war, had been gladdened by the birth of a son, whom they called Peter. Just outside the village the tarmacked road turned to cobbles which presently, what a relief, made way for a soft and bumpy track of sand. The fir trees on either side receded in places and formed a picturesque but, because of the steady rain, somewhat melancholy background for what real estate agents call spacious villas, gloomy houses with a lower part in red brick and an upper story in dark brown stained wood.

They stopped in front of one of those houses. Peter's father opened his window and looked at the house. "Summer Delight," he said, and that was indeed the name that was painted in round white letters on a big gray boulder near the fence. "Summer Delight," Mr. Gimberg repeated, and there was something about the way he said it that made Peter feel lonely, as if he were lost and couldn't find anyone to show him the way.

This loneliness soon turned into a shyness so awful it almost blinded him. He and his father were standing in the living room of "Summer Delight"—the front door led straight into the living room—and they were face to face with a frightened girl, the most beautiful girl he had ever seen, even in the movies. She reminded him of the princesses in the fairy tales his mother used to read to him when he was a little child. In these books the princesses had always looked like annoying spoiled brats, but now that he was looking at one in the flesh he realized he'd been wrong. And even if he hadn't been wrong, even if she was annoying and spoiled (which hardly seemed possible), her faults were glossed over by her beauty, as the sun enhances prisons as well as playgrounds, alleys as well as garden cities with its golden light.

"Aren't your parents home?" he heard his father ask, and the girl, who was a little older than Peter (maybe a year), stepped back and said, "No, sir." We really aren't burglars or murderers, Peter wanted to tell her—but his tongue refused to form the words—while his father explained to the girl that he used to live in this house, years ago, and that Peter (who blushed furiously and, hating himself for it, stared at his feet) had been born there, in that small room upstairs at the front. They went upstairs. The girl followed them hesitantly and Peter, who walked behind his father, cursed the rule of etiquette that said it wasn't polite to let ladies go upstairs first, because he felt that, at any rate in this case, it would have been more polite to let the girl go first, because it was her house and because he and his father, even though they did have an excuse, were nevertheless intruders. And what was much worse—it turned out that the room in which he had been born (by the hissing glaring light of a carbide lamp) was now her room, and he felt more uncomfortable than ever.

He hoped she would realize that it wasn't his fault, that this was all his father's idea, that he, Peter, had very little to do with his father, who lived in Belgium and whom he didn't see more than three times a year, that he would never dream of doing this to her, that he never (but this only occurred to him years later) would intrude into the present lives of complete strangers to try to recapture his own past with which he himself had broken all ties.

"Is it still so hard to turn off the tap?" Mr. Gimberg asked, and the girl frowned and looked at the washbasin, as if she were see-ing it now for the first time. Then she walked to the washbasin, unsure whether this was what was expected of her, and turned on the tap, let it run, and turned it off, and said softly, "No, sir," but only Peter saw and heard it, because his father had opened the window, leaned out, ignoring the rain, and a while later he said, "This was the first thing you saw, Peter, and when I held you up to show you the garden, two German soldiers came up that path through the snow, but I had the proper identity papers, and any-way I had you and you were only a few hours old and you know how Germans are with children. No, I suppose you don't know."

But Peter wasn't listening to his father. It took his full powers of concentration to keep his shyness within reasonable bounds. He looked at the girl, who was running her index finger along the side of the tap. He followed her glance and was delightedly shocked that the reflection of her eyes was focused on him in the mirror. His father turned around, sighed, looked at his watch, and said, "Come on, it's time to go."

They drove the rest of the way to Zwolle at top speed, but Peter was hardly impressed, in fact he barely noticed it. Nor was he impressed when they arrived at the room in the respectable Zwolle hotel (smell of dusty carpets and camphor, the dried-out earth of the dark green ferns in the hall). It had lost its fascination for him and could not give him that nice excited feeling he had looked forward to before they started out. There were two beds in the room, a double bed, which his father claimed for himself, and a couch, which was assigned to Peter. The rest of the furniture consisted of a big brown mirror-fronted wardrobe, two kitchen chairs, and a small narrow table under the window, which looked out over the well-kept garden where orange garden chairs, standing on white pebbles, glistened in the rain. In the distance, beyond the drab rooftops of little houses, between two trees, Peter saw a church clock. Ten past two.

Mr. Gimberg washed his face, put on a clean shirt, and made an appointment with Peter to meet him in the room at half past five. Then they would eat together and perhaps go to the movies, Peter would have to look and see if there was anything interesting, a musical maybe. "Here," said Mr. Gimberg, "I don't have anything smaller, but don't go and spend it all!" and he gave his son a ten-guilder note. When he was gone, Peter stood looking out of the window. It had almost stopped raining. White clouds like clenched fists floated across the sky, but between these clouds and behind them the sky was a faded blue, like an apron which has been washed very often. A starling alighted on one of the orange chairs and pecked at its feathers.

He walked through Zwolle and thought about the girl. They were standing in the room again and were looking at each other in the mirror. I'm sorry my father was so rude, he said. In the background, the hazy contours of his father disintegrated into nothingness. The girl smiled. Are you alone? Peter asked. She nodded. I'm alone too, he said. My father's in prison in Antwerp and my mother's buried in a cemetery in The Hague. He drove with the girl in the Studebaker and they overtook all the other cars and his eyes held hers in the mirror.

He passed a cafeteria and although he was hungry he didn't dare go inside because some teenagers were standing around, leaning nonchalantly on their low, shiny motorcycles, looking at him, silently and disdainfully. And when he wanted to go into a grocery a little way further on to buy a bar of chocolate, he realized that he did not dare do this either, because all he had was the ten-guilder note his father had given him, and the grocer would think: How did that boy get so much money? and call the police. He strolled on, and looked at the pictures in the showcase of a small movie house, where a Laurel and Hardy film was playing, that he had already seen in The Hague. But in the next movie house there was a musical, and he memorized the name of the theater, for that evening.

He saw a splendid car parked in front of a large café, with red numbers on a white license plate, and it was his father's car. He crossed the street because his father was there on business and wouldn't want to see him now. When he turned the corner, almost at a jog trot, he saw the railroad station. He could have cried from anger and sadness at the stupid way he had wasted his afternoon by staying in Zwolle (but it was now almost half past four and at any rate too late) when he could have taken the train to Epe and gone to see the girl.

He went back to the hotel and seated on the edge of his bed he stared at himself in the wardrobe mirror. He saw a skinny little boy, wearing trousers that were too wide for him (his first pair of long trousers) and a jacket that was too short; this is the way all nice English boys are dressed, his mother said. He closed his eyes and the girl crept into his body and made his skin blush. The sky was overcast again, suddenly the rain started lashing viciously against the window, the streetlights went on all over Zwolle, that's how dark it was, and his father, smelling of alcohol, came into the room.

Later that evening, at the end of the film, when the singer kissed the dancer, whom he had loved all the time, tears filled Peter's eyes. It was already after ten o'clock. In front of the theater a bunch of noisy boys were making rough advances to some giggling, screeching girls. At the hotel, the night porter was reading a book he had borrowed from the library. In the room Peter got undressed and his father taught him how to hang his trousers over a chair properly, without ruining the crease.

The next morning the sun was shining and there were no clouds. They drove back to The Hague. "We're going via Elburg," said Mr. Gimberg, putting on his pigskin gloves. "And in Harderwijk we'll stop and eat some eels." Please Father, Daddy, Papa, what should I call you, can't we go via Epe, Peter thought, but he did not dare say it. Let's go via Epe and see the room where I was born yesterday.

Translated by Sheila Vuijsje.
Reprinted from *Delta: A Review of Arts, Life and Thought in the Netherlands* (Autumn 1969, Volume 12, Number 3), published by the Delta International Publication Foundation, Amsterdam.

HUGO CLAUS

The Black Emperor

WANAMAKER had one marble left, the milky white one with the orange rivulets. Piers, the tall boy playing with Simon, poked Wanamaker in the ribs. "Well, Wanamaker, don't you dare?" he asked.

Wanamaker nodded and looked toward the courtyard, where the teacher was already moving over to the bell with long, slow strides. The teacher headed for the bell as if he had worked out precisely how long it took to get there just as recess ended. It mustn't be allowed to vary even one minute from recesses on other days.

He slapped Simon's right fist with his open hand. "Even," he said. They yelled like a couple of madmen, and Simon flashed his dirty, moist hand open.

The bell rang, and they went and stood in line while the noise and the chatter died down and the young teacher of the highest class clapped his hands. Wanamaker thought of what his Mama would say, now he had lost the marble with the orange rivulets.

"One more time," he said close to Simon's back and in Simon's neck that had soft white hairs and was long like the neck of some soft, pale animal.

"You haven't got any forfeits left," Simon whispered without turning his head, while the line moved on and they shuffled over the uneven cobblestones of the courtyard.

Wanamaker said, "I've got a secret," and it was the last thing he possessed, and a minute later he had lost, because it was odd again, and he walked into the classroom poor and bare among the stained and yellowed desks and the maps of Asia and Europe and

8

thought that he had nothing left in all the world now that Simon with his dirty, sticky hand and his bird's head would meet his friend the Negro.

When it was four o'clock, they both went to sit in the park on the green wooden bench Wanamaker singled out. In one of the row of identical houses along Rooseveltlaan, a woman opened a top-story window, and the panes glittered like flashes of lightning. "I'm sad," Wanamaker thought.

They talked about homework, tensely, almost excitedly, as if there was nothing else to talk about. Then Simon asked, "Where's he from?"

"From Africa," said Wanamaker. "He hunts tigers there."

"Did he bring any with him?" asked Simon.

"Yeah," Wanamaker said. "He sells tigers and snakes and crocodiles to the circus." He said "crocodiles" very loud, and wondered whether Simon realized he was calling him a crocodile.

They both looked at the smoothly cut lawn where a municipal gardener was spraying water with a rubber hose. A man walked by and they saw that he had holes in his socks. "He didn't eat all his potatoes today," said Simon.

Wanamaker didn't answer and watched a woman wheeling a baby carriage. "Ha-ta-ta-ta," said the woman.

"I mean, because he still has two in his shoes," said Simon, but Wanamaker didn't laugh.

Hundreds of insects buzzed in the round-clipped trees and the bushes. A man rode past on horseback. Two policemen slowly came toward them, their bodies swinging from left to right.

"Someone should go up there on the statue and sit behind King Albert on his horse," said Wanamaker.

"You, I suppose?" said Simon, and he gave a nasty laugh.

"No, just anybody."

"People would pretty soon notice the difference," said Simon.

"Maybe," said Wanamaker.

"And does he dress like white people?" Simon asked after a while. He tried to balance his schoolbag on one foot. Wanamaker looked from Simon's thin foot, in its black, polished, pointed shoe, to the boy's pale knees, then back to his own, scratched and covered with patches of eczema.

"Yeah," he said, "but in Africa he dresses like his tribe. A red band with feathers in it round his head, and a long gown with a leather belt around his waist. And he has his curved knife, too, and his shield."

"A band with feathers, only Indians wear that," said Simon.

"In his tribe Negroes wear it too," said Wanamaker.

"Did he let you see his shield?" Simon asked.

"He only has that in Africa," Wanamaker said.

"Does he live here in town? Where?"

Wanamaker didn't answer. Where else could a Negro live but in a tent hung with leopard skins; and where else could he, Wanamaker, live but in a house that smelled of onions and pee and where he had to sleep, eat, and do his homework in two rooms with his Mama. With Mama who dressed and undressed him, combed his hair, kissed him, cleaned his eye, placed food in front of him, in the morning, at noon, at four o'clock, and at night, and polished his shoes, and brushed his clothes, and what all didn't she do. And shouted, "Jan, where are your gloves? Jan, have you finished your yogurt?"

After half an hour of waiting and drawing names in the bench with their slate pencils that scratched more than wrote, Simon suddenly said, "He's not coming. I knew all the time you were a dirty liar. You don't know any Negro, you've never even seen one."

The sun was lower now: it made a red fringe above the roofs of the row of houses, and under the gaze of Wanamaker, who was sad, bright-colored patches of orange and lemon yellow moved slowly down along the sidewalls into the gaps where houses had been bombed out of the row.

"Don't be so cross," said Wanamaker. "Just wait, he'll come."

But Simon didn't want to wait, and with one quick movement he got up and hit Wanamaker on the shoulder with his schoolbag. Wanamaker looked up at Simon, frightened by his long, white, twisted face.

"You're really cross," he said.

Then Simon hit him again, and this time he swung his schoolbag round by the strap so hard that the corner, probably where his pencil box was, caught Wanamaker on the chest. Wanamaker got up and grabbed Simon by the hair.

"You ugly one-eye," yelled Simon, "let me go," and he jerked loose and was about to run off, and while he was already bending forward to start to run (and would have fallen, if someone hadn't held on to him), he bumped into a grown-up man who took hold of him by the shoulders of his coat and lifted him up for a moment, so that Simon's long bird's face was hanging between two big folds of his coat.

"Uhuh," said Simon while he straightened his clothes with a cough.

"Wait a minute," said a deep voice that sounded to Wanamaker (the way it always did) like the voice of a father or an elder brother, which he couldn't have, of course.

"Wait a minute," the voice said again, and Simon sat down right in front of the man, who had a brown face beneath his gray felt hat with a heavy shadow under its brim, a face the color of a dark brown, unpolished shoe. He inspected the two boys closely, not unkindly, the boy with the white skin and the freckles and the one with the black patch over his left eye, and then he asked, "What are you fighting about?"

Wanamaker said, "Nothing."

"Oh," said the Negro, and he laughed, and Wanamaker looked (the way he always did) at the chapped lips that moved and folded open.

The Negro straightened his bright red tie, then fastened his fawn-leather shoes on the edge of the bench where the boys were sitting. He had swift, light brown fingers with rings and pale fingernails that shone. He was wearing a camel's-hair coat and a canary-yellow scarf, which was no way to dress for summer, and then Wanamaker knew that his friend was going away, that he would sail on a ship to some place where it was cold and he would need the thick, ocher-yellow coat, some place where he would find new friends, and so forth.

"Are you going away?" asked Wanamaker.

"Yeah," said the Negro, "I can't stay very long. I have to go somewhere."

"On a ship?" asked Wanamaker, or rather he said it, as if he were completing the Negro's unfinished sentence.

"No, where'd you get that idea, little dove?" said the Negro, and looked surprised. "I have to be somewhere in town at seven o'clock."

Then he winked at Simon and said, "How are you?"

"This is my friend Simon," said Wanamaker.

"Hello, Simon," said the Negro.

"Hello," said Simon in a tiny voice.

The Negro laughed hard and then bent over Wanamaker—who looked at the shell of his ear and the shape of his skull and the dark rounding at the back of his head with its fuzzy hair and thought, "Where's he going in town? Who's he going to see?"—and he brushed the tousled hair back from Wanamaker's forehead and said, "So long, little dove."

"Why did he call you little dove?" asked Simon.

"Cause I'm his friend," said Wanamaker.

"He asked how I was," Simon said quietly, and then, "do you see him every day?"

"I wait for him every day. Sometimes he comes, sometimes he doesn't."

"And what do you do together when he comes, Wanamaker?"

But the one-eyed boy got up and slung his cardboard schoolbag over his shoulder. They shuffled over the gravel path together and raised clouds of red, dusty sand as they kicked a wad of crumpled newspaper back and forth. They separated at the bridge.

When Wanamaker got home he ate three slices of bread and then yogurt (the yogurt that his Aunt Bertha brought from the shop where she worked, and that makes little boys as strong as lions). Then he started doing his homework, but before long he stopped and took the pencil dripping with spit out of his mouth and said to his Mama (because she would hear it anyway from Simon, who picked him up every morning to go to school), "Mama, Simon and I met a Negro."

But his Mama was cutting out a piece of blue material from a paper pattern and didn't look up and didn't answer.

Then Wanamaker took out his sketchbook and for the hundredth time carefully drew a dove, with an eye that was much too big: it looked like a dog's eye.

Translated by James S. Holmes and Hans van Marle.
Earlier versions of this story were printed in *The Literary Review* (Spring 1964, Volume 7, Number 3), published by Fairleigh Dickinson University, Rutherford, New Jersey, and *Delta: A Review of Arts, Life, and Thought in the Netherlands* (Spring 1970, Volume 13, Number 1), published by the Delta International Publication Foundation, Amsterdam.

JEF GEERAERTS

Indian Summer

. . . AND instead of lying half-benumbed in the orange light of
the hot tent in order to escape the mosquitoes, I absolutely must
make a different daily timetable, to force myself to the necessary
discipline, for instance to drink less water, or to absorb myself in
all kinds of complicated tasks, perhaps there will be a chance then
that the gurgling water in my stomach won't immediately start to
run in rivulets down my back when the temperature mounts in
the afternoon and the mosquito net is black with mosquitoes, or
I should try to pretend to myself while chewing dwarf-willow
leaves that the juice tastes of spinach and is therefore rich in
vitamins and most of all I mustn't drift into a state of panic by
hysterical thoughts of wonderful food, more and more I get out of
breath at the least movement, even if it's only shifting slightly on
the mattress, pumping air into it is hardly possible any more, I'm
a trembling old man with a throttling pain in my joints and my
gums bleed and when I raise myself to look outside (to see if
they're arriving yet, if perhaps the plane is coming) I feel so sick
that my mouth fills up with spittle and my forehead becomes
clammy with sweat and I start shivering and panting, in Herrbergsdålen that woodcutter asked me in halting German to give
him a rough indication of the route on the map, in the event of
a rescue operation, the only inhabited place apart from Herrbergsdålen is Värgaren, a Lapp and his wife live there, he said,
a fisherman who receives his supplies every three months from the
seaplane of the Forestry Commission and to my question whether
there were bears in the area he replied yes and he pointed on the
map to an area called Nord-Borgafällen, there's nothing, nothing
there, only reindeer, elks and snow, he said, have you got a good

14

compass? That was sixteen days ago, perhaps he's forgotten us, I'd better recite the names on the 1:200 000 map once again, carefully: "Trykt-av-Generalstabens-litografiska-anstalt-Stockholm" in a singsong voice like the characters in a Bergman film, Swedish ordnance survey maps are openly for sale, here they don't fear an enemy attack as they do in the baroque south, hurriedly reciting the row of names is the exciting memory game which must keep my mind resilient so that I won't succumb to a cosmic panic as always at twenty-three hours when the sun disappears in a white, livid Saturn shine below the flattened snowy top of the Barkanyakk and the shadows slowly grow longer until I can no longer see where they end and the lake called Sjougden congeals between the mountains and the mosquitoes will sleep for four full hours, only three days ago I became active at that moment, I'd cooked the last remaining packet of soup, Knackbrot there hadn't been for a long time, nor raisins and . . . yesterday I pressed the last four pills that were left one by one from the plastic container and sucked the sweet coating, Sunday-Monday-Tuesday-Wednesday (Scorpio! Scorpio!) and I no longer have enough strength to put a new supply of dry birch bark on you while the hard lump rises in my throat because kissing is no longer possible, last night or rather twenty-four hours ago, at the moment when the sun was a slice of yellow in the sky *and approached* and the moon rose visibly and I was as always suddenly aware of a rarefied endlessness in which the earth floats like a disk, while the landscape lies rigid under a sun without warmth and at about half past one it rises again in a prehistoric silence above an unreal Cambrian landscape with motionless spruces, ponds, lakes, mountains, no birds, no life, in which you suddenly have to turn round because someone is watching you, the grinning Lapp with the slit-eyes from Värgaren who when you look at him dissolves in the marsh, twenty-four hours ago her features were still beautiful, quiet, her skin taut, brown, her hair shiny, her hands, her hands . . . with a birch twig I carefully chased the mosquitoes and flies away, she was the only woman with whom I would have dared go on such a mad journey through the wilderness, *Jämtland, that must be Lapland,* she said, *what a wonderful name for Lapland,* with her attentive little face, happy, enthusiastic, she followed my

finger on the map and spelt the names which I now keep repeating to myself in the correct order: Dajmasjön, Blierekij, Afvasjön,
Gubbsjöhöjdon, Klöfverfjället, Genjegetjem, Steurjenyuolta, Kör-
fåsen, Hjerpegalten . . . yesterday the gangrene on the leg hadn't
grown black yet and . . . looking in the notebook, the impressions written down during the journey, *the color of the copper
roofs in Helsingör is a venomous green like a green mamba* and
afterwards, while approaching the Swedish coast, standing by the
rail on the boat: *the flat shiny atomic energy station, whose thin
metal chimneys don't give out smoke, a hydrogen bomb has
destroyed Sweden,* we would drive through a charred, cracked
land, but they turned out to be gasoline depots, smokeless and
hygienic like everything in this country, it drizzled under a light
gray sky, but as we drove further northwards (sometimes six hundred kilometers a day through uninhabited forests, past lakes,
across narrow wooden bridges, past rust colored wooden farm-
houses without people, the air pure, rarefied, cool, *polar air,*
finally along deserted smooth earth tracks through forests of fir
trees) it became hotter, oppressive, windless, the mosquitoes became unbearable, the sky was completely overcast, the sun shone
like copper behind a thin layer of clouds, at the last gas station the
half-naked Swede, who spoke English, said he'd never seen anything like it, the thermometer marked eighty-eight degrees in the
shade, that was at the time when we drove virtually naked
through the monotonous landscape of rigid, thinly strewn pine
trees, following the example of the few Swedes who were tearing southwards at great speed with reindeer antlers tied to their
luggage racks and with the headlights on, the end of the mid-
summer night in which everything is permitted, after two days
your small breasts were as brown as your shoulders and your hair
tied up in two buns, young, playful, Marianne, and at about eight
o'clock in the evening we'd be hungry and invariably we found
a wonderful, lonely spot with fir trees and short grass and a mountain stream with icy cold, soft water which makes the soap foam
and polishes the teeth while you drink, and then I'd put the tent
up while you prepared the evening meal, with swift, accurate
movements, chattering all the time, full of plans for the great trip
into Jämtland, the bear trip, the reindeer trip, the bottle of white

wine lay in the stream to cool, because we ate French food, toast with smoked salmon and Chablis, while we pretended it was champagne with lobster, the bottle clattering in the silver ice bucket and afterwards fried potatoes with steak and salad and a bottle of Bordeaux and then I made a fire of birch bark and fir wood, *a fragrant fire,* and we smoked and breathed and drank water, it was as if we were dehydrated, even at night we often got up to drink, we stole through the dim night like naked spirits and drank, flat on our belly from the stream, not a leaf moved, it was close, not even the mosquitoes hummed, in the north we could see the faint shimmer which mesmerized us, we felt very relaxed and happy, we lay naked on top of the sleeping bag, dreaming, slept briefly, woke up, asked each other if we were asleep, and then we smoked a cigarette which we handed to each other, sitting tailor-fashion, we hardly spoke, we listened to the silence and when at about half past two it started to get light and the sun glittered coolly above the forests, we got up and stretched ourselves and yawned noisily and walked naked into the forest, the floor of small needles and moss was moist, we washed each other on a rock while the water brushed past us, from where did it keep coming? We felt like Germanic forest gods and I sang with a resounding voice: *"Duu saagest's!"* from St. Matthew's Passion and imitated an approaching bear with clumsy movements and appropriate grunts till we rolled on the ground, choking with laughter and kissed each other and . . . and then I boiled water on the wood fire with slow, ritual, amorous gestures, for coffee, strong coffee, and you fried bacon and eggs and we drank that fantastic milk from carton pyramids, everything slowly, relaxed, free from original sin, there was no God, only we existed and the earth was there too, fire, water, air, cosmos, then we hadn't been bewitched by the landscape yet, that only happened on the fifth day, on the day when we decided to climb the mountain of the spirits, the Barkanyakk, to put the spirits in a favorable mood I first had to beat an imaginary trolls' drum and sing the holy songs, recite texts from the Edda, first drumming softly, imploringly, *dooboodooboodoob* . . . faster and faster, higher, sharper, and I had to ask our constellations, Scorpio, Pisces, love, death, violence, longing for Evil, the universe, the Void, and ask whether the moment was auspicious for the trolls of the Barkan-yakk and whether the fatal day of Ragnarök wasn't near and utter death cries and go on drumming feverishly *dooboodooboodoob!* and scream hoarsely and finally roll on the ground in a trance and wait breathlessly for the spirits to answer . . . then we took food for a day with us in a rucksack, the mountaintop seemed very near, but when we came out of the birch wood a vast plateau stretched out in front of us with dwarf willows and a maze of little lakes, pools and streams, every step through the marsh made a sucking sound, it took four hours before we got to the foot of the mountain, there we put dry socks on and other boots, we ate hastily, you were already tired then, and most of all nervous because of the mosquitoes which were humming around us in clouds, and then we started to climb, every quarter of an hour you asked to have a rest and you were panting, there were black shadows under your eyes and you stubbornly refused to take glucose, you drank too much water, my undershirt was wet with sweat, even the rucksack was soaked through on one side and at about two o'clock it grew even hotter because there was no longer any vegetation, nor water, and the sun was reflected by the granite so that the eyes hurt, at the top there were no mosquitoes and we sat there for an hour in silence on a rock with our feet in the snow and then we suddenly heard the thumping of hooves, we looked up and at about fifty yards' distance a small herd of reindeer was coming towards us, you jumped up, and pulled the camera out of the rucksack with jerky movements, *reindeer, rein-deer, the answer of the trolls,* you whispered and your whole face was radiant and your eyes, those eyes of yours, black with long, straight lashes, and you ran off and took photographs, the reindeer got wind of us and nervously swerved round, down the slope and you ran after them, yelling, and then I saw you fall, you didn't get up and you called for me in a frightened voice and when I reached you you were still lying with your face down, your right leg was twisted and stuck tight in a crevice and when I lifted you you screamed with pain and then I saw, a splinter of bone was sticking through your slacks which were red with blood and you clung to me and said *don't leave me, I don't want to stay alone, stay with me, don't leave me,* and then I lifted her on my shoulders, the leg was dangling down, we had no antiseptics, we had no rope, no wood to make a splint, I tied up the leg above the knee with a shoelace, fortunately she only weighed ninety-eight pounds, I put her on her stomach on top of my rucksack, hooked my right arm behind her left leg and held her left wrist, she groaned continuously and begged me to do or not to do all sorts of things, definite things, promises for life, during the descent, then through the marshes, the long search for the tent, eighteen hundred feet below, far, far, by the lake called Sjougden which I could see in a white haze and when we got to the marshy plain with the lakes I'd been exhausted three times already and three times I had recovered with difficulty thanks to the last glucose and at the first brooklet I drank my stomach full and gave her to drink from my hand and there were gnarled birch shrubs and I cut off four sticks and with fresh birch bark I tied them round her leg and she bit my arm with pain and I had to help her to pee and when I saw it I cried but it took another eight hours before we reached the tent, in the dense birch wood her splinted leg got stuck all the time but I just didn't look at it and she lost consciousness and I fainted and was covered with beard moss and fell down at least ten times and by the lake dawn arrived in the air with swarms of mosquitoes and puddles and it was already warm and I'd lost direction, I said wait here, I'll go and look by myself and then I'll come and fetch you, because I was hungry and trembled with weakness, *no, don't leave me stay here we'll die here together,* you said, your face was pale, twisted in creases I had never seen before, Marianne, in a few hours you had become ten years older, I'd gone more than two kilometers wrong, in the tent I frantically mixed some instant pudding and raisins and drank two cans of grapefruit juice one after the other, gobbled the pudding and drank water till I couldn't drink any more, hung the bloodstained undershirt on the tent pole, prepared pudding for her and walked unsteadily, spitting, coughing, to the place where you lay, you were hitting savagely at the mosquitoes which were going for the blood and I fed you some pudding with a little spoon but you couldn't keep it down, it came out of your mouth in little gulps and you cried, during the walk back to the tent I felt stronger and I was able to carry you in my arms like a bridegroom carries his bride, in the tent you lay staring at the roof at first and the next day the pain started and you wouldn't let me go for help in Herrbergsdålen, when it became unbearable I poured water on the wound and you grew very thin because then the fever came, sweating, your teeth chattering under two sleeping bags, throwing them off and sweating again, I held your head, your hair was matted together, wet, and you smelled and you looked at me with hollow eyes, your lips were cracked and you gulped water like an animal and the wound started to go green, but I didn't tell you that nor did I tell you that amputation was the only way, the knife was razor-sharp and afterwards I would cauterize the wound, but I was incapable of doing it, after four days there was no more food, the sixth day I came into the tent with water and a sickly smell hit me in the face so that I had to go outside again, you were breathing quietly, the leg looked mouldy, the ankle and knee were swollen and all the time I had to hold your hand and talk to you and now and again you cried, the seventh day you had a high fever and you asked for food but there was nothing left and your hands were narrow and bony like those of a woman of ninety, at about eleven o'clock at night you began to rave and to call incoherently and you turned your head this way and that, with a deep flush and bulging eyes, at a given moment I was so tired that I fell asleep and when I woke up there was a strange silence in the tent, I raised myself on my elbow and took your hand in mine and put it on your breast, closed your eyes and went outside, the sun was setting behind the Barkanyakk, the lake, the mountains were immensely familiar, I walked into the forest and returned at once, knelt by your rucksack and took out your towels, pressed my nose in the soft cloth, then your sponge bag with the scent of you, your underwear, Marianne, my best friend, and when it became light again I opened the zipper of the tent and dared not touch you, I pulled the mattress out of the tent to the lake and sat looking at you for hours chasing away the insects with a twig, all the time I thought: now you'll never swim in the North Sea again, where is your soul now? is it on the way to the Pole or are you floating in the cosmos like an atom? . . . the next day I walked into the wood and started gathering birch bark, which I carefully cut into strips, cork dry, tough, from dead broken stems, and started piling it up on her, only her face I covered with willow twigs, to be able to see it when I sat by her, and then I started chewing willow leaves . . . and when the mosquitoes became too bad I carefully covered her face and had to go back into the tent, into the orange heat and I had to try to sleep or not to think or recite the names once again and sometimes swallow the painful lump in my throat away, but when a brown liquid came out of her mouth yesterday and her belly began to swell to above her belt, I went to the wood with my last strength and gathered as much bark as I could and now it is almost zero hour and I can go outside again, first to drink from the lake and crawl to you on my knees, the match splutters and I hold it under the bark at the four corners, it flares up fiercely and it begins to rustle and creak and hiss and snuffle, black smoke rises vertically and in great wonder I say: Dajma-sjön, Blierekij, Afvasjön, Gubbsjöhöjdon, Klöfverfjället, Genjeget-jem, Steurjenyuolta. . . .

Römnäsmyran, 12 July, 1967
Knokke, 12 July, 1968

ALIENATING COMMENTARY TO THE STORY *Indian Summer*,
INTENDED FOR THE (ATTENTIVE) READER

When you read the date (or rather the two dates) at the end of the story, you will notice that I was in northern Sweden on July 12, 1967. This was not a coincidence. There is a particular background to this fact. During my stay in the Congo I often wandered through the jungle and the savannah, sometimes accompanied by trackers and bearers, sometimes not. In those days I had a passion for hunting dangerous wildlife: elephants, buffalo, leopards, baboons, wild boars. The fact that I could no longer do this in Europe gave me a strong sense of nostalgia for those happy years. To me, hunting was not only the killing of animals, the experience of a titillating thrill during dangerous moments, it was also the realization that a few men, hunting far from the inhabited world, would, if necessary, unhesitatingly hazard their lives for each other (my hunter Sopio had once come to my aid in a perilous situation and I to his when he had been a bit too audacious with a wounded buffalo). There was more, however, and it was this in particular which gave an unusual dimension to our hunting parties: the dialectic of intense life versus violence and death led me before, during, and after the killing of big game to an overwhelming sense of communion of my sharpened senses with the wind, the sun, the earth. It was a kind of return to a primitive way of life which only prehistoric man had known, it was a series of initiations, but initiations with adverse effects: each time a bit of civilization fell away from me and I felt myself approaching closer and closer to the paradisiac state of innocence. Nor did each initiation give me a feeling of confusion, but during a few seconds a violent sense of happiness would burst out inside me so that I started to dance and sing, something which my black hunting comrades understood very well, because after the exertions of the hunt we would eat and drink well, and after the meal the hashish pipe would go from mouth to mouth. Anything was possible then. Ha, that was life!

This much in order to make you understand my journey to Lapland better, attentive reader.

After about seven years in Europe I felt so sullied by Western culture (I had read much, written much, drunk much, traveled much, restlessly made love, I had studied philology, philosophy, and history for four years, etc. . . . with only one bright spot: a few good friends with whom to talk) that I began to feel a growing yearning for purity, a longing for the Lost Paradise. For unknown reasons Lapland began to be the symbol of this lost purity: there one could still find water, air, forests, plains, mountains, vast uninhabited areas where the lonely wanderer with rucksack, map, and compass could ramble for days on end. I imagined my little tent on the shore of a lake where I would be able to fish in peace, go for walks, prepare my food, breathe, think in a still, grandiose landscape which at night was bathed in the strange glow of the never setting sun. That was how I imagined it.

Reality turned out to be rather different. Indeed the forests were endless, the silence impressive, the plains desolate, and during the long treks with rucksack, map, and compass I felt small and lost in all this vastness. But the weather was abominable. Sometimes I had to shelter for hours under a pine tree which finally started to drip until I was soaked through. In spite of waterproof, greased boots, I had wet feet almost all the time. My lips were chapped due to the biting mosquito-repellent cream and if I didn't put the stuff on it was unendurable. Camping quietly by a lake was therefore impossible, fishing was made unpleasant because of the incessant need to slap hands and face, sunbathing was only possible in the mountains and there it was too chilly, the weather could suddenly change from windless and warm to stormy wind and icy cold gusts of rain, so that one had to stay in one's tent for two days, only coming out now and then to kick the tent pegs into the ground once more or to repair the guy ropes. The only bright spot was a boat trip to North Cape and afterwards the climbing of the Glittertind with a group of Norwegian climbers in the majestic mountain region of Jotunheimen, the Land of the Giants from Peer Gynt.

In July, 1968, I had gone to Knokke for some days with the intention of writing a story about Lapland. On July 12 I was walking in the dunes between Het Zoute and Cadzand, there was a strong wind but the temperature was mild. And there I suddenly remembered that exactly a year ago I had been on my first great trip in Jämtland. This realization gave me a shock, I experienced a kind of cosmic consciousness, I had never before felt anything like this, and with a kind of rarefied, floating feeling in which one's surroundings no longer exist (the prelude to *having to write*) I returned to Knokke, locked myself in for a day and a night with the map in front of me on the table (the map I had used on that particular trip) and a piece of birch bark beside me at which I sniffed now and then; I first wrote down a few names on a sheet of paper (the string of Swedish names which the main character recites twice) and then, at one go, the story you know.

It would not surprise me if you had discovered other dimensions in "Indian Summer" and another kind of initiation, it is even probable that you have. One more thing I will disclose to you: the burning of that woman is the (unavailing) destruction of yet another disappointment after the confrontation with an impossible dialogue between myself and the earth.

Don't therefore read the following, but rather re-read "Indian Summer" in the light of my commentary.

ELEMENTARY INFORMATION FOR THE BENEFIT OF
THE WRITERS OF (BAD) REVIEWS

What does "Indian Summer" mean? "Indian Summer" literally means a period of warm or mild weather late in fall or in early winter, but in fact it is a hot, dry summer which lasts until far into fall. The connection of this with the content of the story is obvious: in Lapland the sun virtually doesn't set from May 15 until July 15 and in the story the temperature is, moreover, abnormally high. Why this analysis of key words? Perhaps I've let myself in for a difficult job here, but at least it might possibly lead one of the prominent critics to write something sensible about my stories within the foreseeable future, something which so far hasn't happened, not to my knowledge at any rate.

Half-benumbed: Meant as a kind of pointer to the later events. If I had left "half-benumbed" out at this stage, one might possibly have thought that the main character, lying in the hot tent, was for instance reading "The Coladrinkers," that he went on to play with his toes and ended up by masturbating. Of course this was not the case, but I selected these three fictitious activities very carefully in order to suggest the progressively mounting degree of accompanying pleasure (from zero to Mach-2).

Orange: All good tents are orange. I don't know why, but it is a fact and a fact is a fact and one must always take account of the facts. One year guarantee on the zipper.

The mosquitoes: If you have read "Never Sleep Again" by W. F. Hermans carefully, a novel which one of you has called "boy-scoutish" (evidence that he writes about things he doesn't know about, as a result of which fact alone W. F., who actually did wander about Finnmark with a rucksack, becomes a towering giant beside this crab louse), you will probably remember that the action of the book takes place in a wild, uninhabited, region of northern Norway, which in the brief summer is infested by billions of mosquitoes, due to the swamps. The region in which "Indian Summer" is set is not so far to the north. The story is set in Jämtland, in northern Sweden, a wild, mountainous forest area with many lakes and swamps, which in summer is fairly unpleasant because of the mosquitoes.

Make a different daily timetable: He hadn't done this so far and he thinks, quite rightly: better late than never. Calvinist version of Epicurus' famous proverb: "Never put off till tomorrow what you can let someone else do today."

The necessary discipline: In spite of everything the main character of the story (yes, we're still talking about him) is a westerner, conditioned by Christianity, who thinks that militant self-discipline will save him from insanity or spiritual slackening, more or less like shipwrecked voyagers who ask each other examination questions in the lifeboat or sing pious hymns, so that the moment when they start eating each other is postponed by a few hours.

Drink less water: He drinks too much water.

Complicated tasks: He is an intellectual and therefore well practiced in cerebral hysteria.

In rivulets: If you drink too much and the peripheral temperature suddenly rises, you'll start to sweat.

Dwarf willows: Tough willow shrubs, growing to a height of one foot (*Salix alba*) with silvery leaves, with which vast swamps in Lapland are covered. Very troublesome to make your way through, because the twigs form tough knots. This prevents the hiker from walking nonchalantly or with a shuffling gait, like James Dean or herds of churchgoers. Like all leaves, those of the dwarf willow have a rather special taste. As we are primates (apelikes) and not herbivores (grass eaters) our stomachs protest usually already after the third leaf. This is why I cunningly suggest the taste of spinach, a vegetable for which I personally have a great predilection, because of the many vitamins it contains, but critics who don't like spinach are at liberty to choose beans, kale, or turnips, according to their tastes.

Hysterical thoughts of: You see, an intellectual soon loses his cool, his instinct gets the upper hand after a very short time. Then he undoubtedly begins to think of decadent things such as a cool glass of sherry with an olive, oysters with Chablis, bits of toast with smoked eel and some Chassagne-Montrachet, *entrecôtes* roasted over charcoal with superfine garden peas and a bottle of Chateau Margaux, *crêpes flambées au Grand Marnier*, mocha, Fine Champagne, and a Henry Upmann.

For the critics I suggest tomato soup, potatoes with leeks, and a pork chop (gnawing at the bone, lovely), a glass of Seven-Up and pudding with raisins for dessert, everything prepared and served by the wife. If little Liz or Pete can't get through it, she wipes the plates clean with a few broad sweeps of the fork and whoops, in with it, a good little pig always empties its trough, my dear mother used to say.

Everything that follows, until the passage in parentheses, is detail which only serves to contribute to the atmosphere. They are therefore important, indispensable, *organic* details. Without these details the atmosphere wouldn't be what it now is, that goes without saying.

(*to see if . . . the plane is coming*): The main character apparently expects help from the well-organized Swedish rescue service which traces clumsy hikers benevolently and free of charge. Airplanes, helicopters, and hundreds of volunteers are brought in to search vast areas. This sort of thing would be unthinkable in Belgium, because even in *wild* areas such as Duke's Wood or the High Peat District there is not a spot to be found anymore where you can't hear a church bell tolling somewhere in the distance. On the High Veluwe in the Netherlands it's even worse: every week the trees and bushes there are examined, dusted, and counted.

Herrbergsdålen: Woodcutters' post at fifteen hundred feet above sea level, 64° 42′ 30″ north latitude, 3° 21′ 40″ east longitude. If you take the relevant map (47 RISBÄCK) from the series "Generalstabens karta över Sverige," you will easily find this spot, after some searching.

Värgaren: Wooden house on the shore of lake Värgaren (577.5 m), situated at 64° 48′ north latitude, 3° 22′ east longitude. It is fairly lonely there and the nearest supermarket is at Frostviken, about thirty-seven miles to the south as the crow flies, but this doesn't mean that you therefore have to starve in Värgaren. The lake is teeming with salmon trout and in the forest one comes across deer, elks, and pheasants. There are also lots of reindeer, but they belong to a few rich Lapps.*

In the higher areas there are bears and wolverines. An allusion

---

* Together with Alaska and Graubünden, Lapland is the only place in the world where capitalism reaches into the higher mountain regions.

to this is made in the name Nord-Borgafällen, a vast mountain area roughly around the point 64° 58′ north latitude, 3° 6′ east longitude.

Compass: Indeed, because a map without a compass is like a car without gas, you can't do much with it. One might possibly take one's bearings from the sun, but this is precarious in Lapland and you will still need a wristwatch which tells the right time. With a compass you solve all these problems in a jiffy. This explanation will have to suffice; it is rather complicated to explain in detail how exactly one travels through an uninhabited region with a compass and a map, and moreover it might bore some critics rather quickly, which I wish to avoid. To the main character of the story it was all so obvious that he can afford to mention it only casually in passing: rather like Hemingway's iceberg, nine-tenths remain invisible, but they are there all the same.

"Trykt-av . . .": This is printed at the bottom of every Swedish survey map 1:200 000. "What small scale!" you will probably exclaim in surprise, and quite rightly, too. Indeed, Belgian survey maps are made to a scale of 1:20 000, but then you must remember that if you have lost your way in Belgium, there is a café on almost every corner.

Baroque: This adjective has virtually nothing to do with the seventeenth-century movement in art which was a direct append-age of the Counter-Reformation, characterized by excessive curls, violent light-and-shadow contrasts, jerky movements, restlessness, anxiety, popes in golden bedsteads full of skulls, military cam-paigns with fire and cross, Spain, Flanders, fire-spewing jesuits, loudly laughing devils, people dying at the stake, creaking bones, tearing tendons, shouts for mercy, thudding blows, blood, shit, vomit; in brief: a thrilling time.

I use this adjective because in Sweden bishops live worthily in wooden houses, keeping their mouths shut, the park round the royal palace is open to the public, the Brahmin caste has been done away with for good, sex has been integrated as a normal element in the community, and violence has been declared taboo.

Cosmic panic: You never feel this in your study, that's why I won't say any more about it.

Knackbrot: Swedish national dish. Easily digestible. De-liciously crisp. Wholesome for young and old. After intensive research and numerous tests the Swedes now make their Knackbrot from wheatmeal in which the wheat germ is kept fully intact. It is rich in vitamin B_1 (or thiamine). It contains few calories. It replaces bread and toast. Excellent for reducing. One hundred grams of Knackbrot contains:

Water	3.0 g
Digestible proteins	13.4 g
Digestible lipids	9.4 g
Digestible glucose	61.4 g (including 6.25 g sugar)
Kitchen salt	0.5 g

One rusk weighs about twelve grams and contains fifty calories. *Knackbrot enthält alle Vitaminen und grundsätzlichen Bestandteile des Vollkorns.* Knackbrot contains all the strength and goodness of whole wheat. May be used in place of bread and toast. Crisp Crunchy-Appetizing

Knackbrot è uno cracker dolce con farina integrale. Leggero, è contiene elementi vitaminici del chicco di grano.

Alexis Carrel wrote in his famous work "L'Homme cet inconnu" the following: "The public has been made to believe that white bread is superior to brown bread. The flour has been more and more completely 'refined' and has thus been robbed of its most useful elements."

Thanks to this text I eat Knackbrot every day and I have become a faithful reader of this eminent scholar. In this context I also read his epoch-making book: "Les Miracles de Lourdes" and was so impressed that I was promptly converted to Catholicism. This is why I hasten to withdraw the mischievous assertion that Catholicism is *"a sect of old women and children which is slowly but surely dying out"* (p. 104 in *Werk van Nu 2* [*Work of Today 2*], *" 'I am a left-wing bourgeois,' "* Manteau Publishers, Brussels/The Hague MP 45). You see how far-reaching the effects of eating Knackbrot may be and how salutary for body and soul. Eat therefore Knackbrot!

Pills: And here comes the first clear sexual allusion in this story. Considering my well-known obsession in this field—a reproach I get thrown at me regularly—it has taken a fairly long time before the Catholics among you were able to exclaim: "What bad taste! Can't we do without it just for once, for God's sake?" You may be glad that it took such a long time, but I protest most violently against the accusation of bad taste, you might have been justified in using this term if for instance the main character had been eating condoms out of sheer hunger, but that wasn't possible because he'd left them behind in Herrbergsdålen. Now I ask myself with malicious amusement what you will say when you read my autobiographical novel *Gangreen I (Black Venus)*. There I have been filthy on purpose. There's pornography for you. Excepting shit-eating, bestiality (or zoophilia *), and necrophilia you can find just about everything in it. Buy it, boys!

Scorpio: In the time of year when the cold begins to prowl the earth and the sun descends into its grave, the constellation of Scorpio, the eighth sign of the zodiac, makes its entry (October 23 until November 22). Brown leaves flutter about and form a soft death-carpet. They will decay and, together with the humus of the earth, form a compost for the fermenting resurrection of new life in spring. The scorpion is the only animal which can kill itself by suicide. People born under this sign do in fact unite the qualities of three animals in themselves: the scorpion who carries poison in its tail, the serpent who aggressively spits the poison out of its mouth, and the eagle, the Phoenix with its sharp, watch-ful, cosmic vision. These people display great independence in their thinking. They do not want to be hindered in their activities by others. Their courage and stubbornness are unbelievable.

Scorpio is a fascinating sign, decidedly the strongest of the zodiac. These people penetrate deep into the essence of others. They are highly intuitive, but reserved, cunning, and sly. Often they don't shrink from battling with dishonest means. They do everything with great intensity; they are possessive and jealous and at the same time they can make incredible sacrifices. They are curt and grim, they yield to nothing. In love, the emphasis is on sexuality. It is difficult to change a Scorpio: only the hard blows of fate make any impression on him. One has to bow before his decisions, otherwise there is trouble. He acts with self-

---

* Personally I find this form of sex the limit. I utterly agree with Frederick the Great when he gave the following judgment in the case of a cavalryman who had made love to a mare: "This individual is a pig. Transfer him to the infantry."

confidence, ruthlessness. Some people display excessive energy in danger. Scorpio thrives on danger.

A famous Frenchman once said: "You'll never achieve anything unless you have a devil in your body." Well, Scorpio is possessed by the devil, for good as well as for evil. Eroticism and aggressiveness, life and death are the four key words of this sign. He grumbles more than three Cancers together and that is saying something. He listens absentmindedly to good advice and as he listens he plans rebellion against the established order. He is a born rebel. He lets people talk and without realizing it he turns out to be an anarchist one fine day. He will like a person or dislike him, and nothing can alter his opinion. He is hard to himself. He does not forget insults and his revenge takes time and is well planned. He is strongly bound by his passions. Unfaithfulness of his spouse he does not tolerate. One often finds individuals among them whom one might call "oversexed." They are turbulent and tormented, restless, always busy with something, always fertile and creative. The Scorpio is a perfectionist. He does more work than three other people together.

He quickly sees the gist of something and one can't fool him. He is often superstitious. If a Scorpio woman is in love, she practices all her coquettish, seductive tricks; she is a kind of *ange noir*, a *femme fatale*, a Carmen who throws a flower which she has held between her teeth, into Don José's face with the words: "If I love you, then watch out." In her heart she wishes that the man will tame her, but she defies him. Once a Scorpio is dissatisfied he is dangerous. He himself is undisciplined and untidy, while he demands strict and punctual behavior of others. The Scorpio "smells" money. He spends much and then suddenly becomes mean. Money can take the place of a means of power, a substitute for libido.

A Scorpio and a Pisces understand each other without uttering one single word or even seeing each other. They are better at living with each other than at talking with each other; they understand each other intuitively and are moved by similar desires, even though they may experience these differently. (See also below under Pisces.)

Cambrian (Latin Cambria, i.e. Wales): The oldest of the five periods, subdivided in Upper, Middle, and Lower Cambrian, into which the Paleozoicum is divided. In Britain, where the entire C. has had a marine development, one can make a tripartite division with the help of fossil trilobites into Olenellus-, Paradoxides-, and Olenus-layers. In Europe one also finds the Cambrian for instance in Scandinavia, Scotland, Ireland, Brittany, the Ardennes, the Black Forest, Spain, Bohemia, Sardinia. In North America, where the Cambrian is widespread, there is a tripartite division into Georgian, Acadian and Potsdammian, approximately coinciding with the European classification. The C. is the oldest geological period in which clear remainders of plants and animals have been found. (According to radioactive measurements the C. began about 550 million years ago. It lasted for about 100 million years.) The fauna was still very limited. Trilobites and brachiopods were predominant but it is possible that there were also already quite a few other invertebrates of which no fossil remains are known. Vertebrates were most probably not yet in existence. Of the flora of this period only some algae are known. (General Winkler Prins Encyclopedia, Volume Two BENC–COMO 1956, p. 525.)

Why did I choose this period to describe the impression which the landscape made on the main character? You'll never guess. So I'll tell you. In the first place because the name CAMBRIUM, if you pronounce it lovingly and musically, is very melodious and I am basically a man who will sacrifice everything for beauty. Secondly because I love the countries where the Cambrium raged very much. Scandinavia because here one is free to walk about naked, Scotland because of its whiskey and its beautiful women, Ireland because of its unshakable faith, its clandestine loose morals and its green fields, Brittany because of its beautiful cloud formations, the Ardennes because of the lovely ham, the Black Forest because of the neatly marked touristic walks, Spain because the Law has given way to the Virgin, Bohemia because I am a Bohemian at heart, and Sardinia because I would love to own a piece of land there to build a luxury hotel on.

Helsingör: Small harbor in north Denmark where you can take the ferry boat to Sweden.

Green mamba (Dendraspis): Family of rightly feared poisonous snakes from tropical and southern Africa, more than two meters long, living in trees. Apart from the formidable poison-fangs there are no ordinary teeth in the upper jaw. In the lower jaw there is at the front a catching-tooth and at the back a number of smaller teeth. (General Winkler Prins Encyclopedia, Volume seven MAAN–OVAR 1956, p. 66.) As you see, I have a vast encyclopedic knowledge.

Hygienic: Life-philosophy of the Swedes. This first struck me when I saw in an antiseptic supermarket in the cool town of Gällivare a myopic old lady examining the prices of the packets of meat with a gigantic magnifying glass. In this context I wrote a series of articles about Lapland (which have rightly become famous) in "Het Laatste Nieuws" ("The Latest News"): "A Swede moves only his tongue and his teeth when he talks and if it were possible to speak without making these irritating movements he would be much happier. A Swede always looks in the other direction and if his look accidentally meets another human being his hair stands on end and he writhes in discomfort. A Swede painstakingly avoids contact, talks with other people as little as possible, and only touches objects he has honestly paid for. Why drunk Scandinavian sailors in foreign ports should be counted among the most feared savages is still a mystery to me. Coughing and blowing your nose in public is dreadfully rude. Even bursting out in laughter leads to icy cold looks. Traffic accidents are chiefly caused by reindeer crossing the road. In a supermarket it is as quiet as in a court of justice just before the verdict, a post office looks like a pharmacy and in a pharmacy tall bespectacled figures in spotless white coats move about as if in an operating theater. Talking loudly is discouraged by law but there is no-where any sign of the police because everybody scrupulously follows the letter and the spirit of the law. The ordinary Swede proudly hoists the national flag on Friday evening on the flagpole at his wooden holiday cottage somewhere in a terribly remote spot on a lake (one of the ninety-six thousand) or in the middle of a forest or preferably on an island where he can fish, read and be silent, undisturbed. The forest is in fact the only place where the Swede really feels at home: even politicians have a ramblers' hut in the woods where they can clump about to their heart's content in rubber boots, tartan shirts, and unshaven, something which in Belgium would be almost unthinkable. Religion on the other hand does not seem to interest the Swedes overmuch. About 100 percent of them may be nominal members of one sect or another, but only 2 percent attend church services ("the pinnacle of hygiene!" J.G.), which has as its immediate result that the immaculate wooden churches do not pose parking problems by taking up too much space, nor cause traffic problems on Sunday when the faithful come out, as is sometimes the case in Belgium.

Virtually naked: Or altogether naked, it doesn't matter. One can do this freely because there are in this country (I mean Sweden) no peeping toms. You need not look far for the cause: there are no confession boxes where one learns to peer through holes at a very young age.

Chablis: Racy, white, lightly perfumed Burgundy, poetically called "oysterwater" by the Dutch, another indication of their common sense.

Naked: The second clear sexual allusion. To lie in a tent *naked!* One doesn't do a thing like that because it isn't proper. In marriage it may be allowed under certain circumstances, although it should never be encouraged, but there is absolutely nothing in this story to suggest that the two characters are united in holy wedlock. Why young authors nowadays should be conducting a systematic subversive action against our morals, is a mystery to me. Personally, for instance, I only take off my panties in the toilet and also on Saturdays when I wash myself and change my underwear. On Saturday evening my husband usually carries out his conjugal duties too, so that there's no extra bother. (Statement of the wife of a Catholic critic to an intimate friend.)

Naked: Why would you want to walk around naked in a forest, for God's sake. It's so stupid one can only laugh at it. Only madmen would do such a thing. The author probably does it merely for show, because it has absolutely nothing to do with the spirit of the story. He would do better to carry out his responsibilities as a family man, rather than go off to Lapland with a strange woman. (Jos Ghysen * for the regional radio of Limburg.)

---

* Popular philosopher with a family.

and . . . : Fourth clear sexual allusion and moreover a no less than *dirty* understatement. Are they making love here or aren't they? We are asking ourselves this question. This sows doubt in the hearts of the young. Sowing doubt in every field seems to be the task which the young dirt-and-lust writers have taken upon themselves. You ought not to read this. It will not enrich you, and that is after all the task of literature. (Curate J. Stevens during a talk to young engaged couples in the series "Looking together in one direction.")

Fantastic milk: With butter and water the only foodstuff which is both nice and cheap in Sweden. The white bread, in airtight wrapping, tastes of foam rubber, the cheese spread contains sugar and coffee extract, the pudding contains mainly gelatin, the marmalade mainly water, the beer mainly coloring, the meat mainly hormones, the eggs mainly folliculin. In snackbars there is a smell of deodorants which is dispersed efficiently every five minutes by synthetically smiling white *frøkens* softly manipulating computers which in their turn produce edible ware to which one then has to try to give a taste by means of applying, free of charge, all kinds of ketchup, mustard, Worcestershire sauce, celery salt, etc. Wine and spirits are sold in special shops, at exorbitant prices. The bottles themselves are packed in white and red checkered paper bags, so that one is so conspicuous in the street that the Swedes, clearly disturbed, turn the other way. No other place in the world contains more lonely drinkers than Sweden.

Trolls' drum: Drum to allay or propitiate trolls. Often used by Lapps. A troll is a malevolent, demonic creature from northern mythology.

Edda: Name of two collective works from Old Icelandic literature, the old poetic Edda and the later prose Edda. The oldest poems probably stem from the time of the Vikings and were written down toward the end of the thirteenth century. The work consists of fifteen epics about gods and seventeen about heroes, all of them in alliterative verse of various constructions. The younger prose Edda or Snorra Edda is a manual in verse and mythology, written by Snorri Sturluson (1178–1241).

Pisces: My constellation (Jef Geeraerts). I was in fact born

February 23, 1930, at half past four in the afternoon on carnival Sunday. My ascendant is the Lion and this is a rare combination, as all handbooks about astrology will tell you. As you see, you simply need a bit of luck in life. Napoleon too attached much importance to it. For instance, if he wanted to promote an officer to general, he never asked how brilliant he was (he could be sure that he was), but whether he was usually lucky.

In the time of year when storm and rain, frost and thaw rage about the earth in a flood, when all things are deserted and lonely, but when new life is being prepared (under the earth the seed germinates, the sap rises in the plants), everything is without form and withdrawn in darkness, an empty silence full of hope and faith, at that moment the last sign of the Zodiac (February 19–March 20) makes its entry. The symbol of the Fishes represents two fishes which belong together, one of them swimming upward, the other diving into the depths. Their mouths point in opposite directions. This is the split character of the Fishes. They belong to a kind which is difficult to describe. They are at all times the lonely stranger, they do not care for possessions, they feel nowhere at home and let themselves be swept along on the tide of life because they are curious about the capriciousness of fate. They are restless. They constantly want to escape from the circumscribed world, they live in a mist, they live in a bond with the invisible, they are fishes which glide and suddenly turn around, stay still in the current, suddenly to dart away like a flash of lightning. They are always intently busy with something, especially in order to confirm something within themselves. They usually live very frivolously, full of swarming plans which are not carried out because they can never attain perfection. Toward enemies the Pisces has a very effective weapon: gaining time. It is the sign of self-deception. Usually they are without self-interest. They wish to serve. If they don't succeed, they flee. They throw money around because money is of no importance to them. They are suited to be true craftsmen leading primitive lives. As all Water signs, whose oversensitivity is well known (Cancer, Scorpio), the Pisces knows the despair of life itself. The Cancer makes it into a comedy, the Scorpio settles accounts with it, but the Pisces is made great by it. They are full of understanding when others need them, otherwise they hardly see their fellowmen. They are usually a mystery to the people around them. A Pisces is most in his element where it is quiet and where he can work and make a mess without being disturbed. Pisces don't care for their clothes. They slouch through life. They will be fanatically in love with an old jacket and a dilapidated hat and break all the rules of fashion by paying no attention to them. The heart of a Pisces is full of longing. Love strikes and overwhelms him. To him freedom is the most precious thing on earth. He is very fond of good food and delighted with little presents. He can go without everything, except the small token of affection. In a large company he keeps his mouth shut and is almost churlish because of his absent-mindedness. In the open air and in seclusion he feels at ease. Among them there are many popes and artists in numerous fields, but literature and music predominate strikingly. These artists, moreover, put everything at stake in order to achieve their goal with total disregard of success.

Ragnarök: The destruction of the world in the Edda poem called Völuspa, interpreted as the struggle of the gods against giants and monsters, announced by Baldr's death. People and gods die because of the actions of Loki, Fenrir, and the universal serpent; the world goes up in flames and the earth sinks away in the ocean. A kind of Northern Apocalypse, but without horses because it was too cold for horses in Norway.

Pee: Not a way of writing the letter p but a verb.

Instant pudding: Pour half a pint of cold milk into a bowl. Add contents of the packet. Whisk vigorously with an eggbeater until the powder is dissolved. Pour the pudding into a dish or pudding glasses, then leave for fifteen minutes until set.

Your underwear: This is beyond all limits! Sexual obsession isn't enough, no, here he comes with one of the filthiest aberrations: fetishism with women's underwear.* That is what happens

---

° "A third form of clothes fetishism, which is pathological to a higher degree, is the following, which is the most frequently observed. It consists in this that it is no longer the woman herself, even dressed in a certain way, who is the sexual attraction in the first place, but the sexual attraction lies in a particular piece of feminine clothing, and the representation of this garment, accompanied with pleasure, is detached from the image of the woman and takes on an independent value. This is the true domain of clothes fetishism, where an inanimate object, an isolated garment, is used for its own sake for

when irresponsible publishers throw a cheap edition of that dirty book by Krafft-Ebing on the market. Such things always have fatal consequences. The popes of the Renaissance knew better: when a new popular edition of the Decameron was published, it was promptly put on the Index. This was not the case, however, with the luxury editions. This distinction was a very wise decision on the part of Our Mother The Holy Church; for centuries she has been very conscious indeed of her vast task concerning the moral health of the faithful. (Anonymous reader.)

Zip fastener: One-year guarantee.

Conclusion

Catholic critics will undoubtedly have noted that in my stories God is dead. I might reply to this famous sally by Nietzsche with an equally sharp dictum, namely *God is not dead because he has never lived,* but I won't, no, the matter is too serious in my opinion. Somewhere I spoke about Hemingway's iceberg. Well, this applies to the case of God as well. You don't see him anywhere in my stories, but he is implied everywhere. If the Catholic critics can't guess this, their religious feeling must be in a sad state indeed. In order to refresh it, I therefore advise them most strongly to read the famous book by Father Giovanni Cascaminetti, S.J.: *L'Eglise apostolique, universelle et catholique, preuve suprême de l'existence de Dieu.* It is a standard work which should figure on the bookshelves of every intellectual.

---

the excitement and the satisfaction of the sexual instinct. This third form of clothes fetishism is also the most important in legal medical respect. In quite a few cases, it is a question of under-garments, which are particularly appropriate, because of their intimate nature, to lead to such associations." (p. 351, Dr. R. von Krafft-Ebing, *Psychopatia sexualis*, Paris. Payot, 1950, 906 pp.)

In the story "Indian Summer" there is no mention of "satisfaction of the sexual instinct" and as Jef Geeraerts often uses the method of understatement, we are therefore in the dark about it. In any case, we think it's rather risqué. Besides, the sniffing of the underwear of a *dead* woman is not mentioned by Krafft-Ebing, but it is at least as morbid and revolting as the case mentioned by Diez in *"Der Selbstmord"* mentioned on p. 24. Here a man tears women's underwear to pieces and has an ejaculation as a result. (*Notes by a reader who has made a thorough study of the subject.*)

Translated by Adrienne Dixon.

JACQUES HAMELINK

A *Pause in the Thunder*

SWAMP I knew René suffered from migraine—his mother had
warned us often enough to go easy with him, not to hit him, for
instance, or make him angry without cause. And that's precisely
what we had done now and then, because, aside from his knowing
everything there was to know about the swamp behind the village,
we boys weren't too fond of René.

He could be stubborn and high-handed, and yet quite often he
was extraordinarily dim about things we understood first go. He
was a very mediocre pupil at school, shining only in botany and
zoology. As a matter of fact, those were probably the only subjects he tried his best at. Yet it has to be admitted that you
couldn't show him a single plant without his knowing its name
and the sort of soil it grew on. He often even knew its Latin
name as well, though we suspected him of kidding us on as far as
that was concerned.

At home he had a collection of dried plants, and he must have
spent a lot of time on it—at least, you never saw much of him
outside school hours. He was a show-off in a way, but, strangely
enough, one who only boasted about things he was ignorant
about, or didn't have himself. You would never hear him talk
about the swamp, where he often used to roam about, alone, or
accompanied by a shadowy figure, some older man from the
village. Nor would he talk about his collection of plants or the
tropical aquarium he had at home.

He didn't say a word about the things that really interested him.
And if you yourself were to mention them, he'd act superior, as
though it was above you. He always gave you the feeling he was
showing you only one side of himself, that in his private, secret

world he was someone quite different from the boy who played with us, who could quarrel over a bit of kite string or some small debt incurred when the fair was at the village, and whom we weren't to upset, because then he'd be sick for three days and come back slouching across the playground, his face more like a mask, the movements of his lean body more wooden than ever.

So he was a rather strange boy, yet no one could have foreseen that his being different would lead to such a catastrophe. As a matter of fact, it's not certain whether his complaint really was the cause of his strange way of behaving.

Of course, you could argue that none of it would have happened if that morning, on the day of the tragedy, a morning toward the end of the summer vacation, when we'd all been bored to death for weeks, Marc Kanoffel hadn't suggested that we all go off to the swamp after dinner. But it's useless saying that now. Besides, I know, even if I can't explain it, I know for sure that it would have happened in any case. At some other time, in some other way, maybe—it makes no difference: it would have happened for the simple reason that it had to, it was in the air. And I'm now beginning to see that I was aware of it too, that whole afternoon.

Marc Kanoffel was the leader of our gang. He was big and strong for his age—fourteen. If one of us others had suggested that we go into the forbidden, enticing swamp, the proposal wouldn't have met with much enthusiasm. But now that Marc, the blond savage, the self-assured leader, wanted to, we forgot our fear that they might get to know of the excursion and give us a far from friendly reception when we got back. For we wanted to appear tough—especially to him. It had now become a grand adventure, full of forbidden delight and thrilling, nerve-racking anxiety.

It must have been about eleven in the morning. We were leaning against the wall near the dairy just opposite the school, in the only street our village could boast. We older boys would usually congregate there during the school term, telling jokes or passing remarks as girls from our school walked by, arm in arm. When Marc suggested that that afternoon we should all go "behind the village"—this was our euphemistic way of referring to the area our parents and teacher had placed strictly out of bounds—we looked surreptitiously to see how René reacted and saw him look away, as if he hadn't heard, his rather oldish face— that had the same dingy brown color both winter and summer— expressionless. If he wouldn't come along the plan would fall through. Marc was our unchallenged leader and it would have been absurd to appoint René Dooms, one of the least of us when it came to agility, good sense, and muscle power, in his place. But we all knew it: if René doesn't come, even the rebellious Marc who after all had stolen the bell from the teacher's front door and switched his saddle for his handlebars, so he must have thought he'd gone crazy when he tried to ride off on his bike, even Marc will back down. After all, he's no more familiar with the swamp than we are. He's just as scared of it. Only maybe he's more fascinated by it—that's why he's our leader: he has to be daring, a devil-may-care we others look up to.

René—I can see him before me now: that typical toss of the head as he began to speak, a tic—suddenly swung round, as though bored by the idea and merely giving in to our looks of entreaty, and said: "I'll come."

He sounded a bit hesitant—he was no easy talker. There was something wrong with his tongue and he had been in the hospital for it some time back. But at that moment, with those two words, he sealed his fate, and the only question I'm left with is whether a higher decision hadn't already been arrived at concerning the fate of this particular human being, and whether that little sentence of his wasn't merely his unconscious acceptance of it.

After he'd agreed, he turned round and looked away from us down the street, which was empty, and uneven, and sunny, and beyond which, invisible, yet quite near, lay the mysterious, steamy swamp, stinking of blossoming and of death, that made our blood uneasy in those last days of summer.

The sky began to cloud over a little that afternoon, when a group of about ten of us, each equipped with a stick and a water bottle, left the village behind us. Before us stretched the level land. Over the swamp the sun was a great burning yellow disk with uneven edges. There was little or no wind. The country- side dozed peacefully on its way toward the autumn, advancing quietly, and already making its presence felt in shorn, bare fields and an indefinable ethereal quality in the air surrounding things.

For a time we followed a narrow, uneven ditch, passing a farmyard, where two men were looking at a tractor, and turning off to take a little path along which the grass and stinging nettles grew tall and thick among piles of rubble that had probably come from the neighboring farm. In the deserted potato fields, which stretched out on either side of it, an old man was bending down, looking for any that might have been left lying there. We waved our arms wildly and shouted out to him. He straightened up and looked our way for a moment, one hand feeling his back as he did so: a scarecrow come to sudden, stiff life.

After half an hour or so, we arrived at a low-lying field bordering on the swamp, and Marc told us to wait. Some of us didn't want to, but Marc told them right away that, in that case, they'd have to look out for themselves and they obviously weren't keen on that idea. We sat down in the grass, drank a bit from our water bottles, and consulted together.

In the distance I could see cows moving about in a meadow. A green beetle was crawling up my bare arm, making his way between the hairs as though through a sparse forest. I held out a blade of grass and the little creature crawled up onto it. Then I shook it off inside the collar of René's shirt.

"Damn," he said, when he felt it tickling him.

Marc said we better cut that out.

René finally succeeded in getting rid of it and it seemed to me that it was only now that he was beginning to show any interest in our adventure—I remembered that he hadn't waved and shouted with us at that solitary potato-scavenger. He lay chewing on a stalk of grass and leaning on his elbows, listening, with eyes closed to slits against the sunlight, to the others' confused babble. It struck me even then that though, on the whole, he definitely wasn't any more mature or wiser than the rest of us, he had a certain calm about him which we lacked and which made him seem older than he actually was. He, the boy who was nervous, withdrawn, apparently felt at ease, less scared than usual of our taunts and blows.

Kneeling in our circle, Marc gave us a brief and businesslike explanation of the game we were going to play, and I looked with a kind of awe at this boy, who was no older than myself: at his unbuttoned sport shirt, under which he wore nothing else, at his long, supple body and his lank, straw-blond hair, which he would stroke away out of his eyes every now and then with a careless brush of his hand.

One of us was to go and hide in the swamp, though he didn't have to stay in the same spot all the time. He was supposed to be a bandit on the run and the others had to look for him. If he evaded capture for half an hour, the others had lost and the game would begin all over again, with another boy playing the bandit.

One boy didn't agree with this idea. He was a rather big boy, with thick lips and black, curly hair, but I've forgotten his name, and those of the others, now. He proposed that we should form a line across the swamp and one of us try to get through it without being detected. But Marc stuck to his plan, which, he said, would be more exciting for everyone.

Another boy, easily scared and not feeling too sure of himself so close to this forbidden area, asked if the fugitive would be allowed to hide as well in Pick Creek, the most treacherous part of all.

"Why not?" said René, suddenly aggressive. "It's mighty fine there, all tall reeds. I've often been there with Theo." Theo was the swamp warden, an old farmer fallen on bad times who'd been given this job and who roamed about in the swamp for days on end.

"And what if we meet up with him?" another boy asked.

"What if we do?" René challenged him. "You don't think he'd drown us, do you?"

"My father says that two boys were drowned in Pick Creek once. They'd gone there to cut bulrushes," the boy answered.

It made us all feel kind of uneasy: we'd heard that story too. It was a fact. They'd been quite black in the face, those two, when their bodies had been recovered. The carpenter had had to get them into their coffins right away. They swelled up like balloons.

But much rather than confess to our secret fear, we shouted out that he was crazy and should shut his trap and cut all that old wives' prattle. Marc kept a disdainful silence, conscious of his responsibility, and was determined to continue as planned.

René said any cowards had better piss off. He jumped up, more lithe, more agile, it seemed, than usual. Here he was in his element. The fact that the thought of Pick Creek made us all pretty uneasy, even Marc, who was probably making sure he didn't lose face in his presence, filled René with a sharp joy. You could see it in his eyes, which had something harder, brighter, in them than usual, and in the small, determined lines that had appeared around his mouth. As if this kids' enterprise was a thing of great importance, which it probably was, too.

At that point we felt he was stronger than Marc, who had dropped back in our thoughts to second place and seemed to sense this, confirm it even, by asking René if we should start, what he thought about it?

"He's not coming with us," René said, pointing to the boy who was scared of getting near Pick Creek. It was his condition for taking on the job of guide.

We agreed. No one stood up for the boy, even though every one of us but René probably agreed with him. But René had now got us where he wanted us.

If none of us had cared what the others thought about him, he—and maybe Marc—would have gone into the swamp alone. The haunting thought of those two boys who had been drowned, with their tongues bitten off and their huge, puffed-up bodies, cast a shadow over all the fun. But we were ashamed of confessing it to one another, and especially to Marc and René. And so the hunt-the-fugitive game was on.

The only honest coward had been cried down. And we told him to remember us to our parents, should he be thinking of telling on us, the dope.

EXPLOSION René tells us to take off our shoes and socks. We obey. The bottles are left behind as well. Feeling no thirst, René unscrews the cap of his and empties out the contents: a dark brown stream of cold tea.

Then, armed with our sticks, we move fast across the field. A single, sagging thread of barbed wire, attached to posts of all sizes and here and there to projecting branches, is all there is to protect the cattle from the treacherous bog beyond. We climb over it.

Already the ground begins to be marshy. The grass seems taller and greener and is no longer a thick mat but grows in tussocks, between which you can see the brown, porous soil that turns black where our feet have trodden. Mud.

Before us, a dense belt of reeds, cut down to half its width on this side. Farmers have been here to collect reeds to lay over their potato heaps. From beyond this wall-like barrier comes the cry of waterfowl.

Moving cautiously, to avoid stepping with our bare feet on the stubbles, we continue on our way. René in front, and no longer saying a word. Nor do we. The tension has become almost tangible. We're on forbidden ground now. Then we're standing, with the unmoving reeds all round us, before a small pool, about a foot deep. The bottom is choked with rotting plants. René is picking his way ahead, carefully but confidently.

I suddenly become aware of the silent threat hanging above us. The sky is gray, mottled with patches of paler light. In it the sun is a vague, impotent circle. The wind has dropped now. The reeds stand in line, motionless. The cry of a bird. Once.

Just the sound of our feet, slopping in porridgy soil. Daunted, through an immense sea of silence, the bottom visible, we wade on, like a line of geese, accompanied by our shadows, the disfigured shapes of our bodies.

Then we've reached the fringe of reeds on the other side of the shallows. The ground rises and becomes firmer as we proceed. And into the silence, that has closed over us like a globe of glass, our silence, René suddenly sends a wild cry. "Oohoo!" he cries, like one possessed.

We, freed at one stroke, shout with him. The noise of it sends up birds everywhere that speed away with clacking wings, flying low above the plumy reeds. Waterfowl (or rats? or some mysterious, invisible creatures?) beat the water with wings or legs.

The sky has darkened still further. It looks as if it's going to rain. But René won't hear of postponing it now. The game is about to begin.

We penetrate deeper and deeper into the heavy-odored vegetation. There are bunches of dark green foliage, taller than we and with yellow blossoms whose scent is suffocating. And plants with broad scalloped leaves spreading out low over the ground. Now and then a tawny water rat scurries into hiding just before our feet. Then there's a pollard willow, with its roots all exposed and a hollow trunk split down its length, the mold all fallen out of it. What is this tree doing here? Insects buzz.

All of us sense disaster in the air, advancing, building up, getting ready to burst. This is a no-man's-land. We can smell it. I run the tip of my tongue round my dry lips. The water bottles are lying back there.

Yet René doesn't seem to be affected by it. He shouts, does things, claps his hands. We all resent it. It's not right. He's brought us here. *If anything happens, he'll be the one to blame.*

What *can* happen? Suddenly I recall that night on the beach, where we camped last summer. We've built a campfire. We're stamping round a washed-up tree trunk we've drenched in kerosene, bawling out wild war songs. Late-night strollers along the beach stop and watch the show we're putting on. The glow of the fire in the hollowed-out trunk is dying down, and René, bending low over the final embers, begins to shout out hoarse cries; the medicine man, attempting to exorcize the flames, and who, in some manner unknown to us, is now invested with power. I shiver, uneasy about what our playmate is doing with the great, dark forces of the sea, night, and fire, about an alliance of which he forms part but from which we are excluded. And I shiver again now.

I know the others are aware of it too. This time it must be the approaching rain, the impending thunderstorm, that is working him up to this pitch. At any rate, he's standing now with arms raised, shrieking at the sky. Has he gone crazy? But the game's about to begin.

The tree's our base. We must wait near it till René has hidden himself in the depths of the swamp, the part unknown to us. He disappears, plunging with hasty steps through a breathless silence in which we are left behind, small and subdued. A short while later that "oohoo" cry of his sounds in the distance. It is the signal for us to go over to the attack.

We soon overcome our initial anxiety and our group breaks up. Now the "oohoo" sounds are coming from several spots in the swamp—it's our way of keeping in touch with one another. From the sound of them we must be moving forward in a broad arc. On my own now, I wrestle a way through masses of spiky-haired leaves.

"Oohoo!" I hear to one side of me, quite near. "Oohoo!" I call back. "Oohoo!" is being shouted all over the place in long, cracked cries.

I'm getting ahead pretty quickly, and yet it seems as if something else, besides the resistant vegetation, the squelching mud, the fronds, is trying to impede my progress. It's as though I'm trying to force my way deeper into a tough, resilient silence, that's closing in on me, nearer and nearer, with every step I take. I call out: "Oohoo!" but the sound comes up out of my throat as if I were being strangled. "Oohoo!" comes the response, and I start off again.

If I were alone, I'd panic, and, without bothering to look where I was placing my feet, I'd run straight back to where I imagined the safe, open meadow lay. But is that field now ahead of me or behind me? Is it on my right, or on my left? I've lost my bearings. The hunt continues. My only guides to space or time now are reeds, water, the odors of the swamp, of unidentified flowers, and the silence—in which you can hear your blood pulsing through your veins. Your private space, an internal time, that has become eternal, that stands still.

I notice that I've landed up on the extreme left of our line. The cries of the others are coming from my right, most of them from fairly far off. I recognize Marc's voice—firmer, stronger than those of the other boys, which now sound to me like a chorus in which no individual voice can be distinguished.

Suddenly I'm running with muddy feet over short, velvety moss. Then leaves again, fluffy heads of seed, rising in clouds. I spit them out of my mouth. My shirt is sticking to my back. I bite my tongue by accident as I run. A sweet taste.

I've broken through the barrier like a savage, young beast, sometimes advancing sideways, thrusting branches and leaves aside with both my hands, my body lashed now and then by a branch swinging sharply back. I lost my stick ages ago.

Then I'm standing in front of a mirror of utterly motionless water, thick and shiny as oil, on the surface of which bubbles, like little marbles, are moving round and round.

A sort of little river, about a hundred yards wide, winds out of sight on either side of me, disappearing between reeds and yellow irises. This, I know for sure, is Pick Creek.

At that very moment, I catch sight of René.

He is sitting leaning against the steep bank on the other side, which seems to form a natural dyke. His feet are in the water, which is making rippling rings round his ankles and holding him there, a prisoner. He doesn't look up or around him. He's forgotten all about our game.

Everything acquires the sharp outlines of a vision. If your eyes saw things like this for long, you'd go blind.

He bends forward a little, his elbows on his knees. He's got something in his hands. A box of matches. He slides it open and strikes a match. He bends over still further and holds the lighted match down so that it is almost touching the black surface.

Then the world becomes light and dark, a deep, basalt blue. It happens so quickly that the two colors are actually simultaneous. A reddish glow speeds low across the water, burns itself out in rolls of flame.

A tremendous balloon bursts. The force of it flings me to the ground. Clouds. Blue. Black. At almost the next moment I'm standing up again. I can see, breathe, feel.

But the sound's gone.

LIE DOWN   René is standing upright on the far shore. Or isn't it René? I'm staring so hard I can't be sure to begin with. A thin, dark human body, lean. Like those figures I've seen in the museum in the town, made of wire. Primitive, yet alive, mobile. His arms are hanging down his sides, clumsily, limply.

Yes, it's René. But no longer the old René. An animated doll, a puppet, making automatic movements learned long before. He's gazing at the water. His eyes are huge and bulging in a head that's grown far too big. The body beneath it seems twisted. He keeps staring ahead of him into the water and goes to take a step forward. He lifts a leg. But what incomprehensible tiredness has come over him? He seems to shrivel up under the invisible burden of a world of sleep weighing down on his shoulders.

He hesitates, staggers. The hands grope out for something to hold onto. He stands swaying on his feet, like a sleepwalker. Then he takes a step forward and the surface of the water is splintered. With a tremendous effort, as though iron chains have been fastened round his ankles, he drags himself forward.

I watch, become an eye, no longer conscious of my body.

There is neither pain nor despair in his bulging eyes. Simply a terrible pondering, a probing concentration that contains all the thinking of generations of men. A pondering which penetrates down to the muddy roots of the water plants, to deep down into the spongy bed of the creek, effortless, yet which is now hard put to it to force its own body to move. As though with each step he is sinking down a further couple of feet (yet the bed is of sand, I see), he struggles on.

Then he falls forward. I imagine he's lost consciousness. Slowly, with painful jerks, he sinks to his knees. The water is perhaps eighteen inches deep. Did he, in that split second a moment ago, get burns I can't see? He continues to kneel there for a second or two: a priest engaged in his strange ritual. The eyelids have now closed over the eyes. With the utmost concentration he considers for the last time the thought that is eluding him. Then he sinks further forward. The stiff hands grope out for the smooth bed of the creek. Find it. The fingers spread out under the water. The legs stretch backwards.

For one moment he is resting on hands and feet. A bizarre gymnastic exercise, aimed at keeping head and body dry. Then the body sinks too, the head last of all: a rigid mask, the eyes shut, about the mouth a mixture of contentedness and pain—but it's the contentedness that seems to dominate. What is playing there about the mouth—I watch it with something approaching awe—may possibly be a smile.

Slowly the greasy water smooths over the place where the mirror has been broken. Two, three bubbles rise to the surface: big, like eyes that close.

And then I am able to shout once more.

I scream the air to pieces, as if, at that moment, I myself were being born. It's as if I'm being thrust out of a womb of warmth and silence. It's cold. But the storm, I see, is moving away.

Already the sky, still dotted with heads of thundercloud, is growing brighter.

Bubbles are floating on the surface of the water.

A light breeze is advancing through the forest of reeds.

From every corner my cries are being answered.

FOAM-RUBBER DOLL   Breaking through the belt of shrubs that line Pick Creek further up, Marc comes running toward me along the water's edge. He's as pale as death, and I can't stop my legs' trembling either. An electric current is shooting through my every muscle.

"An explosion!" he shouts. "Someone's trodden on a mine or something. They say there are some here."

It leaves me cold. I don't even believe it.

"René," I mutter, and point across the water. I can hardly get the name across my lips.

"What?" Marc asks, panting.

"He's fallen over," I say. "Into the water." How can I explain to him what's happened?

"Face first," I add, foolishly. "He didn't come up again. Over there, on the other side."

Marc is as shocked as I am and begins to look around him wildly.

"We must do something," he says, and then begins shouting his "Oohoo!" cry again to the others. Their answers come from quite nearby.

A couple of moments later we are standing there, a small, mud-bespattered, shabby band, with torn shirts, some of us with cuts and bloody noses—the explosion flung some face downward onto roots and stumps—pale and shivering, all bunched together and staring across at the far shore. Nobody knows what to do to begin with. We'd like most of all to run away as fast as we can, but René is lying over there in the swamp. He may still be alive. Though there's not one of us that believes he is.

"He only went under a minute or two ago," I tell them. "If we act quickly . . ."

Marc has now recovered some of his self-control.

"We'll form a chain," he says, "and hold on to each other. I'll go first."

Resolute, he steps into the stinking black water, on which, near the edge, small, white flowers are floating. Carefully, sounding the bottom for firmness with his stick, he goes further. We follow. It's all right. The sandy bed holds firm. There's no mud. This water doesn't seem to be part of the real swamp we've been coming through. It's obviously more of a creek.

We move cautiously, putting first our toes and only then the flat of our feet on the bottom. We're halfway by now. A sort of sick disgust at the idea of being sucked down into it takes hold of me. But the creek proves to be no deeper than a couple of feet and the water's already coming less far up our legs.

Under the surface lies a yellowish, oblong shape.

We stop there.

Some wade, still with the utmost caution, to the edge. The others stand still. As though it's all been decided on in advance, Marc and I bend down and heave up the pallid form out of the water. It seems to have become weightless. Marc takes the head, I the feet, and at the same moment each of us notices the monstrous transformation that has taken place. The other boys take fright and are up on the bank in a flash, where it seems safer than here, in the mysterious, rippling water, with this horrific thing.

We drag the body to the narrow strip of sand at the foot of the steep bank and lay it down.

One boy, on the verge of tears, immediately says he wants to go home, but is silenced by Marc's savage "Goddamn!"

It's too much for all of us. Our thoughts close ranks. The thing lying there isn't one of us any more. It is hostile—because it scares us.

On the white sand lies a strange, lightish gray, wan something, as streamlined as a fish. The legs taper off toward the feet. The feet themselves have become small, unrecognizable stumps.

The flesh is spongy, with dilated pores, and long, liver-red colored stripes run down it on either side. A foam-rubber doll, whose head lolls gently to and fro at the end of a neck that has shriveled to the thickness of a thumb. We gaze with horror at the grotesque head saying "no": an indescribably deformed lump of congealed pulp, green and yellow, like a fruit. A flat, round melon, a crooked, spongy moon, without eyes, the nose caved in, and out of what has been a mouth but is now a mere hole, a protruding, curled-up tongue, pure white with brownish edges.

And the worst of all is that, in spite of everything, this being still seems to have something gay about it. The head wiggles slowly in the rising wind, and about its sea-plant mouth a sort of scarcely discernible, vegetable laugh seems to be playing, a mocking laugh that makes the sweat break out on me.

The boys stand there paralyzed. Even when Marc goes to say something his voice catches in his throat.

One of the boys can't avoid being sick and almost chokes in his vomit.

I look at the thing on the ground: a frightening statue that at any moment may come to unexpected, horrible life.

Should we try artificial respiration? one of us asks desperately. No one swears at him. Marc, no longer a prey to horror, has found his tongue again.

"That won't be necessary," he says in a broken voice.

I know he's trying to understand it too; but he can't. It's not possible. Shall we ever be able to understand this? Shall we ever become wise, old, ripe enough for that?

Maybe we're here by election—like the preacher tries to explain to us at confirmation class, rather than by chance.

Once we've heaved it up out of the water, we're scared to touch this creature again. We are prevented from doing so by a fear of poisoning, of being infected by some unnameable germ.

We must get back to the village now. Where no one will ever understand this thing; not the doctor, not our parents, no one. But perhaps the teacher. . .? "Nonsense!" "But we didn't kill him. . . ."

No one in the world will be able to understand this. Our little group shares a terrible secret to which we don't even know the answer.

Suddenly I realize I've got to urinate. It does me good. The moist sand immediately sucks up my water, and my belly is relieved of a scorching tension. It hurts, because I've held it so long. Frothy little bubbles are left on the sand.

The doll, which I imagine is secretly gloating over our return journey and sticking out its horrible tongue still further behind our backs, nods its head incessantly on the end of its rubber neck.

Then Marc tells us to get a move on. We leave.

In the swamp frogs croak contemptuously as we go. An owl hoots out its subdued cry. A chill mist, rising up out of the mud, closes in on us, dulling our thinking, our constant thinking of that one thing.

My head feels dizzy, as though I have a fever.

PEACE   What do I know? What can I do but guess? What have I to say when I get there? I've got hold of the idea that that thing is not really dead. Dead, yes—in the ordinary, every-day sense of the word, but not in the other. In some weird way I know it still exists, in a way that is almost frighteningly peaceful, in a way that comes closer to the rhythm of earth and night and water. And that at this very moment it may be laughing at me, with a laugh that differs in no wise from weeping, because such distinctions have now disappeared.

A strange excitement forces me to go on writing.

This day has gone differently from other days. Close to this house bulldozers are biting away at the soil, digging the course for a new canal. There, among the piles of earth, I found the fossils of plants and animals. Age-old tree trunks lay piled up in great heaps. It was as though I were descending into a lost, but still intact, prehistoric world, that was drawing me in, silent and malign. I spent hours with that ancient, black soil, with weirdly shaped stones and lumps of wood. The tall cranes, silhouetted against the sky, were the heads of mammoths, moving slowly across the horizon through a morass of mud and vegetation, plumping onward on ponderous, gigantic feet.

High up in the sky, clouds were blowing across on a hurried voyage to an unknown destination. What am I looking for here? A silence that exists no more, nowhere? A vegetable breathing which fills me with fear, yet calls me, irresistibly, on?

Stretched diagonally across my life, lies an inhuman corpse that infects the soil and plants with corruption, but that continues to live on: a terrible sign.

Maybe it is for this I am searching along this torn-open piece of the earth's skin. Maybe it is this I am trying, reluctantly, to retrace, to look at again, now I'm a grown man—to see the mystery of it "in the flesh," to resist it, and so break the spell in which it has held me. Maybe what I'm looking for is one and the same thing as that which lodges in sores and scabs, in cancerous tumors, in boils, in pus. In people with open, quivering wounds, monstrous; with vegetable feet that have suddenly become rooted in the soil of their own front gardens, and who stand smiling, still astonished.

Maybe it is the reason why I'm scared of people with skin diseases, all mercurial scaliness, of lepers with hands and feet rotting away—because very soon now they will turn into fish covered with scales, or into seals, dreaming in the sun on the sandbanks in the estuary. What I'm looking for may be the germ of all this, the undemonstrable cause, the virus that can never be localized in any laboratory.

Did René succumb to an urge he was no longer able to master and which led him on? Or did it happen to him all at once? I don't know.

Suddenly I'm overwhelmed by the feeling I'm wading through the swamp as he did that day. A wild presentiment takes possession of my brain. I can hardly move a foot. Cold with sweat, I sit down on a tree trunk which has lain buried here for thousands of centuries.

Time has passed. It's afternoon.

At last I've recovered sufficiently to be able to make my way back home.

There are holes, white, ageless, in the sky.

Has what began years ago, what time has stood still for so long, arrived at last, through me, at its consummation? And is that why, as I sit writing this, close at hand the thunder is beginning to rumble, all at once, unheralded by a darkening sky, a stillness in the air? As though that unbearable absence of sound which commenced that afternoon long ago, is only now about to end, a former equilibrium about to be restored?

Translated by James Brockway.

HEERE HEERESMA

From Your Evil Ways

We're perishing, captain, we're perishing.
Captain, we're perishing from sorrow and misery.

HE'S lain down in the low brush like a dying man. The hang-over's so severe he no longer bothers about beetles, ants, or spiders. That's me, his thoughts go, well, more or less, caving in before my own eyes—and you can hardly call that an observation worth mentioning on this morning, that's fine and summery: fresh, sunny, a golden sky, through which the Sabres stationed in the neighborhood have been screaming since it became light, landing and taking off again, breaking through the sound barrier with dull booms and chasing over the treetops in formation. Down below, watching things through the undergrowth and keeping his eyes fixed on the road to the station, the leaves of the small, star-shaped plant brushing against his lips, he sees columns of military vehicles approaching, turning off and dis-appearing into the opening in the barbed wire on the other side of the road down which he's come. There's a fair number of delivery vans too, belonging to the laundries that have set up business hereabout, attracted by the softness of the water. Yes. It's a new day all right—and here he was, hanging and floating rather than actually lying on these thin, strong twigs.

Only a moment ago, staggering, spitting out bitter saliva as he went, he'd left the attractive timber house he'd entered during the night with Ondrau, thinking it was some exclusive hotel or other. In a room crammed with furniture and lit only by the obligatory standard lamp, shedding its light over a comfortable sofa with cushions in flowered material, he sat down and lay listening to that disturbing creaking in the ceiling and floor. Through some open door or window a soft night wind was wafting in winged insects and the howls of nocturnal animals. The scent of woods and heather penetrated even as far as here, into this creaking timber interior. How would the gentleman present take it if he were to stand up and walk out, just to get the feeling of springy moss under his soles and have the twigs snap back against his coat, as, of course, they would. With a dazzle lamp and a club to stun the life out of it! It seemed a good enough life to him.

The need to do everything a different way for once, not exactly to do it all over again, but simply to introduce more variety into life, seems to be affecting even Ondrau. For some time now he's been standing rather unsteadily with the bottle—sherry, the only liquor immediately on hand—hovering above the earthenware mugs, until with sudden resolution he conjures up two exquisitely shaped, fluted glasses out of an exceptionally beautiful, gleaming sideboard and, still smiling, comes and sits down beside him, handing him a glass that's brimming over with sherry. "Grande!" he cries, raises his glass, bends over toward him, and is just about to make God may know what gesture when both glasses are whisked out of their grasp by a pair of hands that shoot out of the darkness above their heads and are almost entirely concealed within the sleeves of a purple dressing gown.

This shock is possibly even more violent than the one he got when Ondrau shortly before this had parked his Peugeot among the trees along a completely deserted road through the woods, switched off the headlights, and begun by the light of the dashboard light to read out of his pocket diary, in a rather misty voice, several profound reflections jotted down during his trips for one of Western Europe's largest wine importers. Even during Ondrau's unavoidable fit of sobbing, head down on the steering wheel, after he'd confessed about his lamentable trip to Germany a year before—where Zeiss, instead of consoling this notorious boozer had quite simply shown him the door—even then he'd been expecting him to make a sudden snatch under the seat at any minute and land him a blow with a hammer. "Is it so long

ago we last met?" he'd cried, struggling to get the door open as
he did.

Drink, fortunately, heals the wounds of shock and consterna-
tion speedily and effectively. The dressing gown leads the way
without saying a word into the sparsely lighted hall and up the
stairs, while the house continues to creak in all its joints and
seams.

"I'm ascending to heaven!" he mutters, stressing each individual
word, shrunk back into himself—completely shriveled up, if the
truth were known.

Two steps ahead of him, in this dressing gown which reaches
down to her feet and makes her look curvier than—from the look
of it: neck, ankles—she's got a right to, goes Ondrau's wife.
Behind him and below, the ever-laughing, moist-eyed, intelligent
degenerate, Karel Ondrau, who now looks as though he's been
struck by lightning, standing waiting on the round mat in the
hallway, head lowered as though deep in thought—or entirely
indifferent to the proceedings—contemplating maybe what foul
trick he'll play next on who knows whom: well-dressed in his
pale suit, on which, at chest height, there is now a large, red wine
stain with an irregular edge, while on the smooth, rather wide-
legged trousers there are patches of soil at the knees—result of
the disastrous attempt at digging in what later proved to be the
garden, where, some vague recollection told him, a bottle of
cognac ought to lie buried. This, despite frantic digging with
the car jack, had remained elusive, while the bottle they'd taken
with them came to grief owing to an unfortunate maneuver which
landed them one on top of the other.

"Christ, what a mess!" How long have they been climbing this
miserable staircase? (Three quarters of an hour—the time required to write the narration since: "I ascend to heaven!" etc.)
There can be no iffing and butting in this situation. Besides, he
feels like a wet rag, weak at the knees and actually, in brief
flashes, very drunk indeed.

This is how things go when you have to show loyalty. There's
no foreseeing where the trouble'll end. To have to suffer the
silent scorn of this woman so far from his familiar haunts! And
that in the woods of Guelderland—or is it somewhere near Zeist?

Driven for hours through nocturnal meadows, a spooky business. A taxi perhaps?

"Can I call a taxi?"

They're standing on the landing that runs around the hall upstairs, right under the ceiling. A two-story house, with a sloping roof probably, ideally insulated, pigeons fouling the beams between floor and rafters and stored household items maybe.

"There's the toilet."

Remarkable—hadn't he asked quite clearly for a taxi? Maybe it's true, after all, that if you only drink enough you become unintelligible to others.

"There's no call for laughter, my good man, or are you proud of causing all this commotion in the middle of the night? You're no better than a common burglar!"

Would it be a good thing to tell her yet again that he's a guest of her husband's, a young man with plenty of excellent opportunities still ahead of him, comes from a respectable stable, with first-class connections and resounding names in the family, in short: a person who's liable to become very nervous indeed if unable to wash his hands at the appropriate moment? Like her, with her smooth face and especially those gestures, which betray the sheltered environment from which she comes, still not touched by a thing, inviolate, probably not even a child, because little ones could constitute a threat to the suppleness of her immaculate belly.

He gives her a peaceable little prod in one arm with a finger and almost falls over the banisters and lands up in the hall below before getting a sudden, choking fit of coughing under control with a handkerchief.

"Have you gone out of your mind!" She flings open a door as though they've got to enter some hall. Bending forward, with a rapid movement of the hand around the doorjamb—as though the mere approach to the threshold might give rise to unsavory thoughts involving him—she switches on the light.

He's already put his hand to his eyes before this, in a primitive gesture of self-defense, like people who expect to be struck by lightning—so naïve!

Here we are again—it's always the same. A guest room. The inverted glass bowl on the ceiling in which a 40-watt bulb is burning. The chilly bed. Under the gay bedspread, the clammy sheets. Smell of cellar vaults. Opposite: leaded panes, the closet, its door ajar, containing inviting clothes hangers—welcome, welcome!—of various models, flakes of whitewash on the floor of it and snowlike on the linoleum in front of it. Forgotten vacuum cleaner parts in a corner, wastepaper basket, ashtray, wobbly little table and oh, oh, the gleaming washbasin with the mirror of cheap, wavy, rippling glass.

Muttering "Nice mat you've got there," he steps uncertainly into the room, the door behind him swooshing to in reply—firmly but politely closed. No slamming of doors in this house. He opens the windows wide to begin with—quite a job, complicated little catches sliding along narrow grooves in which little nuts fit little bolts. If you don't handle them carefully enough the glass clatters against the window fastener, which can produce a respectable crack.

Outside, the night is very convincing. Not a glimmer, not a sound anymore. Not even a hum, only an enormous movement behind the motionless trees (so far as that is feasible, of course, and it is, as many will gladly confirm who are familiar with trees and preferably whole groups of them)—and a mist which is rising up from the ground but is detectable by the mucous membranes only—the heavy, sickly odor of roses, comparable to the sweet smell of corpses.

Making water forcefully in the washbasin, he decides he will lie down on the bed fully dressed, so as to be able to leave the house immediately at the crack of dawn; if need be, through the window and accompanied by the marble inkstand proudly on display on the wooden mantelpiece.

As he sits bent over, undoing his laces—for why should he deliberately dirty the bed?—as long as he knows what he's doing, it's better not to on account of the impression it makes and then, the bed's the nest in which he can dream without fear of overdoing things, walking on tiptoe, and other exaggerated behavior —the door suddenly shoots open and a precisely ironed hand towel sails into the room. "Look now, how thoughtful!" he calls

out rudely in the direction of the door—now already closed again.
They still know what's right and proper here, even if death's only
just round the corner.

Unfolding the towel and holding it under the tap is done in
a jiffy—twist it round his head like a turban and he already feels
like a different person. It soaks his shirt and broad patches of
wet spread out over the floor. With a jump he lands on his knees
in the bed, which receives him with a shriek, and in this attitude
falls promptly asleep with the rapidity with which natural
disasters take place, his head in a mattress as thin as paper.

Sweating from every pore, opening wide in one terrific scream
for air, he breaks out of a coma in a moment of shock, leaps up
and stands next to the bed.

Heart attack? The gripes? Fit of delirium? He remembers,
sees himself lying against the ground among the trees on the side
of the road along which traffic is pouring, lots of army trucks,
which disappear through openings in the barbed wire opposite.
They are coming slowly nearer, in a file on either side of the road,
the young men clothed in gray combat uniforms. Linen belts
around their young bodies sag down over their hips under the
weight of many highly functional-looking things. The rims of
their steel helmets cut a line across boys' faces now grown grave.
Under their arms they carry their small, lethal submachine guns
like walking sticks. From the tail of the column, hidden from
view by a bend in the road, comes the sound of dogs barking.
They're not singing of Rosemarie this time but scouring the
surface of the road and carefully lifting up the branches along
the margin. They do it so gently, so attentively, they might be
spying on a little brother while he sleeps.

"Who's there?"

He sees himself in a flash, his eyes wide open, peering into the
dark.

There's a rustling sound by the door and the ceiling light clicks
on. To his relief it is Ondrau's wife he sees standing there in the
dim light, still in her dressing gown.

"Lights out!" he hisses. "Air raid!"

She seems nervous. He hears the light switch click three times.
The light goes out, then on, then out for good.

"Do you regret your scandalous behavior?" He whispers and tries to guess her movements. She is standing still.

"Silly man. Oh, how creepy it is here. You're a real puritan!" A conclusion which has a ring of triumph about it, even if delivered in only a whisper. Is she a neurotic? That too?

"I feel awful," he groans. Water has to be drunk, and as soon as possible, to get this nausea under control. He gropes for the washbasin, trips over the little table, for a moment feels himself in great difficulties, then grabs hold of the basin, turns on the tap wildly, and drinks.

"Can you manage? Can I help you?" It sounds really kind and helpful, sincere, too, and—there's no denying—rather suggestive.

He lets her wait. His tongue no longer reacts to the icy tang of the water, but his stomach quiets down. Good, this hangover has really got a grip on him now—that's clear beyond all doubt. The only thing: alcohol. Either that or . . . resignation.

She still hasn't budged, at least, not so that he could detect the movement, and yet she is drawing closer all the same. When she speaks, the sound comes from the middle of the room.

"Karel's always ill afterwards. Then he goes and sits in the bath all day and takes cold showers. Both hot and cold. The whole day long. It drives me crazy. I can feel the pump throbbing in my head."

It's not mere whining but genuine, pure, undiluted despair. It doesn't alter the fact that she's approached the bed now without a sound and sits down on it gingerly. He hears it creak. He clings on tightly to the cold rim of the washbasin, dismayed. He's not in the mood.

"I'm paralyzed." He forms the words but there's simply not sufficient breath to make them audible. To add to all this misery here comes a not unappreciable bang from somewhere below in the house, followed by a respectable vibration which communicates itself to everything—the walls, the window, the ceiling, even to his teeth.

"Karel isn't awake, is he?"

"No, of course not! He's sound asleep. You can be sure I see to that."

She feels at ease. What was that she said? You can be sure

I see to that? So she doesn't merely wait, sly and cautious, but pays more of these nocturnal visits. Wouldn't she otherwise have said: I've *seen* to that? What a bitch. Or perhaps it's her way of contending with a premature menopause? How should he know?

His exhaustion has gone even though he feels dead tired. For his part she can go on pestering him till the break of day. The shuddering doesn't cease or die down till he feels the tap. He puts all his force behind it when he turns it off and hears the washer crack. The silence which ensues is almost too awful to bear. He wants to lie down, massage his temples.

"I'm going to lie down," he says ominously.

She says no word, makes no movement.

He wades through the dark toward the bed, the lair of the fox. If he manages to avoid immediate contact that will be a big gain to start with. How long a night lasts. It becomes even more puzzling when he discovers he can stretch out without hindrance. Is it he or she who thinks himself pursued? Who is to be the dupe?

She certainly has not drawn back; so far she hasn't approached any further than the very edge of the foot of the bed. Is she listening carefully to his breathing as he is listening for hers? If he can move a little he'll be lying more comfortably. He spreads out his legs, too hesitantly for it to be natural, and his foot discovers her warmth, approaches her stealthily, and, for the rest, with indifference.

She bobs up and down. "Don't wriggle about like that. Let me sit in peace for a while. I've had so much to do today."

"What have you got in your mouth? You're sucking on something."

"My necklace. Nothing special."

He can hear a string of beads rattling—glass or amber.

"Oh, come here then."

She acts as though he is forcing himself upon her, giving her little prods and kicks, whereas in reality he has done nothing but lie quite still since he registered her warmth down there. She takes hold of his ankle, changes her position, waves with something, puts his foot under her dressing gown resolutely, as though it were the obvious thing to do. He can feel her ribs, his heel in her lap. He regrets ever having removed his shoes.

"Oh, dear. I say, you're as skinny as a young boy."

"You can do worse than get a skinny one."

"Don't be so dirty. You're common. And let go of my foot."

She doesn't move. She remains silent but considerably less impressively than the night. It's simply *her* silence, lacking any destructive effect, anything but eloquent and no, not impressive. Nothing special doing, as ordinary as the songs lunatics launch upon spontaneously. Mass litanies any nurse working in an asylum can tell you about. Enough to scare outsiders, but to insiders simply a sign the weather's on the change. He's not going to let her outbluff him or land him with guilt feelings.

"You're trembling. What are you doing?"

Oh, Lord, deliver us from this clandestine whispering. She's quivering like a leaf in the wind.

"You're not crying, are you?"

"Why don't you want to look at me?"

"I've looked at you already. Nothing to write home about. You look well turned out. In your late thirties—though you're older. You have pretty hair, small, blue, insignificant eyes. Slender. No doubt play a lot of tennis. Probably a good swimmer. Go on plenty of walks. Doesn't appeal to me. Shouldn't think it appeals to anyone much. You must have great gifts otherwise Ondrau'd never have married you. You wear the pants—am I right?"

"I wish you hadn't said that," she says, meditating and stroking the soft, and in any case rather sensitive skin of his instep. "I didn't want to impose myself, but you two needed to be punished tonight. And now. . . ." She hesitates. Then suddenly: "Now you're trampling on my heart."

It doesn't even sound exaggerated in her mouth. No, liberating, sharp, as if for once she's said exactly what is at stake.

In the dark, with a chattering woman on the bed, he has no wish to overlook the seriousness of the moment or the significance of this night, rich in secrets confided, yet that doesn't alter the fact that he's struggling all the time not to burst out cheering— a marvelous feeling, truly relaxing, and most likely connected with all manner of fermentation processes going on in his blood— not to revel in shouting out: "You silly slut!" and things of that nature. The sensation, however, of having the power in his own hands for the moment prevents him from overloud talk. She wouldn't understand it anyway. How can she know anything of the grand, rapidly changing moods that are the result of a day on the booze?

"Don't be so upset. It only leads to scenes. I have never met anyone so far who could show me any injury, however slight, that could be directly related to trampling on the heart. Take my word for it—as long as no physical violence is involved, it's nothing to worry about."

Her voice betrays impatience.

"You men are all the same. Talk—you can all do that. But when something really gets started, you don't know what to do. All I want is for you to look at me"—and truly cantankerous: "Oh, forget it. You don't think I'm up to much, anyway."

"Are you crazy, woman? Just put on the light and doctor will take a look and see what's the matter."

She gets up and walks across the room, slippers flapping, without bumping into anything.

"No, there's a flashlight here. You can see the light for miles around outside. The curtains aren't all that good."

She finds it without any difficulty at all, touches his shoulder, feels down the arm he has raised in self-defense and presses a smooth plastic staff into his hand.

"Wait a minute while I sit down in front of it. Don't switch on till I tell you."

The thin mattress lifts, the mesh acting as a conductor of some busy activity.

"You're a wizard at finding things in the dark. And in the guest room too! Not usually very familiar territory in a house."

"Why do you always have to talk as if you're in the pulpit?" she asks, murmuring, busily occupied with something.

He tries out the flashlight, shining it into his eyes, which, being oversensitive, promptly begin to water. Puts the top of it in his mouth and imitates a bear, hoping it'll make her laugh. Jokes are pure poison at the erotic feast. Where laughter rings the yearning body might just as well go hang itself.

"Hey! It's already growing light!"

He shines the beam of the flashlight out of the window enthusiastically, feels he wants to get up and go for a walk in the woods, but too brusque a movement sends him dizzily back into the pillows.

"Don't, you fool!" she says nervously.

"What's it matter? Who can stop you from shining a flashlight out of a window—a searchlight for that matter?"

"The airfield's close by. Look, come here with your flashlight. What d'you say about that? Come on, say something!"

The shock of his life!

She's sitting opposite him, her legs crossed, the dressing gown and what she's wearing underneath it pulled down, a mass of loose tapes and clasps and rolls of lingerie round her waist, and facing him with a tensed, almost aggressively arched back. But what she's exposing is not a head with swaths of heavy, ash-blond hair tumbling down over her face, but a gleaming skull. She's as bald as a billiard ball!—no, more feminine: as a grapefruit. It's so fragile, tender and naked, so shamelessly revealing, he could have wept for minutes on end.

When he remains silent, switches out the flashlight and hides his eyes for a moment in the hollow of his arm to protect it from the light now growing brighter outside, she murmurs: "What are you thinking of now?"

He parries the direct invitation to comment with: "A pointless question put at the wrong moment."

Her silhouette is outlined against the window as slowly, taking her time, even a little coquettishly, lazily—she knows he is watching her—she adjusts her clothing, ending with her wig, flicking it out with an elegant gesture of her two hands, like columns of smoke and dark fire. With expertise and, so it seems to him, shamelessly.

"I admit my first reaction was crazy."

"What was it?"

"That you'd been on the wrong side in the war. But that was twenty years ago."

"And then what you felt was pity for that poor, little woman!"

"Yes."

She laughs heartily.

"That's exactly the way every man reacts. Console yourself,

you don't have to take pity on me, though I won't object if you do. What does it matter *what* it is that stirs you up? All that matters to me is finding out what I can get if I should happen to want it. And that is exactly as much as any other woman."

"A bitch, after all," he says quietly and deliberately. "Spoiled and useless."

"Hey—where do you think you are?"

She's standing before the light of the window and points her hand upward, accusingly, to where he's perfectly aware there's merely an empty attic.

"I don't let anyone insult me. Not Karel either, who lays me flat on the bed and thinks of someone else while he's doing it."

"Good luck to you, sister! And close the door properly behind you!"

He steps out of the bed, walks over to the washbasin and drinks. A hefty after-thirst. When he turns back to the bed she has disappeared. He falls asleep.

How long has she been absent when, from the open door, she warns him: "Get up. You must get going and don't hang about either. I've some urgent errands to do."

The air is fresh and cool, the view enchanting—woods all around, another of those "attractive" bungalows in the distance. Chic district. He tries to restore himself with water, but it's useless. It's some time before he ventures to leave the room after hanging about on the edge of the bed. Karel needs her, of course, on account of the money, and to have someone around when he collapses. He longs for a cup of coffee. The house creaks merrily under his feet, but otherwise all is silence. From the clock in the hall he discovers what time it is. Good God, twenty past six! He would give much, much indeed, to be able to creep back into bed. But not here! There's something, an emanation, an atmosphere, in this house that reminds him of a hymn: "Laden as I am with guilt . . ." or something of that sort.

It's some time before he decides to open a door and stands in a large room which affords a view, through open French windows, across a broad lawn bordered by trees. He vaguely recognizes an adjoining room, partially closed off by a curtain. Over thick, old-fashioned carpets he walks gingerly toward the garden. A small terrace of flagstones, comfortable chairs, a table with a glass on it and a breakfast plate. So this is where they sit and enjoy the beauties of nature. He curses—a habit after a day spent in the taprooms. He drops down into a chair with a little groan. He just can't take drink. He needs thirty-six hours to recover. To shore up his spirits he tells himself how nice it is here, the birds singing, the salubrious atmosphere, but promptly pulls his head in between his shoulders as two fighter planes suddenly rip over him out of the blue. Ondrau'll be lying in bed, he thinks, and she'll do all she can to keep things that way. Till then. Every time he met Ondrau he thought: this time's the last time. I'll never see him again. He'll drive himself straight into a hospital bed—drunk as he is tonight.

Near the gate he comes across the spot where they dug last night, looks at the bruised shrubs, a flattened rosebed and strips of torn-up turf and shakes his head. They went to work like madmen!

"Yes, a pretty sight! You've certainly abused your hospitality!"

She's standing leaning against the doorjamb, her arms crossed, wearing a tweed walking costume that makes her look efficient and a trifle mannish. He takes a furtive glance at her hair. There's nothing to betray her miserable secret. He wants to say that no one understands better than she the art of putting a person at ease, but he holds his peace, silenced by the aplomb— all the right on *her* side—that radiates from her person and comes across so very well.

"Er . . . Karel . . . could I . . . ?" he begins, but she cuts in.

"Karel left hours ago!"

The answer is accompanied by a boom from somewhere below in the house and a resultant rattling of the windowpanes.

"He did? Well, in that case I'll be getting on my way again."

"Do."

She is impregnable.

"Which way do I take?"

"Through the gate. Turn left."

"How far is it?" He gets up with a little groan. Not even a cup of coffee or a large glass of ice-cold lemonade.

"A good hour."

From now on Karel's the biggest prick in the world.

They've loosed the dogs, which are now trotting round playing in the low undergrowth. When they find him here they'll gladly tear him to pieces. Bending over, he makes water in a circle all around him, imitating the example of smugglers with trackhounds on their heels. He hopes at least he's remembered the putting-off-the-scent technique correctly.

Even before he is able to see the car he recognizes it from the sound of its diesel engine and that vicious horn. The boys of the guard platoon range themselves on the side of the road. She rips past. He can see she's wound down all the windows from the way her head scarf is waving about in the breeze. There she goes—direction station. Looking for him? No one'll believe that. That many problems and emotions on top of each other just aren't feasible. Desperate, he lifts up his body and whistles on trembling fingers. The young men, fresh sweat patches already visible on their gray overalls, look up astonished and then begin— ashamed?—to call off their dogs.

Translated by James Brockway.

ANTON KOOLHAAS

A Hole in the Ceiling

I

NOT one of all the people who used to live in the house knew exactly when the hole in the ceiling was made. At any rate when the real estate agent, who terrified everyone in the house, lived there it wasn't there yet because aside from the dents he made in some of the doors he took good care of the house. When things reached the point where he came home drunk nearly every night, his wife left him. Later she was granted custody of the children but that didn't last long because they were just about ready to go off to college and they didn't go out of their way to see their mother, later on. Still it was only when he not only kicked at her door when he came home at night but also at the children's door that she left him. His delight at manhandling his wife was already decreasing somewhat, but his desire to beat the children because they never spoke to him any more did not decrease.

It was strange that the woman had chosen the largest room of the house as her bedroom. It had a door leading to the bathroom; perhaps that was the reason, for she bathed terribly often. It is possible that she grew very fond of the idea that she could do as she pleased in those two rooms without being disturbed. She often locked the door to the hall. She must have been often terrified of what could happen in the daytime and especially at night.

Does fear become part of a room like that?

She certainly must have thought that everything in her bedroom including the floor and the walls and the ceiling revealed traces of fear. When she gasped because she heard his black

68

high-buttoned shoes on the staircase, it seemed to her as if everything around her held its breath. She never knew what to do: the light on or off. In the dark the waiting was unbearable, but if there was light shining under the door, perhaps that was what lured him inside. If she had the light on she always stared blankly at the ceiling.

When the demolition men came to the house, later, they said, "You can see the painters didn't use to earn more than five cents an hour. What could you pay for a ceiling like that nowadays!"

It had certainly been quite a lot of work. First there was an arched border of stucco where the ceiling met the walls, very painstakingly done, and then the ceiling itself. Against a green background there was a border of garlands in light purple and in each of the four corners the profile of a woman. In the middle of the long as well as the shorter borders there were figures in bas-relief, lion heads surrounded by those same whirling little garlands. At least those on the borders of the width of the room were clearly lion heads, but those on the longer walls of the room aroused justifiable doubts. Presumably a young inexperienced painter had been given an opportunity to try his hand at it. They looked more like camel heads than anything else. They also could have been wolves and it was only if you looked at the lion heads on the short borders for a while and then suddenly turned to the other ones that you realized they were also supposed to be lion heads; the ones on the short borders looked very much like lion heads and it was obvious that the man who had painted the ones on the long borders had tried to copy them. However if you only looked at the ones on the long borders you could very easily take them for camels. When the woman was terribly frightened, her glance darted timidly from the figures on the long borders to those on the short ones to see if perhaps both of them weren't meant to be entirely different animals after all.

When nothing happened and the house was peaceful so that she could safely assume that her husband had gone to sleep without further ado, she sometimes smiled at the camels who at these moments were more decidedly than ever certainly not lions and who peacefully looked out into the distance, across the desert for example, a wide open space without a single distraction. A few times it had happened that this peacefulness was only an illusion and that her husband had in fact furtively tiptoed to her door in his stockinged feet and began banging on it in an alcoholic frenzy with his shoes which he had in his hands and banged so violently that there was reason to fear the door might give way and shatter into splinters so that she'd be better off simply opening it. The camels quickly turned back into wolves or lions or even into ani- mals that don't exist and the woman's eyes shot past all the figures and flowers on the ceiling and all the things on the floor and on the walls and the remains of her fear must have clung to these things.

On the worst night of all the woman fled. Alone. Later she fetched the children. Shortly afterwards the real estate agent died, the papers referred to him as an upstanding man, and the house was vacated because of course the woman didn't want to return to it although every so often her thoughts did stray to the camels.

Afterward other families lived in the house and the deteriora- tion must have started then. The real estate agent who was now in charge of the house knew how much the woman hated to have him ever mention it and tried to bother her as little as possible with talk of repairs that were in fact very urgently necessary. It must have been during this period that the hole in the ceiling appeared. It was a triangle. The sharpest corner was in the ingeniously made stucco edge and the base of the triangle fol- lowed the line of the border with the purple garlands. You had to look at the ceiling for a while before the hole caught your eye. Once you saw it you wondered how it could have got there because the rest of the ceiling was in remarkably good condition.

After the woman's departure the room had never again been used as a bedroom and no one ever again detected the distinct discrepancy between the lions and the camels. Then a dancing school rented the house. Since the room with the hole in the ceiling was the biggest room, it was there that the dancing lessons were given.

All you could gather from the brochures about the dancing school was that the lessons were intended for pupils from well- to-do families. Mr. Vinkerts, the owner of the school, made it very clear every time a new class was assembled for the first lesson that his was the only dancing school where a pianist provided the music instead of a record player and that he would retain the services of Mr. Poortemans, as the pianist was called, until his death to provide musical accompaniment at the lessons.

This statement did not alter the fact that at the second lesson Mr. Poortemans no longer honored the school with his presence and a very ordinary record player was used. Several of the pupils wondered what could have happened to the old pianist after that first lesson and assumed that he had taken ill and lay neglected in a bed of rags in his little attic room.

Whenever a dance was over the girls withdrew to one side of the room and the boys to the other. They peered at each other from a distance and made meek attempts at conversation until the record player tossed them headfirst into a new dance. Then the boys crossed the room to where the girls were, each boy picked a partner and they started dancing, all the while looking at Monsieur Charles, a Belgian, who was Mr. Vinkerts' assistant and who, assisted in turn by his wife, led the actual lessons.

It was in the interval between two dances that a boy, Evert Jan, saw the pook! Evert Jan was an extremely shy boy who attended the dancing lessons with the greatest reluctance. He never said a word to the girls he had to dance with, nor did he ever speak to the boys in the short intermissions between the dances. Toward the end of the hour-long lesson his shyness reached an intolerable peak because of course he was well aware of the fact that he hadn't said a single word all evening and he also knew the others couldn't have failed to notice this. So in the last ten minutes he started talking to himself to make it clear that the complete absence of any communicative utterance on his part did not necessarily signify a complete absence of any signs of life whatsoever. However the words he spoke to himself, accompanied by exaggerated mouth movements were words completely devoid of any significance. They were words snatched from the piles of words at Evert Jan's disposal and immediately tossed back on the pile after they served their purpose. "Strong," he sometimes muttered quite clearly, or: "Nice," or: "It creaks," and he glanced around timidly to see if anyone had perhaps drawn any conclusions.

One evening his shyness was so overwhelming that he frantically took refuge in staring at the ceiling and continued to do so when the next dance commenced. He looked at the garlands and the lions, but his gaze was so fixed upon those in the center of the short borders that he failed to discover the peculiar discrepancy between the lions and the camels. Evert Jan looked at the dancing boys and girls to see if anyone was aware of his stares. Monsieur Charles had already taken the prettiest girl in the class in his arms, something he did rather often, and when he noticed that several of the boys were jumping around rather disrespectfully he scarcely interrupted his fancy turns to call to one of them, "Ysbran, you're hopping about too much!" thus drawing attention away from himself to the clumsy leaps of this élève who, excited by Monsieur Charles' immodest but graceful dancing, was doing crude injustice to the music and behaving like a wild stallion.

Although Evert Jan was already in high school, he would have preferred the punishment of writing a lot of senseless lines as extra homework to a dancing lesson like this. He wouldn't have to look at the ceiling in a strange house, he could sit alone at his desk; alone in a room scribbling the lines one after the other and as the evening progressed he'd feel his satisfaction grow at a feverish pace because the quantity of identical lines increased so beautifully. He would leaf through the pages of his notebook and enjoy feeling all those pages, nice and thick when you had them all between your fingers, a veritable flood of pages if you let them glide off your thumb.

"*Je remercie ma popsy wopsy,*" Monsieur Charles shouted in a humorous jumble of Gallic spirit and priggish joviality. The dance was over and the prettiest girl of the class fluttered back to her girlfriends. The lesson was over and the pupils rushed for the door. Evert Jan had to stop his peering at the ceiling and leave. He was slow about it and his eyes wandered once more past the garlands. Until they suddenly stopped.

His fear of being surrounded by the other boys and girls in the hall dissolved into thin air. His eyes were glued to the hole in the ceiling and the darkness inside of it. In the hole he saw a brown pointed snout and two very bright tiny eyes that looked straight into his. The snout disappeared immediately and only the triangular hole remained and the darkness within it. It was so dark that there could be no mistake about the light brown color of the little snout that had moved.

No doubt about it, something light brown had moved in the hole. Evert Jan had fleetingly seen the pook that lived between the ceiling and the floor of the room upstairs. That was stranger than he could ever suspect because nobody ever sees pooks.

The boy walked quietly to the hall to put on his coat. He said goodbye to the boys and girls who were still standing there and stepped out onto the dark quay with the light brown snout still before him and the way it moved, the swiftness with which it looked out from the darkness in the hole and withdrew when it noticed it was being watched. Evert Jan tried to recall the expression in the animal's eyes, but it had all happened too fast for him to see it.

The pook Johannes had been living between the ceiling and the upstairs floor with his wife Laura for years. They came there when the wife of the real estate agent still lived in the house and shuddered with fear as she waited for her husband to come home along the dark quay. The hole in the ceiling wasn't there yet and pooks walk so quietly and in general live their life so quietly that she couldn't possibly have heard them. They make much less noise than mice although they move much faster. One of the things that delighted Johannes was that he could run zigzag across the huge surface of the ceiling all night long without making the slightest sound. Laura hardly ever did that anymore. She was already old when they settled in this big, peaceful place.

The ceiling was attached to broad wooden beams. In between these beams there was straw and Johannes and Laura lived off this straw.

They had brought a substantial number of offspring into the world in their lifetime. Very smooth black pooks with soft skin and pointed snouts and intelligent, very observant eyes which revealed a good deal of common sense even in the very young animals. When they grow up, the pooks' black coats turn light brown. They live in the dark and as long as they remain black it is almost impossible to see them. The light brown color makes it easier. Nevertheless by the time they turn from black to light brown they have developed such speed, agility, and skill at hiding that no other living creature can ever succeed in seeing one of them. They sense any vibration of the ground or of the air so that they can detect the approach of any other animal, be it ever so small, before they can be seen.

Pooks are apparently content with just the company of other pooks. Each time a new litter was born, Johannes was beside himself with joy. He and Laura trained them together but only after they had stayed in the nest as long as possible with all the little ones swarming about under them. It was only when the children had reached considerable proportions and had more or less forced their parents out of the nest that Johannes and Laura conceded that the world was indeed larger than the nest. As soon as the little ones had climbed out for the first time, Johannes began to warn them against this or that. Of course he didn't do this by producing any sort of sound, but by swishing his sturdy spatulalike tail into the air. This didn't make any noise but it did cause a slight rush of air that put the little ones on guard and they grew accustomed to never leaving the reach of these rushes of air on their first expedition. With three or four little ones close to them, Laura and Johannes set out on their first scouting expeditions. In the beginning they crept slowly, but as the little ones grew to understand the necessity of silence and invisibility and judgment and common sense in their little eyes increased, it went faster; until the little ones could run across ceilings and attics and through deserted cellars and adventurous holes in the wall and hollow parts of the foundation quite as swiftly as Johannes himself. Just before dawn they always returned to the nest with their parents and resigned themselves to the fact that Laura and Johannes insisted on spreading out on top of them before falling asleep, no matter how uncomfortable and crowded it became.

But a short while later the moment came for them to go forth on their own. Even when only one of the little ones had gone off on his own, as soon as they felt he'd been gone too long Laura and Johannes sat down back to back with their bodies pressed very close to each other. They didn't move and hardly breathed and in a thoroughly wretched state waited for the adventurer to return. When he was back they perked up their ears which had been flat against their neck all that time and they flung themselves passionately but silently on top of the little ones in the nest.

Those were terrible times, because when there is a litter of six or eight little pooks and they reach the stage where they often go out on their own, sometimes all of them together, then it often lasts as long as twenty-three out of the twenty-four hours that make up a day before they are all back home and consequently their parents have very little opportunity to eat or sleep.

By the time the young pooks had grown up, Laura and Johannes were always so weak and helpless that they didn't have the strength to delay the final departure of their children in any way. It sometimes happens that when pooks leave the parental nest the parents die of exhaustion. It never got to that point with Laura and Johannes although after bearing all those litters it did get to the point where Laura hardly ever got up and moved around and she had Johannes bring her food and there was absolutely no question of any more children.

The last time Laura and Johannes had sat waiting with their bodies pressed tightly against each other, shuddering in fear because for ten days and ten nights there had been no sign of the little ones, they were so exhausted and close to death that the strength it took for Johannes to go away from Laura and stumble off in search of food was hardly less mighty than the strength it takes to produce life itself. If life had allowed them to wait there for death to come, this would have been an act of mercy, but in forcing them to begin again, no mercy was shown. The new stream of life would forever be tainted by the fear they had experienced. Nevertheless Johannes regained his old speed within a few days and managed to persuade Laura to eat a few mouthfuls.

After that they often sat back to back with their bodies pressed to each other, but no longer shuddering and terrified of what might have happened to their offspring. Laura was devoid of all emotion since she was always in a daze and would die soon, but Johannes, in his solitude, felt a pang of fear now and then out of sheer habit perhaps or because all the litters they had ever had became one in his mind, one tiny little pook who yearned for adventure, knew no bounds, and often met with calamity.

After the woman left there hadn't been much noise in the room. Various families lived in the house at the same time and most of the noise now came from the floor above the pooks. You could tell the house was not being kept as clean as it used to be by the fact that mice sometimes appeared, compelling the pooks to go into hiding. Life above the ceiling was not eventful. There was however one event worthy of mention.

On the evening prior to the night that was to become the reason for the hasty departure of the woman, she was so frightened by the intentions of her husband who had telephoned her several times from his club, that she walked over to the enormous green and black marble fireplace that stood like a monument built into one of the shorter walls of the room. She tried to push aside the heavy iron screen that blocked off the area inside the fireplace because she wanted to see if it would be possible to crawl into that space and hide. The dark space behind the screen made her shudder in terror, but it wasn't nearly as bad as the plans he had revealed to her over the telephone. She could move the screen aside far enough to see that there was room for her to fit in back of it. She tried to slip in between the sharp edge of the screen and the wall. It was certainly possible and once she was inside she'd have to pull the screen back in place with her fingers so no one could see it had been moved and that someone was perhaps hiding behind it.

But while she was in the process of trying to step inside and pushed the screen aside even further she realized that if her husband couldn't find her he'd be sure to go to the children and take revenge. She decided to abandon the plan and was just about to put the screen back in place when it was already too late and her husband began banging on the door.

When he came inside he subjected the entire room to a careful inspection as if he suspected something. He saw right away that she must have been tampering with the screen and detected her intention of hiding behind it. He walked over to the black screen, grasped it in his two hands, and jerked it from the fireplace. He lifted the whole screen and swayed and panted and flung it into the room. He cut his hands on the sharp edges but he didn't seem to notice it; at any rate he didn't let it bother him because he walked over to the fireplace, bent down, and shouted "boo hoo!" into the chimney opening a few times as loud as he could. He panted as he straightened up and then he went for his wife.

The moment the real estate agent roared into the chimney opening, the pook Johannes was overcome by such strong vibrations that he shook himself loose from Laura and sat down a few feet away from her to try to get his trembling under control.

It seemed to him that—although he hadn't seen it with his eyes —when the screen was removed from the fireplace, a wall had disappeared in his inner being. Something had changed and pooks have such a delicate sense for detecting the most minute alteration in the light or in the air or in anything at all in the atmosphere or in their surroundings that the sudden opening of the chimney pipe threw Johannes into a state of utter confusion. His hind legs jerked so violently against the wood of the beam he was sitting on that he had to lie down on his side to prevent making a sound for the first time in his life.

Then it quickly quieted down in the room because the man's rage subsided and the woman fled.

The screen was however never put back in place. The chimney hole stayed open like a dark cave in the room. The wall around the hole was painted an elegant dark brown and obviously no one saw any reason to cover it with a screen. However the change which had taken place did not cease to upset Johannes. The fact that the house now had a new character and was tenanted by new people with new smells and new sounds failed to impress Johannes nearly as much as the disappearance of the screen in front of the fireplace and this obsessed him to such a degree that, without sharing his secret with Laura, he launched a scouting expedition.

He didn't go so far as to attempt to descend into the room.

What he did do was gnaw away the straw and then a piece of the wooden beam that held up the ceiling in a corner where an arch of stucco reached from the wall to the ceiling. It was a lengthy task, especially since he had to go about it in complete silence, inaudible even to Laura who would have been greatly perturbed had she known what he was doing because pooks do use various materials to build their nests, but they never bring about any alterations whatsoever in their surroundings.

Johannes gnawed all the way through the beam and then with his hind legs he carefully scraped at the layer of plaster until it became thinner and thinner. After he had spent months in this way, his efforts were rewarded. One day when the door to the room slammed shut with a violent thud due to the wind, a small triangle fluttered out of the ceiling. There was a hole.

The space the pooks lived in was totally changed by this. The vague trace of light that until then had indicated that it was daytime was suddenly transformed into a clear ray of light that shot upward in the corner. Laura and Johannes couldn't stay there any longer and had to set up their living quarters in the farthest corner on the other side of the room where it was still dark enough for pooks to live their lives without being detected.

Sometimes however Johannes crept stealthily to the hole at night and looked down into the big dark area that was the room. Of course he never stuck his snout over the edge. For him to look actually meant to feel. He tried to feel what had happened when the screen disappeared from the fireplace. He felt how there was no movement in the room and he heard how the furniture creaked and didn't become lost in the surrounding darkness. This room where the air moved about softly due to the draught from the chimney pipe became very familiar to Johannes as time passed. It was only when he was completely familiar with all the movements and silence and creaking in the room that he let his sense of feeling move where the air was moving, into the chimney pipe. Each time he approached the bounds of the fireplace he shuddered uncontrollably just as he had the moment the real estate agent snatched away the screen. These shudders were still so powerful that after having experienced them for a few seconds he always started edging backward until he was back in the dark depths where he could squeeze up tight to Laura. He calmed down there as Laura pressed herself closer and closer to him and cautiously relaxed her tail which always stood up straight and tense whenever Johannes was not next to her. Johannes relaxed too.

Laura had nothing beside Johannes and Johannes actually wouldn't have had anything beside Laura if it hadn't been for that hole in the ceiling which got more and more of a grip on him and even upset Laura, although she wasn't aware of the facts, whenever he wasn't sitting next to her. It was only in this position that the two pooks achieved peace of mind, two throbbing hearts, the two of them with warm blood, and they sat so close to each other for such long stretches of time that their blood was as the blood of one animal and their heartbeat too.

When Johannes felt a new attack of restlessness and broke away from Laura, first he ran around, fast as lightning, just as he used to, and he brought her food and he ran back to reassure her and delude her into thinking that everything was still the same as it always had been. Each time he dashed away he went a little bit further, and then returned with the speed of a bullet, until finally he went all the way to the hole. Laura waited for him to return, her tail tense and erect, in somewhat of a daze but at the same time despondent because she could never follow him any more.

Thus Johannes got into the habit of visiting the hole and thus he even went so far as to poke his snout over the edge and look down. Of course he shuddered in the most terrible way but there was something even stronger than his terror: the opening of the chimney pipe.

Something lived there.

Not a pook.

Whatever Johannes had felt moving about there was much bigger. Nevertheless it was a creature that must have something in common with pooks. The darkness that emerged from the chimney pipe was dimmer and deeper than the black that Johannes was familiar with. It was a darkness he wouldn't dare enter without hesitation. In no time his light brown color would be conspicuously bright. It would be suitable for only a very

short stay. Just long enough to pass through. It would not be
feasible to survey the area and feel what was in it the way
Johannes could feel his way in the kind of darkness he had known
until now. This darkness was so stifling and dense that it would
be impossible to feel anything at all. It was even denser than the
darkness Johannes had ventured into in thought alone when his
exhaustion was so great that in his terror he preferred death to
a new attempt at life. Something moved in that darkness of the
chimney pipe!

And Johannes, who on that night had peered for the first time
into that new darkness and had shuddered uncontrollably, edged
his way back to Laura a few hours later and sobbed.

The creature that moved about in the chimney pipe every now
and then was a gormol. It had been living there for a long time
and it was on the night that the screen in front of the fireplace
had been removed and the real estate agent had shouted "boo
hoo!" into the chimney pipe at the top of his lungs that the gormol
came down the pipe for the first time. At the bottom of the pipe,
still invisible from within the room, it had stayed in the same
place for four years. Like a monstrous bulge in the wall of the
chimney pipe one might think, at least as long as it didn't move.
And it barely moved. Only the pentagonal mouth opening rustled
along the wall. The gormol eats soot and its calcareous mouth
scrapes it off the stones and gobbles up the little pellets. But
other than this nothing about the gormol ever moved, although
within a few months one would be forced to admit that its position had shifted slightly. Nevertheless Johannes sensed and heard
the imperceptible movement of the creature in the chimney pipe.
And although he had never seen a gormol the nature of the movement he sensed in the chimney pipe and the scraping noise the
mouth made filled him with horror of the animal in the dark.

At the same time he knew that he would someday get a glimpse
of the creature and that it would come even closer to the opening
when the silence in the house had increased to such a degree that
the gormol would be able to emerge from the depths of the darkness. After all it had come down from somewhere high up in the
chimney pipe as soon as the screen had been removed. Judging
from the vibrations that Johannes felt at the time, it must have

descended very quickly indeed. It was clear that the creature intended to come further. Maybe even all the way into the room.

This didn't happen until the house had deteriorated quite a bit and was vacant for half a year, before Mr. Vinkerts rented it for his dancing school. Johannes was not on the lookout when it happened and the first thing he heard in his corner above the ceiling was the gormol's right legs moving back and forth across the tiles under the mantelpiece where the stove used to be.

Johannes cursed himself for not being more alert and ran to the hole but not before he made a lot of detours and brought Laura her food. Once he had neared the hole he didn't go to the opening right away. First he tried to sense what the gormol looked like now that it was in the room. Because he felt very clearly that the chimney pipe was empty.

There was no trace of the sound that the mouth made as it scraped off the soot and no sign of tension in the gormol's feet. Besides the calcareous claws on the tips of its feet, the gormol is also equipped with suction cups that it can clasp to the wall if there is nothing for the claws to hold onto.

On the tiled floor Johannes sensed something moving back and forth. In convulsive jerks. Once more there was a sob in the pook's throat and then more carefully than he had ever moved before, he slowly edged up to the hole in the ceiling.

As soon as the tip of his snout crossed the edge of the hole— not even his eyes: Johannes couldn't see anything!—the vibrations stopped. The gormol stood still. It must have heard something or maybe it saw something move a fraction of an inch in the dark: the tip of Johannes' snout at the edge of the hole.

Johannes didn't move at all any more. He didn't shake with fear because as soon as there is real danger pooks are no longer afraid and they stop shaking. He hesitated however before going any further and giving his eyes a chance to look down into the room.

He thought it over.

The creature down there had seen him. He could withdraw the outermost tip of his snout from the edge of the hole and slowly back away in the darkness. If he were to do that, there was a good chance the animal downstairs would also withdraw back into the chimney pipe because it didn't know whether what it had seen moving was a threat or not.

The gormol must know that the circumstances under which the pook lived didn't differ so much from its own. But perhaps, just as Johannes, it would want to see these faint signs of life which it had sensed, almost too vague to be real and yet too clear to be a product of its imagination, confirmed by the sight of an actual creature. Johannes listened with every bit of him that could listen. The convulsive jerks against the tiles started again. After a while the sound was even more violent than before. It was a sad pointless movement like the way an epileptic moves. The motive behind the movement was pure aimlessness. Johannes rushed forward now and extended his head so far over the edge that his eyes could see.

In the darkness below him, on the border between that darkness that was in the chimney pipe and the darkness of the room, he saw the animal!

It was a creature made of chalk and scales with the height of a cinder bin and about as wide as two of them. It would have resembled a crab were it not for the dorsal vertebrae that protruded in the middle of its back. They were big dull black vertebrae and the four legs that were attached to them on each side exposed deep slits with something blood-red and moldy inside of them. These slits looked as if they had been chopped in the bone with a hatchet years and years ago to expose the deadly pale marrow spotted with dried-up clots of blood. At the tip of each of the eight, three-jointed legs there was a little lump of flesh with a long hooklike claw that made it possible for the gormol to get a good grip and to climb. Just before the vertebrae began the head tapered down to a funnel-shaped snout covered with calcareous scales that ended up in the pentagonal mouth opening flanked on all sides by flat scissorlike feelers that moved to and fro with no apparent purpose. In back, just behind the last vertebra, the body tapered down again and the scaly tip was pressed to the floor when Johannes got his first glimpse of the gormol. This hind end seemed to be fringed with shiny jet-black stones. In front, just before the first vertebra, on a raised ridge on the snout, one eye was visible. This eye was looking at Johannes when he first saw the animal. The shudders stopped again once Johannes poked his head over the edge. The creature stood still, completely still, with its right legs on the tiles and its left legs braced against the wall so that its body sloped upward to the wall. Suddenly there was no sign of movement at all. The eye didn't move but it looked.

And Johannes' eyes looked back.

Thus they observed each other without either of them moving a muscle. The gormol had descended from a darkness just as infinitely black as the shiny jet on its hind end. The pook, light brown and soft, had come from the darkness above the ceiling, much less black than the darkness in the chimney pipe but nevertheless dark enough for a pook to hide in. Now they looked at each other in the dark room that must have seemed very light to the gormol because even for Johannes it was dangerously light. But they didn't withdraw and their eyes remained glued to each other. They hardly breathed. They stayed like this until both of them felt the end of the night approaching. The gormol was the first to disappear. No matter how inconspicuously Johannes could come into motion and how quickly he could dart off, even before anyone could notice he had moved at all, this was nothing compared with the way the gormol moved. Johannes was better trained to sense any alteration or movement than any other animal, and yet that animal below had all eight of its feet against the wall before he noticed any shift in the position of the eye looking at him. Like a shadow it slithered upwards so silently that the scraping sound the gormol made later when it was eating soot was piercing by comparison.

Johannes also withdrew. He didn't sit down next to Laura because of the violence of the shudders that shook his body once the gormol had disappeared.

It wasn't the first time he couldn't stop trembling in terror. This time it was panic, fear that Laura might disappear, the last one who could leave Johannes, Laura whom a trembling pook yearns to protect and share his warmth with.

II

Although Mr. Vinkerts definitely saw the hole in the ceiling when he rented the house and didn't consider the bare chimney pipe to be conducive to the intimate atmosphere of the ballroom, he left both these things as he had found them. It would be extremely expensive to have the ceiling repaired and the open chimney pipe provided a cheap means of ventilation, an asset not to be ignored. A few chairs were placed in front of the fireplace, their legs right up against the tiles, for the pupils to relax in and work up energy for the next dance.

On the other side of the room was the piano Mr. Poortemans was to play until his last dying breath and next to the door was a counter where thirsty pupils could buy a bottle of lemonade if they so pleased. They never bought anything at all because their conception of well-to-do differed considerably from that of Mr. Vinkerts, who charged the most outrageous prices at his lemonade counter. At the formal Christmas and Easter balls the children had very little choice in the matter and the tinkling of bottles and glasses could be heard. The school wasn't terribly lucrative and while Monsieur Charles supervised the lessons Mr. Vinkerts, who always sat behind the counter just in case, drifted away into his own private dreamworld. The people next door wanted to enlarge their office and since this house was the only obstacle to their plans Mr. Vinkerts intended to stay there with his young dancers as long as possible. Sooner or later they would be sure to offer to buy the house in order to tear it down and build a fine extension to their own office.

At the next lesson Evert Jan's eyes were glued almost continually to the hole in the ceiling in the hope of seeing the pointed brown snout again and the eyes that had looked at him, but nothing of the sort happened. He gazed at the small triangle above his head fervently and with such devotion that in the end he was nevertheless convinced he had detected various minute signs of life. Monsieur Charles couldn't help noticing the peculiar position of his head and was worried about this poorly gifted pupil skipping so many dances. *"Evert Jan, le fox trot!"* he shouted unexpectedly barely a few inches from Evert Jan's ear. He called a girl who was standing on the other side of the room and started blushing as soon as the next record started. *"Mademoiselle Truus, vous formez la contrepartie, allez hop."* He himself again chose the prettiest girl in the class and from the middle of the floor he

shouted instructions to Evert Jan and Truus who, locked awkwardly in each other's arms, would have loved to sink through
the floor and disappear. Either Evert Jan or Truus always feigned
a small defect in their shoe and with their finger poked into the
side of the shoe they limped off the dance floor in the middle of
the lesson, as ice skaters do to tighten their skates. If it was
Evert Jan who had beaten a retreat in this way, he spent the rest
of the evening in a chair in front of the fireplace, if possible.
Toward the end of the lesson the whirling around grew wilder,
the cheeks redder, Monsieur Charles' shouts bolder, and the
attention for the few pupils who had cut themselves off from the
rest extremely minute.

But one evening after Evert Jan had retreated to a chair and
sat staring at the hole in the ceiling, under a spell of the darkness
beyond the hole, he was suddenly overcome by indescribable
fear. Chills went up and down his spine, he felt an ominous
hollow deepness behind his back, and while he kept the rest of
his body stiff and motionless to avoid being conspicuous he tried
to look behind him.

The red tiles had a soft glow to them in the lamplight; the deep
brown wall that bordered the fireplace lost its color in the darkness at the top, and that darkness that continued upward seemed
somehow stale and contained a threat that knew no bounds.
Evert Jan felt the warmth of the room, turbulently in motion
because of the dancers, sweep past him. It ascended into the
darkness. Evert Jan had danced in that air, just like the others.
It also contained some of his warmth. The air had enveloped him
and had flowed between him and the girl he danced with. It had
brushed past their foreheads and touched their eyes and filled
the awkward space between them. Evert Jan was alive and the
girl was alive. He had held her hand and his arm was on her back
just as hers had been on his but they had moved each other like
objects. Objects with eyes and with a life force that moved both
of them but hardly belonged to them and, like the warm air that
disappeared into the chimney pipe, it was merely the relic of
exuberance.

That disappearance into the dark was irrevocable. And exuberance can become a shortcoming. And the life that is animated by

exuberance that does not come from within can, once this exuberance has disappeared, become utterly confused and forlorn. And the arms that were now tossed loosely around each other and were afraid of touching life in the object would some day yearn for real embraces in the hope of regaining the exuberance that disappeared into the chimney pipe after brushing past Evert Jan, warm and whirling.

From within that darkness fear gripped him, strongly, as if the loneliest of all monsters were about to appear and seize him and torture him, now that for the first time a bit of his life was lost to him and wouldn't return from the darkness that sucked in his warmth. The fear was suddenly so powerful and disconcerting that the boy stood up. Although the last dance had already started, he crossed over to the girls' side of the room, to Truus again, *la contrepartie,* who clutched her bag as if she was about to emigrate, now that it was almost time to go home. Evert Jan bowed and the girl said there was no point to it any more but she might just as well have held her tongue because Evert Jan steered her onto the dance floor in among the others.

Mr. Vinkerts put all six bottles of lemonade back in the closet. Monsieur Charles shouted *"fini!"* and presently the lights were dimmed. Both Johannes and the gormol waited for this moment. The gormol lowered itself down the chimney pipe and Johannes took his position at the edge of the hole. They looked at each other. The gormol came all the way into the room and at a steady pace it made its rounds under the counter and along the glass disks under the piano legs which it brushed up against with the scales on the side of its body, and then back again along the other side of the room to the tiles under the fireplace. Sometimes it crossed straight across the room and Johannes heard the lumpy little feet on the mosaic woodwork of the dance floor, dull thuds, with the ticking of the long nails as peculiar accompaniment. When it was back on the tiles the gormol always returned to the same position it had been in when Johannes saw it the first time; diagonal against the wall, and its dull black body made those same shuddering movements. In the meantime their eyes were constantly glued to each other.

Laura died. One night, when Johannes had looked at the

gormol for a very long time, she was cold when he came back to her. Johannes dragged her to the space above the ceiling of another room and buried her in the wood and covered her with chunks of plaster which he loosened from the straw.

There was nothing left for him but the hole in the ceiling. As soon as the lights went out after the dancing lesson he dashed over to it without further delay. He sometimes contemplated climbing down into the room but he bore in mind that then he, an old pook, would be doing what he'd always been afraid his children would do when they went out to seek adventure and left him behind trembling with fear. Besides it was contrary to the nature of a pook to approach another living creature in this way. So he stayed where he was although it struck him that now that Laura was dead it didn't make the slightest difference which species of animal he belonged to. His life was there and the only other life he knew of belonged to the gormol.

The gormol didn't come down every night. Sometimes it just stayed where it was. Then he had to sit there and feel and in this way approximate the gormol's position in the chimney pipe. When it was impossible for him to achieve any certainty about it he hung over the edge by his hind legs to peer into the chimney pipe. But he saw nothing and this behavior alienated him from the customs of his species.

Who knows if the black chalky creature also thought of Johannes on the nights it spent in the chimney pipe? Almost no one knows anything about the gormol. They multiplied, since they existed. The males sometimes crawl over eggs in the darkness of the chimney pipe, eggs that a female laid there, perhaps a century ago, who knows. They fertilize the eggs without being aware of it or without even being aware of the fact that they crawled over a sooty smoky egg.

On the nights that the gormol didn't come down it stayed in the chimney pipe because its eye was so deeply absorbed in the blackness that it couldn't tear itself away from it and because that pitch-black darkness is really the only thing the gormol is interested in, and due to its suspicion that no darker blackness is possible, it is the only thing that provides it with a certain sense of pleasure in the atrocious construction of vertebrae, scales, and stony legs, and because a blackness like that relaxes the fleshy feet at the tips of the legs and eases the muscles behind the claws which cling to the wall like dead metal clamps and absorbs the gormol and makes it one with the dead material it clings to. Sometimes when Johannes waited for hours in vain for the animal from the chimney pipe he started trembling as in the old days. And although the black monster had not appeared and their eyes had not met in silence, that trembling—even though it sprang from fear—still gave him a certain happy feeling just because this peculiarity, characteristic of his species, was still a part of him.

Then it came to pass that the gormol found a place where the blackness was so black that it relaxed completely and even the jet-black scales on its hind end stopped glittering. It didn't budge for months. This period was too long for Johannes and his fears and the pook died. All those months he went to the hole in the ceiling every night and waited and trembled. In the end he was so alienated from his customs and instincts that he even looked down during the dancing lessons and it was on one of these occasions that the boy Evert Jan spotted him.

Of course the pook realized that he had been spied because for a split second he had looked into the eyes of the boy. The eye of the gormol, and one could only tell it was an eye because it bore a vague trace of life in the midst of the dull black scales and because it had a dim glow in it as it sought a new direction, had become dear to him; but the light and troubled eyes of the boy, dilated with fear but still much too vulnerable, aroused his anger; a worried kind of anger that made him dash zigzag across the ceiling as in the old days. He was caught in the act by those eyes, caught yearning for a fellow creature. The eye of the gormol had never caught him this way, it was more a peephole into an existence of greater darkness and obscurity than a pook needs.

After this unexpected event Johannes felt an unpleasant tightness in his chest. For a few minutes he sat panting in the spot where he used to sit with Laura and he noticed that without actually being aware of what he was doing he crept to this spot when he couldn't go on any longer. After his adventure with the gormol he was suddenly thrust back into the midst of his former life, Laura, the little ones, the successive litters. He stayed there. Viewed from this point, peering through the hole at the gormol seemed little better than a vice. His loneliness provided an excuse, but his behavior was nevertheless contrary to his true nature. What business does a pook have with a gormol?

The dancing lesson was over, the light was out, but Johannes stayed where he was and neither dashed nor crept to the hole. He did think about the creature. Perhaps on precisely this night it had appeared again and sat slanted against the wall, jerking about aimlessly on the tiles.

Then again perhaps it hadn't appeared this time either and stayed in the horror of the chimney.

Perhaps in fact it had never seen the pook at all. Johannes wanted to see the gormol's eye down there on the floor. He wanted to feel the animal's presence. He looked in the direction of the hole. Like a bubbling spring a lighter kind of darkness surged upwards out of the darkness of the room.

Possibly, possibly . . ., Johannes thought but he didn't go over there. He shuddered because he sat alone at the spot where Laura had always waited for him, he sat alone without being able to ever look forward to anything again; disgraced for all eternity now that the gormol had abandoned him, at a moment of expectation, to the eyes of a boy which were clear, bright, and ignorant. Lost and forlorn in the darkness above the ceiling with a hole in it.

Johannes didn't shudder any more and he dozed off, even before he slowly began to crawl about in search of a pook to cuddle up to. With closed eyes as one unborn, he looked around just as his heart stopped.

III

When the gormol came down again the dancing school had long since been shut down. The house was empty, awaiting its demolition that was to start very soon. It was so quiet there that the sounds of the house itself were the only ones to be heard. That must have been the reason the gormol came to its senses from within the deepest black it had lodged in until then, completely one with the wall. It ate for several days and nights and then it came down. It resumed its slanted position on the tiles and started making slow jerking motions. Its eye did not look at the hole in the ceiling. The gormol was in motion all night and then quickly climbed back up.

After that it came down more often and resumed its expeditions through the room. Always along the edge because Mr. Vinkerts had removed the inlaid floor from the middle of the room and the gormol could no longer tap its nails against the wood. There was nothing left in the house except one glass disk formerly placed under a piano leg and an empty lemonade bottle. The last mover, who left the house with a chair on his back, had drunk the contents of the bottle and Mr. Vinkerts, who was carrying a few small things, had forgotten the bottle in spite of the deposit. Sometimes the gormol crawled on top of the glass disk and let itself sag down in the middle until it felt its scales creaking. On rare occasions it clamped the suction cups of its eight little feet to the empty bottle and when it let go the bottle rolled around and around on the floor. Sometimes it spent the whole night in the chimney and sometimes the evening found him clenched to the wall just above the floor, now and then tapping a tile with one of its hooked claws.

One evening Evert Jan walked past the house with his girlfriend. "I used to take dancing lessons here," he said. They stopped and looked at the house. It was clear that it was empty although a few of the windows still had curtains hanging. "I would have liked to have seen you at a dancing lesson," the girl said. Evert Jan went to the porch and lifted the lid of the letter slot to look inside. "A house like this is just like one of those shells where you can hear the sound of the sea," he said, putting his ear to the slot. "Suddenly I know exactly what I was like then."

"Tell me!" the girl shouted and, laughing, she in turn held her ear to the letter slot. Suddenly she stood up straight. "I really hear something," she said, shocked.

"What?"

"Something rolling."

"Maybe a bottle of lemonade trying to lure us inside," Evert Jan said. He listened again but he didn't hear anything.

They stood side by side again in front of the door. The girl shuddered. Evert Jan led her off the porch and was standing right behind her on the quay when they looked at the house again. It was packed to the very roof with darkness. "What could it have been that I heard?" the girl asked. Now Evert Jan shuddered. "Sometimes when you look at a place like that, a place that used to be so familiar, it's suddenly as if it's forbidden territory. Really forbidden," he said.

It was quiet in the house. The pooks were dead and in the chimney pipe there was only the gormol, that forgot it had ever seen a pook or had come across any other living creature. The darkness of the chimney emerged into the darkness of the room and Evert Jan thought of the evening he looked in back of him and, of his own free will, danced with a girl.

"Are you coming?" he said.

"Dancing lessons," the girl said. "What a lost paradise."

The men who came to wreck the house had an easy job of it. Every time they broke open a floor, light splashed between the planks into the darkness, and every time they tore down a piece of a wall, plaster and dust whirled, white and sparkling in the sun, high up into the radiantly bright sky.

All the darkness that had been in the house, all the dark corners and nooks were flooded with bright light by just one blow of a sturdy ax and surrendered their most intimate contents to the daylight and the blazing sun.

There was one wrecker who sensed the strange glory in this violation of all those dusty and tired planks and stones that were exposed to the light, in the somber pattern of the wallpaper, the boards torn loose, the painted ceilings, especially the designs of the garlands in the big room with the lions and camels in between. They disappeared in big chunks in clouds of plaster and debris and whoever found them still in one piece could have laid them side by side to see exactly where the apprentice painter had failed in imitating the work of his boss. But no one bothered to examine the pieces of this house. Wheelbarrows carried the debris to trucks and the whole house was carried off in boards, plaster, stones, straw, paper, and grit. Until they were down to the big chimney pipe, that ran along the adjacent house.

The mantelpiece had already been taken apart and the black

and green marble had been carried off somewhat more carefully than the other parts of the house. It was almost time to stop work and a piercing ray of late afternoon sunlight grazed the wrecker's ax so that it sparkled each time he raised it for another blow at the chimney wall. Big chunks, gray on the outside and black on the inside, came plunging to the ground where the suddenly exposed black disappeared almost completely in the white of the plaster that whirled around in the debris.

Suddenly the wrecker saw something move within the white of the debris and the stones. It must have been deep under the stones that were suddenly tossed into violent motion by something that made a powerful dash forward. It couldn't be a rat or a cat or a dog or any other living creature that he could possibly associate with a house. Nevertheless there was something there. Something sinister, invulnerable, and big, that made a hurried dash under the stones. A gigantic insect, the wrecker thought, a monstrous beetle, an atrocious crab, a terrifying spider. His blood went lukewarm and he was limp all over. But he lashed out at the moving stones with his ax. And when whatever it was moved on he swung at it again and again and with more force now and the limpness disappeared and made way for panic and fear at the threat of everything that is unknown in life and suddenly viciously asserts itself. The movement under the debris and the heavy sharp chunks of stone continued in the same direction. The wrecker had to run a few steps in the trail of whatever it was that dashed through the debris to take aim and strike again, his blows getting wilder and wilder. He wanted to call his mates and in fact anybody at all within hearing distance because he was afraid that what was crawling there would be revealed to him alone and he already knew he wouldn't be able to bear it.

He made another bounding attack and chopped at the stones with the steel blade with frantic intensity to put a stop to the movement and kill the monster so he could call the others and, with them at his side, venture to look under the stones. But it didn't help. The trail went on and even surged to a peak when it neared the wall of the adjacent house.

The wrecker was drenched with the sweat of fear. The thing he was terrified of beholding aroused at the same time the fear of being forsaken and alone from now on, forever. His face was twisted with anguish. The gormol appeared from under the debris and scrambled up the wall.

"Oooh!" the wrecker screamed and reeled around, wild-eyed, to give the other men time to come closer and also to get his eyes off the gormol, in the hope that the sight of other human beings would give him the courage to swing at the monster again with his ax. "Aaah, ooooh!" he gasped again but the ax did not strike.

He wouldn't have hit the gormol anyway because it was already up near the top of the wall near the roof of the other house. It was a monster, a living creature the likes of which the wrecker had never seen before, nor heard about, nor could he imagine that anyone else had ever seen anything of the sort. It disappeared over the edge of the roof. Then there was nothing left. Except its trail that still formed a clear ridge of stones across the debris. The wrecker called the other men by name. They looked at him from the distance and saw right away that there hadn't been an accident. The wrecker let go of his ax. He couldn't stop shivering. He saw his whole life before him, his wife and his children. He thought of all the things that could happen to his wife and his children and to all the other people and he thought of the unknown and unseen things in life and he looked at the ridge in the debris and saw the stones moving before him again when the gormol passed and without daring to look he saw the gormol appear again with a movement as noiseless as the shifting of a shadow and dash up the wall with its chalky monstrous body.

He understood that he had seen something more terrible than had ever been seen before.

The other men finally came over to him. They saw that their friend was white as chalk and staggered through the debris like a broken man. They asked what was the matter and he pointed to the ridge of stones in the debris but they didn't see anything unusual and watched him walk away.

The house is gone. They have already started work on the foundation for a new house.

Monsieur Charles went back to Belgium where he now owns his own dancing school. Mr. Vinkerts is a secondhand car dealer. Mr. Poortemans hasn't passed away yet, although the real estate agent's widow has. In spite of everything the children still had her buried in the family grave next to her husband. Evert Jan's engagement party was a big success.

The wrecker chose a different trade. He has become very withdrawn and taciturn. He lives in the country and as evening falls he often sits in front of his house in the twilight. He watches the clouds float by. The heads of lions are there and of camels and human figures that disappear in silence. He often stays in his chair until it is completely dark.

His wife comes to him and almost without fail she says, "Are you still sitting there? You almost gave me a fright. Come on in!"

"Yeah, I'm coming," he says. He stands up and she takes him by the hand and leads him inside to where the rest of the family is sitting.

Translated by Sheila Vuijsje.

HARRY MULISCH

The Horses' Jump and the Fresh Sea

MAY this account concerning the mythology of the former Isle of Schokland, situated in the eastern part of the former Zuyderzee, serve in order to provide an insight into the downfall and the great salvation of the human spirit.

I

When Gustaaf Nagelhout was thirteen years old, he fell in love with a fair-haired girl, the daughter of an airline pilot. From her father she had inherited the distant, light blue eyes, looking beyond the horizon; from her mother the full mouth of teeth. She was gay and sturdy, wore a light dress, and yes, indeed, her hair in pigtails, and on her head, yes, on her head a straw hat! On the way to Mr. Scharr, M.A., a retired teacher who coached him (he was still in elementary school, had doubled the first as well as the third class), Gustaaf saw her for the first time. There she came, blonde, light blue, and dancing . . . as if struck by lightning he stood stiff in his shoes, trembling and with open mouth, unable to move.

Even a long time after she'd gone out of sight, Gustaaf Nagelhout still stood there with his satchel. He had grown pale and felt a thousand tears pricking behind his eyes. It seemed to him as if now, at this moment, his life had begun. It began with waiting, long and silently, in a busy street. Everything else, the past, had disappeared, had politely tipped its hat and taken its leave. Gone were his parents, his hobbies, his friends, school—everything had been smothered, singed by what he had just seen passing by and turning the corner. Even if he'd have to wait all his life, Gustaaf Nagelhout wouldn't move a foot and would stay on the spot, waiting for her to come back. It was rather an absurd spot where he was standing, nailed to the ground; in front of a stationery shop and a window with ladies' underwear. There he stood, and waited like a monument; a deep conviction told him that he would never see her again if he as much as moved an inch from the sacred place where he had seen her first.

The passersby had to go around him in a circle. Sometimes elderly ladies or gentlemen came straight at him, assuming that he would step aside for their age. When there was no question of this, they snapped at him angrily. A wrinkled old granny, who found him as a rock in her path, even began to tug at him doggedly and to push up against him, and finally threatened him with her umbrella. But Gustaaf Nagelhout did not yield. He was due for his lesson at five o'clock and it was nearly half past, but he never gave it a thought, however afraid he usually was of Mr. Scharr's shouting. When Mr. Scharr was angry, his saliva would spurt out of his mouth and he would turn red as a tulip under his close-cropped gray hair. Gustaaf's eyes remained fixed on the corner where she had disappeared, minute after minute.

After three quarters of an hour she was suddenly back in the street, swinging a parcel; in the other hand she held her hat. How did Gustaaf feel? Here I am! Here! Here I am! he would have liked to shout, but remained silent, trembling, and tried to overpower her with his eyes. Did she look at him? Yes, she looked at him. Did she smile? Yes, she smiled, but before that she had been smiling too and she went on smiling. When she was very near him she crossed the street. Gustaaf turned on his heels and after a few seconds suddenly wanted to run after her, but remained fixed and gave a scream. His feet were asleep, long pins and needles stuck through his soles up to his knees. Like a walker with wooden legs he started the chase but there was no question of catching up. Why should he, anyway? As if he would ever dare.

But he did find out where she lived: opposite the pond not far from his own house. In the grass, at the water's edge, he looked at her house for a long time. Sometimes he saw her in the living room, especially when dusk fell and the lamp was turned on.

Lying on his belly Gustaaf Nagelhout stretched his arms out to her, imploringly. He wrinkled his forehead and whispered strange and forceful words, and then he let his head fall in the wet grass and sobbed convulsively. When her mother drew the curtains she herself came outside again to clear away some toys; another girl was helping her, apparently her sister, also blonde, and light blue, but younger and totally useless.

Only when it had grown completely dark, well gone nine o'clock, Gustaaf went home, broken. In silence he underwent the questions and the scolding, and even the next day he wasn't afraid of Mr. Scharr's shouting. In the hard-cover punishment-book, which the old man had made him buy after their very first lesson, he had to write one hundred times: *"Erroneously did I, ass's foal, assume to have the right to forsake my duty."* He wrote without thinking or grumbling and had finished before he knew. What did duty mean compared with his love? Duty evaporated in this love like ether in the free air and there was no holier duty than this love. Don't people say that it's wonderful to be in love? This is one of the deceptions with which the elderly poison their own life. They can't be in love any more—and how wonderful it was to be in love!—wonderful youth has gone . . . and with this thought they are already resentfully dying. If ever Gustaaf Nagelhout died it was in these weeks, with love; if ever life in him was attacked, molested, damaged, it was then. To have to exist face to face with a secret, unattainable possibility of bliss! What was the sense of school, of play? His days were hollow and void; emptily the light hung over his world; in the evenings he lay in the grass in front of her house, wretched and desolate, and stretched out his arms. The nights were sleepless and filled with weeping, alternating with hours in which he lay on his back, as if dying with thirst, motionlessly staring into the dark.

Yet he did get to know her soon. A boy from his class, whose father was also a pilot (there were many pilots living in this district) let himself be persuaded, with payment, to bring him in contact with her, although he himself thought she was an awful creature. She was called Bessie. The classmate went catching minnows with her in the pond and Gustaaf, who'd been waiting at the corner with thumping heart, happened to pass by. The boy called him, so he could look at her closely for the first time—but mainly he smelt her, a soft, pink, warm smell. Suddenly as limp as a rag his knees gave way and he tried with all his might to check the fearful trembling which shook him from head to toe. Speaking was out of the question, with one hand he had to keep his clattering jaws under control. When his classmate said something to him, calling him emphatically by his name (he'd been paid for this), he could only nod in reply. Sometimes he glanced at Bessie's sturdy legs, on which there were tiny blonde hairs, or at her face, but he never dared to do so for more than a moment. She, for her part, seemed to have forgotten him already. Her hat lay in the grass. Ghostlike the fishing nets waded through the deep green water. There were already lots of minnows in the jam jars. Then suddenly the classmate turned his net inside out and picked up his jar. He announced that he'd had enough of it and said good-bye. This too had been arranged and paid for. In the minutes that Bessie went on fishing, Gustaaf tore his brain trying to find something to say, but there was nothing to be found in a single hole or corner. He was no longer trembling so much, he now felt on the point of bursting into tears of helplessness. Bessie had walked to another corner of the pond with her net, a long way further on. As much as he was concerned with her, so little did she bother about him. Without saying anything to him, she too picked up her jam jar after a while and went to the house on the other side, dragging the net behind her.

Then Gustaaf called after her: "Your net is trailing on the ground! Bye-bye!" And laughed.

She briefly glanced back at him, but didn't reply. She didn't stop the net from trailing. Only when she'd already gone into the house, Gustaaf saw that she'd forgotten her hat. White and lonely it lay in the grass, a few yards further on. He looked at it for a moment; then with a jump he sat down beside it. Breathing hard with excitement he was thinking of what he ought to do. Should he take it to her home? Then he would still have a chance to talk to her! But he dismissed it at once: her mother might answer the door and send him away with a thank-you. And suddenly a strange thought occurred to him: would she have forgotten the hat if she didn't care about him at all? With large eyes he looked at the sacred object. He could give it back to her another time, when she was alone! But then he must take it away at once, before they came to look for it! He stretched out his hand but dared not touch it. Then he suddenly pulled himself together, stuffed the hat under his arm, and started to run.

At home he threw himself down on his bed and pressed his nose into the hat. At once he was surrounded by the same soft, warm smell of that afternoon. He closed his eyes and seemed to be floating away, he didn't know where. . . . Until suppertime he lay there without moving. When his mother called him he started and for several seconds didn't know from where and why he was being called and who was calling. . . . And when later that night he went to bed with the hat he knew that whatever Bessie's forgetfulnes might mean, he would never return the hat to her.

Soon it was clear that the money he'd spent on the encounter had only gained him a hat. Nothing had changed. When he met her in the following days, or passed her, she gave no sign of recognition. You might have thought that if one has met someone, if one has to a certain extent been out fishing with someone, and even sees him sometimes lying in the grass in front of one's house, that one would at least *recognize* that person. But not at all. Although she smiled whenever she saw him, she also smiled before and after—she simply smiled all the time.

Everything he did remained fruitless; even a psychological ruse to which he finally took resort. It was a variation on an old theme. He knew that other boys who were in love with girls chalked on the paving stones: CORRY IS SWEET—JAN; or WILLY IS SWEET—PIET. He had never done it himself, not because he didn't dare or because he felt himself above it, but because he thought it could have no effect, or, worse, the opposite effect. And therefore he wrote, one evening after dark, in many places between her school and her house, not BESSIE IS SWEET— GUSTAAF, but GUSTAAF IS SWEET—ANNEKE. He also wrote it on the walls. Trembling with expectation he watched her the next day. Had she read it? Did he notice any hope-giving jealousy in her face? Did a base desire to push out Anneke awaken in her eyes—a cunning meanness which would benefit him? It was impossible to say. When he saw her again in the afternoon and watched intently what the expression in her eyes would be the moment she noticed him, she smiled, as ever, and did not look at him a moment longer than usual. Perhaps she had already forgotten his name?—Nothing had changed. But the next day Mr. Scharr stopped him in the road. "Come with me," he said.

The old man was taking his afternoon walk; stooping he leaned on his walking stick which was covered from top to bottom with tin badges from Valkenburg and the Ardennes. Every now and then he would stop and flick a pebble from the pavement with the ferrule. Late in the evenings he would go out for a walk too; you could see him walking along in the dark, sparks spraying up at his feet.

Gustaaf went with him in silence. Suddenly he blushed deeply because he realized what was coming. A moment later Mr. Scharr pointed his stick at one of Anneke's declarations of love and looked at him from aside. His head bent, now in *his* turn red as a tulip, Gustaaf looked at his shoes. And then Mr. Scharr took him to all the places where it was written, tapped on the pavement, pointed at the walls, and said: "The poor child loves you. Tell her you need all your time for your work. Tell her you've got other things to think about than puppy love, considering that your chances of passing the entrance examination are already reduced to a minimum."

GUSTAAF IS SWEET—ANNEKE. . . . And suddenly, in broad daylight Nagelhout began to sob and hiccup with regret, remorse, hatred, love, loneliness, longing, and wept hotter tears than ever before. . . .

When it became clear to him that all his efforts were bound to end in failure, he started to think of suicide. He began to realize that his life was doomed to the same gigantic degree as to which it should have been blessed and beatified. That smiling, blonde, light blue mystery—it crushed him. His whole life went to pieces. At school he got one low mark after another. There was little doubt that he would fail to pass the entrance exam. His father had long ceased to speak to him and his mother said indifferently: "You just carry on." And Mr. Scharr, too, more and more often had the opportunity to send his saliva flying through the air. The punishment-book was rapidly filling up; in some passages Anneke was declared guilty a hundred times; he was being punished with this dead phantom which he had thought up in his lonely love in order to give his longing heart a chance with the living. He hardly ever spoke. He didn't play with his friends any more. Silent and pale he sat bent over his meals and only spoke when he was asked something and hardly even then. Most of his time he spent in his room, or on the dunes, where he stared emptily ahead. But after he'd been thinking of suicide for some days, he knew he'd never do it. Suicide was a fantasy, a game, like the hazardous rescue operations from fire or the skillful piloting of burning aircraft, with which his mind had occupied itself at first. The more he felt attracted to the thought of death, the more he felt that although death might always remain his best, his closest friend, he himself was very much alive and that if he was ever going to kill, it would be a living person who was doing the killing, that he would kill and become guilty out of his love for life, in the same way as one can let live with deadly intentions. And he would never kill himself—more or less like that.

And then, one night, when the flavor of these feelings had pervaded his mind, waking up with a shock from a kind of stupor, the hat under the blankets, something dawned on him which was so far from being a game that he no longer dared to move—murder.

To murder Bessie.

Like a stone he lay between the sheets. Downstairs his parents' bed squeaked like a dying animal. He began to shiver with fear and cold. To murder Bessie. Slowly he sat up, with wide eyes, shaking his head very fast in the dark, clutching the hat in his hands. Murder Bessie, murder Bessie. Then he felt his mouth filling up with saliva and a moment later he began to vomit. When his mother rushed into the room, and soon afterward his father, he was half hanging out of the soiled bed, crying and raving. When the doctor arrived he was still raving; sweat stood on his forehead. He had a high fever and the doctor said he should stay in bed for some days. When he'd been told about the boy's strange behavior in the last few weeks, he said it was probably a case of nervous exhaustion.

"Exhaustion?" the father repeated. "What could he be exhausted from? If I were exhausted . . . but he? Every day he comes home with bad marks! . . . What's that absurd hat doing in his bed?"

The doctor made a movement with his hand and went home to go back to sleep. He had long since given up trying to bring fathers to see reason. Neither the father nor the mother could discover any sense in the raving which went on, at intervals, for three days and three nights. Death was mentioned often, and Mr. Scharr, who walked around at night with fire at his feet, and a girl called Bessie, who smelt nice and caught fishes . . . and that on the streets was written: BESSIE IS DEAD—GUSTAAF, and that Mr. Scharr pointed at it with his stick and looked at him askance without saying anything.

The fourth day the fever went down. Quietly he lay on his back, looking at the ceiling. Was anything in the world so familiar as the pattern of cracks in the plaster? He thought of Bessie whom he had wanted to murder. Bessie—he loved her. But differently from before. He no longer cared that she didn't recognize him and had forgotten his name, that to her he was in no way distinguishable from others. He would never lie down in front of her house again, or write anything on the street. Her hat had disappeared—it didn't matter. He would give her up, just like everyone else had to give her up and in this way he would always go on loving her.

A few days later—it was a warm, sunny spring—he was allowed to go out for the first time. A bit pale and thin, somewhat oldish, he went for a walk around the neighborhood. All the time he felt that his legs wanted to take him to Bessie's house by the pond, but he resisted. He did stay near her street though. It must have rained recently because there was no trace of his chalkings anywhere. With his hands in his trouser pockets he wandered through the streets for more than an hour and was beginning to feel very tired. He noticed that he was all the time walking round the pond in wide circles.

Suddenly he saw his classmate, to whom he'd paid his pocket

money; he was sitting on the edge of the pavement in front of his house. Gustaaf called him from a distance but got no answer. The other boy seemed surprised to see him outside. When Gustaaf sat down beside him he stood up, and looked toward the corner of the street where a funeral procession appeared.

His chin resting in his hands, Gustaaf too watched the slowly approaching carriages. The wheels creaked and the horses were wearing large black shrouds hanging almost to the ground. The shroud of the huge black horse in front of the hearse was stitched with silver. A man across the road took off his hat in passing. Suddenly the curtain in one of the carriages was pushed aside a little and a hand appeared waving briefly. The classmate waved back, looked once more at the hearse, and sat down again.

"I wasn't allowed to go," he said. "That was my mother. I wasn't allowed to watch in front of the door either."

"Who's being buried then? A pilot in a crash?"

"A girl I know. The daughter of. . . . Hey, you know!" he called out, "Bessie! She was run over!"

Then the following happened to Gustaaf Nagelhout.

After being unconscious for two, three seconds, he came to, before his body had had time to collapse. He stood up and started to walk home fast, without actually running. His head was sticking out in front of him, as if he was on the scent of something; as if he was only walking in order not to fall. His gait was a bit like that of an idiot.

At home he found his way upstairs without running into his mother. In his room he stood swaying, turned around with mowing arms, and grabbed the hard-cover punishment-book from the table. He also snatched a few pencils from the open box and put them in his pocket. Holding the book in both hands he went down the stairs again.

"Gustaaf, is that you?" called his mother from the front room. "Don't go out again now, you've just been ill."

Without answering her—probably without even hearing her— he walked through the kitchen into the garden. On the lid of the trash can lay Bessie's hat, dirty and creased. He picked it up, ran through the gate, and once in the road he started to hurry like mad, rushing through the streets and across the squares like a criminal on the run. Some passersby looked behind him to see what was chasing him. Soon there was more space around him, he had come to the edge of the town. Everywhere among the blocks of houses there were large, square fields, surrounded by roads; soon they would be building here. The rolling fields were densely overgrown with grass and weeds, sometimes also with bits of tree trunk which were sprouting again, bushlike, forming small enclosures. In one such field, in such an enclosure among the green, Gustaaf fell down.

For a minute he lay on his back, exhausted. Ants were beginning to crawl over him and here and there a bee hummed. On the other side of the field, where the land was more open, they were having riding lessons. A few horses with slender girls on their backs walked in a wide circle around a short man in riding breeches. Sometimes he shouted something and then they trotted, turned, or stopped.

Suddenly, the straw hat on his head, Gustaaf Nagelhout was writing. He knelt down and sat on his heels, holding the book in his lap. Bending over he wrote with a light blue crayon, continuously, in rows underneath one another, as always in this book: *"Bessie is dead, Bessie is dead, Bessie is dead. . . ."* He wrote fast, and yet clearly, legibly, not once did his handwriting fade to a bare indication. He filled two pages, three, four—then unexpectedly this sentence followed: *"Erroneously did I, murderer, assume to have the right to reduce Bessie to a minimum."*

And after that, while the galloping horses made the earth drone syncopatedly, the following story appeared in the book:

"I had grown stiff all over and I was standing there waiting very quietly; the old woman came up to me, she was very nasty and started to push at me but I couldn't move any more. She was completely black and she wanted to hit me but she didn't dare because she was a little scared of me standing there so quietly. I wouldn't have minded killing her, because I wasn't allowed to move. But I wasn't allowed to move so I couldn't kill her. I would have loved to kill her so I could have waited even more quietly for Bessie, and because I couldn't kill her because I wasn't allowed to move so that I could wait for Bessie, she killed Bessie and she killed me and I killed Bessie. When I'd been wait-

*ing all alone for a long long time Bessie came. I wanted to shout
out very loudly but I couldn't. She smiled and I wanted to go
after her but I'd been nailed to the ground and the nails were still
sticking into my feet so I could hardly walk. But I lay down next
to her by the water, I couldn't help crying because I loved her so
much. The sun was going down. Father was very angry and
didn't speak to me any more and the sputtering old man with the
flames around his feet made me write lines. A hundred million
lines, I had to write lines all my life, he turned as red as fire and
yet and yet Bessie is dead, Bessie is dead, Bessie is dead, Bessie
is dead, Bessie is dead. Because she never really looked at me
everything became hollow inside and the sun a bit of rubbish. I
became so homesick between my legs and every evening I lay
crying by the pond. His father was a pilot too, just like her father,
I gave him all my pocket money and he went fishing in the pond
with her. But I trembled so and I couldn't say anything, she
didn't even look at me but later on I took her hat away and took
it to bed with me every night. I could never say anything. Then
I started writing with big letters as if somebody else had written
it I am sweet, but no she didn't see it no she didn't, only the man
with the fire, he pointed at it with his stick and looked at me and
all of a sudden I started to cry and I wished that the whole world
didn't exist. Everything is so awful. Then I often went to sit in
the dunes and I wanted to kill myself. But then I thought, it was
very dark,* ONE NIGHT, *Bessie, I'm going to kill Bessie. When
I was thinking that everything became as cold as ice and I got
very frightened inside and I don't remember what happened after
that."*

The horses were now tearing around at a gallop across the
whole field. Fluttering and laughing the girls flew past in the
wind; where Gustaaf was kneeling the ground vibrated under
the hooves. Sometimes, when the horses came thundering past
near him, kicked-up lumps of earth were strewed over his paper.
Nobody remembered that he sat there behind the foliage; the
running boy of a while ago had been forgotten.

He wrote:

*"But then I saw the ceiling and I knew every bit of it; I felt
so at home. Who was Bessie? Who was Bessie? They had taken*

*the hat away but I didn't care very much. I didn't care about
anything any more. Bessie had never really looked at me, later
I went for a walk. I walked round in a circle all the time but
on purpose I didn't go to her house to lie down by the water and
to look if I could see her. I didn't care about anything, I didn't
care about trying to pass the entrance exam, I'm so many years
behind already. I'm older than everybody else. I went all over
the place to see whether I could find anything I'd written, to rub
it out, but you couldn't see any of it anymore, it had all gone.
Then I saw my friend and I sat down next to him on the pavement but he didn't even speak to me. Then very slowly there
came around the corner, with a very big black cloth on his head
a very big black . . ."*

And at this moment the earth where he was sitting began to
rock and to heave, someone gave a long scream, and while there
was this scream the branches opened out and as a judgment a
gigantic jumping horse broke through the foliage, gazing down
panic-stricken at the boy with the straw hat, writing there under
his hooves. The girl sailed with widespread legs above the saddle,
with her left hand she was still holding the reins, the right one
she raised behind her. . . . Like a black damnation everything
crashed down on Gustaaf. Several yards further on the horse
somersaulted in a tremendous swing, his legs floundering. The
girl was hurtled through the air and did not break her neck until
she landed on the paved road. But Gustaaf, bleeding, rose up
again, he shook his torn arms above his head and shrieked: "I
have become a great magician! Watch out for me! Watch out for
me! The vansevane claps for the vansevane! Clansepole!"

II

Now—Gustaaf Nagelhout has gone mad and is no longer of
interest to us—our narration has to mention a certain baker's
deliveryman who came to cut grass for his rabbits in the field in
the evenings. He had already filled a big bag when he found the
trampled exercise-book. He leafed through it to see whether he
could find a name and address anywhere, but without success. The
name Wodan on the inside of the cover could hardly refer to the

owner. (In contrast to his friends, Gustaaf Nagelhout had had a strong fear of writing down his name, a strange longing for anonymity, which made him leave all his possessions unsigned— or maybe a longing for illusion, which sometimes led him to sign with incredible barbarian pseudonyms.) The deliveryman soon discovered that his find was a punishment-book. There were the strangest phrases, repeated a hundred times, as if they were eternal truths, like: *"Whosoever takes obscene words into his mouth, finds himself on a slippery slope,"* and: *"I don't do my homework, I am not worth that I live,"* and: *"Erroneously did I, ass's foal, assume to have the right to forsake my duty,"* and: *"Bessie is dead."*

This last one surprised the deliveryman somewhat. He leafed a bit further and came across a narration, a story, a kind of account. It had become too dark for him to read the light blue words. He put the book on top of the cut grass, lugged the sack onto his bicycle and rode home.

He didn't think of it again until the next morning, when he went to feed the rabbits. Filling the racks slowly with one hand, he held the book in the other hand and read the story. When he had finished he raised his eyebrows and started to chuckle.

He got on his bike and cycled to the bakery; all the way the grin did not leave his face. He had taken the book with him. As he was waiting with his colleagues for the bread to be brought out, he went from one to the other and let everyone read the book. Only a few laughed, some only nodded and turned away.

This didn't spoil his enthusiasm in the least. He was the first to ride off with his carrier-tricycle and that morning he read aloud from the book, at every door. Some, among them many servant-girls who liked him, giggled and chuckled too; others, mostly mothers and housewives, began to look sad and didn't seem to appreciate it; a few pointed to their foreheads.

The deliveryman simply couldn't stop. He read the story from a to z in the kitchen of the multimillionaire margarine manu-facturer P. Listening to him were Ans the housekeeper, Neel the maid, Fiep the waitress, Piet the gardener, Gijs the butler, Hein the silver boy, and Ubbe the chauffeur.

Ubbe Joziasse, to be precise. He was leaning against the

colossal whipped-cream machine and listened attentively. When the deliveryman had finished reading and looked around in expectation, he first saw Ans's sad face. She had folded her hands in her lap and was gazing through the window into the park. Neel was picking her nose but stopped when she noticed that he was looking at her. Only Fiep burst out laughing and began to dance round the table with mirth. Piet kept gazing at him with big eyes, as if he was waiting for more—as if he thought that the real stuff was still to come, after that last, half-finished sentence. Gijs pulled his cuff out a bit more, moved one eyebrow, and left the kitchen with dignity. And yes, Hein was sniggering. But Ubbe, Ubbe Joziasse, he pushed himself away from the whipped-cream machine and walked out of the house with a puzzled expression on his face.

In the park, on the way to his home above the garage, he wondered what precisely had moved him so in that story. (The bread deliveryman is no longer of any concern to us, our account takes leave of him; at the age of sixty-three he died in Zwolle in violent pain.) Ubbe couldn't make it out, perhaps it was something from his childhood which he had forgotten. Something which had happened or hadn't happened but should have happened, and which therefore in a certain sense had happened now, in his emotion. And he also felt a strong but equally inexplicable urge to tell his father what he'd heard, to the old Joziasse, Gnodde Joziasse, who lived with him above the garage. Ubbe climbed the stairs and stood in a corner of the room. With a heavy heart he looked at his father; he couldn't bring himself to break the silence. The old man sat straight as a ramrod in his chair by the window; a heavy, very old man. An enormous beard covered his chest, his hair hung down on his shoulders—its color was deep gray, there was too much strength in him for it to grow completely white. The Joziasses . . . were they not the last and only Schoklanders left? With his head half turned away he watched his son sharply from the corners of his eyes.

"You want to tell me something, don't you," he said, "why don't you speak?"

"Yes, I, just now . . ." stammered Ubbe, "the bread deliveryman . . ."

"Don't stammer so."

"No Dad."

Ubbe swallowed with difficulty and looked fearfully at his father.

"The bread deliveryman found an exercise-book," he began again. "He read something from it. It was about a man who'd gone stiff, he wasn't very old yet, and he was attacked by a witch. He wanted to kill her but he couldn't move anymore. He was waiting for a beautiful woman with wonderful hair, who was later murdered by the witch, or by himself, I didn't quite get that. And when that woman came he wanted to shout with joy but he couldn't do that either. And then, oh yes, she was smiling all the time and then he wanted to go to her but he couldn't because he'd been nailed to the ground. And then he lay down at the edge of the lake, Dad, and he started to cry. And when it had gone dark he called for his father but his father didn't answer." Ubbe waited a moment, his lips were trembling. "Then there came a burning man who was spitting fire and he punished him. He was never allowed to speak again, he had to write, all his life. And she never looked at him," said Ubbe and made a passionate gesture with his arm, "and the sun became small and cold! Every evening he lay crying at the edge of the lake, and he was homesick between his legs."—This term Ubbe had fixed firmly in his mind. "But then he gave all his money to someone else whose father was a pilot just like her father and he went out fishing with her on the lake, the son I mean. He himself was on board too, the man who loved her so much I mean, but he still couldn't speak and then he stole her hat to take to bed with him. That's how the deliveryman read it, don't blame me please. And because he couldn't say anything he started writing who he was but she didn't read it, only that burning man read it and pointed at it so that he started to cry again and began to curse the whole world. And in the end he sat in the dunes and wanted to kill himself. He wanted—he wanted to drive into a tree, Dad, so he'd be finished with everything! He wanted suddenly to turn the steering wheel," panted Ubbe, turning an imaginary wheel with his arms, "and drive head on into a tree at full speed!"

The old man by the window began to shake a little, perhaps

some ailment was beginning to bother him, or perhaps he was smirking in his beard. He didn't take his eyes away from his son.

"But one dark night!" Ubbe shouted passionately and took a step forward, "he thought, no, not myself, I'm going to kill her! And then suddenly everything went as cold as ice and he was frightened to death. But later he looked up and recognized everything so he felt at home again and became very calm. The hat had been stolen but he didn't care. He went for a walk, he didn't care about that beautiful woman any more—that's to say—he—And everything he'd written had disappeared too. In the end he sat down beside his friend, the one from the boat, that fishing boat, you remember, the one in which they'd been out fishing, but he got no answer. Then slowly something very large appeared, with a big black cloth on its back. . . ." Ubbe spread his fingers and took a deep breath. "I don't know what it was," he said and was silent. It was clear that the story moved him even more now than when he'd first heard it.

Motionlessly the old man sat in his armchair, plucking at his beard with two fingers.

"Did you make it all up?" he asked after a while, narrowing his eyes.

"But Dad," said Ubbe. "It's the truth!"

Gnodde Joziasse nodded and seemed to be pondering.

"I'm telling you, you've made it all up," he said again. "From beginning to end."

"Oh Dad," said Ubbe, "then I've made up the truth!"

Not long after this Ubbe crashed head on into a tree, together with the margarine manufacturer. When Gnodde Joziasse heard the news, he at once wrote a short letter and started to pack his suitcase. Fourteen days later, it was a sunny day, he received a reply, and Gnodde Joziasse traveled to the coast of the former Zuyderzee, then already called Ijsselmeer and cut off by a dike from its great mothers, the North Sea and the oceans. He traveled by train and then by bus; the last stretch to the beach he had to walk with his suitcase. He walked slowly, but straight as a ramrod; his beard and hair were blowing in front of him as if they were being pulled toward the water. The sun shone warm on the deserted sand which stretched right and left to the horizon.

The lake was smooth and empty, only an old, half-rotted fishing boat was anchored about thirty yards from the shore, waiting for him. On board were his four brothers: four very old bearded men, whose sons had all died. The ragged, dirty sail moved gently in the soft wind, and silently they looked at their brother as he was slowly approaching across the beach and began to wade through the water, holding his suitcase in his arms. Sea and beach . . . nothing else moved anywhere.

When Gnodde had reached the boat, one of his brothers took the suitcase from him. He himself stayed a moment longer holding on to the rail, up to his waist in the water, and looked up at the bearded four in their rags.

"Hello Odde," he said, "hello Slikke, hello Ubbe, hello Stobbe."

"Hello Gnodde," nodded the brothers.

"You're late," said Stobbe, "you're the last one."

Gnodde smiled in agreement and raised his arms. Then the four old men bent over the rail, laughing, and pulled their brother into the boat.

Gnodde, wet as he was, sat down in the front of the boat and Slikke sat down at the helm. When the others tended the sail, the wreck slowly began to move. A moment later it was at right angles to the shore and gradually the land began to recede. . . .

For a long time not a word was spoken in the old fishing boat, which was letting a good deal of water. The sun caressed the lake and everywhere in the boat there sat an old man with hair down to his shoulders and a gray beard. Gnodde did not move, his clothes were already drying. It was very quiet; only the squeaking of the mast could be heard, and the water lapping against the hull. . . .

The Joziasses. Because Schokland was small and marshy, and because the sea swallowed large sections of bog at every high tide, the island was evacuated in the previous century, by order of the authorities; for their own safety the few hundred inhabitants were resettled on the Isle of Urk or on the mainland. But in spite of the order the Joziasses had always returned to the deserted, worm-shaped island and lived among the more and more decaying and moldering fishermen's cottages, finally amid vast ruins, through which the wind shrieked. After their wives had died and they themselves were too old to go out fishing, they went to the mainland, to their sons who died there one after the other. One after the other the fathers returned to the dead island of ruins, built a cave with the grown-over debris, and lived there, cold, dark and in silence. Gnodde was the last one to return.

When Gnodde had been quietly watching his brothers for a long time, he bent over, put his finger in the water on the floor of the boat, and licked at it. At once he began to spit and wiped the finger dry on his beard, nauseated.

"Still less salty," he cursed.

"Sugar water," grunted Odde.

And all the brothers spat over the railing, with indignant contempt. Slowly the land receded to the horizon and as the boat moved on, Gnodde looked at it musingly, over his brothers' heads. The weather was as soft as velvet.

"Do you remember," he started, when the coastline had merged with the horizon, "how we used to sail here, every one in his own boat, with nets and helpers? Nets for the herring. Helpers for the herring."

"Nets for the herring," repeated Stobbe, musingly.

"Helpers for the herring," sighed Slikke at the helm.

"And we often met each other here on the water. Sometimes Ubbe and Stobbe would meet, or Slikke and Obbe, or Odde and Stobbe, or I and Ubbe."

"And one night in September," said Ubbe, "in 1869—there was a storm and the sea was rough, we all met, all five of us. And although all our boats were damaged we climbed the masts and shouted to each other in the dark, above the violent elements."

"Ah," called out Stobbe, "the violent elements."

"And you remember how surprised the boys were," said Odde, smiling.

The other four smiled too, and looked at each other.

They were silent, the smile remained on their faces for several minutes, but then it slowly disappeared and gave way to a somber, serious expression. The boat groaned and let a lot of water; deep in thought, Ubbe, Stobbe and Odde began to bail mechanically with rusty cans.

"It was still a *sea* then," said Gnodde with controlled anger, "the water was salt and a home for herring. That blasted dike wasn't there yet, that abominable work of the devil." He had risen to his feet and pointed to the north. Softly his hair and beard waved in the wind. "Now it's all fresh, it's only fit for tadpoles and goldfish, our water." He cursed again and sat down.

The others went on bailing in silence; Slikke sat motionless at the helm.

"From then on our blood lost its strength," Gnodde resumed, as if he was talking to himself. "Sugar water. . . . All our sons died on the shore. Mine drove into a little tree in a little car." He looked up into the mocking faces of his brothers, he himself too smiled contemptuously. "Only we have remained what we were. People like us will no longer exist, everything comes to an end. With us Schokland will die."

The sun was going down and created a pink glow in the west. The wind had become still; only now and then there was a flutter in the sail. Slikke was still steering but he knew that they were lying practically still and that the boat was leaking.

While the others were slowly bailing with their cans, Gnodde looked down at the water beside him.

"Soon grass and wheat will be growing down there," he said, "and the bastards will send their cows to graze there and will run after their chickens. With their horrid little ploughs they will crawl about on the bottom of our sea where we only deign to go when we drown. Schokland will become a somber hill in the fields—and no one will remember what a human being is. . . ."

At this moment Stobbe dropped his can in the water and sat completely still, tears running down his cheeks into his beard.

Gnodde watched him for a time with his old eyes and then nodded, looking at his feet: the water was already reaching up to his ankles. He looked around and peered at Schokland, which was now a short line on the horizon. But at once he looked in front of him again, into the boat, a happy expression on his face.

"After twenty years we are together again," he said, looking at his brothers one after the other. He stretched out his arms: "Brothers! This was our father's wish."

At these words Odde and Ubbe also stopped bailing and Slikke let go of the helm. They looked up at Gnodde as if something had just become clear to them, as if these fathers suddenly remembered that they too had had a father, whose sons they were. An intense expectation showed on their faces as if they realized that now was coming what everything was all about—and always had been. The boat didn't move, the water had even ceased to ripple against the hull. Gnodde let his eyes roam across the sky which was turning pale and still more quiet. And however softly he spoke, it was as if his words filled the whole sky, from horizon to horizon:

"When our father was not yet born, brothers, nor his father, nor his father's father, there lived many gods in the sky above Schokland, and their chief god had as his daughter the beautiful, beautiful Leia, the goddess of the sea. She wore a crown of deer's antlers, which possessed magic powers, and she often played on the beach. On the island lived Binar, a half-god and the ancestor of us all: the father of our father's father's father. One day Binar saw Leia, and he was fatally struck by her heavenly beauty. She laughed as she played on the beach with her crown of antlers, throwing it up high. Sometimes it would turn into a blue bird, sometimes into a black rose, sometimes into a small moon. But her father was looking down from the heights above Schokland and saw how Binar was overwhelmed with love for his daughter. And because Binar was only a half-god, and his daughter a goddess, he sent the witch Foki down to nail him to the ground and to strike him dumb. Foki did so and Binar could not move a foot and was mute. With all his yearning heart he wanted to go to Leia, but he couldn't; he wanted to sing to her with the voice of a forest, but there was no sound coming from his mouth. Powerless and with breaking heart he had to watch how Leia laughed and played, and vanished. With bleeding feet, wounded by Foki's nails, he dragged himself to the sea, fell down, and stretched his arms out toward her. . . . And Binar wept bitterly until sundown."

It was growing redder in the west; the sunlight began to trickle onto the water and streamed in a broad, blinding beam across the lake to the boat, where the old men's faces were kindled by the glow. Gnodde looked at Stobbe, who was crouching in the middle of the boat; the water reached up to his waist and his beard sucked it up greedily. Gnodde felt the water rising around his calves. It seemed to him as if he heard his own words rustling away on the horizon.

"When night had fallen," he continued softly, "Binar called plaintively for his father, a wretched human who had been allowed to break many commandments; who had seduced a goddess in order to beget him, Binar. But his father did not come. The sky began to burn and there appeared, from the north, Geidallr, full of flames, pointing at him with his staff, and while Binar tremblingly saw fire blaze from Geidallr's mouth he was condemned to a lifelong sentence of writing, because he, a half-god, loved the goddess of the sea. Because only gods are allowed to love goddesses, or humans, like his father—never a half-god; for the half-god, too much human for the gods, too much god for the humans, there is only loneliness.

"Then Binar began to write all along the beaches of Schokland, from north to south and from south to north he wrote on the shores of Leia. And always he saw her, but she never saw him, and it was as if the sun became a moon and did no longer have its own light but received it from elsewhere in shame, as an alms.

"But one day," said Gnodde, raising his scarlet face, "one day Binar decided to defy the gods! He gave all his possessions to Gorr, the son of one of the sky-gods. Gorr used his powers on his behalf and together, the three of them sailed out to sea: Leia, Gorr and Binar—in a fishing boat they sailed, the father of all fishing boats. And they had a miraculous haul of fishes, brothers! Of their own accord the herring jumped from the sea into the boat! But Binar still could not speak to Leia, Foki's curse continued in undiminished strength. And then he stole Leia's crown of antlers, he gained from it the magic power to write as no one has ever written before or since: he raised it to the sky and wrote with the clouds!" Gnodde shouted with rapture, raising his arms. "With the clouds he wrote from east to west across the sky, that he loved her! That he loved her!"

He shouted it and then was silent, breathing hard. The boat was now sinking fast. Stobbe sat up to his shoulders in the water; the waves rippled over Gnodde's thighs and also the others were only half visible. But no one took any notice, all eyes were fixed on Gnodde, who as he spoke became redder and redder in the sun, which was now touching the water.

"But Leia saw nothing," whispered Gnodde. "She did not look up. She smiled in front of her—why should a goddess look up toward heaven? But Geidallr, accursed, he looked up and read it and pointed toward it while the flames were seeping out of his mouth. Then Binar went to the beach, spread his arms, and began to roar and to curse the world. And then the thought of death occurred to him. He crept to the dunes, looked at the sea, and saw the thought of death approach—but not for himself . . . for her! Death, death to Leia. Death to the sea. Then all the letter-clouds piled up into a fist and struck him down and he turned into transparent ice." Gnodde swallowed and could no longer speak. Suddenly he had seen Schokland, right ahead of him. It had moved along the horizon, from one side to the other; the boat was slowly turning on its axis.

"Much later he woke up," continued Gnodde hoarsely. "It was night. He lay still and looked up at the stars, he recognized all the stars and felt at home in the world as in a safe haven."

Stobbe stood up in order to go on listening to him; the water dripped down from him on all sides. Ubbe, Odde, and Slikke had also got up and finally he himself stood up too. The boat lay very deep, the water was as high inside it as outside; only the rail could still be seen, a large oval ring a few inches above the surface, a mast rising out of the water and five old men inside the oval. The sun became green and purple and wavered in its colors, and the water. . . .

"Binar walked along the beach, Ubbe," said Gnodde, his voice choking with tears, looking each of his brothers into the eyes. "His crown had been stolen, Odde, and what he had written had vanished. He met Gorr, Slikke, in silence he sat down beside him, in silence, they didn't say a word, everything was so quiet, Stobbe, so quiet. Then slowly something gigantic appeared, black . . . death . . . the . . . the. . . ."

Suddenly the boat began to sway gently, the rail disappeared under the water and now only the mast and the motionless sail could be seen, and the heads of the five old men. They were sinking fast, their heads seemed to be floating on the lake in rings of hair; the water was reaching their lips. . . .

"The fresh water," whispered Gnodde and vanished with his brothers in the depths.

At the moment when the pennant on top of the mast was pulled under water, the sun disappeared and at once a deep dusk fell over the plain of the former Zuyderzee.

These are the connections according to which Gustaaf Nagelhout became, at the age of thirteen, the spiritual father of the mythology of the Isle of Schokland, which, however, no longer exists and is today an oblong elevation in the North-East Polder, surrounded by luscious meadows and fields of waving wheat.

May 1954

Translated by Adrienne Dixon.

HUGO RAES

Explosion

IN a field of vision made indistinct by divisions and spots, something is moving, coming up from just below the surface. Its outline is vague, but now it rises to the surface and its shape is
clearly visible. It is an oval body, it twists a bit sometimes and
then shoots forward. Then it stops. An alarmingly still shape.
It disappears partly under a hazy patch, through which it is again
dimly visible. Suddenly it disappears from the field of vision,
from the eyepiece, from view. Wait patiently. Suddenly it shoots
into the circle again. A remarkable contraction takes place. It
expands, shrinks, and suddenly splits. Now there are two bodies.
Asexual reproduction. The bodies will split again, an infinite
number of times. In a few hours they will have reproduced themselves innumerable times, generously and diligently. The dividing
bodies have gone. Now there are little rods. They move or lie
still for a time. One rod touches another at right angles and sails
on. Long thin sticks transparent as glass, others grayish black.
And then the little balls. Between the sluggish rods rotating on
their axes the little black balls shoot back and forth and crisscross,
infallibly avoiding any contact with one another. They seem to
be now rolling, now skating. A bullet, another bullet zigzagging
and quivering in and out of the field of sight. And through it.
Balls. Rods. Ballet of dots and spots. A ball touches a rod and
disappears in it. The signal is now given. A twig eats a ball. Now
eat, eat. Rods eat balls. Drastic changes of shape are now taking
place. The rods are expanding, bending around, becoming closed
circles, rings, flexible elastic rings which bend, move. Between
a ball and a rod; a ring. Living elastic rings under the rods and
black dots. Dot dash, dash, dot dot dot ring dot, ring dash ring.

New things are born. They grow larger or give rise to other shapes, these creatures. Infinite number of adaptations. You can combine them in pots, in beakers, the voice says, feed them well, make a sludge. Living porridge. Living porridge takes on an elastic shape, sticky and elastic at once. You open a pot, pour a little of the sludge out; it hangs from the edge like a living drop of snot. It contracts and expands, pulls itself up, drops again. Grayish blue with a light green or sea-green edge. You take hold of the end, the voice says, lift it up between thumb and forefinger, put it back in the pot. It again takes on the form of a uniform liquid. Sometimes beautiful gradations of color appear. A wisp of pink, a haze of purple, dots of yellow. A wonderful prism, the voice says. Examine, breed, play with wonderful new materials. Always something new. The voice says: recently a fabulous discovery. Living microorganisms in ore, and at that the most lethal ore, uranium. So there are microorganisms that can resist the strongest radioactivity. They live in it. Always something new. Always experiment, the voice says. With living color gradations, with changing forms, microorganisms.

The figures in the street—yes, it is a street—move, walk, hurrying across each other's paths. Large and small ones zigzag about. They are people. Look at them well, gaze. Of course, because I am in the street too. Now I can see it. I am among them. But isolated from them, in the middle of the open street without traffic. All people. All people. A sort of droning begins in the sky. It has an ominous sound. The people look up. The droning comes nearer, gets angrier. The people stop and scan the sky. It is a spotless blue, not a cloud to be seen. Clear weather, but where is the sun? No air machine, no craft visible. The noise has now swollen to a loud rasp. A loud, dry rasp, like a circular saw with a high revolution rate. The people stand speechless, nailed to the ground, listening and looking. Their faces are turned upward. They are trying to discover what is going on, what this is. The rasping roar is deafeningly loud. Nothing to be seen. Roaring aaaaaah eeerrrr. But it is not a monotonous, level sound.

The voice says: look at the painting, look at the artist's work. The human artist works, creates, experiments. The painting has fine color nuances. Sea-green, translucent stuff with light blue misty patches, a wisp of pink here and there. The color moves. Various kinds of people appear in it, evolving into rich browns. Balls become visible unexpectedly and then greedy, active but stiff rods. All kinds of changes occur. Suddenly a black thread shoots through the stuff, becoming less transparent. Unnoticeably at first, the gentle undulation has increased and becomes a lump. Further on something has begun to germinate. A seed. Under the warm lamps and ultraviolet rays a plant has germinated in the red flesh on the left side of the painting. At the bottom the red, semiliquid flesh begins to run over the frame. A rubbery lobe is hanging down. The artist adjusts the position of the painting. Mechanically he sets it horizontal. The red lobe shrinks. In a few hours it will form a ball perhaps. Numbers of spectators watch with fascination the changing forms and gradations of color of the enormous masterpiece.

The droning roar is certainly monotonous. But attentive listening makes it seem to have variation in it. Just as when you listen carefully to the ticking of a clock or the hum of a fine electric instrument or set. The people are standing petrified in the open street without traffic, without vehicles. There are only people, people, with their faces turned upwards, a listening audience, slowly turning eyes trying to pierce the sky, to examine it. The roar becomes louder and louder. More and more vicious. Increasingly ominous. There is nothing to see and the roaring is coming lower. Some in alarm take a step or two backward. But what is the use of stepping backward when something is coming from above and is invisible. Low down the crazy aeeeerrr is no longer bearable, and then suddenly: a tremendous explosion. It seems to last for hours, for if you go up in an explosion, are disintegrated, there is no more time, or the explosion is eternal.

The voice says: the next day the spectators are again standing before the masterpiece. Those who came to look in the night will not return till late in the day, as they are going to sleep now. They look for a few hours and then come back later when new forms have emerged and variations are more clearly outlined. Yes, indeed: the synchronized, dripping plasma feeds the germinated plants and the flesh blossoms, the gigantic bacteria enlarged half a million times with radiation and artificial means.

The artist-biologist, the painter, sculptor, biologist, chemist, team or one-man team creates in a subtle way.

The next day a sort of heart begins beating in the painting. Nicely isolated a piece of flesh lies beating gently and rhythmically. The spectators outside the glass tank can hear the beating through a microphone and listening apparatus. The voice says: the next day the painting, affected by increased temperature and a different arrangement of lighting, feeding, and position, gave off a smell for the first time. Unrecognizable. A soft, cloying smell, not unpleasant, not of rotting or decay. A mild, even rather attractive smell. A smell of plants and healthy flesh mixed.

And three days after the third day, the voice says, the most incredible thing happened for those who happened to be looking at the first living, moving experimental painting in the world. The never expected. The unbelievable. In the shapes, now well developed, and particles, some separated from others, small opening and shutting holes and valves had appeared. Complete silence is enforced in the darkened room, where the living, experimental painting evolves and is fed and looked after under special lamps. Only the great incubator is bathed in light. In perfect peace and isolation, and warmth for hatching, and liquids and drops for feeding, it lives, changes, grows or withers, drooping here and there, the artistic product of man.

Now and then a scientist opens part of the incubator to do something to it. It happened that the people present on the sixth day were witnesses of the incredible: through the loudspeaker which transmitted the heartbeat and sometimes a faint sound of dripping they were suddenly aware of a rustle, a sigh. After that the work of art constantly produced vague noises, a sort of sighing.

The man was now becoming more restless. He turned over and was tired from *the journey*. So they had been on a journey, for a long time. And how restful the house was, empty and deserted, when you entered it again after weeks of absence. How surprising your step sounded on the tiles in the passage, the creaking parquet floor of the living room, the back door which is only now unlocked and swings open with a squeak. And you sit in the garden: quiet, untouched, the grass has grown high, has over-grown part of the path. You can hardly see any flowers in the grass any longer. How fresh it all is and how quiet. The trash can is in the middle of the yard under the shelter. How did it get there? He goes up to it. What is it that smells so? He lifts the lid and jumps back from the black things that swarm out like spattering gravel; fat, dark bluebottles that keep on rising from the bin. He shivers, a few of the hard, fat insects settle on his head, hair, and shoulders. He jumps aside and waves his arms around his head. There are more and more big flies under the shelter, most of them rise into the air, disappear into the tree and over the garden wall into the neighbors' gardens. And the stink. There are no more flies coming out of the can. He goes to the can and looks in with horror; there is a rotting fetus in it. Moral, says the voice, never leave your trash can outside when you go away.

Now the man wakes with a start. He is lying on his back. He opens his eyes wide. Disquiet oppresses him. A nightmare, he thinks. He coughs and turns the sheet over the blanket again, so that he does not have the wool against his chin. He turns over. He is not comfortable and turns over again. He tries to think of something else. Nothing much comes into his head. He dozes off again. He thinks something about a newspaper, he is turning the pages of a large newspaper. Someone is with the police super-intendent. He is saying: my father-in-law is seventy-nine and lives alone in Dennebosstraat and I haven't seen him for several days; his house is shut and there is no sign of life. A policeman was sent with him. Through a chink in the french windows he could see that the septuagenarian was lying with his head on the window seat. The superintendent and the local doctor got into the house over the roof. They went to the old man on the window seat. Under the dead body the doctor discovered a block of wood. He took the block away from under the corpse. Suddenly a shot was fired. The doctor was struck by a bullet in the left hand. Under the old fellow was a small cannon, such as is used by country people for frightening birds. The man had been an eccentric. He had provided the thing with a small barrel and put revolver bullets in it. The thing went off when the wooden block was removed. A small round of cannon fire. The bullet, which had penetrated the doctor's wrist, had to be removed by surgery in the hospital.

A little boy with hideously crooked, deformed legs, hobbles nearer with difficulty. He has a dying, green face. He says: Daddy.

His body is under unbearable tension; heat like an electric current runs through it, increasing in strength till at any moment it may be fatal. It must be a question of seconds.

There is now a very ugly woman nearby. She is staring at him pityingly and while drying glasses she is saying something, but he cannot hear what. Someone with a tortoise's head crosses between them very quickly.

The disaster grows, the disquiet, the uncomfortable fear, grow. He kicks the blankets off and is half-awake. The child is still saying: Daddy. He sits up. I was too hot in bed, he thinks. He looks around the half-dark room. He feels as if some horrible discovery is still waiting for him. He wants to shake everything off. How is it possible to have such a succession of nightmares, he wonders, I did not eat anything late last night. I did not read anything. I am not strained or overtired. Has something happened? He tries to remember if anything happened in the course of the day that could have given rise by association to the forming of a nightmare. He went to sleep again. At once he felt himself threatened. He looked around, suspicious, nerves and senses stretched to the utmost, walking across the deserted street. Suddenly some young fellows, hoodlums, appear in the distance. Their hands are up as if they want to fight. He looks around and sees three more. Now they are with him in a cellar. They lay him down and hiss that they are going to do something to him. We are not going to kill you, we shall just do all kinds of things to you. He cries out, he wants to talk to them, explain to them. But they are beginning to hit him, they take hold of his genitals. He feels the threat of death and calls for help. He has lost all control over his body. He calls out, no one comes to his assistance. He hears himself shout: Nora! As he hears himself calling the name he opens his eyes and wakes. His heart is thumping, he is breathing quickly. I am sweating, he thinks, but his feet are cold.

I will try another position. He spreads his legs out like open scissors and puts his right arm under his pillow with the left half folded beside his chest, so that the arm is supported by the hand, as it were. It is as if his head is too low. He puts it further back, his chin is now sticking out. He lies awake for some seconds but sleep begins to press on him again, just as if the dream has to continue at once. The gloomy atmosphere remains. He feels that another nightmare is going to start. I had better get up at once, he thinks. It is enough to turn your hair gray or give you heart failure. If I do not break up the oppressive atmosphere at once it will never stop. People have been killed by nightmares. As he is getting up one of the metal feet of the bed slips with a cracking noise on the linoleum. Depression hangs around him like a specter's sheet. He has a clear impression that he is dead, a ghost. He breathes deeply a few times and opens the stiff door. It opens with a swish and there is a black hole before him. He advances slowly, blindly, unsteady on his legs and gropes along the wall for the switch. In a flash he thinks: perhaps there is something in the house, perhaps there is a burglar and I heard someting unconsciously in my sleep, had a premonition. He thinks with revulsion and uncertainty, fumbling in the dark for the switch, that he will suddenly feel a person, or bump into a body on the ground. He finds the switch and turns the light on. It gives a flinty click. He tries to overcome the dazzle unnaturally fast. There is nothing to be seen. Step after step of the staircase creaks loudly. Hearing and nerves still stretched by the ominous feeling he looks over the landing and tries to see if there is anything downstairs. In the meantime the unpleasant atmosphere abates a little. He puts on light after light. He thinks: I'll fetch a few bottles of beer from the cellar. That soon makes you sleepy and calm. In the living room he went to the window still half asleep, as he noticed. He drew back the curtain and looked out at the car. There was moonlight and the car was standing there, peaceful and ordinary. The indirect lighting of the hall he had turned out, but the ground floor was bathed in what seemed to be excessively white light. The cellar door groaned a little as he opened it. It also needs a drop of oil, he reflected, and went down the wooden steps. The cellar smelled of cold and of damp stone. From step to step he saw two holes, spaces. He switched on the weak, bare bulbs in both and first cast a glance right and left. Then he took a bottle and then another. At the top of the steps he thought he heard a strange sound, just as he turned out the light. He held his breath and listened. He went into the living room. How strange and dead it seemed. What a strange night, he thought. The nightmares are affecting me, still have me in their grip. Every movement, every sound seems amplified a thousand times. How is it possible? He takes an opener out of the drawer in the cupboard. He shuts the drawer again. He takes the bottle in his left hand and opens it with his right. The metal clinks against the glass, he twists and suddenly there is an enormous explosion, he feels a fantastic pressure and a blow in his face, so that his head is thrown back. He falls to the ground, his feet kick with the toes scraping the floor, one of his ugly leather slippers falls off. He groans for another second, can no longer breathe and does not know anything anymore. The room is filled as if with a vapor, a gas. His body is sound, but saliva runs out of his mouth, forming a thread reaching to the ground. It touches the parquet floor, forms a bubble, and lies there as beautiful as a little convex pond, a pearl.

Translated by Ralph Powell.

GERARD K. VAN HET REVE

The Decline and Fall of the Boslowits Family

MY first contact with the Boslowits family was at a children's Christmas party at some friends'. There were paper napkins on the table, with gay little red-and-green figures printed on them. In front of each plate burned a candle in a socket carved from a half potato turned cut-edge down and covered neatly with dull green paper. The flowerpot holding the Christmas tree was covered the same way.

Near me, holding a slice of bread over the flame of his candle, sat Hansie Boslowits. "I'm making toast," he said. There was also a boy with a violin; while he was playing I almost had to cry, and I thought for a moment of giving him a kiss. I was seven years old then.

Hansie, who was two years older, began wiggling the branches of the Christmas tree with seeming nonchalance, until a branch above a candle flame began to sputter and emit a sharp scorching smell. People shouted, mothers came scurrying, and everyone near the tree was forced to sit down at the table or go to the other room, where a few children were playing dominoes on the floor.

The two Willink boys were there, too. They were the sons of a learned couple who let them go about with close-cropped heads because they were of the opinion that man's appearance is not the essential thing; this way it was easy to keep the boys' hair clean, and no valuable time had to be spent combing it. The cutting was done monthly by their mother with the family clippers— an important financial saving.

It was fine having the Willink boys around, because they would dare do anything. Sometimes on Sundays they came with their parents to visit us. Then I would go out with them to wander around the neighborhood and follow their example by throwing stones, rotten potatoes, or pieces of horse dung through every open window. A wonderful fever of friendship would liberate me from all my fears.

At the Christmas party they amused themselves by holding a burning candle at an angle over someone's hand or arm until the hot tallow dripped on the victim's skin and he jumped up with a scream.

Hans Boslowits' mother saw it and said, "I don't think that's nice of you at all." But his father smiled: he admired the ingeniousness of it, and he didn't have to be afraid that anyone would try the joke on him, since he was an invalid, his whole lower body crippled by disease. After that evening I was to call them Aunt Jaanne and Uncle Hans.

I was very anxious to watch Uncle Hans leave, because I had seen him carried in by two other guests and the spectacle had fascinated me. But at half past eight, already, I had to go home with my parents.

Four days later, it was still Christmas vacation, I went with my mother on a visit to the Boslowits family. The street had a long, narrow stretch of grass down the middle, and we had to walk around it. "Well, big boy Simon," Uncle Hans said, "Hansie is in his room. Go play with him."

When I entered the room Hans asked, "What do you want?"

"To play with you, that's what your father said," I answered, taken aback.

He had on a pair of knickers and a green sweater, he was wearing glasses, and his black hair was plastered down and parted sharply. I looked around the room and caught sight of a small statue on the shelf above the convertible bed; on touching and smelling it, I found it to be a little dog made of soap.

"I made that," he said.

"Oh?" I asked. "At school?"

"By myself," he claimed, "at home, out of soap from the store." But I had already stopped believing him, because he had been confused for a moment by my question.

On his desk was an object that he kept looking at and picking up in a way designed to arouse my utmost curiosity. It was a metal box in the shape of a writing tablet, two fingers thick and a bit slanting, with a push button at the top. The cover was surrounded by a frame with a transparent celluloid window in it. You could write words on the plate. Not only with a pencil, but with a stylus that wouldn't write otherwise, or with a stick; the words appeared in purple beneath the little window. If you pushed the little button everything that had been written disappeared. The possibility that such a thing could exist had never entered my mind.

I myself was given the opportunity to write on it and make what had been written go away with a push on the button. Sometimes, though, the apparatus refused to work, and the text remained wholly or partially visible.

"I'm going to throw it away," said Hans. "It's broken."

"It's a nice thing you can write on and it goes away when you push on it," I said to Aunt Jaanne, who came in just then. "Hans says he's going to throw it away."

"Now he's being bad again," Aunt Jaanne said. "He's going to throw it away because he doesn't want to give it away." All afternoon I kept hoping to possess the apparatus, but I didn't dare make any reference to it.

In the living room, too, were interesting objects. For example there was an armchair that was six feet long, covered with leather and resting on one round metal foot. Because of its easy-to-damage construction I was only allowed to lower myself into it sideways; then I could use my right arm to turn a wheel underneath, whose position determined the angle of the seat.

On the mantelpiece stood two old delft tiles, one depicting a fisherman, the other a skater. Potted plants in little antique copper pails lined the windowsill—there was a small indoor palm, and any number of cactus plants, including a ball-shaped one covered with ropelike growths that Aunt Jaanne called "the plant with gray hair."

We sat down to lunch, and we had knives with yellow ivory handles. The blades bore an elegantly engraved trademark with the letters H.B.L. "What do these letters stand for?" I asked, but my mother, Aunt Jaanne, and Uncle Hans were so engrossed in conversation that only Hansie heard the question.

"The H is for Hans," he said loudly, "and the B is for Boslowits."

"And the last letter?" I asked, waiting.

"But the L," he went on, "yes, the L!" He ticked on the knife blade with his fork. "What that is for is known only to my father, me, and a few other people." I didn't want to bear the responsibility of asking something that for weighty reasons had to be kept secret, so I held my tongue.

After the meal there was something new: a woman came with Hans's brother Otto. I had already been instructed about him by my mother: "The boy is a little backward, so if you dare tease him . . ." she had said.

"Here we are again!" the woman called out, and turned the boy loose like a dog given the liberty to jump up on his master for a moment. He stooped forward when he walked, and he was wearing extraordinarily high shoes with toes that pointed in toward each other. He had on knickers, like his brother, and he was perspiring so heavily that strands of his colorless hair were plastered to his forehead. His face was strangely wrinkled, and his eyes didn't match.

"Well, are you here again, my little fellow?" his father said.

"Yeah," he called, "yeah, yeah father mother!" He kissed them both, and Hans. Then, standing still, he suddenly jumped into the air so hard that everything rumbled.

The violence frightened me, but he appeared to be harmless, as my mother had already told me.

"Go shake hands with Aunt Jettie," he was ordered, and after the words had been repeated for him several times he succeeded in bringing out "Aunt Jettie" and "hello aunt," until they finally got him to say the combination, "Hello Aunt Jettie."

"And this is Simon," said Aunt Jaanne.

"Hello, Otto," I said, and shook his sopping-wet hand.

He jumped into the air again and got a goody; a piece of candy that Aunt Jaanne stuffed into his mouth. Every time anyone asked him something—in the usual way, without expecting an answer—he would shout "Yeah yeah," "Yeah mother," driving the words out forcibly. Someone put a portable phonograph on the table, and the woman who had come with Otto wound it up.

"He stayed dry last night," she said.

"Oh, that's good, what a good boy, Otto; you stayed completely dry, didn't you?" his mother asked. "Isn't he a good boy, Annie?"

"Yes, he's been a good boy, haven't you, Otto?" the nurse answered.

"What do you say now?" his mother asked, "—Yes, Nurse Annie."

"Yes Nurse Annie." After an endless struggle he got it out, all in one breath.

He was busy sorting out phonograph records from a box. He held each one up close to his face with both hands, as though he were smelling it. His nose was red and damp, with a small yellow pimple at the end of it.

"He smells which ones they are," explained Uncle Hans, helping to sort from where he sat in his chair.

"This one," he said, and handed one to Otto.

The boy took the record, inspected it, sighed, and leaned on the table with his elbow for a moment; unluckily he happened to lean on a record, and with a quick little sound it snapped into thirds. I shouted something, but Uncle Hans took the pieces and looked at the label, then said, "A very old one, Otto."

"Old one!" Otto forced out, and put the record that his father had indicated on the turntable.

It was not like the other records: it was brown and thin and looked as if it was manufactured of cardboard or paper. Only one side was playable. Hans put a rubber piece on the turntable rod, because the record bulged upward a bit. When it started to play, a flat voice said, "The Loriton Record, to which you are now listening, is suitable for recordings of every sort. It is light in weight and flexible, and it is three times as durable as the ordinary record."

Then the speaker introduced a dance orchestra. When it had finished playing the voice said, "The Loriton Record can only be played on one side, but if you will check with your watch you will see that it plays twice as long on one side as an ordinary record. And, ladies and gentlemen, the price is no more than half."

Otto was jumping up and down with impatience. His mother quickly chose another record, a small one with a pink label. Two voices sang a song about the three little children.

Outside the windows, a fine drizzly rain was falling. I sneaked to Hans's room, where I looked at the little dog and touched the writing apparatus and wrote on it until I was called to go home.

On the way I asked my mother, "How old is Otto?" "A bit older than you are, pet," she answered, "but remember you must never ask at Uncle Hans's how old Otto is." It seemed to me that the rain suddenly blew a bit harder against us.

I was lost in my thoughts, but I heard my mother add, "They're afraid that Otto won't be taken care of after they're gone." These two bits of information gave me food for days of thought.

Only with the second visit did it become clear to me from the conversation that Otto didn't live there, but at a children's home, and that the woman who brought him was a friend of Aunt Jaanne's who was a nurse at the institution.

It was on a Sunday, and my father went along. When we came in Otto was being talked about in a reprimanding tone. Hans was standing in front of the window and Otto by the antique cabinet with glass doors; Uncle Hans was sitting in a chair beside the table.

"Yes," Aunt Jaanne said, going into the room ahead of us, "we were just talking about Otto."

"Yeah," Otto shouted, "yeah mother!"

"There was a bowl of grapes in the next room, in the office," said Uncle Hans—what he meant was his small study on the street side. "I wondered why he was coming in all the time. And each time he picked off a grape from the bowl, and now they're all gone."

Otto laughed and jumped into the air. His face was glistening with sweat. "Mother doesn't think it's funny at all," Aunt Jaanne said. "You've been very naughty, Otto."

"Otto naughty!" he yelled, his face twisted anxiously.

The phonograph was playing busily most of the time, and the talking grew still more noisy when the Fonteins appeared. I had never seen Mrs. Fontein before, but I had heard at home that whenever she came upon an acquaintance carrying a shopping bag she would hide behind a fence or in a doorway so she wouldn't have to say hello to someone who went out for her own groceries. I had also heard that whenever she was somewhere visiting in the evening she would leave for an hour to go back home and see whether her nineteen-year-old-son had gone to sleep. She was called Aunt Ellie, but grown-ups made fun of her as "crazy Ellie."

Once my mother had gone to see her at home, and she had talked to my mother in the hall, saying that the chiropodist was there; but she had stuffed a gigantic bonbon in my mother's mouth, with the words, "Actually it's one for high society, but I'll let you have it." At home my mother had given only a feeble imitation of her nasal tonsilitis-sufferer's voice, but now I heard the sound unadulterated.

Aunt Ellie's husband, my father, and Uncle Hans went to the study, Uncle Hans propelling himself forward in an extraordinary way, first searching for support with his hands, hunching over, and then letting his frail legs swing forward with a jerk, one after the other.

I followed them through the hall and went into the room behind Uncle Hans. "Was that crazy Ellie there?" I asked Uncle Hans, pointing back in the direction of the living room. Later I comprehended that this question, asked in her husband's presence, must have embarrassed Uncle Hans extremely. He fumbled in his vest pocket till he found a quarter and gave it to me, saying, "You go buy yourself an ice-cream cone."

I went outside just as an ice-cream man was passing. I put the quarter on the cart and said, "An ice-cream cone."

"A five-cent one?" he asked.

"That's all right," I said.

"Or a ten-cent one?"

"That's all right. An ice-cream cone," I said.

"For five cents or ten cents?" he asked then. There was no definite decision reached, but he made a very large one, and I was taking it from him just as my mother came outside.

"He's been naughty," she said to the man. "He's been begging for it." I kept hold of the ice-cream cone. My mother pulled me along with her. "He still has some change coming!" the ice-cream man called out, but we were already inside and the door banged shut. The ice-cream cone didn't taste good, and I was allowed to put it on a plate in the kitchen.

After that, visits were exchanged regularly. On my birthday my new aunt and uncle gave me a metal toy car that wound up, and I tried not to let them know that I was really too old for it.

Usually they spent New Year's Eve with us, and my father would carry Uncle Hans upstairs with the help of the taxi driver.

Uncle Hans's condition remained the same all those years, but I remember that one afternoon at our place Aunt Jaanne said there was a lameness that had begun in his right arm and came back regularly. It was the same year I started going to a junior high school very near the Boslowitses' apartment. The Sunday before the new school year began I went to see them. I was requested to stay for lunch.

Aunt Jaanne was telling her sister that she had put Hansie in a boarding school in Laren, because things couldn't go on the way they were. After the meal, while Uncle Hans was sitting in his study, she said, "When he has a quarrel with his father he puts his hand on the man's head. And that makes him so furious; it's horrible."

She went on to say that a neighbor woman she had talked with that morning over the garden fence had more or less reproached her for the decision, saying, "You already have one boy away from home, and now to send this son away too . . ." "I've been lying on the sofa all morning crying," said Aunt Jaanne.

"She has a nerve to say that," her sister said. "What business is it of hers?"

I said, "Tomorrow school starts there." I pointed in the direction of the building around the corner. "Do you think I'll get homework the very first day?"

"Well, no, I don't think so," Aunt Jaanne said.

Now that Hans wasn't there I hunted through his room out of curiosity, but I didn't find anything of interest. The little dog was still there, but the writing apparatus had disappeared long since.

When Aunt Jaanne came in, I said, "I wanted to borrow a few books," and took up a position in front of the bookcase as though I were deep in reflection. "These." Without thinking, I pulled out two volumes of *Bully and Beanpole,* a children's story about a fat boy and a lean one, and *The Book of Jeremiah Called Michael.* "If Hansie doesn't mind," I said.

"If we don't mind," Aunt Jaanne said. "But we trust you."

"I'll bring them back before long," I said.

Three years before the war the Boslowits family moved to an apartment looking out on the river, a side-canal, and a lot that was being filled in for construction. There was a granite entry-way with twenty steps to climb. From there I watched the large-scale air-defense exercises that were held one day, I think it was in autumn.

The Boslowitses had invited a large number of people to come and watch, and the younger generation climbed through a window at the head of the stairs above the top-floor neighbors' apartment, and onto the roof. Sitting beside the chimney, straddling the ridge, we watched the barrels of the antiaircraft guns on the vacant sand lot spring back for a shot each time a formation of airplanes passed, a moment before we heard the sound. Fifty yards ahead of us machine gunners were shooting from the roof of a large mansion set off from the other houses. The Willink boys were there with us, throwing pebbles they had brought along especially for the purpose. Sirens sounded the air-raid alarm and the sky grew overcast. Then new squadrons of airplanes passed over, flying through the cloudlets of the antiaircraft explosions and discharging green, glowing balls that burned out before they reached the ground. The air-defense fire squad spouted water into the canal and the river to test its equipment. At the end of all the turmoil, an amphibian plane landed on the river and skimmed along the surface, then climbed again, over the big bridge connecting the southern and eastern parts of town. I was highly satisfied with the spectacle. Everyone was given tea with crisp, salty crackers.

Half a year later we moved to the center of town, no more than a ten-minute walk from the Boslowits family, on the opposite side of the river. Now we could exchange visits more frequently. Aunt Jaanne came regularly, and on the afternoons when Otto had no school—he was learning paper mat-weaving and bead-stringing somewhere—she would fetch him from the children's home and bring him along to our place for a bit of a change. Walking home from high school one Friday, I saw them approaching from the other direction, Otto hunched over more than

ever, springing about like a dancing bear on a chain, so that his
mother could hardly hold onto his hand. The eight-year-old
neighbor girl from the second floor was jumping rope, and she
had fastened one end of the cord to the iron fence around one of
the narrow front yards, so she would only have to use one hand
to swing the rope. When Otto's mother turned him loose so he
could gallop full speed toward our house, the girl purposely
stretched out her rope in his path. He stumbled but didn't fall.
The girl let go of the rope and fled before Aunt Jaanne, who was
so furious she could hardly make a sound.

She went upstairs in a passion, right behind Otto, and I followed them. Otto leaped into the hall with a rumble, looking
forward to the few old picture postcards my mother gave him
each time he came. "That anybody," said Aunt Jaanne, "that
anybody could do such a thing—can you understand it? If I had
been able to get my hands on her, I would have done I don't
know what to her." She grew a bit calmer, but kept on blinking
her eyes—a habit I noticed then for the first time.

"Let's go see if we have a postcard for you," my mother said.

"Yeah Aunt Jettie!" Otto forced out, dancing along with her
to the cupboard. She dug out three of the cards from a cigar box.
He sniffed at them and jumped in the air.

"Be careful, boy. There are people living downstairs," my
mother said.

"Where's Otto going?" asked Aunt Jaanne.

"Yeah yeah mother!"

"Where are you going?"

"Yeah mother!"

"No, Otto, you know well enough. Where are you going?"
When Otto had still not given a satisfactory answer, she said,
"To Russia."

"To Russia yeah mother!" Otto shouted.

"You see, Jettie," said Aunt Jaanne, "a professor in Russia has
completely cured a number of children by an operation. So we've
decided that he's going to Russia." Another bit of news had to do
with Uncle Hans's condition. He had collapsed and was in bed,
and his right arm was paralyzed almost all the time. "And besides
that there's his temper," she said. "That's something terrible."

As a more encouraging bit of information, she told us that a doctor who had treated Uncle Hans ten years before had come to visit and had said, "Man, I thought you'd died a long time ago."

That wasn't all the news. They were thinking of buying a new wheelchair for Uncle Hans so that when he had got a bit better he would be able to be outside in the air more and could go visiting here and there without it costing so much.

"But he doesn't want to," said Aunt Jaanne, "because he thinks he'll seem like an invalid then."

"But that's what he is," my mother said.

Uncle Hans did get his wheelchair, despite his opposition, but not until quite a while later. It was a three-wheeled one, propelled by levers that turned the front wheel and guided the vehicle at the same time. It had to be taken from a garage each time, and then Uncle Hans had to be carried down the high stone entryway. He hadn't had the wheelchair long before they rented a ground-floor apartment. It was in the street behind ours. Though it was a dark, dank house, there were advantages to it, since the Block Committee agreed to having the wheelchair stand in the entry, and a friend who was a carpenter made a letter box in a windowpane in Uncle Hans's study so the postman could drop his letters practically on his desk. Going out in the wheelchair was an act of his own in appearance only, for someone had to push him—his thin hands, and especially the right one, had no strength at all.

One Sunday afternoon we—my parents and I—were coming back from a birthday party together with Otto, Aunt Jaanne, and Uncle Hans, and I was patiently pushing the wheelchair. We were crossing a bridge that sloped rather steeply. On the other side of the canal we had to turn left. On the downslope the wheelchair began to go faster and faster; I held it back, but Uncle Hans ordered me to let loose. I obeyed. There was an intersection just beyond the bridge, and the presence of a traffic policeman made it impossible to turn left right away. Vehicles had to wait for the traffic signal, then cross over and line up on the right side of the street.

But Uncle Hans zoomed down the bridge and cut diagonally around the corner without waiting. "You can't do that," I called after him. Right behind the traffic policeman he veered left, but his velocity and the incline made the wheelchair topple over and hit the street with a bang. The policeman and some pedestrians came hurrying up and set the wheelchair upright, with Uncle Hans still in it. He hadn't been hurt at all, but he said nothing, and even after we got to the Boslowitses' he sat at the table in silence, staring straight ahead.

Aunt Jaanne comforted Otto, because she thought he had seen the fall and was frightened by it. "It wasn't father that tipped over, but someone else, wasn't it, Otto; it was some other man, not father."

"Not father!" Otto shouted, and he leaned his elbow on a tea-cup, which broke. It was a gray day with no rain falling, though a still sky constantly threatened it.

On my sixteenth birthday, that same spring, Hansie came along with Aunt Jaanne and Uncle Hans to visit. His mother had decided to have him come back home. "If there's going to be a war, I'd rather have him at home," she said. He was to be a salesman in an uncle's business.

"You say if there's going to be a war, as if there's nothing going on now," my father said. At that my interest in the conversation was aroused. It was true that England and France were at war with Germany, but to my dissatisfaction there had not been any military activities of importance to follow.

From time to time I went to the movies with Joost, the younger of the two Willink boys, and before the main feature there would be some insignificant news shots from the front, with camouflaged cannon standing ready or firing a shot every quarter of an hour. Once there was a favorable exception to this monotony in some shots of the grounded German battleship *Graf von Spee*, beautifully unraveled and shattered. "Horrors of the war, fine," Joost said in a comical tone as a shot from the air gave a last view of the wreckage.

"What I'd like best is short, violent street fighting here in town," I said. "From window to window, with hand grenades and white flags. But not for more than two days, because then it would be boring again."

One evening in May when I went to ask if we could borrow

an electric toaster from the Boslowitses, I found Uncle Hans, Aunt Jaanne, and Hansie together in the twilight. There was a neighbor visiting them. They were so deep in conversation that they didn't notice it right away when I came in. "That means something," the neighbor said. "I say that has a significance. It means a lot more than we know." Confused, I stood waiting at the door to the living room for a little while, till Aunt Jaanne caught sight of me.

"Oh, it's you," she said. "Have you heard that the leaves are all canceled? This man's son has to be back this evening already, and be in the barracks tonight."

"No," I said, "is that so?"

"That's what they said over the radio," the neighbor said.

"Then there's something in the air anyway," I said, and I felt a deep emotion rising inside me. That same week, on Thursday night, almost everyone in the neighborhood appeared in the streets a few hours after midnight. Airplanes went droning over, antiaircraft guns thundered, and searchlights pushed their shafts upward between the thin tufts of clouds.

"They're getting something to put up with again over in England," said a milkman who had concluded that they were German planes on their way to English cities and being shot at over Dutch territory by our neutral military forces. He proved to be right about the nationality of the planes, but the rest of his hypothesis was refuted when we came to realize the meaning of the deep thuds and flashes of light on the southwest horizon.

A little after seven o'clock Aunt Jaanne came upstairs. I wasn't there at the time, because the Willink boys and their sister had come for me. I had gone along to their house, and from the balcony I could see black clouds of smoke hovering above a spot that couldn't be anything but Schiphol Airport.

"It's war," said the Willink girl, whose name was Lies. We went back to my house together, elated at so many thrilling events all at one time. It was a quarter to eight.

"It's war," said my mother. "It's been on the radio already." "What did they say exactly?" I asked. "Oh, I can't repeat it all, you should have listened yourself then," she answered.

Aunt Jaanne sat in the easy chair with a black velvet cap on her head, blinking her eyes. The radio was dead, and we sat waiting impatiently for the beginning of the regular broadcasting day at eight o'clock. It was the custom to introduce the day's broadcasts with a rooster's crow.

"I wonder if they'll do cock-a-doodle-doo the same as usual this morning," said my father, coming in from the hall.

I fervently hoped that the rumors flying through the neighborhood were all true. "Really at war, wonderful," I said to myself softly.

The radio clock began the soft noise it makes before it strikes. After the sixteen notes of the chime, it struck, slow and clear. Then the rooster crowed. "That's really a shame!" said my father.

I was frightened, because everything could still be spoiled. This was probably proof that war hadn't broken out at all. I was put at ease only when it was announced that the borders of Holland, Belgium, and Luxembourg had been crossed by German troops.

I went to school that morning content, while Aunt Jaanne still sat staring straight ahead without saying a word.

At school a solemn mood prevailed. The building was to be used as a hospital, and the principal made an announcement of the fact in the auditorium. After that we all sang the national anthem. The fact that the school was closed for the time being made the day still lighter, as though all things had been made new.

We didn't see Aunt Jaanne again until the next Tuesday afternoon. She came to visit us alone, and she looked pale. "What are you doing?" she asked. "What a smell—is there something burning? Things look pretty bad."

"Pretty bad," my mother said. "They've just capitulated."

We had begun burning books and pamphlets in the stove, and it puffed and smoked from being stuffed overfull. At the same time my brother and my father were busy filling two burlap bags and a suitcase with books. After dark they threw them in the canal.

Everywhere in the neighborhood fires glowed that evening, with new loads of things to be burned being carried up constantly, sometimes chestful at a time. Many other people threw

everything in the canals. Sometimes, in the general haste, this or
that was left lying on the edge. Wandering along the canal in
the twilight, I found a book with a flaming red cover—I have
forgotten the title—that my mother later took out of my room and
refused to give back.

After the announcement of the capitulation, Aunt Jaanne let it
be repeated to her once more and then suddenly went away. The
following day brought two interesting events. Towards noon the
first Germans rode into the city. They were men on motorcycles,
dressed in spotted green capes. A few people stood along the
road to watch them coming over the bridge. Aunt Jaanne had
seen them too, and when she came to see us Wednesday evening
she called them "frogs."

I wasn't at home, because I was busy. Hundreds of fish had
come swimming to the surface of the canals, gulping for air—it
was said because salt water had been let into the canals by mistake. I was catching those in front of the house with a big fishnet;
they made no attempt to escape, and I took home a pailful of
them.

The next day school began again, and the very first evening
I went seeking consolation at a small movie house where that
week, for the last time, there was still a French film. The movie,
Hôtel du Nord, was about a suicide pact in which the boy succeeded in shooting the girl, then lacked the courage to turn his
gun on himself. But the girl recovered, and it all ended with a
reconciliation between them and an acceptance of life when she
came to meet him at the prison after he had served his sentence.
I felt satisfied with the way the problem was solved.

At home I found Aunt Jaanne sitting on the sofa and my mother
pouring coffee.

It was dusky in the room, because the lights hadn't been turned
on yet. Unrolling the blackout paper and fastening it with thumb-
tacks was a cumbersome job. And so I found them sitting by the
pensive light of the tea warmer.

"You have to blackout," I said. "That light shines outside."

"You do it then, will you?" said my mother.

I remember that one window was ajar when I let down the roll
of paper. "Hans sent a letter to an aunt in Berlin, quite a while

ago," Aunt Jaanne said. "It just came back, undeliverable. Moved, whereabouts unknown it said on it."

Just then a gust of wind lifted the blackout paper and the curtain for a few seconds, chasing a piece of paper off the table. I shut the window quickly.

Late one afternoon when there was no school I dropped by the Boslowitses'. It was high summer, and Uncle Hans was sitting in front of his office window in the sun. Almost immediately he turned the conversation to his sickness and a doctor called Witvis, who had already been there several times and wanted to try something new to cure him. "He'll make me run like a rabbit," he said. "You'd like to have a cigarette, wouldn't you?" he asked, and got up to look for the box. "Tell me where they are and I'll get them," I said, but he shuffled to the corner of the room and took a flat, square copper box from a table. "Are you laughing?" he asked, his back turned toward me. "No, honest," I said.

Hans came in and sat down on his father's desk. "How's it going?" I asked. "That selling, do you like it?"

"Today my turnover was near a thousand guilders," he answered.

"Is there any news?" asked Aunt Jaanne.

"News that the Germans are advancing on Brest," I answered. "They're making a terrific hullabaloo on the radio." Then I told them what a fat boy in my class had claimed. According to a prediction made by a French priest forty years before, the Germans were to be defeated near Orléans. "He also wrote that the city on the Meuse will be destroyed," I said.

Aunt Jaanne said, "If you'll bring me the book that says that, I'll give you something."

That same afternoon, not long before dinner, I went to the Willinks for a little while to tell them the latest news from the radio. Just after I sat down in Eric's room the antiaircraft artillery began popping restlessly. Two airplanes glistened in the sunlight, flying so high it was impossible to make out their forms, but only a glittering reflection.

A bit later we heard the rattle of machine guns and the terrifying sound of a fighter plane zooming by close overhead. From time to time when the noise grew too strong, we would hurry inside from the balcony; we could also hear the rattling of the plane's guns.

Then it was still for a moment, and we saw a black swath through the sky with a flaming star dropping rapidly at the point of it. The light was white, like the light of an acetylene torch. Then we saw a second column of smoke beside the flame: the plane had broken in two.

After a moment it all disappeared behind the houses. There were no parachutes to be seen anywhere in the sky. "May God guard those who fare on the sea and in the sky," I said solemnly. No air-raid alarm had been given.

After dinner Hans Boslowits came to our house. "Do you know what kind of a plane it was that came down?" he asked.

"No, I don't know," I said.

"It was German," he declared.

"How do you know?" I asked. "Have you already heard where it came down?"

"Look," Hans said, polishing his glasses with his handkerchief, "we have our sources of information."

"I hope it's so," I said, "but I don't believe anyone can know anything for sure yet."

"We have our sources of information," he said, and went away.

The next day, I'm certain it was a weekday, on my way home from the movies in the afternoon I saw the announcement of the French surrender being posted as a bulletin in front of a newspaper office. When I gave a résumé at home, my mother said, "Then they're asking for an armistice. That's not the same thing. Go to Aunt Jaanne's and tell her exactly what it said."

"It may be propaganda," Aunt Jaanne said, but I could tell she didn't doubt the announcement for an instant. That same evening she came to our place, and it was then that she told us what had happened to her all of four weeks earlier.

One afternoon two Germans in uniform had come in an automobile. "Put your hands up," one of them had said on entering Uncle Hans's room. "Don't be witty, mister," he had answered in German, "I can't even stand on my legs."

They had searched the apartment and then declared that he had to go along. Uncle Hans had gone to get dressed; once they saw him dragging himself through the house his crippled state became so completely obvious they must have realized the foolishness of making an arrest. Then they watched Aunt Jaanne fasten a rubber flask for urinating onto his waist. "They asked if I was the only one that could do that," she went on. "I said I was the only one. Then they wrote down some more and went away again. It wasn't very pleasant though." She blinked her eyes, and a few slight quivers shot through the muscles of her face.

"How is Uncle Hans, anyway?" my mother asked.

"He's not getting any worse," Aunt Jaanne said. "Just now he's able to use that hand to write with again."

"That's something," said my mother.

Summer and fall went drably by. It was after New Year, dull, damp, springlike weather. The second Sunday in the new year the parents of my school pal Jim had asked me to dinner, and unexpectedly I ran into Hansie there. Jim's father was a wholesale dealer in veal and had an amazingly fat belly, but he took things lightly and was a lot of fun. Although he had had three stomach operations, he didn't allow it to restrict him in any way.

"I like everything, so long as there aren't any pins in it," he said at the table. As a gesture of friendliness they had also invited my parents, whom they didn't know.

"I don't read German books any more," said a small gray-haired man when the conversation was on literature for a moment. At once the talk turned to the war and surmises of how long it would last.

"Now I'd say half a year at the outside," said Jim's father. "But actually he's not going to hold out that long."

"The way it's going now, it could last twenty-five years," my father said, smiling.

Hansie, who happened to know one of Jim's brothers, had his guitar with him, and he played a renowned tune, *Skating on the Rainbow*, with a great deal of violence. When talk of the war came up, he said, "It's going to be over this year."

"What makes you think so, Hans?" asked my mother.

He answered, "The circles who keep me informed know very well, Aunt Jettie—I repeat, very well—what's going on."

Five or six weeks later Aunt Jaanne climbed the steps to our apartment, flushed with excitement. "The greenies are catching the boys all around Waterlooplein," she said. "Can Simon go look for me? No, he had better go to Hansie's office and tell him he can't go out on the streets. But wait, I'll call him up. Have Simon wait."

"First come and sit down," my mother said. It was a Wednesday afternoon. We succeeded in calming Aunt Jaanne, "Now go call up Hansie," my mother said.

"I already have," she said.

"Oh, have you?" my mother said.

"I'm going to go around there and have a look," I declared.

"You'll be careful, won't you?" asked my mother.

I cycled quickly to the neighborhood around Waterlooplein and brought back a detailed report on everything. Uncle Hans puffed slowly on his stubby black pipe. "You've got on a nice sweater there," he said in the middle of my account. "Is it new?"

Aunt Jaanne was busy constantly telephoning the office where Hansie worked. He was to stay there at night; I heard her promise to take him bedding and food. At her request I took the telephone. "Don't believe that what you're going to say will be of the slightest importance, high and mighty Simon," said the voice on the other end.

"Is that so," I answered, smiling, because Aunt Jaanne was keeping a close eye on me.

"That woman sure jaws a lot," he went on. "Just tell her for me that she's a horrible old jawer."

The receiver had a very clear tone, so I drummed on the floor with my left foot. "Yes, that's right," I said loudly. "I can imagine that. Fine."

"What do you mean?" he asked.

"That's it exactly," I said, "that in any case you'll be careful— but you are, so I hear. Goodbye. See you." And I put down the receiver, even though Hans had suddenly begun to shout so loudly that the telephone emitted squeaking sounds.

"Well, what did he say?" asked Aunt Jaanne.

"He says," I replied, "that we are all nervous and say crazy things to each other. But you shouldn't be at all worried, he says.

Of course he'll stay inside. He says in a day everything will be over."

"You can talk on the telephone again," said Aunt Jaanne, satisfied. Then she looked out of the window and said, "Don't be worried: it's a nice theory."

Four days later Aunt Jaanne came to see my mother, who was at some friends' somewhere and might be back any moment. While Aunt Jaanne sat waiting for her, the fat magician who lived around the corner also came up the stairs. On the steps he always whistled the melody that preceded broadcasts from London. "You shouldn't whistle like that on the stairs," I said. "It doesn't get you anywhere, and it's dangerous."

After he had listened to what meager news there was, he said, "I think they're going to lose, only I don't know whether it'll be before I'm dead and buried or after." He shook with laughter and went away, whistling the melody loudly on the stairs. He had barely gone when my mother came home.

Only then did Aunt Jaanne say, "Parkman's daughter is dead." She explained how the daughter and son-in-law of a neighbor across the street from her had swallowed poison together. The man had been revived in the hospital and was recovering. "He's screaming, and they have to hold him down," Aunt Jaanne said. Whom did she mean, I thought, the father or the husband?

June was very mild, a bright, sunny early-summer month. One afternoon while my mother was sitting in front of the open window knitting, Aunt Jaanne came in with Otto. She looked pale, and the skin of her face was cracked and chalky, though she didn't use powder. "Mother mother," Otto called impatiently.

"Be quiet a little, dear, that's a sweet boy," said Aunt Jaanne.

She had to tell about something that had happened to a nephew of hers. Cycling through the heart of town, he had violated a traffic regulation and was stopped by a man in black boots, partly uniformed, partly in civilian dress. The man had grinned as he wrote down the name.

One evening a few days afterwards, a nondescript man in dark-colored clothes came to the door. He said that the nephew had to appear at an office somewhere in the center of town the next afternoon because of a traffic violation—in order, so he said, to settle the affair.

The boy went, but his mother went along. At the entrance to the office she was held back, but her son was allowed to enter. After twenty minutes he came stumbling outside, vomiting. There were several welts and bleeding gashes on his face and dirt on his clothes as though they had been dragged across the floor.

For a high fee, the two of them took a cab with rubber tires and a pony to pull it. When they got home the doctor found a slight brain concussion and a contusion of the left shoulder blade, and the collarbone on the same side was broken.

They had let him wait in a little room. The man who had stopped him on the street came in first, then he called in some others, part of them carrying billy clubs. "This is a sassy kid that called me bastard," he explained. One of the others struck the boy under the chin and then all six or seven of them began hitting and kicking him.

"It started all at once," he had told Aunt Jaanne. One man with greasy gray hair kept trying to kick him in the groin. He stumbled in his attempt to avoid the man's blows and ended up lying on his back. Before he could take up a safer position, one of the men stamped on his chest. After he had turned over, someone, he thought the gray-haired man, stood on his back.

Then a bell rang or a whistle blew, in any case there was a shrill sound that made everybody stop; after that he heard all kinds of voices, but he couldn't remember anything about what happened from then on until he came outside.

"You know that Joseph's people got notice of his death?" said Aunt Jaanne.

"No," my mother said, "I didn't know."

"But they had a letter from him from camp, too, with a much later date," Aunt Jaanne went on, "but now they don't hear any more news."

They fell silent. Aunt Jaanne looked at Otto and said, "The doctor has given him some powders. He's stayed dry for two nights already, I heard from the nurse." My mother remembered that she had neglected to give Otto any picture postcards, and she hunted out two of them from the cupboard; one was in bright colors, a view of some foreign city with a pink sky.

When I went to see Hans Boslowits one evening several weeks later, he was busy playing his guitar. He would slap the strings with his open hand and beat up and down with his foot. At my request he played *O Joseph, Joseph,* but I wasn't pleased by the performance because he followed the melody by singing "ta ta ta ta" with too much emphasis, tilting his head up so that his throat was foolishly tensed.

"It's the heartbeat of our society, this music," he said. At that moment someone tapped on the panel of the living-room door. The visitor had already come in the hall; he called out his name loudly and Aunt Jaanne answered, "Yes, come on in, neighbor."

"Mrs. Boslowits," said the neighbor, entering, "I don't suppose you've heard yet that Dr. Witvis is dead?"

"How can that be?" Aunt Jaanne asked.

"I only heard it just now," he said. "It happened last night."

Late in the evening, he went on, the doctor had taken a razor and slashed both his two small sons' wrists, holding their forearms in a basin of warm water while he did it because that prevented pain. After his wife had opened the artery on her wrist herself, he cut his the same way. The order of events was deduced from the position of the victims and the presence of a second razor in his wife's hand. The mother and the children were already dead when they were found, and the father was unconscious. He was given a blood transfusion in the hospital after the wound had been closed, but he died before noon without having regained consciousness.

When I went to the Boslowitses' to borrow half a loaf of bread one Sunday afternoon late in the fall, I found Otto beside the phonograph.

"Otto is going on a trip," Aunt Jaanne said. "Isn't that right, Otto?"

"Yeah mother," he called, "Otto on trip!"

"Where for god's sake is he going to?" I asked.

Aunt Jaanne's face gave the impression of being inflamed by fever. "He can't stay at the children's home or the school any more," she answered. "He has to go to Apeldoorn. I'm taking him there tomorrow."

I saw only then that the sliding doors to the back room stood open, and Uncle Hans lay there in bed. The bedstead had white iron rods, with copper globes at the four corners. The sick man's face was thin, but even so it looked swollen, as though it was moist inside.

On a chair were bottles of medicine, a breakfast plate with a knife, and a chessboard. "I was playing chess with Hans this afternoon," he said, "but Otto was always tipping it over."

He kept to his bed the following days as well, and his situation turned serious. Winter was coming, and the new doctor said that the rooms should be kept quite warm. For a long time Uncle Hans could still go to the bathroom by himself, but eventually he had to be helped.

"He's so awfully heavy I can't do it," Aunt Jaanne said. "Actually he doesn't cooperate."

After New Year the doctor strongly recommended his being admitted to a hospital, and he was taken there early that same week.

"He has it really fine," Aunt Jaanne told my mother after a visit, "and the doctors and the nurses are all so nice."

"He doesn't have any notion of things any more," she went on soon after that. "I don't understand what's going on inside him nowadays. Hansie took him some oranges—he could buy them from someone at the office. He says, father, these cost sixty cents apiece, be sure you eat them. But he didn't eat a single one; he gave them all away. Of course you should share things, but this is enough to make you furious."

"From tomorrow on we have to be inside at eight o'clock," Aunt Jaanne said to my mother one day late in the spring. "Will you go on the evening visiting hours? I can't get back in time and what good does it do Hans if I have to go away again after three minutes? I'll just stay a little longer in the daytime then; they won't mind that."

"He looks good, he's getting fat," my mother said after she had been to visit the first time, reporting to Aunt Jaanne at her place the same evening. But Aunt Jaanne was not much interested. Hansie wasn't home yet, and she asked my mother to go somewhere and call his office, because their telephone had just been taken away.

"Have Simon go to the office and see if he's still there." My mother was at the point of going to carry out her request when Hansie came in. The streets had been cordoned off, and they had been warned at the office. He waited till everything seemed quiet again, but halfway home he had had to take refuge in a public toilet. Finally eight o'clock had come and he had covered the last part, through our neighborhood, on the run.

"We aren't allowed to go out of the city any more," Aunt Jaanne said one night when I came to tell her that my mother couldn't visit Uncle Hans the next Friday evening. "Ask your mother if she'll go see Otto this week."

The next day, a Wednesday afternoon, Aunt Jaanne came to our home. "They're taking inventory," she said. After my mother had asked her to sit down and had poured her a cup of apple tea, she said that the inventory takers had been to all the neighbors in her building—two men, each with a briefcase. They had inspected everything and noted it all down.

They had found the first-floor neighbors' five-year-old son playing with a little dark red toy purse on the stairs. One of the two men took it away from him, opened it, and fished out a nickel five-cent piece and three small silver pieces, then gave it back. "That one isn't a quarter," the child said, "it's something that there isn't any more, my father said."

"You just be very still, little boy," the man had said then. "Very still."

It was impossible to determine whether or not she had heard the knock on her door; at any rate they had disappeared without visiting her apartment.

She asked me to go along with her right away, and she had me pack a Frisian clock, some antique pottery, two carved ivory candlesticks, and the two tiles into a suitcase and take them with me. I carried them to our house and made two more trips to get old china plates, a camera, and a small, delicate mirror.

Every other week, usually on a Tuesday, my mother went to visit Otto in the big institution at Apeldoorn. The first time, Aunt Jaanne sat at our place in the afternoon waiting for her to come back. "How was it?" she asked my mother. "He looks fine," my mother answered, "and he was awfully glad to see me. The nurses are all very kind to him."

"Didn't he ask about home?" asked Aunt Jaanne.

"No, not at all," my mother said, "and he was having fun playing with the other children. When I went away he looked sad for a moment, but that he misses anything really—no, you couldn't say that."

She gave Aunt Jaanne a detailed description of how she was received by the nurse in charge of the ward and how she had given the fruit and cookies and candy to be handed out. But one part, a bag of cherries, she had given to Otto himself when they went walking in the sun along the path in the woods.

"I kept feeding him a few at a time," she said. "But he wanted to take them out of the bag himself. I was always afraid he'd slobber juice on his clothes, but it wasn't so bad." Later, after Aunt Jaanne had gone, she told me that he was sloppily dressed, with his pants held up by a rope instead of suspenders or a belt. "And his shoes," she said. "I don't see how they can fit onto his feet in such a crazy way. There's not enough staff, but the people do their best."

She also told me that Otto had said several times, "To mother."

"Mother is at home; she'll come some other time," she had answered.

"Mother home," he had yelled out then. He had cried when she went away late in the afternoon.

A week later Aunt Jaanne came to our house one evening just after supper. "They're starting to come after them," she said. "They're coming and getting them. No more summonses, they just come and get them. They came and got the Allegro family. Do you know them?"

"No, I don't know them," my mother said.

Aunt Jaanne wanted me to go to the hospital right away and ask for a paper certifying that Uncle Hans was seriously ill. I went, and at the main entrance I was directed to one of the wings, where I handed over my note at an office. After ten minutes I was presented a white sealed envelope and took it home to Aunt Jaanne.

The next evening she appeared for a second time. She asked me if I would go again. "It says in it that he's seriously ill; that should be mortally ill," she said. "I don't know if they'll put that in," I answered, "but we'll see."

After the head nurse had taken Aunt Jaanne's note and the first certificate, I waited a quarter of an hour and was given a new letter.

"Do you know what, Simon," Aunt Jaanne said two evenings later. "You'll have to go one more time and ask if they can make a whole new paper giving the nature of the illness in it. The nature of the illness. And not in Latin; if it has to be, in German, but at any rate so it's understandable."

She gave me back the last certificate, but without any accompanying note. I set off for the hospital again.

"Mrs. Boslowits asks if the nature of the illness can be given in it," I said. "And it's better if it's not in Latin." The head nurse took the envelope and came back a little later.

"Will you wait a while?" she asked. After some time I received a sealed envelope, exactly the same as the others.

I went at once to deliver it, and I found Aunt Jaanne and Hansie both sitting in front of the bay window. The room was almost completely dark. The draperies were open and the curtain pushed aside, so they could see the street from the window.

"Look, that's fine," Aunt Jaanne said when she read the paper.

"Did you think that would do any good?" Hans asked.

"Of course," I answered. "He knows, he knows," I said.

"What are you saying?" asked Aunt Jaanne.

"I was humming," I said.

Not only my mother but other friends of the Boslowits family who dropped by in the evenings spoke about the situation in gloomy wonderment. "It's just like a haunted house," my mother said.

I went there regularly in the evenings, and everything was always the same. I would ring the bell, the apartment door would be unlocked, and by the time I entered the hall, Aunt Jaanne would already be back inside. When I came into the living room, Aunt Jaanne would be sitting to the left in the bay window and Hansie to the right. Once I was inside Aunt Jaanne would leave her post again for a moment to scurry into the hall and lock the door. When I went away they would follow me and lock the door after me, and by the time I was in the street I could see them already sitting like statues in front of the window again. Then I would make a motion of waving, but they never reacted.

One Tuesday morning some neighbors of theirs came to tell us that about half past eight the night before two policemen with black helmets had come. Aunt Jaanne had shown them the certificate from the hospital, and one of them threw the beam of a flashlight on it. "Who are you?" he had asked Hansie. When he had identified himself, the other man said, "He's not on the list." "Both of you have to come with us," the first one had said then.

Uncle Hans said nothing when he heard the news. They thought he hadn't heard or hadn't really understood, and they repeated it emphatically several times. He tried to raise himself up, and after they had put a pillow behind his back he sat looking out of the window. Finally the visitors, a friend of Aunt Jaanne's and her daughter, went home again.

One day some time later a neighbor came to visit. "They are emptying the old people's home," she said. She had watched while hundreds of very old people were carried down the stairs and out of the building to vehicles standing ready for them. One ninety-two-year-old man whom she thought she had known once had called out, "They're carrying me like a king." "The Apeldoorn Woods Institute was emptied yesterday too," she said.

"What did you say about Otto?" I asked my mother when she came back from her next visit to Uncle Hans.

"The truth—that everything was taken away," she said. "He only hopes he's put to death right away. The doctors and nurses stayed with the patients, did you know that?"

"No," I said, "I didn't know."

Early the following week a friend of Uncle Hans's hired a cab and took him from the hospital to an attic room he had been able to arrange for him at some friends' in the center of town. Late that night he also took the wheelchair—the tires had already been stolen from it—from the entryway of Uncle Hans's house. It was only four days until everything in the apartment was taken away, but it was agreed not to tell Uncle Hans for the time being.

He lay there all alone in his new location, but a nurse came twice a day to look after him. Only a few people knew where he was.

During the summer everything went as well as could be hoped

for. But when fall came, another hiding place for Uncle Hans had to be found, because a stove couldn't be used in his room.

They succeeded in obtaining a place for him in an old people's home. The papers would be taken care of.

When he was told the decision, he showed his disappointment. He explained he would rather be taken in by friends.

Sometimes he didn't seem to know what he was saying; one afternoon he said to the nurse, "Do you still remember when I was twenty-seven? No, I mean 1927. I know exactly what I mean, so—" and after that he lay lost in thought.

One Wednesday a friend, a woman who was an artist, was visiting him. "You like that atlas such a lot, don't you?" he asked. "Tell me the truth, now." He had an atlas of the world that was supposed to be very extensive and valuable, and friends had been able to rescue it from his apartment.

When the nurse came that afternoon, he said, "Take that atlas along, I've given it to Ali."

"What nonsense," she said, "it's much too nice to give away."

"Take it along, I said." Then he asked for something to drink.

The following day the daughter of Aunt Jaanne's friend came and found him asleep. "He's sleeping," she said at home. In the evening the nurse came again, found him resting, took his pulse, and left satisfied. The next morning she came back at the usual time and found his body already cold. She lifted up the head; its little tuft of hair felt damp to the touch. The thin mouth was closed, and the glasses gave the face an unreal expression.

"I didn't understand it all right away," she said later. "And I thought I heard something strange, but it was a carpet sweeper on the ground floor."

When she saw the empty box beside the glass of water, she began to comprehend. But she figured out that it couldn't have contained more than four sleeping tablets. The only conclusion was that he had regularly saved one at a time and so built up a supply.

That night the friend who had taken him out of the hospital and the man who had given up the room for him together carried the body downstairs and noiselessly lowered it on a rope into the canal beside the house; it sank immediately, so I was told.

They both hurried back inside the house and waited together with the nurse until they could go home at four in the morning.

In the meanwhile they discussed all things: the distances of planets, the duration of the war, the existence of a god. The two men were also given a bit of information by the nurse: she was able to tell them that Uncle Hans's money could have served to maintain him for at least another year. "That wasn't the reason," she said.

Translated by James S. Holmes and Hans van Marle.
Reprinted from *The Literary Review*, (Winter 1961-1962, Volume 5, Number 2), published by Fairleigh Dickinson University, Rutherford, New Jersey.

WARD RUYSLINCK

The Madonna with the Lump

I

THE old man, the *vecchione* of Romiliano, wouldn't die. For three days and three nights he'd been lying motionlessly, with his eyes closed, in the alcove under the stairs. All the Santinis had died in this alcove, his father and his grandfather and probably also his great-grandfather who had built the house, and because at the beginning of his illness he himself had asked to be taken there, it was understood by everyone that his time had come. But he seemed to be waiting for something, nobody knew what, the revelation of an ancient secret or the return of a cherished memory which would close his eyes and seal his heart.

And so, on the morning of the fourth day, his son Pippo and his daughter-in-law Lucia found him in exactly the same condition as when he had first taken to his bed. Pippo Santini opened the faded green curtains in front of the alcove a little wider and bent over the old man. His breathing seemed calm and regular. Tall and thin he lay stretched out on the goatskins and his gray, unkempt drooping moustache was a horseshoe shadow round his toothless, sunken mouth. The quid of tobacco which he had stuck to the side of the bed three days ago was still there, dried out.

Lucia looked over Pippo's shoulder at the brown, weather-beaten, wrinkled face. Then her glance moved to his chest and settled on the small silver medal which he had received in the year of the first great vintage, because at the risk of his own life he had rescued the son of Baffone the lemon-seller from the violent whirlpools of the river Tarpo. She herself had pinned it

155

to his shirt yesterday, because she was proud of the old man and of his act of self-sacrifice which she wanted anyone who might visit him to remember. She couldn't recall any other Santini, not one of this old family of winegrowers, ever having received such a high honor. "Do you think I'd better polish the medal?" she whispered into Pippo's ear. "It's gotten so dull."

He scratched his stubbly chin with his fingernails and nodded slowly.

"Yes, all right," he said absentmindedly.

She bent over the bed and carefully unpinned the medal from Giulio Santini's shirt. From the adjacent room the sharp, stifling smell of smoldering wood invaded the alcove. Pippo turned around in irritation.

"Where's that smoke coming from? The stupid creature. Tell her to shut the door when she's lighting the fire. Does she want to choke him?"

He hastily drew the curtains, shutting the old man away in the narrow dark space under the stairs. Lucia went into the living room, closed the door behind her, and looked in alarm through the thick smoke at her daughter, who was kneeling in front of the stove with streaming eyes, trying to blow the smoldering wood alight.

"*Santa Maria,* what a lot of smoke! Have you gone mad, Elena? You'll choke your grandpa to death! Can't you learn how to light a fire? And you're going to get married. . . ."

The girl looked up and squatted on her heels. She had the watery green eyes and shiny black hair of the Santinis. The woven raffia sandals which she was wearing for the first time creaked when she rose from her crouched position.

"Is he still alive?" she asked, paying no attention to her mother's outburst.

Driving the smoke in front of her with fiercely waving arms Lucia walked around the table. She pulled the window open and turned round coughing: "Of course he's still alive. You want him to stay alive too, don't you, not for his sake, not because you love your grandfather, but only so that you can get married the day after tomorrow. You ought to be ashamed, Elena, it's selfish."

Elena combed her hair backward with her fingers and said

nothing. She smiled: the day after tomorrow, in two days' time. But if the old man died beforehand, she would have to wait for six months. The smile vanished. It would be autumn and God knows whether Mario Costello might not lose patience and start looking for another girl. She thought of the lovely satin wedding dress, ready in her room upstairs. It had silver butterflies embroidered on it and the white collar stood up like the graceful petal of a jack-in-the-pulpit. She thought of the chest beside her bed, filled with linen and household objects. She longed intensely for the fulfilment of her love and wished with all her heart that the old man would stay alive for two more days, so that Mario need not wait for her any longer.

"Are you dreaming again, you silly goose," grumbled Lucia. "Your father is angry with you, hurry up."

Slowly the girl swept the floor in front of the stove. The wood had finally caught fire; little yellow flames flickered up now and then. In spite of the open window, the heavy smoke lingered under the low ceiling. Lucia had stopped paying attention to it, she took a duster from a drawer and polished the silver medal, meticulously.

Pippo's head appeared in the doorway. "Lucia, come and help me, quickly. The staircase is full of smoke already."

"What do you want me to do?" asked Lucia.

"Help me carry him outside, into the yard. He'll suffocate if he stays in the alcove."

She came at once. In spite of her fat, round belly, which bulged beneath her apron, she followed him with steps remarkably nimble. Together they lifted the old man from his bed. He wasn't very heavy and it took little effort to carry him between them into the yard, where they laid him under the porch, on the bench which was splashed with pigeon droppings, by the pump from which no water had been drawn for a long time because the well near the house had run dry.

"He won't last much longer," whispered Pippo. "Have you noticed how wide his nostrils are? Like a dying mule."

"I ought to trim the hair in his nose," said Lucia.

"Yes," he said.

She bent over the sick man, her face wrinkled so that the little fleshy wart by her left eye lay embedded in one of the crow's-feet like an ant's egg. She looked at him intently for some time, and beckoned to Pippo with a hand behind her back.

"Look how he's sweating, the poor man. Do you think it's the death sweat already?"

Pippo looked more closely at his father, at the furrowed face which was covered with fine, glistening sweat. In the shrill daylight the gray moustache looked like the dusty, woolly fluff of a mulberry tree.

"It might be," he said finally.

They stood there for some time in helpless solicitude, their hands clasped on their bellies, then, silently, went back into the house. It was as if by laying him outside on the bench and by looking at him for so long and so attentively, they had performed a last duty and could do nothing more for him. A sick dog one puts in a quiet corner on a folded blanket, leaves it and forgets it, and as soon as it is dead one digs a hole, then forgets it for good.

Giulio Santini, the man who once did a heroic deed for which he was rewarded by his government with high distinction, was lying in a quiet, lonely spot behind the house, on a hard wooden bench, waiting for something which wouldn't come and of which no one knew what it was.

The sweet, blossomy smell of spring drifted across the yard, mingled with the moist dewy air from the vineyards on the mountainside. Some two hundred yards behind the house rose a sunny slope, a westerly offshoot of Mount Sempiterno, the Eternal One. The vineyards on the terraces, intersected by winding paths, ebbed in green undulations down the mountain flank and sank away into the valley.

The sun, like a golden yolk newly broken from the fragile shell of the morning in the misty distance behind the valley, had risen above the mountainside, glazing the vine leaves on the higher terraces. The soft spring breeze and the sourish muscat fragrance of the vineyards did not reach the old man. He lay on the bench, motionless as before in the alcove, with the peculiar patience and superhuman resignation which sharpen the inner attentiveness of the dying. He obviously didn't notice the difference between the hard, gnarled wooden bench and the soft goatskins of his bed.

He looked like one apparently dead; he was no longer alive and yet he hadn't died yet. The sunlight slanted under the porch onto his sweat-covered face and made it shine like the brown, warm crust of a newly baked loaf. Small groups of girls, coming from the valley and climbing the steep paths to the vineyards, sang the songs they had learnt during the *vendemmia* the year before, and pigeons settled on the ridge of the barn, flapping their wings and fluffing out their white feathers. The broad shadow of the mountain retreated further from the houses, it became smaller and smaller. But the old man heard or saw nothing. His heart was no longer connected with the world, he was gently dying; facing death in exactly the same way as he had accepted life: without worrying himself over it, in the calm conviction that what must be will be.

He lay there for half an hour and as the shadow of the porch reached his eyes a door opened somewhere. The girl was coming across the yard, her raffia sandals creaked. Shyly she stood by the bench, looking with blinking eyelids at the worn, tawny face, the creased skin, the sunken mouth, the drooping moustache, and the Adam's apple jutting sharply from the emaciated neck. She noticed the dark sweat stains on his shirt, near the armpits. Bending over him she listened for his breathing, which was faint, almost inaudible.

A dreadful apprehension crept into her. She went down on her knees and put her head on the old man's chest. His body smelled of sweat and urine, reminding her of the acrid, warm smell of animals which have spent the whole winter lying on dirty, sodden straw in the stable. Filled with an anxious premonition she listened for his heartbeat. She listened for it as she would sometimes, near Hermit's Lane, press her ear to the sheer rock to hear the dull, distant rumble of the Tarpo, the mountain torrent which plunges down the steeps on the other side of the hill. But the only sound coming to her now was the restless throbbing of her own heart. "*Avolo mio,* grandpa, can you hear me?" she whispered.

If he heard her, he gave no sign of it. His eyes remained closed and his arms lay still beside his body. Only his lips seemed to twitch momentarily, fleetingly. Or did she imagine it? She pressed closer to him and stroked his hand. "Are you really leaving us?" she said in a voice at once sad and coaxing. "Don't you remember it will be my wedding day in two days' time? Have you forgotten? It's spring. Can't you smell the spring, grandpa? Say something then. I've been longing for it so much, the wedding, and I've prayed for you to get better soon so that you can be there. But you don't care, do you, otherwise you'd try harder to get better. Why don't you say something, grandpa? Can't you hear me?"

She raised her head hopefully, waiting for him to reply. But he gave no sound. He really looked dead already. She knew he couldn't be; a dead man's hand couldn't be so warm. She bit her lip and got up angrily. She hated him because she thought he wasn't answering on purpose, because he didn't want to be disturbed, selfishly, like all people who were ill, only wanting peace and quiet and forgetting that the rest of the world needs to go on existing. She hated him and felt even more embittered because she couldn't wish him dead, for that was what mattered most to her. He mustn't die.

She swallowed in order to drive away the throttling feeling in her throat. The boys and girls working in the vineyards were singing a cheerful *ritornel;* she recognized the tune and absentmindedly began to mutter the words, but their actual meaning was lost to her. The feeling as if there was suddenly something in her life which was too much drove away the thought she'd had a moment earlier, that something was missing from her life. She couldn't explain it, but it was so. Slowly she raised her hand above her eyes to peer into the blinding daylight, at the hillside. She saw the colorful specks moving about on the paths and among the green foliage, and thought she could distinguish Mario, the son of the locksmith who wrote poetry. She had first met him at last year's *vendemmia,* the annual wine harvest, and she remembered his promise, that same evening as they walked down Hermit's Lane toward the narrow pass. He had said: "It will soon be spring, Elena, and then we'll get married." Now it was spring, the jackdaws had left the valley and Mount Sempiterno stood above the horizon without its snowy cap. It was the season of fulfillment. Could anyone say, "We'll get married in the spring," and then not keep his promise because of the whim of one sick old man who had lived for eighty-three years?

II

On the evening of the fourth day, soon after dusk, Giulio Santini lay cold and rigid and with sagging, open mouth on the bench under the awning. Cooing pigeons huddled together under the roof and the old man's shirt and trousers seemed spattered with big splotches of whitewash. One arm hung beside his body, the fingertips nearly touching the ground as if he had tried to reach for something under the bench. When, after supper, Pippo and Lucia came outside to watch the sun set behind the blue hills of the Signore Dio, they saw him. They crossed themselves, their eyes widening, as if they'd seen the old man alive and well only a moment ago. Then they carried him silently into the house, put him back in the alcove and pinned the polished medal to his chest.

"I wonder why he was suddenly in such a hurry," said Pippo, staring gloomily at his father's closed face which in death seemed to have become smaller and more crumpled.

Elena had run away from the dead body in dismay, upstairs to her room where she burst out sobbing. Through her tears she looked at the white satin dress on the chair by the window. The high, stand-up collar drooped limply like a wilting flower and the silver butterflies had closed their wings. A trace of light still found its way into the room from outside, a faint opaqueness; but it lingered behind the window, slowly merging into the unperturbed, soundless evening.

She hadn't felt any compassion for her grandfather yet. She cried, not because she would never see or hear him again or because the rocking chair by the stove would now remain empty, but because his death crushed the first great expectation of her life. Like all young people she abhorred the idea of death in general, as the senseless, incomprehensible terror disturbing the order of daily events and casting a strange shadow on the faces of the living. Yes, she thought of the dead as mean and demanding, unreasonable in their selfishness. But toward the old man, who had chosen his time so inconveniently, she also felt great bitterness. Not only was he taking the past with him into the grave, but the future as well, and she could not forgive him this. She didn't mourn for the past because she had no place in it, but the coming weeks and months were full of special promise for her, and so it was unjust that someone should rob her of this happiness just because his own life had come to an end today. Tears rolled down her cheeks. She sat on the edge of the bed, looking at the lamp on the wardrobe which spread a drab yellow light into the room. From the stony coolness downstairs sounded the wailing of the neighbors, the Fugazzas, who had come to pay their condolences. She also recognized the bleating voice of the *sagrestano* who had come to measure the body and discuss the preparations for the funeral service. The hullabaloo which would go on until Giulio Santini was entrusted to the earth had begun. And the day after tomorrow, when it would all be over for everyone but when it should really have started for her, the oppressive silence in the house would crush them all.

She raised her head, listening for Mario's voice, because the news of the *vecchione's* death would spread through the village like wildfire. The thought of seeing him tonight was painful. She dreaded meeting him when their mood could only be sad and despondent. She imagined him taking her head between his hands and saying with his wistful smile, so tender that it made her dizzy: "It will soon be autumn, Elena, and then we'll get married." Just as several months ago he had said: "It will soon be spring." But she didn't want to get married in the autumn. A wedding should be full of brilliant light and exuberance and an intoxicating urge for life—how could this be so in the sad season of autumn?

Someone was coming up the stairs; the steps creaked. She didn't even bother to smooth her hair and dry her tears. Lucia entered the room. A black shawl covered her shoulders, her eyes were red from crying.

"Elena, aren't you coming down?"

Elena looked at the fatty wart by her mother's eye.

"Has Mario come yet?" she asked, turning her head away.

"What are you thinking of?" answered Lucia grumpily. "Dreaming of Mario while downstairs the holy candle is burning for your grandpa. You haven't even been to look at him yet."

Elena shook her head disconsolately.

"I don't want to see him," she said.

And with a sullen look on her face she added petulantly: "I've never seen a dead body and I never want to either."

Lucia came a step nearer and clasped her hands in indignation. "*Santa Maria*, why are you telling me such lies? You were there when my mother died, your grandma. Or don't you remember? When I was your age I'd seen more dead people than live ones. And I must say I've learned to be less afraid of the dead than of the living. Be sensible, Elena, come downstairs."

Elena hardly listened to her mother. She stared at the quivering light of the lamp on the pale wall opposite her and shook her head obstinately.

"Leave me alone," she said, "I don't want to see him today, can't you understand?"

Her mother heaved a sigh, and glancing at the wedding dress she went on, half angrily, half soothingly:

"I know what you're thinking. *Corbezzole*, is it the old man's fault that this happened just before your wedding? Do you think he asked for it? Do be reasonable, Elena. Well, if you don't want to come downstairs you can stay where you are. But don't forget: your time will come one day and God knows what you'll be thinking then. Maybe you'll count yourself lucky to have just one of your children near you in your last hour."

With a somber face, her hands on her bulging, swaying stomach, she left the room. Elena heard her go down the stairs, it seemed to go on for ever, it was as if she was descending into a bottomless abyss.

Meanwhile the *sagrestano* must have gone back to the village because down in the valley the church bell started to toll. Elena still hadn't moved. She was sitting on the bed, her fingers plucking at the blanket. A vague shudder of excitement went through her body. She was thinking of the Madonna with the Lump, the *Madonna Bubbonica*, the miraculous alabaster statue in the choir of the church at Romiliano which had been the object of special adoration in the last few years. Every year there was a growing stream of pilgrims to this quiet place of grace: sick and handicapped and healthy people alike, who had heard of the statue's mysterious powers and often came great distances to find a cure or to beg for personal favors.

The small, lasting miracle which distinguished this alabaster saint from all the other statues of the Holy Mother was a mysterious swelling on her forehead, a lumpy thickness which according to some people had arisen when the sculptor, in a drunken trance, had kissed her there. But the Madonna's fame had only begun to spread outside the village a couple of years ago when she had spoken to a girl suffering from spotted fever and had cured her miraculously. She had appeared in a dazzling light and was supposed to have said: "Because your soul is pure I will purify your blood as well." The girl had run home at once, to her mother, who was in the kitchen cooking risotto for the festival of the Resurrection. She'd been amazed to see that the fever spots had vanished from her daughter's skin and she had gone down on her knees to thank the *Madonna Bubbonica*.

Elena was thinking of this while in the church porch the *sagrestano* was jumping up and down trying to catch the swinging bell rope which had slipped out of his grazed hands. He was wondering what mysterious message old Giulio Santini might have been waiting for before leaving this life.

Elena got up and walked to the window. The moon shone on the hills and the tiled roof of the barn shimmered like the wet, scaly back of a sea monster.

When she had looked at the evening for a long time and the booming sound of the bell had finally died away, she turned from the window. Her eyes had grown wide and gleaming from staring at the moonlit mountain. She tidied her hair in front of the mirror, put on a kerchief, and blew out the lamp.

III

Pippo was telling the Fugazzas how thirty years ago his father had rescued the son of Baffone the lemon-seller from the Tarpo. "And the government gave him a silver medal as a reward, with his name engraved on it in full," he concluded and reached for the wine jug on the table.

Emilio Fugazza was hearing the story for the third time, but he nodded in admiration as if it was the first. He twirled up his ginger moustache and said: "Yes, there you are: courage and self-sacrifice are always rewarded." His wife Marta narrowed her little fox's eyes and said nothing. The black bone rosary lay in front of her on the table and the brass crucifix glimmered in the lamplight.

After a while, Lucia broke the silence: "Pippo, when is the *curato* coming? Didn't the *sagrestano* say? I haven't any candles left and where am I to get holy water from?"

"You heard what the *sagrestano* said," replied Pippo. "The *curato* left for Reggio d'Ilfonso this afternoon to discuss the repair of the choir screen. He won't be back till tomorrow."

"Not till tomorrow!" Lucia exclaimed. "For God's sake, how am I going to get candles and holy water? You know he's got to give his permission."

"You can have some holy water of mine," Marta Fugazza reassured her. "I've kept some in a bottle, you never know when it might come in useful."

"Thank God, you can help me out, Marta dear," said Lucia, relieved and grateful.

The men were smoking their pipes and drinking Sempiterno wine. Pippo Santini shook his head sadly from time to time.

"It's hot in here," said Marta. "You must be very well off if you can light the stove in spring." She wound the rosary around her wrist and peered at the stove, which radiated a gentle red glow.

"We're not well off, God knows," Lucia said apologetically, "but the evenings are so chilly."

"Hush," said Pippo, "someone's knocking at the door."

"You're dreaming," said Lucia. "I can't hear anything."

Pippo took his pipe out of his mouth and called: "Come in." The door opened slowly and the handle did not turn back straight away, as if the visitor hesitated to come in. "You see, it's Mario," said Pippo, rising from his seat to welcome his future son-in-law.

Mario silently embraced Elena's parents and patted Lucia encouragingly on the shoulder. She burst out into sobs: "So you've heard. I'm glad you've come. . . ."

The Fugazzas sat there mutely, staring at the table top, at the yellow wine stains in the wood. The light fell on Mario's bronzed, sinewy neck and on his oddly small ears. He had the same ears as his father, little mouse ears.

"Isn't your father coming?" asked Pippo.

"He's coming later," said Mario. "Actually, I'm not supposed to tell you this, but he's writing a funeral poem for your father."

"A funeral poem? How good of him." Pippo was touched.

"Your father is a wonderful man," Lucia agreed, with tears in her voice.

"A locksmith who writes poems, whoever heard of that," muttered Marta, fixing her sly foxy eyes on young Costello. "I've heard of a teacher who could make locks, but that's different." The beads of the rosary moved swiftly between her fingers.

Emilio sniffed noisily as he slowly drew the outline of the wine jug in the air with his index finger.

"Don't you want to see him first?" Pippo asked Mario.

Elena's fiancé nodded and the two men left the room.

Marta watched them go without emotion, cleared her throat and turned to Lucia: "When's he going to be buried? Have you decided yet?"

"The day after tomorrow," said Lucia.

"So you'll find the bearers on your doorstep instead of the wedding pages. Well, that's life, isn't it. Man proposes, God disposes."

In a neighboring farmyard howled a dog. Emilio, whose face was dark red, pushed his chair further away from the stove. Soon Mario and Pippo came back into the room. The locksmith's son joined the others round the table; he didn't mention the dead man, like the others he listened to the doleful wailing of the dog. He kept moistening his dry lips with the tip of his tongue. Finally, with a timid look in Lucia's direction, he asked: "Isn't Elena in?"

"Didn't you see her?" asked Lucia surprised. "She went to church to pray for her grandpa's soul. She's been crying all evening, until a few minutes before you came. No, she must have been gone longer than that."

"I didn't see her," said Mario, disappointed.

"She probably went down the Via di Salvatore," suggested Pippo. "It's the quickest way down into the valley and the most beautiful one as well in the moonlight."

He struck a match and relit his pipe.

"Did you come by the Ponte dei Amanti?"

"Yes," said Mario.

"You see, that's why you missed each other."

The howling of the dog suddenly switched into a vicious barking and then they all heard quick footsteps, approaching the house at a run.

"Someone's in a hurry," Emilio remarked drily.

All faces turned toward the door, which was suddenly thrust open. Elena appeared in the doorway, somewhat pale and out of breath. She didn't come in and strands of pipe smoke floated past her out into the dark. Her eyes met Mario's and she kept looking at him with a wide, bewildered gaze. She looked frighteningly strange, as if she was going to smile at something she alone saw, in Mario's eyes and then beyond him on the whitewashed wall. But the smile didn't reach her eyes. Her eyes had an unusual expression, reminiscent of pain and happiness at the same time, like the look of some martyrs on prayer cards.

As she stood there motionlessly, as if in a trance, Pippo finally spoke:

"What's happened? You look so strange. Has anything frightened you?"

His words didn't reach her. Her kerchief had slipped down to her shoulders. There was an oppressive silence in the room.

"Don't just stand there. Shut that door," Lucia told her impatiently.

Slowly, absently, the girl did as she was told. Mario had got up from his chair and took her by the hand. "Are you ill, Elena?"

She withdrew her hand gently and shook her head.

"But say something, what's the matter with you?" Lucia burst out in irritation.

"She's been looking at the moon too long," said Emilio. "The moonlight can confuse the mind."

"You'd swear she'd seen the devil," Marta put in, pressing her crucifix to her breast in conjuration.

Elena seemed to wake up from her stupor. She sat down on the chair which Mario had pulled up for her and at once reality overwhelmed her: the lamp; a big, luminous mushroom; the wine stains on the table top, the familiar faces, the familiar sounds of the voices belonging to those faces, and in the background the stove, the rocking chair, the flakes on the whitewashed wall. She let her eyes slowly wander around the room, like someone returning home from a long, distant journey. And while everyone was watching her in curious expectation, she said calmly:

"I've seen the Madonna."

Pippo took the pipe out of his mouth with a jerk. Bending forward, he asked in a hoarse voice: "The Madonna, did you say? Where?"

"In the church," Elena answered quietly, gazing dreamily in front of her. "She was beautiful, I've never seen anyone so beautiful. In fact, I'd imagined her quite differently."

Emilio Fugazza peered pensively into the bowl of his pipe, at the glowing red embers, and when he looked up he saw a similar glow in Elena's eyes.

"I told you, didn't I? She's out of her mind," he muttered, scratching his neck with the stem of his pipe.

None of the others uttered a word and Elena continued: "She was sitting in the center of a big light, not like a living person but like a white cloud with the sun shining behind it. The light itself wasn't like anything else on earth, far more beautiful than the light on the mountains at sunrise. And everything about her was unbelievably white and brilliant and so unreal, I thought one could die by looking at her, just by looking."

The Santinis and the Fugazzas and Mario Costello looked at her with open mouths, their amazement growing with each word, and when they'd heard everything they believed her. They were convinced that no one could invent such a thing, and they were overcome by an intense emotion which made them look at the girl as if she herself was a supernatural apparition, a small, wonderful madonna, surrounded by the shine of the lamp, dreamily sitting before them with her hands folded in her lap.

"What was she like then? You said she was so beautiful. Did you see her eyes?" whispered Marta, her lip trembling.

"I didn't pay attention," said Elena. "It's hard to express it, you've got to see her with your own eyes to know what she looked like."

"Did she have a lump on her forehead, like the statue?" Pippo wanted to know. His eyes bulged and he restlessly moved his shoulder blades as if his back was itching.

"I think so. But it doesn't matter. She was beautiful."

Lucia Santini hadn't managed to say a word so far, she was so impressed. She didn't do what the mother of the afflicted girl had done, she didn't go down on her knees and it didn't occur to her to thank the Madonna either. Perhaps she didn't think of it because she couldn't see any outward sign of grace about her daughter, like the disappearance of the spots with that other girl. She sat there as if struck by God's hand. First she didn't believe it and then she did, and in the end the tears came to her eyes. She really didn't know whether to be proud or grateful or only happy, and because she didn't know she became very excited and after a while she burst out into a kind of affectionate wailing.

"Holy Angel! I'm only just beginning to realize it. Elena, my darling, is it true what you're telling us, did you really see her? Have you really seen the Madonna with the Lump? Are you sure you haven't been looking at the moon too long? Are you feeling all right? Holy Mary, I hope you're not making it all up."

"Shut up, woman," Pippo snapped at her. "Why should she be telling us a pack of lies? Give her a hug instead, you don't seem to realize what an honor this is for all of us."

Mechanically Lucia threw herself into her daughter's arms, stroked her hair, and went on repeating: "I'm sure you'll be made a saint one day."

Pippo and Emilio watched in silence, chewing the mouthpieces of their burnt-out pipes with their strong beaver's teeth. Mario still said nothing; he looked at each in turn, in silent awe, but mostly he looked at Elena's dreamy, smiling face. But whenever she looked at him and tried to catch his eye, he cast his eyes down, as if he was embarrassed to be engaged to a girl to whom the Madonna had appeared.

Then Emilio, who had been twirling the tips of his moustache between his fingers, came up with an unexpected question. He spoke in a voice uncharacteristically vehement, like someone who has seen the light of revelation but who hasn't altogether rid himself of a burdensome guilt.

"Elena, didn't she say anything to you? Haven't you got any message from her?"

Elena slowly put her hands together. The curious faces around her didn't seem to disturb her.

"Yes, she did," she said. "She did say something to me."

Lucia and Marta uttered a cry of surprise.

"Good gracious, child, why didn't you say so before?"

"What did she say?"

"Weren't you allowed to tell anyone?"

Pippo banged his fist on the table. "For God's sake, how do you want her to tell us if you don't let her speak?"

Elena closed her eyes as if to collect her thoughts and when she opened them again everyone was quiet.

"Yes, I can still hear it clearly: 'This is your grandfather's day, but don't forget that the day after tomorrow it will be your day.' That's what she said. At first I didn't understand her, but later I knew what she meant."

She threw a quick, stealthy glance around her and saw the startled faces and then the many shadows flowed together and came upon her as one great darkness. She heard exclamations of surprise and excitement but didn't understand what was being said. Someone gently touched her shoulder and she shrank back, as if the contact hurt her.

She thought: I don't hear Mario. Why doesn't he say anything? She felt as if she was no longer present in the room, and hastily looked up. The darkness tore open and she saw him. He was watching her, but it struck her that he didn't smile and that he didn't look as happy as she had expected.

IV

Like snow water in the spring, finding its way down the mountainside into the valley, disturbing the villagers' sleep with its incessant murmur, the rumor of the miraculous vision had spread through Romiliano in the night. The valley awoke, windows were lit, and on the roads and in the narrow village streets where the moon cast its shadows there was a growing, restless movement of people gathering for a great, exciting event. Like worms leaving moldered wood they emerged from their houses and soon flocked together in a silent procession wending toward the church.

The Madonna behind the cast-iron choir screen received them with a gentle smile and welcoming, outstretched arms. The choir was festively lit as on a high holy day by the glow of countless candles in their holders and the feet of the statue were hidden in a cloud of fragrant flowers which pilgrims had left there the day before. Illumined by this brilliant whiteness were the raised faces of the men and women kneeling on the granite floor under the ex-votos on the wall, quietly moving their lips in prayer, their hands around the railings of the screen.

In the porch the noise of shuffling feet was constantly growing, it was as if a gust of wind from outside was rustling through a heap of dust, paper, and dry leaves, chasing them through the open doors into the nave and making them flutter about wildly.

As soon as the *sagrestano* became aware of the gathering crowds, he remembered what had happened after the first vision, now some years ago, and he hastened to close the choir screen. But when he saw that the flow of people into the church continued unabated, and that the screen threatened to collapse a second time under the weight of the crowd thronging in the aisle, he was suddenly taken by fright. The passionate adoration and fanatical rapture expressed on their faces made him even more afraid. After a desperate, fruitless attempt to get the situation under control by bolting the doors, he sent off an urgent telegram to Reggio d'Ilfonso, imploring the *curato* to come back at once.

Two hours later the *curato* arrived in the village, in a hired carriage driven by a sleepy *vetturino*. The leaves of the oleander tree in the church square looked lacquered in the clear moonlight. When he got out and saw the crowds, and especially when he caught some of the excited conversations, he understood at once what was going on. A few moments later he was given a full account by the *sagrestano*, who had been waiting helplessly in the vestry.

The *curato*, an elderly man with a rigid, inscrutable expression and a surly looking mouth, knew at once what to do. He took off his coat, pushed up the sleeves of his cassock, and left by the door leading to the sanctuary. The *sagrestano* heard him address-ing the people; his voice was low, calm, and full of self-confidence. He called them the pilgrims of darkness, warned them against the errings of rash faith, and finally admonished them to go home and wait for the day. And all those people, pressing against the screen, listening to him in silence, must have bowed their heads in shame and gone away obediently, because soon afterward he reappeared in the vestry and said: "You'd better close the doors now, so that they won't come in again." He said it casually, as if he'd merely gone out to wash his hands.

At dawn the *curato* left the house. He was carrying an oblong parcel under his arm. He walked through the village without hurrying, up the Via di Salvatore, and soon reached the Santinis' house. As he had expected, there was an unusual commotion outside the gate. People he had never seen before, apparently from surrounding villages, were jostling by the entrance, curious, hoping to catch a glimpse of the girl who had been granted such a special favor. A few women from the neighborhood were walk-ing away from the house, cackling and gesticulating, their faces sallow in the morning twilight. When they saw the *curato* enter-ing the yard, they stopped in their tracks and turned around, keeping some distance behind him.

In the Santinis' living room the lamp had been burning all night. Some ten people were sitting around the table, yawning and drowsy. Apart from the Fugazzas and the locksmith and his son, there were Leonzi the blacksmith and the Serafini sisters with their sharp vulture faces, who had the reputation of always making straight for the smell of a corpse.

In the midst of this sleepy gathering was Elena, the center of all the talk. Together with Marta Fugazza she was praying her rosary, firmly holding her head erect in an effort to conquer her sleepiness.

When she saw the *curato* she started. But, taking no notice of her or of any of the others, he went straight up to Lucia and Pippo. After expressing his condolences and saying a few words of encouragement, he handed the parcel he'd been carrying to Lucia and said, without any reference to recent events: "I've brought you some candles and a flask of holy water." Before

Lucia could thank him, he went on to say that he'd come to visit them mainly because of their bereavement. He had a gift of choosing his words in such a way that they also expressed what he left unsaid, and the Santinis understood that apart from wanting to pay a last farewell to the *vecchione*, he also meant, without saying it in so many words, "The living will get their turn as well."

Pippo accompanied him to the alcove and withdrew respectfully into the background. In the flickering light of the remaining candle stump, the priest knelt by the old man's body. Pippo noticed a hole in the sole of one of his shoes.

After a few minutes the *curato* rose, smoothed his bushy eyebrows with his index finger, and asked Pippo, in a voice permitting no contradiction, to go and fetch Elena. "I want to talk to her in private," he said.

And although he clearly said, "in private," there was no doubt that he meant to include someone else; and this was also an allusion to the old man.

"At your service, *signore parroco*," said Pippo, hurrying out of the room.

Some time passed before Elena entered, uncertainly. The *curato* fixed his cool, inscrutable eyes on her and with a brief flexing of his finger ordered her to come nearer. When she was standing close before him, she cast her eyes down. The candle flame sputtered. Their shadows were tall on the wall opposite the alcove.

"You've made up a nice story," said the *curato*, looking at her penetratingly. "Don't you realize that you've done the Madonna a terrible insult which nothing can wipe out unless you withdraw all this nonsense?"

"Why do you say that, *signore parroco?* I haven't made up anything," Elena answered calmly.

She looked past him at her own shadow on the wall; her head was huge and had a faint penumbra.

"Don't you dare to look at me?"

At once she looked him boldly in the eyes and it struck him that she had the same watery green eyes as her father, muscatel eyes.

"What did you actually hear? Can you repeat the words?" he asked, his eyes still fixed on her.

She bit her fingernails and it seemed at first that she didn't want to answer. But after some hesitation she repeated, in an almost indifferent tone, the words which since her return from church she had said at least twenty times: "This is your grandfather's day, but don't forget that the day after tomorrow it will be your day."

The *curato* lowered his head to his chest, still looking at her. "Did she speak in Italian or in Latin?"

"In Italian. If she'd spoken in Latin I'm sure I wouldn't have understood her."

"Was she wearing a blue cloak or a white one?"

"I didn't notice. I remember she was completely white, and shining, rather like a cloud with the sun shining from behind it. But I don't know if she was wearing a cloak."

For a few seconds he looked at her in silence, then asked her several more questions, for instance whether she hadn't had a headache afterwards and whether the Madonna had made herself known by name. Her frank but restrained answers impressed him more than he let appear. He didn't ask anything about the swelling and this surprised her somewhat, but she didn't mention it either.

Finally he muttered something to himself and she understood that the interrogation was ended.

"Elena," he said, "dare you swear by your grandfather's head that you've told me the truth? Dare you do so, here in this room? Dare you swear by the cross?"

She peered into the alcove where the dead man lay, the old man with his thin, lined, wrinkled face like a brick baked for so long that it had cracked. She held her breath and made a timid movement.

"Don't you dare?" he asked again, in forbidding challenge.

Dragging her feet she went into the recess under the stairs. Her sandals creaked as if she was walking on frozen snow. The medal on Giulio's chest glittered in the moving light. But Elena paid no attention to the silver object; her eyes rested on the brass crucifix between the dead man's fingers. She stared at it for a long time, the exhaustion of the whole sleepless night overwhelming her at that moment.

The hand with which she touched the cross trembled slightly. "I swear it," she whispered.

The *curato* cleared his throat. "What do you swear?" he asked in a loud voice.

"That I spoke the truth," she added weakly.

She quickly withdrew her hand and turned half around. The candle went on hissing into the silence, burning a black hole into it, a small dark scorch mark in eternity, of which the old man was part from now on.

"I'll marry you tomorrow," the *curato* suddenly decided. "Not because I believe you, but because it makes no difference to me. But remember, your offspring could be cursed till the end of time. Think of Solomon's words: 'A false witness will not escape punishment and one who utters nothing but lies will perish.'"

He snapped his fingers and she had a feeling as if he was snapping a jackknife shut behind her back. She didn't move and gave no answer. In the next room someone yawned loudly.

V

The day to which Elena had been looking forward with impatience and yet with a heavy heart had dawned clear above the valley. And as the weeders were climbing the vineyard, laughing and singing as usual, the sky had already become high and blue. She had often heard the winegrowers say that a day which starts without clouds won't end without rain—but she had her own belief which was simple enough; it told her that God had created heaven and earth but left it up to people themselves to work for their own happiness. She hadn't forgotten the *curato's* warning, but she preferred not to think of it just now. This was the day which had been specially made for her, of which the old man had tried to rob her, in the fear that otherwise his death might have been pushed into the background.

She turned away from the window and admired herself for the last time in the mirror, lovingly stroking the shiny satin of her dress, examining her own smile. The silver butterflies on the bodice spread their wings as if trying to fly toward the collar, which stood up like a flower. A ray of sunshine moved across the lightly clouded mirror, was reflected in the cut-glass edge and glittered around her impeccable hairdo like a mother-of-pearl diadem.

She took a few steps backward and thought she looked breath-takingly beautiful and at that moment she knew for sure that Mario would never want another girl.

Strengthened by this thought she went down the stairs, the train of her dress rustling against the wall and on the steps. At the foot of the stairs her mother and father were waiting for her. Pippo was wearing his best suit, which was a bit tight under the arms. His razor had left a blood-red scar on his cheek, which he kept touching.

"My goodness, you're pretty," he said, looking her up and down. "As if you hadn't been blessed enough, the Madonna gave you beauty as well."

Lucia, who was dressed in black, with a sweet-smelling nosegay of lilies of the valley on her breast, pushed him aside impatiently.

"Are you making speeches already?" she grumbled, and turning to Elena: "Are you ready at last? Mario is here."

Elena smiled faintly. Everything she'd been thinking and feeling a moment ago, in her room, now seemed meaningless. As she walked past the alcove, followed by her parents, she saw to her relief that someone had drawn the curtains. She knew that the old man couldn't see her pass by, that he couldn't stealthily raise his heavy cork eyelids to watch her and maybe, at the last minute, yet prevent that which he had purposely died to prevent, a few days ago.

In the living room she was overwhelmed by a strange white-ness which shimmered all around her: the bouquet in Mario's hand, Mario's immaculate collar, the white covers on the chest of drawers and the rocking chair. With her eyes closed she strug-gled for a moment against this overpowering whiteness, which probably struck her with such vehemence because she couldn't forget that it had taken the place of the expected black shrouds. Mario embraced her. She put her cheek against his and looked over his shoulder into the self-satisfied face of Emilio Fugazza, who had consented to be her witness. The locksmith and Leonzi the blacksmith, who was Mario's witness, had arrived as well. Because of Giulio's death the Santinis had decided to let the wedding take place without any pomp and circumstance and so they had invited nobody except the bridegroom's widowed father and the two witnesses.

Emilio banged his fist on an imaginary closed door and called out boisterously: *"Evviva la sposa!"* But the exuberance died on his lips and his face contracted in tiny wrinkles as everyone looked at him in surprise. He'd obviously forgotten all about the old man. In order to give himself an attitude he twirled the points of his pomaded moustache and nudged the locksmith: "What about your surprise? You haven't written an ode to the bride and groom by any chance have you?"

Elena heard him and glanced curiously at her future father-in-law. He answered with a reassuring wink. He didn't say anything but patted significantly on his inner pocket.

Quickly she looked away, feeling uneasy and not quite knowing how to behave. The floor heaved under her feet and a terrible premonition cast a shadow on the reckless joy with which, fruitlessly, she attempted to infuse herself.

She clutched the bouquet and felt the fragile stems crack between her fingers.

Someone said: "Elena is overcome." The horrible feeling passed, her head cleared, and she turned to her mother:

"What are we waiting for?"

"For the carriage," said Lucia. "We ordered one after all, your father insisted. But it looks as if that lazy *vetturino* has overslept." She said it in an apologetic tone, as if everything had been hurriedly arranged at the last minute, which was probably true.

Almost at the same moment Pippo gave his daughter a gentle nudge and said proudly: "Look outside. Have you ever seen so much interest taken in a wedding? We shall have to close the gate soon. You're famous, you see? I've heard that lots of people have come all the way from Streppo and Reggio d'Ilfonso to see the wedding of Elena Santini, you know, the girl who's had a vision of the *Madonna Bubbonica*."

Elena glanced timidly out of the window and saw that the yard was black with people. She reflected on her father's words and one sentence in particular stuck in her mind: Elena Santini, you know, the girl who's had a vision of the *Madonna Bubbonica*.

And then she thought again: famous, I'm famous. She didn't know what was coming over her; it didn't make her happy, on the contrary, she could have cried. Perhaps it was because of that horrible premonition.

"Elena, *cara mia*. . . ."

She started from her thoughts and smiled automatically. "Mario. . . ?"

"I want to talk to you," he whispered.

Before she understood exactly what he wanted of her, he took her by the arm and pushed her gently in front of him toward the kitchen.

He closed the door behind them. The voices of the guests suddenly sounded blurred and distant and she awoke from the strange unreality with which this day had started for her. Without much effort she was suddenly able to see things in their natural context and in true relation to their surroundings. She saw the china cups, the plates of sugarloaf and thin slices of candied-peel cake waiting on the kitchen table, and nearer by, the correct number of knives and forks laid out on a towel.

Mario took the bouquet from her and put it behind him on the drainboard. She looked at him questioningly and when she saw his hands reaching for hers and his imploring eyes looking at her, she knew what to expect.

"Elena, you didn't make it all up, did you. . . ?"

Ever since her return from church, the night before last, he hadn't spoken to her about it and she had thought he believed her. But she saw the shadow of mistrust darkening his face and suddenly it dawned on her that he had been worrying about it all the time.

"Did you speak to the *curato?*" she asked, her lips tightening.

He shook his head. "No, but imagine my position. I feel as if I'm getting married to some kind of saint, some being which is far above all ordinary earthly love. Don't you understand? It's all become so different."

She stared at him with a vacuous look; his mouth opened and shut and she heard the sound of his words and she saw them as well, as if they were concrete, visible objects, not sounds but images. And then she became afraid. She felt defenseless against his quiet frankness.

"Would you rather have me say it wasn't true?" she mumbled.

"I honestly don't know what to think of it," he sighed. "I think it would be just as difficult to marry a saint as . . . a . . . as a. . . ."

"What do you mean? Say it"

He finally let go of her hands.

"Well," he said, "a desecrater."

Her blood began to thump against her temples and it surprised her that she could go on thinking calmly. Solomon's words came to her mind again: "A false witness will not escape punishment and one who utters nothing but lies will perish."

"Mario, you don't know what you're saying. Do you think I. . . ."

"I asked you something and you haven't even answered me yet," he interrupted her. "Did you really see and hear the Madonna?"

She avoided his eyes, which desperately tried to meet hers. In the living room, behind the closed door, the blacksmith raised his heavy, droning voice. She suddenly felt as if she was locked inside a stiflingly small room, whose ceiling was slowly being lowered, pressing on her head.

"Perhaps . . ." she said hesitantly. "Do you think I might have imagined it?"

She wanted to know how he'd react to it and peered at him through her eyelashes. He'd moved a step backward to the sink and an unruly lock of hair fell across one of his little mouse ears.

"Jesus Christ, you really did invent the whole thing," he uttered with difficulty. "You've told us a lie, Elena."

"Mario, what's come over you? Let me. . . ."

"You've told us a lie," he repeated, not listening to her. "You've taken a holy name in vain in order to get your way, you've deceived your father and your mother and me in a disgraceful way and you didn't even respect the dead, your own grandfather. How did you have the nerve?"

"Mario," she stammered, "what's the matter with you? Nobody knows, only you. . . ."

His face shifted inside the outline within which she had seen it all the time and then it suddenly wasn't a face any longer. It was a big, moldy gray sunspot dancing before her eyes. She had never even seen him annoyed, and this unexpected outburst of rage paralyzed her.

"Yes, I'm the only one who knows, and the fact that apart from me God will witness against you doesn't even seem to bother you," he went on, more and more vehemently. "You actually feel safe, don't you, after swearing by the cross, after insulting God and desecrating the memory of your grandfather, you perjurer!"

Just as pain only reaches an injured limb after the first moments of numbness, the significance of his words took some time to penetrate.

"So you did speak to the *curato* after all?" she said.

He didn't deign to answer her, put his hands to his face and moaned softly: "Oh Elena, how could you fall so low?"

In the yard a pigeon flew off, clattering its wings. Automatically her eyes moved toward the window. The ceiling pressed ever more heavily on her head and she hoped the carriage would soon come, so that everything would go as planned. Because she still believed that even this terrible intermezzo would alter nothing of the direction and course of the destiny she herself had brought about.

When after a while he took his hands from his face, it seemed to her that his mind was made up. "Today it's your day, indeed," he said, "but I hope you've got enough sense at least to understand that today there'll be no fulfillment of your expectations. This isn't a beginning, Elena, it's an ending."

With trembling hands he pushed back the unruly lock of hair and went on:

"You've brought disgrace on me, you've brought shame on your whole family, and even if you were willing to take all those lies back publicly, you can't put it right again. Everyone will point his finger at you, and spit at you, you'll be despised, an outcast, and you'll never be able to wipe out the shame. It may well be that God's anger will follow you all your life. There'll be a curse on your children and on all their children after them, and nothing you do will be of any consequence. Didn't you think of that, then?"

She looked at him speechlessly. He was still standing with his back against the draining board; his hands moved backward to find support on the edge of the zinc top. Everything he said shocked her profoundly but she couldn't believe that his decision was irrevocable. She thought he wanted to frighten her, to push her away from him in order to forgive her the more magnanimously afterwards, and so she said, with desperate urgency:

"I only thought of one thing: our love, Mario. Are you going to renounce me now, because out of longing for you I sacrificed my salvation?"

"Unfulfilled longing keeps love alive, but a lie destroys it," he said.

She realized how unapproachable he was and suddenly she hated him, with the same senseless, uncontrolled hatred the old man had aroused in her when he lay dying under the awning, in the face of death oblivious of the future of those who would survive him.

Her fear died away and she felt a feverish warmth rising in her. "I thought you were a man, but you're a pathetic coward," she said hoarsely. "You're afraid of gossip, you don't dare to take your happiness in your own hands, you're too feeble and spineless." Bitterness and resentment and pain at the humiliation welled up in her like something which had been accumulating in her heart for a long time and which now suddenly found an outlet: when she noticed that her words, although surprising him, didn't wound him, all her feelings were discharged in a terrible rage. Her face glowed and her brain seemed to swell under the violent weight of confused thoughts. One single thought detached itself from the knot and started to whirl about in her head like a fiery circle, a burning Ferris wheel.

Her hand made a quick grab. She saw the white of the towel and the steel-blue shine of the knives and forks and she heard their clatter. Her head thumped against a hard, rough silence as if against a wall.

"Elena," he exclaimed, alarmed.

In his eyes there appeared an expression of incredulous amazement. He remained motionless, his back against the drainboard, and he made no effort at all to ward her off. With unbridled force she thrust the knife into his chest.

"If you don't want me you won't have anyone else either!" she shrieked, loudly as if she had to shout someone down.

No sound came from his lips, his eyes bulged glassily and his knees gave way so that he slid down, like someone kneeling carefully, the upper part of his body erect. His hand rose feebly toward the knife, but fell back at once. He rolled on his side, slumped against the draining board, his legs curled up, with his mouth wide open, gasping for breath.

She bent over him in blurred concern and didn't recognize him. Her lips parted slowly and she looked down on him as on someone she had never seen before. Even his name she didn't remember, her memory seemed frozen.

Behind her she heard the door handle move. Her mother's voice had a hard, sharp sound as of splitting wood: "I hope you're not quar. . . ." The voice faltered and leapt into a scream of horror.

Elena didn't turn round. Everything that happened now happened in another world, infinitely far away, beyond the boundaries of her consciousness. A confused hubbub came toward her, the hoarse shouts of men and the shrill, frightened screams of a woman and a wild trampling as of a herd of cattle driven toward her.

She listened to it with her head raised, a ray of sunshine flickered in the copper frying pan above the draining board and shone into her eyes. She bent her head sideways, there was a throttling feeling in her throat, her hand sought support on the edge of the table and then she was sick all over the china cups and the plate of candied-peel cake.

VI

In the Santinis' yard the growing, menacing crowd was being held in check by carabinieri. In the front rows there were the matrons of Romiliano, noisily giving vent to their anger. Marta Fugazza, who was standing right in front, narrowed her fox's eyes and said: "I knew it! I had a premonition! I knew it would turn out badly, the little hypocrite!" Behind her, the Serafini sisters were pushing; their vulture's faces were dark and tight with inquisitive expectation and in their thin, craned necks the restless beat of the artery was visible. One of them, the elder one, asked: "Is he dead?" Emilio's wife was turning this way and that like a shrieking weather vane in a rising storm: "Thank God, no, he's not dead, but I doubt whether he'll survive. His lung has been damaged; he's thrown up at least half a bucket full of blood. Didn't you know? Emilio got to him first and saw it all, it must have been a terrible sight, everything was spattered with blood, the floor and the sink and the table legs. Just imagine it! The poor boy hadn't even lost consciousness, he kept asking to be taken to the church, to the Madonna. Perhaps he'll even ask forgiveness for the little monster, I shouldn't wonder."

The bystanders listened in breathless suspense. Now and again they joined in with wails of horror or exclamations of surprise, meanwhile never for a moment taking their eyes from the house where the gruesome incident had taken place.

The carriage, which had by now arrived, stood deserted in the road. The horses nervously threw back their heads, making the bells on their reins jingle. It was an incongruously gay sound in the oppressive gloom of the morning.

When finally Elena appeared in the doorway, accompanied by two carabinieri, a deathly hush fell for one brief moment. But soon there was a deafening outburst of howling and jeering; clenched fists were raised and there seemed to be no end to the shouts of rage and revenge.

"*Bricconcella!* Little witch!"

"*Sacrilega!* Desecrater!"

"*Assassina!*"

"To the gallows with her! *Dalla forca! Dalla forca!*"

Terrified, Elena looked at the contorted faces. Her white dress was stained with blood and dried vomit. Hesitantly she stepped down from the low threshold, hampered by the train of her wedding dress, and at that moment the shadow of a large, frothy cloud began to darken the valley. Shyly she looked upward, she saw the sun hiding behind the cloud and she knew that the wine-growers were right, that human happiness was indeed bound by omens.

A sneering voice nearby made her start. "Yes, go on, look at the sky, maybe the Madonna will come down from heaven again to help you!" She was knocked on the shoulder and someone croaked like an old parrot: "Today it's your day, bride of the devil!"

Hunching her head between her shoulders, she walked across the yard with thumping heart, protected by the carabinieri. The howls which followed her all the way through the dense crowd swelled into a savage roar.

She closed her eyes so as not to see the malicious, irate faces and when she opened them again she saw the smooth bodies of the horses and the carriage, festooned with colorful paper streamers, and then a strange pain, which she had never felt before, pinched her heart. The sun came out again, shining through the foliage of the olive trees along the road as if through a church window, and flashed like lightning on the barrels of the carabinieris' rifles.

Some people followed the girl as she was led away, shouting and sneering, but most of them stayed where they were, craning their necks and waiting impatiently for the door to be opened again and for Mario Costello to be brought outside. Gradually, tempers cooled and the general mood of horror and outrage gave way to one of pity and commiseration. Leonzi the blacksmith, who left the house a little later, was besieged with inquisitive questions. "Make way!" he shouted. "For God's sake keep the way clear. We're taking him to the church, he wants to ask the Madonna's forgiveness. Where is the *vetturino?*"

"Here!" answered Marlocchi, the half-grown coachman, using his whip to push aside the bystanders, who were like a high wall, concealing the dwarflike figure.

"Will you take the boy to the square, please?" Leonzi asked him.

The dwarf looked up helplessly at the robust blacksmith, scratched behind his ear, and said doubtfully: "I hope he won't soil the carriage. Is he losing much blood?"

But before he had made up his mind, the door opened and the injured man was carried outside by his father and one of his friends, Giovanni Portolani, a young vine pruner. A stretcher had been hastily improvised from two curtain rods and a piece of canvas. The locksmith, his head bent, walked out reeling. He was a broken man; with the utmost effort and with faltering steps he dragged his son and himself to the carriage, and then turned away, overcome with grief.

Willing hands lifted Mario up and carefully hoisted him into the gaily festooned carriage which was to have taken him and Elena to church but which was now only taking him, without his bride, without witnesses. Marlocchi frowned at a drop of blood on the footboard. He spat in the sand and said nothing. At a sign from Portolani, who had joined Mario inside the carriage, he climbed onto the driving box and gave the horses a light tap with the reins.

"*Lento! Guarda a voi!*" Leonzi called out to the dwarf. "Gently! Careful does it!"

Slowly the carriage and pair moved off and at the same time the silent waiting crowd began to stream toward the road. At first only a few people followed the gently swaying vehicle, but soon the others joined, one taking his cue from the other, as at the start of a church ceremony.

At the head went the locksmith and the blacksmith, closely followed by the Fugazzas and the Serafini sisters, and behind them came the boys and girls who had left the vineyards, the matrons of Romiliano, the wine growers from the valley with their broad-rimmed straw hats, the men and women from Reggio d'Ilfonso and the mountain village of Streppo. It was a silent, sad procession winding its way along the silvery green olive trees toward the Ponte dei Amanti. It was a funeral without a body, a wedding without a bride.

On the way, new groups joined them from time to time, among them a small gathering of pilgrims from Torre del Greco, led by a thin, bony woman with a black eye-patch. The horses' bells jingled gaily and the bright blue banner of the pilgrims swayed above the yew hedge.

The tied-up may roses in the front gardens smelt of honey and the rosemary bushes sent their clusters of white flowers creeping through the trellises. The houses and gardens and trees sloped downwards into the valley, from where the church spire, like a glistening spike, rose slowly above the rooftops, ever higher and steeper.

In the piazza, in the shade of the oleander tree, the head of the procession came to a halt. The dwarf on the coachman's seat turned around and watched in silence how Portolani and the blacksmith carried the injured, semiconscious man, who was groaning softly, from the carriage. They put him on the canvas stretcher and carried him carefully into the half-dark church porch. The winegrowers took off their straw hats, the women started to finger their rosaries, and then they all followed the bier, at a distance, swarming out into the church like humming bees.

The *curato's* head appeared above the swinging door of the finely carved confession box and the *sagrestano,* coming out of the vestry with a candle snuffer, stole toward the choir screen, a look of horror on his face, and closed it. Emilio Fugazza went up to him and whispered through the railings "Open it, you don't need to worry, nothing will happen. He only wants to ask the Madonna's forgiveness."

The *sagrestano* wavered and said: "He can do so just as well from the other side of the screen." As he was saying this, he felt a hand on his shoulder. The *curato* stood behind him; moving shadows flowed across his face like dark water. In a quiet voice he ordered the *sagrestano* to open the screen doors. Soon afterward Mario was lying in the choir, under the miraculous alabaster statue. His head rested on a brocade hassock and the palms of his hands, facing upward, looked like the pale, rigid plaster hands of the saints in the choir gallery. From the corner of his mouth came a trickle of blood, which seeped under his shirt collar.

The crowds were surging up toward the screen. In the front, pressed against the railings, was the locksmith, his large, sad eyes fixed on the stretcher. He didn't weep and his lips scarcely moved, but his jaw trembled in an effort to contain his grief, and the knuckles of his hands, clutching the railings, were white. Perhaps he remembered the funeral poem for Giulio Santini in his pocket, and the wedding poem for his son in his other pocket, and perhaps he was beginning to understand that the thoughts

and feelings which a man might entrust to paper were meaningless and false, because God's invisible hand wrote his own
indelible words on top of them when he thought the time was
ripe.

Mario Costello awoke from a green twilight which was like an
imageless dream. An odor of bitter flowers and wilting foliage
surrounded him and when he tried to breathe it in deeply, the
pain stung in his chest like a splinter of broken glass. First he
imagined he was in the vineyards, on the green mountainside,
near the sky, near a high, wide spaciousness full of the warm
light of spring. And when he raised his eyes the first thing he
saw was indeed a soft, white glow, bursting open between his
eyelashes like a star with long, needle-sharp rays. But then he
smelt the molten candle wax and something reminiscent of the
sickly odor of incense, and he slowly opened his eyes wider. He
saw the nimbus above the *Madonna Bubbonica's* head and the
pink face, inclined toward him, with the gentle smile, and
finally he saw the welcoming, outstretched arms. The statue
moved and became alive before his eyes, radiating an irrational
beauty which moved him deeply and a strangely painless love
which made him feel happy. For he vaguely remembered that
there had been in his life a love which had been painful and a
beauty which had wanted to destroy him, and which had therefore been rational. As soon as this memory had taken complete
possession of him, as a past, but relived reality, he understood
where he was and why. "*Santa Maria,*" he prayed, "she had made
your holy, pure name into a lie; I am ashamed of her, take this
shameful sin away from her. . . ."

The words welled up from his heart like air bubbles, bursting
before they reached his mouth. He trustingly looked at the statue
which floated on a white cloud of flowers, and then, for the first
time, his eyes saw the lump, the strange swelling on the
Madonna's forehead. As he looked at it, his senses were confused by a vision: the swelling burst open. A thick, treacly
substance oozed out of the alabaster head, congealing in mid-
flow, like the slow drip of a candle. An immeasurable happiness
poured into him when he saw this. And this happiness was more
intense than the pain in his body, which was dulled by it. He

immediately understood the meaning of the vision: the pus, secreted by the swelling, could be nothing other than the evil, the sinfulness, the impurity, driven out by the power of an infinite love—the Madonna had purified herself from the shame of defilement. He knew she had heard his prayer. He smiled, and there was no sadness in his smile.

Marta Fugazza grabbed Emilio's arm.

"Look, he's smiling," she whispered.

"Yes, he's delirious, this must be the end," Emilio answered with a nod.

The locksmith and the blacksmith, and all the others who were silently, anxiously standing behind the screen, saw Mario's smile. They hoped that at last the miracle would happen, and involuntarily they raised their eyes toward the motionless statue. But they saw nothing unusual and they too believed that the end had come, that this was the smile of those passing into the next life. The *curato* knelt by the bier and wiped the blood from the young man's mouth with a handkerchief. An unreal silence fell, stretching like a wide web under the vaulted roof. The breath of death blew into the web and the shadows of the flickering candle flames danced on the walls.

The light invaded Mario's soul like a benevolent warmth; he rose up the mountain, along the green slopes, toward the blue, cloudless sky which had never been so near.

Translated by Adrienne Dixon.

JOS VANDELOO

The Day of the Dead God

THE first atom bomb on Paris produced a big blast, literally and metaphorically. The operation was apparently successful, at least in the eyes of the bold men who had taken the initiative. The Louvre, the Arc de Triomphe, the Palais de Chaillot, the Rodin Museum, Sacré-Coeur and other military targets had been completely destroyed. The Eiffel Tower had been buckled and near the top even partially melted by the enormous heat.

By a remarkable coincidence—as always in disasters—a peasant from the region of Rambouillet had the fright of his life that day. He was a simple man, like all peasants. Uncomplicated, without neuroses (he'd never heard of Freud or Jung), with a good appetite and healthy bowel movements. He'd made the unfortunate error of having been born on that very day, although it must be added that sixty years had passed since then. So on that luckless morning it was his birthday and consequently he was a little happy. His only daughter-in-law had just presented him with a gas-fueled cigarette lighter.

Because he was of a rather mistrustful and suspicious nature, especially concerning things like gas (and probably also daughters-in-law) he went outside to try out the glittering present for the first time in the open air. Cautiously he pressed the button with his calloused thumb. At that very moment the first atom bomb exploded over Paris. The peasant from Rambouillet failed to understand how his small lighter could produce so much light and such incredible heat. His eyes wide with amazement, he looked at the shiny object in his hand. For one moment he was frightened and pleased at the same time. The next moment he was only frightened and blind. And probably a bit angry with his daughter-in-law as well.

When a little later the second bomb was dropped, the surprise effect had gone. So had most Parisians. The city was a stinking, burning, smoking ruin. Above it towered the gray heads of the two mushroom clouds. The loud crackling of the flames, the noise of collapsing buildings, the terrible groans of the dying and the continual explosions were the only sounds in the murdered city. It was a dreadful situation.

But Paris hadn't been the only target. Operation "Light in the city of light" hadn't been an isolated incident. It soon appeared that atom bombs had been and were being dropped all over the place. Bonn had been as utterly destroyed as Paris. Perhaps it had all started in Bonn? Later, a strange, almost incredible rumor spread.

The rulers of a small country which had always been contemptuously disregarded by the great powers, rejoiced in the secret possession of just one single atom bomb. The high production costs had nearly resulted in inflation and devaluation. No one knew anything about it, apart from the ministers, the generals, and their sweethearts. It was a military secret which was carefully guarded and cherished. But one day the government of that country was affected by a sudden, inexplicable burst of pacifist sentiment. The rulers put their grave heads together and met in secret session at night. They were of the opinion that something should be done urgently to protect world peace, to put an end to discord and to the Cold War.

After a series of stormy meetings, during which the patriotic string was strummed not without merit by some, it was definitely decided to disarm unilaterally. In order to give a good example to the bigger powers, the wise rulers of this small country decided to destroy their one and only atom bomb. It is easy to understand that this decision was taken only after a storm of counter-arguments and reproaches. The conservatives dragged in practically everything: the young, the old, religion, national honor etc. But it was a democratic country. So there was not only corruption, but also a party with a decisive vote. And a majority in this party agreed with the doves.

Immediately a solemn but firm telegram was sent from the parliament building to the supreme commander of the armed forces: DESTROY BOMB.

It went on to say that this decision had been signed by the prime minister on behalf of the entire government.

Unfortunately, something must have gone wrong in the transmission of this yet so lucid, terse, laconic communication. When the supreme commander of the armed forces received the telegram he read to his astonishment: DESTROY BONN.

He was an extremely loyal servant of the fatherland, otherwise he would never have got where he was in the first place. To him, an order was an order. The telegram indicated urgency.

It never occurred to him to check that this gruesome order was indeed correct, even though there were always three telephones on his desk. Two black ones and one white one. On the contrary, he put on his general's hat, hitched up his trousers and did up the brass buttons on his coat. Then, with appropriate sternness as befits a good general, he inspected his uniform in the mirror. Presumably he found everything in order according to regulations, because he conferred a superior little smile on his reflection. The inspection completed, he started issuing orders in a grim voice. He wanted to do his utmost to conclude the business as quickly and as correctly as possible.

Naturally, there was nothing in it for him in the way of promotion; he had already reached the highest rank. He only wanted to put the prime minister and the members of the government in a good mood, by his impeccable devotion, thus safeguarding his high rank and ditto pension. Because one never can tell with governments. And of course he also wanted to show, to the public at large that is, how effectively and efficiently his army could act when an order was given from above.

Ten minutes after the arrival of the telegram a military aircraft carrying the precious, unique atom bomb was on its way to Bonn. This dashed the illusions of the director of the military museum. In his heart and in his museum he had long since silently reserved a place for the national atom bomb. Alas, nothing would come of this now. A precious piece was lost to posterity.

A short while later the pilot was able to report with justified pride that the order had been carried out accurately and to perfection. The aircraft returned to its base unhindered. The supreme commander smiled happily, drank a double whiskey and awaited the congratulations of the prime minister.

The pilot had not exaggerated in his radio report. Bonn had indeed been reduced to almost nothing. The waters of the Rhine churned and swirled like a spuming Icelandic geyser. Even for a formidable figure like the chancellor, who normally could stand up to a few knocks, the bomb had been too heavy.

Meanwhile the French hadn't been idle. Fast as lightning they had retaliated, proving beyond doubt the effectiveness of their own nuclear weapon.

The Germans, whom naïve souls believed not to have any atom bombs, didn't permit the destruction of Bonn and the tragic death of their chancellor to go unpunished. Not only did the magazine *Der Spiegel* immediately come out with a special edition—which was promptly confiscated on account of the undermining of army morale—but the Germans experimented fruitfully with nuclear bombs of their own manufacture. Because Germany had no uninhabited island, nor a desert, and because they had no taste for the unhealthy curiosity of outsiders, they had never been able to carry out tests in the past. Pessimists thought this was a disadvantage, but experience showed that even without previous tests everything went off very nicely.

Within a matter of hours everybody was busy throwing atom bombs or busy dying. Egypt grabbed the opportunity to drop a few bombs on Israel. Israel retaliated instantly and rightly with a product of her own manufacture, at least as effective as the Arab bombs. Because Israel first thought that Jordan had made the assault, the wrong country was attacked by mistake. This led to immense misunderstandings and gigantic chain reactions. By that time pandemonium reigned all over the world.

China, with great accuracy and a sense of justice to match, dropped ten bombs on America and ten on Russia, because it didn't want to favor either. Equality for all remained its lofty slogan even now.

The Americans hit back swiftly and grimly, but because of the hurry a few bombs missed their target and landed on Japan. For this error, some of the technicians responsible were called before a commission and temporarily suspended.

A bomb of unknown origin fell on Scotland, causing some annoyance among the English. They promptly started a search for the unknown sender with a view to a quick settlement of the account. The search came to an abrupt end when the next load came down unannounced on London. For once the speakers in Hyde Park were at a loss for words and Soho was bathing in a festive red light even on this Sunday morning.

In Vietnam, Indonesia, South Africa, Malaysia, Greenland, Tibet, Australia, and everywhere else atom bombs were being tested with more or less success. Suddenly everyone appeared to possess nuclear arms, as well as enemies to use them on.

Even countries like Albania, Algeria, and Upper Volta joined in the terrifying race, not without fruit. In Berlin each sector proved to have its own nuclear weapon, although it must be added that these bombs were lighter (and therefore of inferior quality). A large number of African and Asian countries possessed, beside chronic famine, an expensive atom bomb of their very own.

The world was suddenly filled with light and warmth. Even the night was brilliantly white with the blinding fire which was reflected by a ceiling of mobile black clouds of smoke. After twenty-four hours of confused struggle, insofar as one could speak of a struggle, there were few bombs and few people left. Even so, the strange war continued for several hours more. Everyone was licking his wounds and looking around for something to be salvaged. It was hardly worth the trouble. The injured, the blind, the burned, the radioactive died in their multitudes.

In the course of the following days fewer and fewer people remained alive. Some went about with old gas masks on, others crawled along the streets like beaten dogs. Finally there were those who on no condition wanted to leave their cellars or shelters. In brief, it was a dreadful situation. The earth was burned and covered with hideous sores and bruises.

Then a strange rumor spread. None of the survivors knew or could guess where it came from. But one day someone said that the unceasing, hellish explosions had so severely damaged the universe that the sun, the moon, the stars, and the planets had been destroyed and that even God ("the good old man in the clouds") had been killed in the holocaust. This was a strange, even an exciting piece of news which moreover had far-reaching consequences. The faithful no longer needed to believe and even to the unbelievers certain things had lost their meaning. There was nothing left. Everything was suddenly very simple and un-important and there was no longer any discord among men. Centuries-old religious quarrels came to an end at once. An old village priest who had been spared disenchantedly put on a yel-low raincoat over his sober dark suit. There was no point in it anymore, he shook his head, people had scattered everything to the winds, fools that they were. A leading anticleric encourag-ingly and sympathetically patted him on the shoulder. Together they dashed away a tear at the thought of the good old days, the days before the bombs.

As long as the fires were blazing everywhere, it wasn't so noticeable that the sun had disappeared. But gradually fire and light began to fade, which made life more difficult for the sur-vivors. They tried to keep the fires going as much as possible, so that they had sufficient warmth and light at least in some places. There were plenty of corpses everywhere to replenish the piles. For the time being there was no shortage of that kind of fuel. But with respect to hygiene and health the situation was worsen-ing. Epidemics were breaking out because the piles of bodies were not being cleared away fast enough. A few old, scrapped gas ovens were therefore temporarily reopened and some former camp specialists even turned up to offer their services. Their spontaneous offer was gratefully accepted because they had a special technique and worked at an amazing speed. However, one of these fellows had to be sacked because he was constantly searching for gold teeth in the victims' mouths, with a small pair of pliers. He hadn't got a dentist's diploma, although admittedly he had acquired a certain skill in this field. Some of the casual helpers thought they noticed that these veterans performed their duties not without relish. However, there was no proof whether this impression had any firm foundation in fact (perhaps it was only imagination) and nobody had the time or the inclination to look into the matter.

As mysteriously as the rumor about the dead and meanwhile almost forgotten god (for such is the fate of the dead), another rumor sprang up. It was said that all survivors of the great massacre had to go to Central Africa for a census. They would have to use whatever means of transport were still available. This was no easy task, but man is tough and ingenious. Naturally, it took some while before everyone had heard about it and had found some means of starting the journey. Besides, the number of travelers became smaller and smaller. Only the strong managed to keep going. Children and old people perished miserably on the way. For many it was a terrible journey, exhausting and almost inhuman.

On arrival, people greeted each other with cheers and joy. There wasn't a trace of racial prejudice or any other kind of discrimination anywhere. Everyone was happy with his skin, no matter what color.

The leaders, who were self-appointed, as is right and proper, had chosen Leopoldville as their meeting place. No atom bombs had fallen in the Congo, with the exception of Katanga, of course, which contained most of the country's natural resources. Even so, there were comparatively few Congolese left. They had exterminated each other relentlessly in long, bloody tribal wars and mutual mass killings. Interested parties from outside saw to a supply of modern, up-to-date arms. There had been just as many casualties as there would have been if a few atom bombs had been dropped, but of course, using such an old-fashioned method, they'd needed a good deal more time. Malnutrition, disease and fever had thinned their meager ranks even further.

The survivors gathered in the Baudouin Stadium, a huge arena which wouldn't be needed for sporting events anyway in the near future. It was only half filled. There were a handful of blind and crippled people at the meeting, who doggedly refused to give up the struggle. They were presented to the public as intrepid heroes and were rewarded with a loud ovation. One of the blind men wore a whole string of decorations dating from some bygone war. Someone asked what had become of King Baudouin. A superfluous question. The atom bomb which fell on Brussels had not only put an end to a Eurovision broadcast (probably a football match or a royal wedding, the only things in which Eurovision people are really interested), but also to Baudouin and most of his subjects. And large numbers of European civil servants, well-dressed and well paid, had met their death as brave citizens, without realizing it.

There were relatively few people left in Western Europe. In Oslo and Copenhagen, in Amsterdam, Lyons, Zürich, Strassbourg, Milan, and elsewhere there had been a lavish profusion of bombs. In Rome, the Holy Father had been among the casualties and there was as yet no replacement.

The question concerning Baudouin led to a brief discussion in that corner of the stadium. One person said that the bomb which hit Belgium had been dropped with the express purpose of putting a stop to the language war which had been dragging on for years. If this really was the case, which seemed somewhat doubtful, the foreign intervention had been successful. After the bomb hardly a word was spoken in Belgium in any language whatsoever.

When at last the survivors were all quietly sitting down, when the conversations and gesticulations had ceased, the people were offered a word of welcome, for lack of anything better. The leaders were seated at long tables in the middle of the stadium, with microphones in front of them. Surprisingly, there was no one from the press. No newspapers appeared at that time. Yet there was plenty of news. Quite enough material even for an interesting daily miscellany, or a lofty or blood-and-thunder editorial. No, the reason for their nonappearance lay elsewhere. Not only were there not enough people, who moreover spoke a variety of different languages, but above all, there were no longer any advertisements.

First of all, a number of appeals were made to the audience. Many people asked permission to speak, to make so-called important announcements, most of which amounted to nothing much. The meeting went on for hours. The speakers got bogged down in endless arguments. Because of this, the mood didn't exactly improve. On the contrary, it worsened even more when one of the survivors made the unfortunate move of bringing up the question of guilt. Indeed, who exactly had dropped the first bomb? It wasn't so simple to find out. There had been that story about the small country with its mad disarmament plans, but there was no hard evidence. The speakers juggled with dates and times to their hearts' content, but it didn't solve anything. One person calculated according to Greenwich time, another made an eloquent plea based on Central European time, etc. Maps were spread out and with grim, flushed faces the opposing factions pointed out places and shouted out names of towns. Someone hysterically started to sing his country's national anthem, waving his national flag. Struck by the disapproving looks around him he fell silent and shrank like a slug under salt. The argument became more and more heated and no one saw a way out. In any case, the prime witnesses were nearly all dead and therefore doomed to eternal silence.

Chaos increased, especially because the word "time" had aroused sleeping dogs. A few enterprising fellows took it as a wonderful excuse to suggest a new calendar. An Italian made a fiery plea in favor of returning to the Julian calendar. When he had finished, a Greek went on interminably about lunar years and lunar months. Nobody could make head or tail of it, partly because he spoke in Greek. Moreover, he kept his mouth much too close to the microphone.

Members of the former United Arab Republic insisted forcefully that the guilt of the Jews should be publicly declared. This again led to a terrible fuss. There were about thirty surviving Jews who were understandably sick and tired of having to act as scapegoats. Their indignation was profound and sincere and they reacted with startling vehemence.

Obviously, another scapegoat was now needed. Every country, every nation, proved to have an archenemy somewhere, sometimes even within its own borders, who was now brought forward as the miscreant. There were lengthy arguments, among deafening noise. In the turmoil an Egyptian was pushed down the stairs and in the fight which followed a Cuban lost half of his luxuriant beard. An ex-member of the Ku Klux Klan with a knife chased a black man.

Slowly it began to dawn on everyone that a satisfactory solution would never be found. They were all just as divided as ever. Even the most incorrigible optimists, if such still existed, would have to bow their heads in defeat before this sad, negative truth.

Amid the excited crowds in the stadium there was one quiet, inconspicuous man. It was hard to guess his nationality. He might have come from some small island in one of the oceans. Nobody knew. Nor did it interest anyone; everybody was far too busy with other worries. The man was very simply dressed and was carrying a rather worn traveling bag. Nobody knew or could have guessed what was in this bag. In fact, the man had brought a miniature atom bomb along. It wasn't a big, impressive specimen, but it was a quality product all the same. As the quarreling and arguing continued, the endless jabbering started to get on the man's nerves.

Unobtrusively he opened his bag and took out the shiny, red bomb. Nobody was looking at him, he really wasn't important. He didn't get himself involved in the rumpus and was therefore of no interest to anyone. It was people who could shout and roar who were needed, people with elbows and thick skins. The man looked up at the sky, which didn't look too good, and then at the leaders and the people around him. They didn't look too good either. Fondly he stroked his little bomb and let it explode.

Immediately everyone present recognized the sound, the light, the heat, and the pillar of smoke. That was the last they ever recognized, because no one escaped.

From that moment the earth was again a total wilderness, as it had been in the beginning of time. And at once the moment was ripe for a new creation story. It was the dead god's great day. When he looked around he muttered angrily into his beard: what a mess. This didn't sound very intellectual, but then he was only a poor carpenter's son and had never had the benefit of a scholarship. Immersed in thought he wandered about the devastated earth. Finally he decided to create a human being. So he took some earth and some water (both a little radioactive, but he didn't think that mattered) and he carefully modeled a human body. It was a woman, a very beautiful woman even. When she had been brought to life, she smiled sweetly and coquettishly at her creator, but he had other things on his mind. In order to avoid all sorts of complications, he let her go back to sleep. With his scalpel he swiftly and expertly cut through her rosy flesh and took away one of her ribs. From this one rib he made, not without effort, a robust man. Underneath her delicate, well-shaped left breast there was now a long, thin scar, but it didn't bother her. There were no other women around to look at her in disdain.

Once his act of creation was completed, he let them go off together in peace. They got on well with each other right away, although there were some things they had to get used to. Also, she felt at first some pain under her left breast when he caressed her. But this soon passed.

When the creator had made sure that there were no apple trees or snakes about anywhere, he felt happy and relieved. A feeling of great calm came over him and it was as if he had done a really good deed.

Meanwhile, Adam and Eve went looking for a quiet spot, which wasn't hard to find. They nestled down in the grass and everything could start afresh. Because everything was different, and yet exactly the same.

Translated by Adrienne Dixon.

The Sons of Pepe Gimenez

"Es triste a no poder más
el hombre en su padecer,
si no tiene una mujer
que lo ampare y lo consuele:
más pa que otro se la pele
lo mejor es no tener."
                    José Hernandez

I

HE raised himself once more in his agony, he stammered something, and fell back like a felled tree while trying to point to the door with both arms.

This was how old Gimenez died, Pepe Gimenez, high up on his *rancho* in the Andes.

The sons had been dozing. The thud woke them with a start. With the *mate* jug in his left hand and the blackened water kettle in the other, Mario went to the dark corner of the hut where Pepe Gimenez had just expired in his stinking bed.

"*Bueno,*" grunted Mario, "*murió el viejo*, the old man is dead." Cacho also went to have a look.

"*Sí, está muerto,*" he confirmed. "*Pobre viejo,*" he added.

Mario eagerly sucked the hot *mate* into his stomach, spat a squirt of yellow juice across the earth floor.

"*Pobre viejo,*" he agreed.

"We must bury him," said Cacho, quietly.

"*Sí,*" nodded Mario, "next to his *vieja*, by the rock."

That was all. The brothers had nothing more to say. They shrugged their shoulders and Mario, walking back to the fire in

200

the middle of the hut, tossed the jet of water into the narrow neck of the *mate* jug.

Each lowered his massive one-hundred-and-eighty-pound body onto a groaning chair, took turns in taking a swig from the *bombilla*, and at intervals they glanced aside at the dead man, as he lay motionless, with glassy eyes and his fists clenched on his chest.

When the *mate* began to taste of water, they rose. Mario took the shovel and Cacho fumbled in the half-dark for the pick, and then they walked toward the rock, Cacho behind Mario. There they had buried their mother, the *vieja*, but it was so long ago that they weren't sure where. That day the *viejo* had been in a worse temper than ever. Their *vieja* had taken less time to depart than the old man. Hardly two days after she had vomited blood, the boys had had to dig her grave.

"*Ay vieja, ay mi vieja*," the old man had moaned and after the funeral he had gone to the village to get drunk. The boys had gone to fetch him there and they'd had a hard time of it on the long journey home.

What Cacho scratched loose with the pick, Mario shoveled aside with a lazy lurch. It was tough, dry soil. They made slow progress. So high in the mountains one can't work fast anyway, even if one wanted to. The air is too thin. In any case, Cacho and Mario were in no hurry. They never were. They didn't even know what hurrying was. In the mountains there was plenty of time. The *viejo* had an old pocket watch but it didn't tick any longer. Did it make them unhappy?

When they had dug a hole, not so very deep, they could tell by the sun that it was noon. Their shovel and pick they left by the grave and they trundled back to the hut, to the shade under the *patio* where a hunk of goat still hung in the meat safe. The meat was old and dry. Tomorrow Cacho had better kill a fresh animal.

Mario made a fire and placed the grill on it. Again they started drinking *mate*, taking turns, without looking at each other, sullenly staring at their hands. The *viejo* was dead now, and outside, where they were sitting, his chair remained empty. When Mario drank, Cacho looked at the old, sagging chair, and when Cacho drank, Mario looked, stealthily, as if it wasn't allowed, but neither said: what a pity that the *viejo* is gone.

By the color and smell of the goat's meat they could tell it was done. They had never eaten anything else in all their life, but the *asado* of a *chivito* always tasted good.

Their eyes met as their hairy left hands reached simultaneously for the meat, cutting a chunk off with their big knives, their *facones*. For one brief moment their eyes met and it startled them. It was as if they had both caught a glimpse of hell, and their life was certain to become a hell, they knew, now that the *viejo* had gone. Because as long as he was there, no quarreling had been tolerated and the hatred, the irrational, blind hatred which the sons of Pepe Gimenez bore toward each other had expressed itself by each completely ignoring the other. They didn't even know why they couldn't stand each other. They didn't ask themselves that question. In turns, during spring and summer, they would stay for two or three weeks, sometimes for a month or even two months, with the herd on the Cerro Redondo and they had never talked so much to each other as at the *viejo's* deathbed.

They started eating. With the fingertips of the left hand they held a piece of meat by the end, and with their right hand they wielded the long, pointed knife. It cut noiselessly through the charred goat's meat, brushing narrowly past their rough black moustaches, right in front of their cold, malicious eyes, which were red with smoke, perhaps also with hate.

With their massive legs, crouching on creaking little chairs hardly eight inches from the ground, they looked like repulsive, cannibalistic buddhas. They let the meat slide into their mouths like a boiled fish, cutting away what wouldn't go in. That was the way they had learned to eat. With the wine, cheap though it was, which went with it, they weren't at all lavish. When Pepe Gimenez went to the village he'd occasionally brought home a bottle, but the village was far and they weren't rich. Only at the New Year and at carnival time they drank wine. But then they drank until they were drunk, angry, and belligerent. They had both hoped with all their heart that the *viejo* would die when they were up in the mountains. Both had hoped, if necessary, to be alone with him, but old Pepe Gimenez had long felt his end to be near and he had ordered both of them to keep watch. Even when the *viejo* lay dying, the sons still didn't dare resist him; but that the old, life-weary man had wanted to reconcile them at his deathbed, they didn't grasp. To them, it had merely been their father's wish that they should both be at home when he died. They had obeyed without further ado. For the very last time.

"I'm the oldest," Mario had wanted to say, but he simply couldn't get the words past his lips. It would have been tantamount to saying: Now I'm the one who gives the orders. He didn't say it because Cacho would have given the same reply as always: Twins are twins. So they're equally old. Even though you were the first to be born. In any case, there's no one who knows which of us two was born first.

But Mario did know. The *vieja* had told him once, and so Cacho ought to obey him. Because Cacho never would, Mario said nothing. So they both remained silent, peering at each other, eating, and drinking *mate* at intervals. And they were looking forward to the moment when the *viejo* would be buried, and when Cacho would ride off to the Cerro Redondo, two days' traveling away.

Mario trampled out the fire and they went back to the hut. They wrapped Pepe Gimenez in an old poncho and carried him, Cacho by his legs and Mario under his arms, to the shallow pit they had dug by the rock. The body fell with a dull thud to the bottom and the first shovel of earth covered the white face of their *viejo* completely, reaching into the thick, gray hair on the narrow forehead.

Cacho nailed together a cross, crooked and lame, and planted it on the hillock on top of Pepe's grave. Then he turned, took up his pick, and went behind the *rancho* in order to saddle his horse. He heard Mario taking the young goats to their mothers in the compound. They bleated with hunger.

Mario returned to the hut when he saw Cacho galloping off in the direction of the Cerro Redondo. He took a candle end from the wooden chest by the door and went out to light it in a crevice in the rock, where it wouldn't blow out. There the candle burned, in honor of the *Virgen de Lujan* and at the same time to ward off the evil spirits which had designs on the dead man's soul. Mario thought it was right and proper to light a candle. And also that it was his duty to light it, because he was the oldest.

And that evening Mario crept into the only bed in the lonely, gray-mud house where it still smelt of Pepe Gimenez. This too, he must do, he thought, being the oldest.

The screech of a night bird sounded vicious as a curse and on the fresh grave by the rock an armadillo was gnawing on a half-burnt goat's bone. A fat toad crawled toward the warmth of the hut and tried in vain to cross the uneven threshold into the room where Mario lay gazing into the dying flames as if he was seeing visions.

Now that Cacho had gone, he mused about his newly acquired riches, and how he would tackle things from now on. Tomorrow he must go to the *pueblo* without fail, to report the *viejo's* death to the police and in order to have all his possessions made over to Mario Gimenez. He smiled at the flames at the thought of Cacho. Cacho had better not get worked up when he got back. He, Mario Gimenez, was the elder of the two; the *vieja* had told him so.

"Fair is fair," he said half aloud. Pepe's horse whinnied softly in reply.

Toward dawn Cacho tied his horse's front legs together with the leather thong he carried with him on the saddle. Like an animal he crawled into a small cave, snuggled comfortably into his poncho, and fell asleep.

II

After four days Cacho finally found the herd of goats on the south flank of the Cerro Redondo. The eighty goats were scattered about searching for food. When they heard him they became restless and began to form one close group.

Four rawboned hounds came rushing toward him, teeth bared, without barking, for watchdogs in the *Cordillera* don't bark. They attack with unsparing fury. They fight till they win or die. They darted down the slope and when they recognized him leapt up against the horse. Cacho hit them savagely round the ears with his *rebenque*. He looked for the little Indian boy to whom Mario had entrusted the herd about a week ago, and then he saw him, a speck by the shelter, a little fellow like a dwarf with a giant's poncho! The boy suddenly seemed to come gliding down like a ghost.

"*Qué tal, don Mario?*" he squealed from afar.

"I'm not Mario."

The boy giggled shyly at his error.

"Five goats have died," he chattered.

"*Como?*" Cacho threatened.

"Five goats," jabbered the little Indian, trying to stretch his five sausage fingers neatly in a row.

"They fell, don Cacho, over there . . . down there . . . between the rocks . . . very deep . . . so deep."

He spoke Spanish with difficulty. The other little arm now appeared as well from under the closely woven poncho, in order to show Cacho where and how deep down those five goats had fallen.

"There," he pointed once again. It must have been very far indeed.

"Five goats!" roared Cacho. "Then you won't get any money, do you hear! Or do you think we pay fellows who allow five goats to fall into a crevasse, just like that?"

The little Indian blinked. He knew it was no good arguing and that he'd better keep his mouth shut if he didn't want a beating with Cacho's *rebenque*. So now he wouldn't be able to buy a guitar. His dark eyes became moist.

"It wasn't my fault, honestly."

"Nothing doing. No money," Cacho burst out. "Bring me some *mate*." Like a sprite, the little Indian tripped friskily ahead of the horse toward the shelter.

"Have you done anything except sleep?"

"Yes, I slept often," the little boy admitted sheepishly.

"I'm hungry."

"*Sí, señor*, I'll roast some *chivito*."

A little later he returned with a slaughtered goat, dragging it along by a hind leg.

"First give my horse to drink," Cacho ordered, drunk with joy at finally having found someone who obeyed him.

"*Sí, señor*," the little Indian said again, with humble politeness. The boy unsaddled the horse, gave it to drink and saw to the food, while Cacho kicked off his boots and stretched himself like a sultan on the dirty lair. He scratched his hairy chest with both hands. It amused him enormously that the little Indian obeyed him so slavishly. Perhaps he could keep the little fellow with him. For a small consideration. The thought of Mario infuriated him. It annoyed Cacho always having to take his brother's opinion into account whenever he wanted to take a decision. As now, with that Indian boy!

"Dammit!" he cursed aloud. "I'm my own boss, the same as Mario."

"Did the *señor* call?" The little Indian came running.

"Get out!" Cacho bellowed, kicking the boy outside.

"*Señor, señor*," he heard presently. "The meat is done. May I please come in to get my things?"

"Come and get them!" the fat man taunted, lazily. "Well, what are you waiting for?"

The little Indian, beyond the reach of the hairy paws, stole toward his canteen which was tied in a gray cloth.

"May I?" he squeaked again meekly, pressing anxiously against the wall of the hut.

"I said so, didn't I," Cacho laughed and went on scratching contentedly in the black hair on the white, flabby stomach.

"Stop!" he suddenly thundered.

The canteen clattered to the ground. It was empty, Cacho saw. The little Indian stood as if petrified with fright.

"Here's some money," said Cacho. "And take a piece of *chivito* for your mother. And ask her if you can come again. Do you live far?"

"Far?" faltered the little Indian, not comprehending at once. "Far? Ten miles, twenty, maybe more. Very, very far."

"All right, I'll forgive you those five goats," said Cacho, entering into one of his rare good moods. "But you'll have to come back to work for me. *De acuerdo?*"

"*De acuerdo, señor! Sí, sí*, I'll come back."

Cacho heard the small, bare feet scampering on the rocks and later the rattling of the canteen. He tried to calculate how much money a herd of eighty goats might represent.

That morning, that first morning as ruler of the *puesto*, Mario crawled on hands and knees round the smoldering fire, blowing into it with all his might. He gathered some dry wood and went on blowing till he saw flames. Then he went outside to pee. He stood for a time looking at the sky with the intoxicatingly wonderful feeling of having been reborn that morning as an *estanciero*. It was all his: the hut, one big room without a window and with a door which was never closed, the well for which other *puesteros* had always envied Pepe Gimenez. Of course, it wasn't much, Mario was well aware of it, but it was all his. Over the fire, the kettle started to boil. Into the first *mate* of the day Mario threw a whole soupspoonful of sugar, because this was a special day. He went out to the *patio* to sit in the sun and tried to estimate how much had come into his possession through the death of his *viejo*.

First of all, there were Pepe's as good as new, black, soft-leather boots. And his heavy belt filled with foreign coins. And his *asado* knife with the silver hilt, and the black bolero with the silver buckle, the silver spurs, the silver-mounted stirrups. It was more than Mario had at first imagined. He immediately abandoned his *bombilla* and went inside to look at his treasures, like a miser. With nervous jerks he pulled the old trunk from under the bed. He knelt beside it. He held the wide riding breeches slantedly up against the light, he let the glittering spurs jingle, he kneaded the new boots like modeling clay and tried on Pepe's black hat. Then he threw everything on the bed, kicked the trunk back into place, and went to the well to draw water. Washed and shaved, decked out from top to toe in the old man's finery, he went out to look for Pepe Gimenez's magnificent horse. He'd seen it only yesterday, frisking about somewhere in the valley, with its front legs tied together. A beautiful horse, thought Mario, and a good horse too. The *viejo* had paid a lot of money for it. How much had it been? Well, the horse was also his now. A nervous *tibiano*, white with large dark patches. He went down to the valley, his *rebenque* dangling from his belt like a sword, listening to the creaking of the new boots, the right one of which was beginning to feel tight on the instep. But this was, Mario knew, because he usually wore his own comfortable *alpargatas*.

It was a long while before he saw the *tibiano* grazing and it took even longer to get hold of him. The horse hadn't been mounted for two weeks. During these two weeks he had tasted freedom to the full. With his tied front legs he hopped about like a rabbit and Mario, nearing exhaustion, could only manage to get him to a standstill when he hesitated before the shallow stream, the wild, shallow mountain stream bordered by a strip of soft green grass.

The *tibiano* was still wearing a rough leather halter. Mario stroked the horse until he finally felt the trembling body coming to rest under his hands. Then he tied the long leather lasso to the halter and gently pulled the horse along to the *rancho*. There he had put the *viejo's* splendid saddle ready. Mario trimmed the *tibiano's* unkempt mane, he cut and polished the hooves, combed the tail, and brushed the gleaming, healthy hide. He talked to the *tibiano* like a young man to his sweetheart, with words no one else is allowed to hear.

It took a long time before the horse was saddled and harnessed and Mario took a few steps back to inspect him at leisure. He tried to remember the horse's name, but couldn't, strangely enough. He'd give him another name. Domingo, for instance, yes, Domingo, because yesterday it had been Sunday, he thought, and because yesterday the horse had become his, he would be called Domingo, Sunday.

"Domingo!" he called, but the *tibiano* went on nervously rubbing his nose against the post of the patio. He'll get used to the name, Mario consoled himself. "Domingo," he kept saying, "Domingo, Domingo," coaxingly, cajolingly. He fumbled at the tall saddle which Pepe had bought in Chile, he inspected the silver-mounted stirrups with the leather leggings, and with a bold thrust of his knee in the horse's ribs he tightened the belly-band a bit more. He took his time, he couldn't get enough of it, he'd never enjoyed himself so much in all his life. He kept looking at the splendid horse, which only yesterday had belonged to the

viejo and which was his today. He walked round him, talking
and talking, as if he'd drunk too much *grappa*. But it was getting
late. They had to go to the village, the two of them, four hours'
distance.

"*Vamos*, Domingo," he said, taking the long reins in his left
hand, and nimble like a jockey, vaulted his huge body into the
saddle.

"*Vamos*, Domingo."

So they trotted to the village, a horse and his rider, alone in
the endless accumulation of mountains and rocks, alone in the
distant valleys without shade and without roads, a speck, moving
toward nowhere.

It was far into the afternoon when the *tibiano* and his rider
entered the *pueblo* by the wide, straight road. The gray, tightly
shuttered houses were blazing in the sun and the wind chased the
sand in shreds of dust across the flat roofs. Mario saw the *pueblo*
from beginning to end, he saw all the houses to the left of the
road and all the houses to the right of the road and the only thing
alive was the faded, blue-white flag, which was tugging at its
flagpole in the *plaza*. Mario thought it was a pity. It wasn't that
he liked people so much, or busy streets, but today they should
have been there, the people who lived here. He also reflected that
these villagers led a pretty lazy life, whereas they, the *puesteros*. . . .

When he arrived at the *almacén*, the Turco's big new store, he
had a crazy impulse. He left the *tibiano* by the step, went over
to the shopwindow, and looked at his reflection, at this *puestero*
called Mario Gimenez. On the pots and pans, the primus stoves
and stable lanterns, he didn't bestow a single glance. He only
looked at that giant of a *gaucho*, whose hairy hands were feeling
the broad belt, who rapturously stroked his black bolero, knotted
his white silk scarf, doffed his black hat in greeting. "That's me,"
Mario chuckled, "and this is all mine. My boots, my belt, my
asado knife and my hat, my bolero, and my gray gabardine
bombacha. I must go to the barber's." He let the money jingle
in his trouser pocket. And he gave another chuckle when he
caught sight of the *tibiano* in the window.

"*Vamos*, Domingo," he said.

They rode off to the *municipalidad,* the pompous looking town hall in the *plaza.*

"Pepe Gimenez is dead," he announced to the superintendent.

The superintendent had suspected as much when he recognized Mario, dressed up in Pepe's best clothes. He knew how ill the *viejo* had been.

A quarter of an hour later Mario stood blinking in the glaring light rebounding from the white façade of the new school, on the other side of the small square. With slit-eyes he scanned the four red-painted seats under the weeping trees in the *plaza,* and he reflected once again that the people of the village earned their living by doing nothing. They were afraid of the sun. They must be lying lazily on their beds, having their siesta, their stomachs heavy from overeating.

The four *grappas* to which Mario Gimenez had treated himself in Pablo's bar hadn't made him drunk. He only had an unpleasant feeling in his head, because it was a long time since he'd drunk *grappa.* No, he wasn't exactly drunk. He told Pablo that the *viejo* had died and Pablo had muttered something about *Dios* and *Lastima,* from which Mario gathered that Pablo was expressing commiseration. But the conversation flagged. It didn't seem to stir Pablo in the least that Mario had now become the sole owner of a *puesto;* a *puestero* with eighty goats, three horses, a house of his own, and a first-class well; Pablo nodded at these revelations as he nodded at any other bits of news. He didn't say: Proficiat Mario, or: You're a man of standing now, Mario. None of it. The man had no idea how to deal with customers. Mario was strongly under the impression that he'd dragged the landlord straight from his bed, maybe from the embrace of his wife.

Although Mario didn't actually get drunk, the *grappa* did make him wistful. And a little angry too, because he felt he wasn't being treated as a *puestero* ought to be treated.

"Are you off already?" Pablo yawned when Mario threw the money on the smudged table. But the *puestero* didn't answer. The chairs and tables whirled before his eyes like spinning tops and he felt a malicious desire to grab hold of the barman and chuck him amidst the bottles behind the counter.

"Tchao," he said gruffly, swaying toward the door.

"*Adiós*," Mario heard Pablo sing, and he also heard the tinkle of glasses on the counter and of coins into the barman's bulging breast pocket.

"I'm never coming here again, Domingo," Mario wanted to say, but instead he thrust his arms round the horse's neck like a pair of tongs and started to sob.

"*Ay*, Domingo," he sobbed, "*ay* Domingo, *pobre de mi!*"

The sun chased the alcohol to his head like a clot of blood but no one would ever have noticed, because he clambered into the saddle like a gentleman. He let the *tibiano* walk up the middle of the road. In turn he saw the houses on the left sway to the right and the houses on the right sway to the left, but Domingo carried him safely on his back. Toward somewhere. Turning into a dusty side road somewhere, over a bridge, into a little square, up to a big, newly painted house with a tiny door. Here the *tibiano* stopped as if he had reached his destination.

"What are you doing?" bawled Mario. "What are you doing now, *carajo?*" He studied the broad, bare façade and the tiny door and in his brain the reddish mist lifted briefly.

"*Putcha*," he laughed suddenly, "*putcha viejo, qué te parió!*"

Like a lame dog he slid to the ground and with the long reins fastened Domingo to one of the rings in the façade. He pressed his hundred and eighty pounds against the door and found himself in a porch where there hung a smell of cheap perfume, wakening long forgotten instincts in him.

As in a strange nebula a misshapen monster appeared, addressing him in a sickly-sweet woman's voice:

"*Buen día, joven*. Good afternoon, young gentleman. The young gentleman desires company?"

Retching, he looked at her.

"Have you got money?"

Unashamedly her eyes examined Pepe Gimenez's clothes.

"*Y el viejo?*" He didn't hear her.

She came up to him, took him by the hand, and led him through a long corridor with many little doors, and she told him about his *viejo*, what an old rogue he'd been and how promptly he'd always paid. An honest working man. She'd rather have one like that in her house than all those fine gentlemen who wanted a lot for little money.

She pushed one of the little doors open.

"Delia," he heard her croak. "Here's a gentleman for you."

III

For five days Cacho tried to find the crevasse into which the five goats were supposed to have disappeared. He searched in caves and grottos and the longer he searched the angrier he grew with the little Indian.

When the little Indian comes back I shall have a wonderful time, he mused. He'd let the boy fetch water, cook *asado,* pour *mate.* It would be a good life, but as he waited for the little Indian to turn up, he searched for the goats which surely must have died by now. He decided to give the sneaky little fellow a thorough dressing down, should he have the temerity to come back to him. He'd first give him a proper beating and then make him haul the goats out of the crevasse, one by one.

Of the seventy-five remaining goats Cacho saw only a dozen or so, but he knew the dogs were watching. Condors he'd seen only very rarely in recent years.

He kept thinking of the little Indian, of the hungry little face under the thick black hair, of the little sore feet under the coarse woollen trousers. He dreamt of how the boy would serve him like an obedient slave. What the boy would earn in cash, was of no importance at this stage. In any case, Indians were happy just to have their keep.

It will be a good life for me, he kept thinking. He thought of the little Indian for so long that it made him feel almost miserable. Cacho finally came to the conclusion that he must have been the biggest idiot alive, not to have made the boy get those five goats back at once. It would have saved him a great deal of trouble.

In the afternoon the dogs became restive. They walked around growling, baring their teeth. Cacho took the old pistol out of the saddle bag and undid the catch, although he suspected that the little Indian was on his way.

At sunset the boy arrived, smiling as if he'd only been gone a short while. He waved his grubby hat. Behind him stalked a llama, chewing the cud with the dignity of a dromedary.

On the llama's back the little Indian had tied his few meager possessions.

The llama looked at Cacho with disdainful eyes and took no notice of the dogs, which were sniffing about his legs mistrustfully.

"Here I am," said the boy.

"What are we supposed to do with that animal?"

"Kiki," the little Indian introduced his llama.

"He's lame," Cacho pointed out.

"Yes, broke his leg. But it's better now. Kiki can carry heavy loads."

"Is he yours?" Cacho asked, interestedly.

"*Sí, señor*, my father gave him to me."

In a brotherly gesture, the boy put his arm round the neck of the still chewing llama.

Cacho wasn't quite sure what he wanted the boy to do first. The thrashing could wait until later. He'd give him that at the first opportunity.

"Put your junk at the back of the room," he said gruffly.

The boy took out a small black cast-iron canteen, a pair of sandals, a pair of trousers, a cap and a flute. Indians are fond of music.

"If you blow on that thing, I'll bash your head in."

"But Mario used to like it," pouted the boy.

"I've got nothing to do with Mario."

Cacho thought it was most peculiar that Mario had listened to the little Indian playing on the flute. He tried to imagine his twin brother, sitting there listening to the whining of a *quena*.

"Mario really did like it," repeated the little Indian, when he saw Cacho staring pensively in front of him.

"Well, I don't. Did you play to him often?"

He asked it almost jealously.

"Not often. Only once a day."

"Well," began Cacho, "if you work hard and if I'm satisfied with you, you may play for me too, some time."

The little Indian put the *quena* to his lips and sucked the air into his lungs.

"Not now!" roared Cacho, disconcerted. "Maybe tonight."

The picture of his brother, listening to melancholy Indian music . . . he couldn't get it out of his mind. Actually, why shouldn't he listen too? If Mario liked music, why shouldn't Cacho? The boy, he saw, was still standing there, begging for a signal, with popping eyes, with too much air in his narrow chest, the flute at his lips. So Cacho, reflecting that apparently it had given Mario pleasure, said:

"Go on then."

Tears of joy ran in rivulets through the gray dust on the boy's brown cheeks. He stood there blowing like a faun, hoping that Cacho might like it.

"Is that what Mario likes?" cursed Cacho, but he went on listening. It was a monotonous tune and it went on for so long that Cacho repeatedly felt an itch to throw a stone at the warbling Indian. Only the thought of Mario made him hide his impatience, but he cursed his brother from the bottom of his heart, and the little flute player as well.

"*Basta!*" he finally called out.

"You like it?" asked the boy.

"So-so," said Cacho. "What's that song called?"

"*Solo tu amor!* Only your love," said the little Indian. "Anyone who hears this song won't feel lonely anymore."

"Yes, it was nice," Cacho said indulgently. He felt it was his duty to say that the boy had played well. He was holding the flute in position again, ready for a second tune.

"*Basta!*" Cacho shouted again.

The faun saw he meant it, and wiped the mouthpiece of his *quena* on his dirty poncho.

"I know five songs," the little Indian informed him, holding up his right hand. "But *Solo tu amor* is the loveliest one."

"Anyone who hears this song," Cacho repeated softly, "won't feel lonely any more." He became irritated, because he suddenly realized how terribly lonely he was. It nearly made him feel gloomy.

"Don't stand there gaping, you little fool, why don't you . . . get away with you . . . out of my sight!"

Philosophically Kiki walked off behind his young master, to somewhere further off, where the little Indian and the llama would share the last *tortilla* which the boy's mother had given him.

' "We'll share it between us, Kiki," whispered the boy. "The *señor* should have been more friendly if he wanted any."

Kiki winked understandingly, chewing the thistles which he'd snatched up on the way, and the odd-tasting object the little master had given him during one of their rests. It only tasted so-so. They walked a long way and when they had shared the *tortilla* fairly and equally, the little Indian took his *quena* from under his poncho and played once more, very softly: *Solo tu amor.*

From then on he was allowed to play it every day and he felt that *señor* Cacho liked it better each time. Every time the song lasted a bit longer, too, but with growing anxiety the little Indian noticed how Cacho was changing. Sometimes he was more gruff, more bullying than usual, and sometimes tiresomely friendly. He was different each day. One moment he would lash out at the boy, throw stones at him or shake him about like a duffle bag. A little later he'd beg him to play the tune again, but especially at those moments when Cacho crept closer by, closer and closer, the boy felt like running away as fast as he could.

Cacho also took to talking a lot, especially to himself, sometimes to the little Indian who only understood half of it.

"This is all mine," he often said, with a wild sweep of his arms.

"Suppose this was all yours," he once asked, "all those goats and the horse and everything you see around you, what would you do?"

"We're only poor folk, *señor*, nobody in our village has a herd like this," said the little Indian, humbly, failing to understand how one could ask such a question.

"*Putcha!*" thundered Cacho, "I'm only asking you what you would do if you were as rich as me."

"As rich as don Cacho," the little fellow whispered to Kiki. He was completely confused. "I'd buy a guitar, and shoes, real shoes for *mamita* and a real doll for my little sister."

He shook his head, which felt giddy with such a grave question.

"You're rich, aren't you, don Cacho? And Mario is richer still, isn't he?"

Cacho felt as if he'd been hit in the face. Why couldn't the damn boy shut up about Mario?

"Push off, you!" he raged. "Get away. You're too dumb to talk to a man like me."

Later, the little Indian sat by the fire again, pouring *mate* for don Cacho, who said nothing all evening except: "You're too dumb to talk to a man like me."

No, there really was no point in talking to an Indian. Didn't even know what he'd do, the stupid fellow, if he was as rich as his master. Then you really must be very dumb indeed, mused Cacho. Not to be able to think even. The thought that he must therefore be cleverer than the little Indian, cheered him a little. If the boy once more as much as mentioned the name of Mario, Cacho would give him that drubbing on the spot. The thought put him in a slightly friendlier mood. He kicked off his boots, scratched his chest with his hairy hands. He stretched himself out on his bed and noisily sipped the *mate* which the little Indian handed to him.

"*Señor, señor,*" he heard, as from afar. It sounded as if the boy wanted to ask him something.

"Are you going to play?" Cacho asked, in a buttery voice.

"Yes, if you'll let me."

"*Vamos, vamos,* play. Go on then, play!" Cacho suddenly burst out. "Play," he said again, hoarsely and threateningly, "play!"

It gave him pleasure to read the fear in the boy's dark eyes, the round dark eyes under the mop of thick black hair. His glance moved across the small, angular face, to the tiny, swift fingers dancing up and down the *quena*.

"Yes, play, that's right," Cacho laughed raucously, sliding from his bed, noiselessly like a panther, eagerly moving toward the boy, who played as if for the devil.

Cacho fell back on his bed, shivering as if in a fever, while the little Indian fled into the night.

While Cacho was saddling his horse, the little Indian and the chewing llama watched him from a safe distance.

"Go and get those five fat goats from the compound," he snarled at the boy.

He was putting his spurs on when the boy returned with the goats. One of the dogs kept them together with angry growls and pushes.

"Come here," Cacho commanded.

The little Indian shuffled nearer.

"Listen, in a few days' time Mario will be here and when he comes. . . ." He stared at the boy in confusion, shook his head, and leapt into the saddle, annoyed with himself because he hadn't had the courage to tell the boy that he should only play for Cacho in the future.

"That Indian is too stupid to talk to a man like me," he consoled himself. This made him feel a little bit rich, once again.

IV

Just as in the past, the sons of Pepe Gimenez "felt" each other already at several miles' distance. This was a lesson taught to them by nature, in a world where people were scattered even more thinly than the lonely, dry trees, growing here and there among the rocks.

They got wind of each other. They knew, each for himself, that soon they'd meet again and that they would be irresistibly drawn towards each other.

In a few hours' time they would greet each other, with that cold hatred in their eyes. Or would Cacho no longer even bother to say *"buen día?"* thought Mario. He used to, even though reluctantly. Because the *viejo* expected him to. So, first Cacho would say *"buen día,"* as icily as possible, and then Mario would answer *"buen día."* That's how it should be, thought Mario, because Cacho was the younger of the two. Now he wondered what their meeting would be like.

He looked out, over the rock, toward the Cerro de Torro, for the cloud of dust which was to confirm Cacho's coming. The dogs were getting restless too. They were pacing to and fro, sniffing the air with their pointed snouts; they were getting irritable, and snapped at one another. Never before had Mario hated his brother as much as now and when he reflected that

Cacho would never consent to taking the sole care of the mountain herd upon himself, he cursed from the bottom of his heart. Mario thought this was the hardest day of his life.

The annoying thing about the long journey home was that Cacho had to reckon with the goats, the horse, and the dog, all the time. His animals weren't spoiled, but even so, he had to give them a rest now and then and a chance to look for food.

They progressed no faster than at a walking pace, southwards, as closely as possible following the bed of the *rio Seco*, where they discovered, from time to time, those places where a pool of water had remained.

Cacho wanted to spare the animals. On the mountain, the goats had become very fat and it would be a pity if they lost it all during the journey. Yet this wasn't his main worry on the monotonous trek in the parching sun. He'd been doing this journey for years. It wasn't worth wasting any thoughts on it. Instead, he was desperately trying to calculate what would be in the trunk under the bed in the hut. He tried to imagine the *viejo*, riding off to the *pueblo* for the New Year's festivities, and as best as he could he drew up an inventory of Pepe's possessions, starting with the black hat, down to the silver spurs. Furiously, he pictured in his mind's eye, Mario parading in the *viejo's* rig.

With his spur Cacho hit out at one of Mario's dogs, which was cheerfully coming up to meet him. A little later he came upon Mario's horse in the valley, which made off in flight before the small caravan, with tied front legs. Cacho watched him for a long time.

"I should have shot the *tibiano*," he said bitterly.

His horse respectfully stepped round Pepe Gimenez's grave, but the goats clumsily knocked down the cross. Cacho irritably flicked his *rebenque* at the stupid beasts. When he reached the top of the hill, he saw the dirty white hut.

Mario was standing in the doorway, legs astride.

The dogs started to sniff at each other, Cacho's abandoning the goats for Mario's bitch. Cacho thought of the *viejo* as he stared at Mario, who was wearing his best *bombacha* and his boots, as if he had just returned from the village.

The horse slowly came into motion again and walked languidly toward the shade of the patio. Cacho heard Mario shout something to the dogs, who had started a fight. He kept thinking of the *viejo*. How he used to wave his arms from afar, to him or to Mario, and how he used to sit and chat under the *patio*. Once again, Cacho felt lonely. He said some inanities to his horse, which was greedily drinking the ice-cold water from the well. With a forceful sweep Cacho chucked what was left in the bucket against the hot flanks of his mount. The horse shivered. Cacho took a cloth and began to rub him dry. He was in no hurry. As he knelt down to rub the horse's belly, he saw, between the legs, Mario leaning against the patio wall. He hadn't heard him coming.

"What about those five goats?" began Mario.

"I'm going to sell them presently."

"From now on I take care of that."

"Don't you be so sure," hissed Cacho under his breath, without looking up, "and don't you think either that anything has changed here after father's death! *Basta* now, leave me alone."

They avoided each other. They each went into a different direction to make *asado*. The meat didn't taste very good and they both wished that they got on better together. Now it was too late. Their hatred demanded more and more and they felt resentful. Cacho had noticed the *viejo's* hat hanging from a hook in the *patio*. He knew for sure now that Mario hadn't been able to keep his paws off the clothes in the trunk. But he couldn't quite understand yet why Mario should want to send him into the mountains for good. Did the fellow really think he could lord it on the *puesto*, forever, while Cacho did all the work in the mountains? Mario no longer had any illusions. He knew his brother. It would be hard, living for two, perhaps three weeks in the mountains without Delia. The thought of the eighty goats made him feel sick. On his return to the village he'd ask the old hag, how about his sweetheart, when would she be free. Obviously, the toothless witch wouldn't like to let the girl go. Delia had many visitors. The old woman had said herself that Delia was very popular with the men, even though she wasn't all that young, and that she'd be very sorry indeed if Delia were to leave

to become Mario's *compañera*. The old hag's blabbering made
the burly *gaucho* so jealous that he felt ill. And on the other hand
he was immensely proud to be the favorite of this woman. Mario
was prepared to give the old woman a few goats in compensation
for Delia. On his return he'd ask the fat *dona* point blank how
about it. She'd have to look around for a new girl. In any case,
Delia had brought in quite enough money already. Now he
wanted Delia to be his forever.

Out of breath, Cacho had to put up with the *tibiano* giving him
the slip every time he approached it. Embittered, he went to the
hut, roughly tied a piece of string through the mouth of his horse,
and a short while later he caught the *tibiano* with the lasso. Mario
had watched it all from afar. He continued to watch Cacho, in
silence, threateningly. He filled the doorway so that Cacho hardly
had any light as he spread out the *viejo's* things on the floor, and
tried on the boots. Mario remained silent when Cacho rode off
to the village like a wealthy *estanciero,* followed by his dog, who
trudged behind the five goats with sore feet. Mario felt miserable
at the thought of being without Delia, for weeks on end.

"The *viejo* is dead," said Cacho, standing by the counter in
Pablo's bar.

"I know," nodded Pablo.

"You do?"

"You told me already."

"*Macanas,* nonsense. I was in the mountains for weeks after
he'd died."

"You came in here to get drunk, wearing your *viejo's* clothes."

"*Mentira,*" Cacho cursed. "Liar! I was in the mountains."

For some time he went on arguing with Pablo, who maintained
he'd seen young Gimenez in his bar, shortly after old Pepe's death.

"It wasn't me!" shouted Cacho. He was spending the money he
had got for the goats liberally on *grappa,* and Pablo prudently
changed his tune.

"Well, all right then," he maneuvered shrewdly. "Maybe it was
your brother."

Cacho clasped the counter with both hands.

"*Mi hermano,*" he stammered, "*mi hermano, sí,* my brother, it
must have been him. It must have been!"

With trembling hand he grabbed his glass and smashed it in front of his feet.

"It was him, Pablo! It was Mario, the shameless dog. In my *viejo's* clothes!" Cacho sobbed, "in the clothes of my dear old father."

"Don't stand there blubbering," Pablo mocked, pouring out another *grappa* for Cacho.

"Mario, hey?" Cacho bawled. *"La puta madre. . . .* I'll get him, Pablo, see if I don't, the bastard!"

At this point Cacho dropped into a chair and banged his flat hand on the wobbly table, whimpering with impotent rage.

He managed to get into the saddle unaided. He let the horse find its own way, knowing that more than once the *tibiano* had carried the *viejo* back to the *rancho* like a sack of wheat on his back. This consoled him. It reassured him. It also allowed him to abandon himself utterly to his great grief and his blind rage. Repeatedly he felt the urge to give the horse a prod with the spurs but he didn't. His subconscious told him that he'd be thrown to the ground at once if he did. As it was, he was reeling giddily in the saddle.

"Hey, you bastard, what are you doing here?" Cacho blabbered, when he noticed the *tibiano* had stopped by the little door in the broad, white house. He tugged at the reins, beating about with the *rebenque* like a madman, and finally the *tibiano,* as if offended, walked back to the big, long road, head in the air.

Very distantly Cacho heard a woman's voice call Mario, but he didn't turn round. He tried to remember if he knew anyone in the village by the name of Mario. But his brain was too tired to think. He only knew one Mario, *por desgracia,* he said aloud, and that one Mario he would shortly have to meet.

V

Mario first noticed the llama, looking at him in philosophical disdain, and soon afterwards the little Indian emerged from the shelter.

"What are you still here for?"

"Don Cacho, hey, don Mario . . . don Cacho asked me. I look after the goats and I. . . ."

"Shut your trap! Cacho actually asked you to stay here, did he?"

"*Sí, señor!*"

"And that animal?"

"Kiki? My llama? He's my friend."

"I hope your friend will keep out of my way. Go and get some water and make *mate!*" Mario said curtly.

He failed to see how Cacho could possibly appreciate the company of an Indo, but when he saw that the dirty little fellow had reinforced the walls of the shelter and cleaned the floor, he didn't mind him staying.

"Are you very cross with me, don Mario?" asked the little Indian with his anxious, squealing voice.

"No. Why should I be?"

"Because of those five goats."

"Cacho sold them. That wasn't your fault, was it?"

"No, I mean the five goats that fell in a crevasse, *señor*. Don Cacho was very cross with me."

"What's that?" roared Mario, and he gave the wailing little Indian the thrashing that Cacho had promised himself he'd give him at the first opportunity.

Cacho chased the dogs from his bed and fell asleep with the thought that there was a smell in the hut of something he'd never smelled in it before. The next morning he woke up with the same strange smell in his nostrils and he searched all along the grayish white walls and on the earth floor. Like a hound he sniffed all over the bed and under the hard mattress he discovered a bundle of transparent underwear. It suddenly made him frantic with desire for a woman. It must have been ten years since he'd last touched a woman. Now he sat on the ramshackle bed, panting, with a woman's underwear in his stiff hands. He scarcely dared look at it. It burned his rough palms like the sweaty body of the whore to whom he had paid twenty pesos, ten years ago. Like a flame this woman seemed to rise from the rosy garments. He saw her, naked and enticing, he reached for her ankles and tumbled with his clammy face into his hands which smelled of something he saw floating mercilessly before his eyes. He buried himself in the garments. His fingers clawed passionately as if gripping the body of a groaning woman. He fell asleep, carried away into a sultry dream. He shivered.

"Show me where it was, *indio de mierda*," Mario hissed, twisting the Indian's slender wrist.

The boy wasn't even crying anymore.

"*Perdone, perdone*," he shrieked only, scrambling up the mountainside beside Mario, on his bare feet. Kiki limped along behind them. The dogs followed passively.

"There . . . here," the little Indian brought out with effort, when they had reached a deep, dark crevasse.

"Get them out," Mario commanded, letting go of the boy who slumped down as if dead. Mario kicked him upright.

"Get them out, *carajo!*"

Trembling with fright the little Indian crawled into the dark cave. When after a long time his head reappeared, he shook it, no, the eyes blinded by the light and wide with fear. He had found nothing. Feverishly, Mario began to gather dry tussocks of grass, pressed them into a clump, held a burning match under it, and tossed the fireball into the abyss. The flame burned for a long time at the bottom of the crevasse, ten yards down. They could see into the farthest corners.

"Empty," whispered Mario.

He grabbed the little Indian, who was about to sneak off.

"We're poor folk, don Mario, I . . . I . . . will pay you back! You're rich. . . . No, no!" he cried in terror.

Even before the flame had died, the little body crashed like a faggot of dry twigs on the hard rocky bottom. Then Mario noticed that Kiki had taken to his heels, lithe like a mountain goat, in spite of his stiff leg.

In vain Mario tried to outmaneuver the llama. The animal was hiding, with the shrewdness of its wilder kinsmen, but it didn't go far from the place where it had seen its young master disappear into the hole.

Every time the son of Pepe Gimenez came near the crevasse, he saw the llama, chewing near the opening, but he didn't manage to get close to Kiki. Instinct drove the animal to flight. It knew it was safe among the craggy rocks and in the countless hiding places in the mountains. There, where the llama went, no horse could go. Mario became frantic. Perhaps, he hoped, the llama would die of starvation. Perhaps it would, but this was an idle hope, stumble into the crevasse.

If the little Indian didn't return home, his family would go out looking for him. They would know where the boy was, near enough. And they would see that stupid llama, always hovering near the crevasse. For a moment it crossed his mind that he might ride back to the *rancho* to fetch his revolver: with only his knife he'd never get the better of the mistrustful creature.

He returned to the *rancho*, constantly seeing the llama as a specter before his eyes. Kiki had become an obsession to him. Behind every rock, in every vale, he thought he could see the llama's silhouette, motionless but for the enervating chewing, ears in its neck. Only the thought that Delia would soon share his bed, Pepe's old, decrepit bed, only this thought freed him from the llama. Cacho was coming along, with a bleating goat under each arm, just when Mario's horse stumbled over the cross on the grave by the rock. Mario briefly bared his head for the *viejo* under the ground. When he rose, Cacho had already turned his back on him.

Mario shaved and washed by the well. He carefully trimmed his thick black moustache and combed his hair like a big-town dandy. He saw Cacho's grin and shrugged his shoulders indulgently. Soon there'd be a woman on the *rancho*, his woman, the woman of the elder Gimenez, a woman who'd sleep with him, who'd wash and cook for him. *Solo tu amor,* he whistled softly.

The twin brothers left simultaneously, Cacho for the Cerro and Mario for the village, for Delia.

"Delia," said the old hag, like a mother saying good-bye to her daughter, "Delia, your Mario is waiting in my room. Go with him. You're free. It's the chance of your life. He might marry you. You'll have a roof over your head. The man's actually in love with you. You know how to make his love last."

"*Gracias, señora,*" Delia said, sanctimoniously.

"It's no good staying here any longer," the serpent smiled. "I can't go on keeping you, you do understand, don't you. I've been good to you, haven't I? Here's some money. Just for you. No need to tell Mario," she added with a sly wink.

She played her motherly role brilliantly. There were even tears in her eyes. "In our trade you've got to be able to weep," she had once told Delia, when the girl had entered in her service. She was pretty good at it herself, thought Delia.

"And if he throws you out you can come back to me, to your *mamita*. I'll find you something to do."

"Who will live in my room?" Delia asked softly.

"She's coming today," the old woman cooed, businesslike. "One from the city."

"Hoho, she's young, is she?" Delia nodded understandingly, picking up her bundle. There wasn't much.

Mario looked at her, somewhat ill at ease. He'd never seen Delia in broad daylight, nor with so many clothes on. She looked nice, with those bright red lips and those sunglasses. He only hoped she could ride a horse. Shouldn't he have ordered a taxi, for this once? Perhaps she expected that. She didn't know yet where she was going.

"There are two horses," he said.

"All right, let's be off then."

Delia was tired. What did she care about a horse! The ugly hag embraced her and kissed her on the mouth. She took the giant by the hand.

"She's the apple of my eye, *señor*. Be good to her."

Mario was moved by her tears. And proud of his new possession.

They were on their way to the *rancho* and Mario was at first at a loss for words. He squinted at Delia, unaccustomed on Mario's horse, at her stockinged legs and her high-heeled shoes which she risked losing all the time. Her bundle of belongings he had tied to his saddle. He thought she was quite a lady.

"My *rancho* isn't very big," he apologized.

She smiled.

"As long as there's room for me," she said.

He was happy. He thought it was wonderful, those high heels and those sunglasses, but whether they were really suitable for the *rancho*, that was another question.

"I'll paint the *rancho*," he promised. "The house is pretty cramped. With two men, what can you expect," he laughed.

"Two men?"

There was nothing for it, he had to tell her. She'd see Cacho in any case, some day.

"I've got a brother, but he's thinking of moving," he lied brazenly. "There's no room for two men. And I'm the oldest."

VI

He didn't see her tears behind the sunglasses. He groped under the mattress and showed her the pink souvenirs he'd begged from her once. There was something boyish about him, the way he laughed. She let him carry on, flaunting his shabby treasures. He puffed out his chest, while she looked up at the roof over her head. She could see the blue sky through it, blurred, through her tears. She took off her sunglasses, kicked her shoes aside, and set to work. She'd learned not to philosophize about her lot. This was indeed her last chance. The last episode of her poor life. So this was the end. She gritted her teeth. Behind her back the rugged *gaucho* was purring with simple-hearted joy, pride, and animal longing. He sweated big stains under his arms and was in her way like a puppy. His stupid remarks made her smile with pity, for him and for herself. At her orders he carried the drab furniture outside, he fetched water, and promised the craziest things, which she no longer believed. She no longer believed any promises. She'd got to know so many men and she knew what it was they wanted.

When they woke up it no longer smelled of Pepe Gimenez in the *rancho*. Not even of smoke and charcoal. She'd turned the place inside out, resolutely.

He lay with his heavy body against hers, his eyes closed, and he tried to imagine what she would do today. Whether she would make any more changes around the *rancho*.

"What's the time?" she asked.

Mario didn't know the answer. He'd never bothered to find out what the time was.

"*Vamos, querido.* You've got to build a little oven behind the house."

"Must that be done today?"

"*Claro*," said Delia, categorically. "We've got to work hard today." She felt relatively happy. She'd tame him like an old, dull billy goat. He'd been without a woman far too long to be master of his senses.

For five days Cacho waited for the little Indian. Then he began to worry. In a corner there were still the *quena*, the grubby canteen, and the sandals which belonged to the boy. They'd been left behind as if the boy was coming back any moment. On the fifth day Cacho started searching for the little Indian in the neighborhood. He found the llama chewing peacefully by the crevasse, and when the little Indian didn't answer his calls Cacho knew something must have happened to him. But it wasn't until two days later that he threw a faggot of burning tussocks into the crevasse.

"Hey, hey!" boomed his voice, resounding against the bottom. The boy didn't stir. Cacho started cursing him.

"You see, *malcreado*, *indio loco*, little wretch, nothing but fooling about, hey!"

He was cross with the little Indian. It was as if the boy had cheated him by falling asleep peacefully in a horrible hole. Just as if he had jumped into the abyss on purpose, in order not to be at don Cacho's beck and call any longer. Out of laziness! Even so, the thought flashed through Cacho's mind that perhaps the little Indian hadn't been playing on the edge of the crevasse. But now that he was dead and irretrievable, ten yards down in a dark cave where he would soon be finished off by rats, Cacho wanted to avoid the unpleasantness of a police investigation. For half a day he patiently stayed on the lookout. Then he shot a bullet through poor lame Kiki's faithful head, dragged the heavy animal over the edge of the crevasse, and also threw the little Indian's scanty possessions down into the depths.

He felt like an intruder. He was standing in front of the hut and heard voices. He heard a woman saying:

"Mario, there's someone there."

They stood staring at each other, the two sons of Pepe Gimenez, the twins. Mario, dressed up like an *estanciero,* with a white silk scarf round his neck, and Cacho still with a kerchief in front of his mouth, against the dust of the journey.

"Who is it, *querido?*" asked the woman, and Cacho smelt the pink underwear again.

It was silent for a moment. Then Mario smiled:

"It's my brother. Come, Delia," he beckoned like a conqueror, "come and meet my brother."

She emerged from the half-dark of the *rancho* and Cacho reluctantly took his hand from the hilt of his knife.

"*Bienvenido,* welcome," the woman nodded. "Come in."

No, Cacho wanted to say, but he pulled his neckerchief off and came forward. Mario and Delia stepped aside. She understood that the brothers hated each other and that there was no room for the two of them at the *rancho.*

She accompanied Mario to the rock.

"This is the last time," snarled Mario. "I don't want to go into the mountains anymore. Why did you let him come in? When I get back, he's got to go."

"You can leave that to me," she said kindly. "Cacho is the younger one. He'll understand."

He trusted her. Until he came near the Cerro Redondo. Then his jealousy made him unable to eat, because he knew what Delia had been and what her body wanted. And there was his brother who could talk.

She walked back to the *patio* to chat with Cacho, who was still lying down wrapped in his poncho, his eyes shut as if he was asleep.

"Do you hate him?" she asked, coming straight to the point.

"Yes," he said curtly.

"Because he's the oldest and therefore has inherited the *rancho?*"

Cacho hadn't spoken to a woman for years. Her indiscreet questions infuriated him.

"He's not the oldest," he snapped.

He raised himself on his elbow. She saw how much he resembled Mario. He might be slightly smaller, slightly less stout, with slightly finer features.

"Are you the oldest then?"

"No," he said. "Is it your business?"

She laughed.

"You're not the oldest and you're not the youngest. Come off it," she said, as if to a schoolboy.

"I'm not the oldest and I'm not the youngest," he sang back sarcastically, "that's right, *señora*. I'm his twin! You see? And I can prove it to you!"

She laughed again. In order not to cry. She realized that Cacho wasn't lying and that Mario had not told her about him on purpose. They both had the same rights.

Delia wearily passed her hand across her forehead.

"Come," she said invitingly, "I'm sure you must be hungry." Cacho obeyed.

He was given soup, vegetables, and meat. He couldn't remember ever having eaten so well. She poured wine for him and he drank, out of thirst, out of relish, and out of love, and gradually he felt as if the lower part of his body became numb. It was a wonderful feeling. Absentmindedly he listened to Delia's voice. She was the second woman at the *rancho*, the first one since the *vieja*. Cacho let her spoil him like a child with measles.

She told him about her life, while Cacho poked in the fire with a stick. He didn't understand what she was getting at. He was thinking about something quite different.

There was a moment of intense silence.

"What are your plans?" she asked him, in suspense. "Are you thinking of staying here, with us, with your brother?"

"I'm staying," he said harshly. "Why shouldn't I?"

He hit out angrily at the flames.

"Why do you hate each other so?"

He shrugged his shoulders. Delia had put her hand on his knee. The question surprised him. He felt the compelling pressure of her fingers. She wanted an answer.

"*No se*," Cacho sighed, "I don't know. We always have."

Again there was that fragrance of her clothes. She was sitting next to him and handed him her glass. With his strong hand he clasped the neck of the *damajuana* and poured.

"Don't talk about him any more, will you?" he asked.

It wasn't a question but an order. She didn't insist, because it would be no good. Her skillful woman's hand ran across his knee. Cry when you wish, it flashed through her head. It wasn't difficult to be sad. Now that her mute plea had failed, there was only one means left to her. It might succeed, or it might not.

"It's getting cold," she whispered. "It's late."

She pulled herself up on his arm, slowly and calculatedly, and when she saw his hungry eyes and his hands over which he no longer had control, she fled into the hut.

He looked so much like Mario.

They didn't speak about Mario. Cacho continued to build the oven, drew water, and went to bed with Delia. He hadn't touched a woman for ten years. His senses were taking their revenge. Delia and Cacho didn't want to count the days, didn't want to talk about the future. They only knew the insatiable, wild desire for each other. They abandoned themselves to this, recklessly, blindly like young lovers.

"When did the *viejo* die?" she asked him one night.

"Why do you ask?"

"No particular reason."

"In the spring," said Cacho. How should he know the date.

"Did you love him?"

"Oh, leave off, will you," he answered testily.

She gently stroked his naked back until she felt he was no longer annoyed.

"He was a good man, our *viejo*, better than us two," he lied, between passionate kisses.

So he was, thought Delia. Cacho couldn't see her smile, a little wryly. She knew so many secrets.

"Didn't he ever ask the two of you to . . ."

"Shut up, shut up," she heard Cacho say. "Shut up, what do you women know about it?"

"*Mucho querido, mucho,*" Delia whispered softly, pressing him more tightly to her breast.

She closed her eyes and let him kiss her.

"Cacho?" she sighed after a while.

"*Sí?*"

"You ought to trim your moustache."

He laughed out loud. She'd never heard him laugh. It was a

minor victory. Cacho was such a very young *gaucho,* coming to her. She warded him off, she knew how to, because she knew her job.

VII

It was an old drum-revolver. Mario turned the drum and gave the thing another thorough examination. With the revolver at full cock he went to lie in ambush. For a whole week he kept watch near the place where he had last seen the llama.

He nearly went mad with the angry shrieks of a dozen chimangos which kept circling above the crevasse, furious because they couldn't reach their prey.

Mario had been lying in the blazing sun. His skin was dry and hard and his lips were swollen. The hot air danced in front of his eyes like a thousand llamas, like Delias and Cachos. Tears ran from his eyes. Perhaps, he pondered at times, perhaps I could sell everything, all the goats and the horses. And if I gave Cacho his share and went to live in the village. . . . He couldn't think. Not even of Delia. He only wanted to shoot that llama, before going back to the *rancho.* After a week he gave up. The llama had disappeared. Mario giddily went to the edge of the crevasse. With his *facon* he lashed out at the troublesome birds, groped for his matches and lit one.

He was bending dangerously over the edge and couldn't stop looking at the little Indian and at the llama lying close by the boy's body. In the reddish glow he saw the *quena,* the canteen, and the sandals. Then he turned over on his side, took Cacho's revolver out of his belt and dropped it in the cave.

"When they find you, *amigo,*" he called after it, hoarse with thirst, "when they find you, you know, Cacho will be the culprit!" Cacho, the cave echoed.

Mario scrambled to his feet and stumbled toward his horse. The dogs were waiting for him, tails between their legs.

"*Vamos!*" he shouted.

He suddenly felt the need to talk to a human being. His head reeled and it took a long, long time before his horse was saddled. He put on his spurs, picked up the last leather water-bag and jumped into the saddle.

Toward evening the dogs were lagging behind and the horse was bleeding from its flanks. They trotted through the moonlit night. Mario allowed himself no rest. Anxiety drove him on, an ever growing, oppressive anxiety. Flecks of foam flew into his face. He tortured his mount continually with the pointed spurs. There seemed to be no end to this ride. It became day and it became warm; he tumbled from his horse and crawled on all fours to the edge of the water. They drank greedily, minutes long, Mario and his horse. At last they went on their way, at a walking pace, toward the cave which was a fixed stopping-place on the journey to the Cerro Redondo.

He didn't even tie the horse's forelegs together, he even lacked the strength to unsaddle it. They slept in the cool half-dark.

"Why don't you go now?" asked Delia.

She saw Cacho dawdling by the *tibiano*.

"Mario is coming," he said, without looking at her.

She heard the disquiet in his voice.

"Mario? He's only just gone. How should he! Can you see him by any chance?"

There was only the wide, bare landscape with a tiny flicker of green by the *río*, down in the valley.

"Can you see him?" Delia repeated.

"He's coming," Cacho snapped. "I know it."

She came close to him, leaning against the *tibiano*.

"Go then," she implored him.

For Mario was coming. She could read it in the small, dark eyes of his twin. She could tell by the carefulness with which he saddled the horse. He tried to smile and took her in his arms.

"Let him come, *querida*, I'm ready."

"But run away then, he's still far off! You wanted to go to the *pueblo*, didn't you!"

She was a woman. She didn't understand that he had to stay.

"There's no room here for both of us."

His malicious grin made her shudder.

"Is that a reason to fight?"

"*Me queres?* Do you love me?" he asked, evading her question.

"You know I do," said Delia, almost inaudibly.

She was also thinking of Mario, who was now approaching the rancho.

"It had to come sometime," said Cacho. "You go to the cave presently, and light a candle for the Virgin. So that I may win."

Delia thought again of Mario.

"Stay with me," he asked.

She put her arms round his waist, clung to him. His heart thumped. He was nothing like as calm as he pretended. Suddenly he lifted her up, and kissed her, fiercely, frantically, because he saw the cloud of dust, which was growing bigger and closer. He saw the small speck approaching like a whirlwind and he estimated how long he could go on kissing Delia and what were his chances of surviving the fight.

Delia didn't see the cloud of dust. She closed her eyes and groaned. She would have to lose one of her lovers, she had reconciled herself to this, but she didn't want it to be Cacho and she didn't want it to be Mario either. Soon she would weep for one of them, and tonight she would sleep with the murderer of her lover.

Cacho felt her start as she heard the thud of the horse's feet. She didn't look around. He felt her nails in his back and he kissed her one last time as Mario was bringing his horse to a standstill scarcely fifteen feet from where they were standing, holding each other in a desperate embrace. Cacho saw the privation on his brother's bearded face, he saw the horse hanging his head. He had a chance. Gently he let Delia get down.

"See you soon," he said. He wanted Mario to hear.

"See you soon," Mario jeered.

Cacho rose into the saddle, fresh and reposed.

"*Vamos,*" he called out to Mario. "See you at the tree by the river!"

They gave their horses the spurs and speeded off. Delia walked to the *rancho*. She looked in vain for a candle.

VIII

Cacho was the first to arrive under the tree by the *río*. He had run like a devil, with the intention of bringing Mario to exhaustion. He let himself slide from the saddle and slung the reins loosely round the trunk of the tree. A few moments later Mario was there. They didn't speak a word. They didn't look at each other. They prepared themselves as if there was a disagreeable little job which they had to get over and done with. Neither displayed any hurry as yet, either to kill or to die. Cacho unfastened his big, cumbersome spurs and looked at his brother who had a terrible journey behind him.

Mario felt dizzy as if he had been drinking. Cacho heard Mario's whistling breathing and saw the drops of sweat glistening in his black beard. He almost felt regret that this man had to die. He felt a bit like the moment just before cutting the throat of a goat.

They put their spurs and their hats on the saddles, they took off their boleros and carefully proceeded to wind their colorful ponchos over their left arm.

Then they stood face to face, the sons of Pepe Gimenez. Cacho was wearing his father's boots, the colorful *faja* under the heavy belt, and Pepe's best poncho round his arm.

They both crossed themselves.

"*Listo?*" asked Mario.

"*Listo*," said Cacho.

Their hands reached for the long *facon*, the pointed *asado* knife between the belt on their back. Again they crossed themselves. With the hilt, angularly and clumsily.

With his left arm in front of him like a shield, Mario made the first lunge. Cacho awaited him like a fortress, ducked like lightning when Mario's knife flashed toward him and got ready to intercept the second thrust. Mario did not dare take the risk. Like wrestlers they began to steal around each other in circles, using the arm with the poncho as a shield, in their hard hand the dreadful *facon*.

"*Te mato*," hissed Mario. "I'm going to kill you."

Cacho laughed scoffingly.

"When, *señor* Mario?"

He took a lithe jump forward, swinging his knife. Mario felt it like a chilly gust of wind past his left cheek. He shrank backward.

"When, don Mario?" Cacho taunted, maliciously.

Let Mario attack, he calculated. And Mario remembered how once, during a smuggling run, he'd come upon a gendarme. An artless gendarme, who'd been just as surprised as he. The man hadn't even had a gun on him. But he knew how to handle a bayonet. It had been a long struggle, Mario consoled himself, and the thought of this gendarme, in whose stomach he had thrust his *facon,* gave him courage.

Then suddenly Cacho lashed out with all his might. His knife tore Mario's shirt to shreds.

"Very good!" Mario jeered, tautening his muscles.

They made their decisive sally at the same moment. They collided with each other. It was as if they wanted to embrace each other like brothers. Body to body they remained standing, very briefly only, then Cacho slumped sideways like a drunk. Mario was still holding the *facon* in his hand. He felt the warm, sticky blood and then he saw Cacho's knife. Cacho had planted it up to the hilt in his brother's belly. But Mario felt no pain. In a daze he looked at the silver hilt, which turned red, at Cacho who was staring at the leaves of the tree. Mario's *facon* fell to the ground with a thud. He grabbed Cacho's knife with both hands and pulled it out of the wound. He took his handkerchief and wiped his hands, while he reeled toward the *tibiano,* as if in a mist. Cacho's hat and spurs he swept aside.

"*Vamos,* Domingo," he hiccuped.

Delia saw him coming. Hesitantly she went to meet him.

"Cacho, Cacho," she wept, sobbing in her hands, when she recognized Mario.

The *tibiano* walked as if in a procession, carefully, as if carrying a wax statue on his back.

"Delia," she heard Mario say with difficulty, "Delia, *mi amor,* it was an honest fight. I've killed him. By the tree."

She saw how pale he was and she thought they must have fought hard. His shirt was hanging about his chest in shreds. He closed his eyes and opened his mouth. Only then she noticed the blood. She daren't come nearer. The blood seeped down the *tibiano's* flanks, forming a dark pool on the ground.

"We are . . . together now," he panted, and smiled painfully.
"Cacho!" cried Delia, "Mario, Cacho! *Pobre de mi!*"

"Together . . ." Mario lisped, and slumped forward. He was lying with his arms round the *tibiano's* neck, his face in the mane.

Delia cried and cried. Through her tears she saw Mario's exhausted dogs, licking the hands of their dead master.

She tied the body to the horse with a leather strap, she took the reins in her left hand and the pick in the other and went to the tree by the river.

She didn't know how deep she should dig in the hard ground. It took such an endlessly long time. It was night before the twins of Pepe Gimenez were lying in the grave. It was morning when Delia arrived back in the *rancho*. She could no longer cry. The dogs were standing around her. Two hundred pesos she had left, the money Mario shouldn't know about. It was just enough for a cast-iron cross and flowers for two graves.

Translation of Spanish words:

Mate: an indigenous tea, the use of which was propagated mainly by Jesuits, after the conquest of South America by the Spanish. *Mate* is especially recommended to counteract the harmful effects of excessive meat consumption.
Bombilla: the cup into which the hot *mate* is poured. Usually made from a hollowed fruit.
Asado: roast meat.
Chivito: young goat.
Poncho: square blanket used as a cloak. Sometimes it has a slit in the middle, for the head. Made of strong, multicolored wool and so densely woven that it is virtually waterproof.
Pueblo: people, but also, as here, village.
Rebenque: whip.
Estanciero: owner of an *estancia* or large farm.
Puesto: usually nothing more than a hut in the remotest corner of a large property. A *puesto* is inhabited by a *puestero*, with or without a family. Usually the *puestero* is a subordinate.
Asado knife: the knife which South Americans use to kill and skin cattle, to cut meat and to fight.
Facon: synonym of *asado* knife (in *gaucho* jargon).
Alpargatas: linen shoes with rope soles.
Grappa: strong liquor.
Gaucho: South American cowboy.
Compañera: female companion.
Damajuana: demijohn, big bottle in plaitwork.
Faja: belt. The *gaucho-faja* is a long, narrow, woven belt, which is wound

round the waist in order to protect the intestines against the jolting of horse-riding.

Chimango: small bird of prey, chiefly a scavenger.

Carajo: strongest South American expletive.

Parabellum: drum revolver.

Tortilla: pancake.

Translated by Adrienne Dixon.

DIRK DE WITTE

A Blind Cat

IT was the only house on the hillside. In the past it had shimmered white through the trees in the orchard. But in the last few
years the color of its roof, walls, windows, and doors had merged
with the surroundings, grass slowly yellowing and withering, no
longer to be severed from nature. As his wife gradually became
less mobile—some ailment or other which she vaguely referred
to as "something in my stomach"—but most of all when he himself found it increasingly difficult to climb a ladder, he had given
up setting the house off from the seasons and the landscape
each spring. It was as if, at an undefined point in time at which
the lines life and death began to join more clearly and per-
sistently, he had felt that the time had come to wipe out all the
traces which he had drawn in his life with her. Altogether there
wasn't very much to clear away. There were no children and he
had often asked himself whether this was a gain to him or an
emptiness, a vacuum which he hadn't been able to fill with the
elements prescribed somewhere in the blueprint of fibers and
blood. He had left nothing on paper, not even the illusion of a
last will. There was only the house which he himself had built
in the loneliness of this hill and the orchard he had planted around
it, which had gradually grown into a wilderness, concealing the
house, absorbing it into the organic curve of growth and decay.
And there was Souki the cat, who had joined them for the last
twelve years, in a separate, faster rhythm, in the process of
decline, who had become blind about a year ago and was now
beginning to dribble as well.

At the bottom of the orchard there was a mossy woodpile on
which green, sticky toadstools grew in autumn and orange, white-

specked fungus. Against this pile of firewood he had built a seat where he would sometimes sit dozing whole afternoons, or simply staring in front of him with Souki on his knees. Souki—a silly name for a cat, but no sillier than Puss or Pops or Balthazar. Even after she had become blind, she still followed him everywhere as he wandered through the fields. But since the woman had kept to her bed, the cat had detached herself from him, staying with her in her room, all day and later also all night. Souki lay at the foot of the bed and only went out briefly in the morning and at night. To make her go, he had to lift her from the bed and put her down in the kitchen. Then she would walk around in circles for a time, miaowing plaintively, but would end up by following him outside. Usually he would loaf around idly for a quarter of an hour or so, among the overgrown shrubs and the grass which hadn't been mown for years. Souki followed him till he went in again. He'd open the bedroom door and from the last store of words remaining to him, draw some long since threadbare cliché. "It's close today. Perhaps there'll be a storm."

In the last few weeks the yellowish gray face on the pillow had begun to look like a wax mask and he couldn't tell how much still got through to her, as if already she was sliding outside the compass of daily perceptions, into a suffocating, withering sleep, in which events only occurred on the inside. The bony hands, the thin legs, the fragile, derelict body when he washed her— it all had fallen into decay so slowly that he hadn't even noticed it, could only recover it from his memories, or measure it by the far too large nightclothes he put on her.

Sometimes he suspected it painfully, unexpectedly glimpsing something of the progressive deterioration, but he compared it with his own stiffened, wizened body, which he could scarcely remember ever having been young and supple.

"Have you been asleep?" he asks softly.

"I don't know, perhaps I have." The voice hardly reaches the walls of the room.

"Do you want anything to drink?"

"No."

"Aren't you hungry yet?"

"No."

In the twilight of the bedroom the whispered words hardly disturb the silence—they form part of this room and the monotony is only broken by the sounds from outside: sparrows and starlings in the cherry trees.

Souki is a black hairy ball of purring tranquillity against the hillock of her feet under the blanket. The man follows the scarcely curving line of legs, belly, breast. The face, from which the bridge of the nose jumps out like a knife.

Her eyes are closed. As if she is asleep. But he knows she's not asleep. She hasn't slept for weeks. What can she be thinking? The same small thoughts as he? That the end is coming, in which all paradoxes are resolved? That she is wasting away, only drawing on forces which are merely vegetable? She probably weighs no more than seventy pounds. And she used to weigh over a hundred and fifty. He can lift her effortlessly from the bed, in order to put her gently on the commode, upholstered in brown oilcloth, which she hasn't used for weeks because she can no longer decipher the signals of her inner organism.

"You just let it come, like a child," he had grumbled at first, but now he changes the cloths which he spreads on top of the sheets without saying anything, rinsing them each day, and putting them out in the orchard to dry and bleach.

I shan't manage to cope much longer, he thinks at times. We're both going to pieces like this. Her temples are sunken, her hands are fingers up to the wrists, it strikes him each time he looks at them. They lie side by side on the blanket, yellow and shriveled —strange, aloof things which can start fidgeting with the blanket at any moment. How long have we had those blankets? Thirty years? Forty years? How long does a blanket last? Then the gasping, difficult breathing starts up again, as if she is entering a fight with the secret intention of giving up. He looks at himself in the mirror of the wardrobe on the other side of the bed. He sees himself, straddling the chair, and notices that he hasn't shaved today and yesterday and the day before. He tilts himself out of the mirror, gets up from the chair. The crotch of his corduroy trousers sticks to the seat. Carefully he goes to the door. When he turns the brown china knob he hears the panting voice:

"Come. Here. Lie beside me."

Souki gets up, stretches, walks across the sharp ridge of the body to the woman's face. She lies down between the hands which start stroking the cat slowly.

Under the regular purring the woman's breathing grows calmer again. Perhaps she'll fall asleep at last, he thinks, but realizes he's been thinking this for the last two weeks. If she falls asleep now, it will be for ever. If she falls asleep now, all sounds from outside will be shut out, every smell, every gesture will be locked away. The way she lies there now, she's almost dead already. The only thing alive about her is Souki, the warm black fur of a cat. It isn't much, but it is life. Life which with the regularity of her heats had expanded into new life twice a year, but which each time he had reduced to the mother cat when he drowned the kittens in the well. Holding four or five kittens under water twice a year for so long that the bodies became wet, fleshy rags which he stuffed into a hole, trampling the earth above them as if he had to hide the humiliating barrenness of his own life deep down in the earth. A secret which each spring burgeoned, yellow-golden, in the forsythia which he planted on the small mass graves. The garden was full of mildly sprouting forsythia, irregularly scattered among the straggling fruit trees.

"Where are you going?" she whispers.

"A little walk."

"Don't stay away long," she says, her eyes closed. "I'm very ill."

"No, no," he answers, almost testily. He walks down the three steps into the kitchen and suddenly swims in the mild air which comes swarming in by the open kitchen door together with hundreds of flies.

When he goes outside, dozens of sparrows and starlings and blackbirds fly up from the cherry trees. He walks down the path to the woodpile, crouches awkwardly on the seat, takes out his pipe and tobacco pouch, and starts filling his pipe. Souki isn't there to claw at the smoke when he lights the pipe. At first he'd been jealous—Souki stayed with the woman on the bed and he was bored on his own in the garden. At first he used to take the cat under his arm when he went out, but he'd stopped when Souki resisted, striking her claws into the blankets whenever he tried to lift her from the bed.

One after the other, the blackbirds, sparrows, and starlings drop back into the trees. He can no longer see them clearly. There is water in his eyes, all the time. That's why he had to give up hunting, years ago now. And also because his hands had begun to tremble. At first he had thought it was simply fatigue, but when he hadn't hit a hare or pheasant for a whole week, he'd hung the gun on the hook over the hearth and he had realized that finally everything boiled down to wear, old age, the end.

He wipes the water from his eyes and the blur has gone for a few moments. Alone to the end, he mutters. In the room he is partially dying. What will it be like when the woman has gone? What shall I be doing here, all by myself?

When he has finished his pipe, he knocks it out on his clog. Heavily he rises to his feet, first to his right knee, pulls up his left leg, clings to the woodpile and pulls his right leg up from underneath. It doesn't hurt, he doesn't feel any pain, but it is as if his body is made of lead, as if his muscles have stretched into useless rubber bands. A man grows old, he mutters, and walks up the path to the house. He leaves his clogs by the kitchen door and walks on stockinged feet toward the bedroom door, carefully and silently turns the china knob, as if he still believes in the miracle that he will at last find her in a sleep from which she will awake cured and well, and will start doing her work again, or simply sit out in the sun.

Souki walks across the bed toward him, miaowing plaintively. "Hush," he says severely. "You'll wake up the mistress." But then he sees her face and knows she will never wake up again. It is as if the bedroom has expanded, as if it has taken on a different spatial relation, with a dimension of emptiness and absence.

From outside the day cuts like a knife between the almost closed curtains.

"Celia," he says. "Celia. What is it? Aren't you feeling well?"

He has always known that she would go just when he was out for a while. He goes to the woman, opens one of the closed eyelids with his thumb. It remains open, languidly, exposing a lifeless, glassy marble. The shadow of death, which had been hanging over her for weeks, now clearly falls across her face. Souki brushes her head against his arm, miaowing ruefully. He carefully presses the eyelid down again, joins her hands together, clumsily folding the fingers across one another because he can't imagine the dead in any other way. He takes his handkerchief and wipes the sweat from his forehead, rubs his gleaming scalp dry.

I'm alone, he thinks. It has happened. The time has come. It has nothing to do with a feeling of loneliness. It is more physical, more the feeling that you're no longer useful, that you only exist partially, less than halved. He puts the handkerchief back into his pocket, clenches his fist, opens it and with something like wonderment and incredulity examines the moving fingers. He opens and closes the hand three times and is amazed that this is still possible. Her mouth sags open a little crookedly. He takes a towel from the bedside table and ties it around the head so that the mouth can stiffen in closed contentment. Then he stands there watching for a time, trying to think of something resembling a prayer, something with a way out. But he feels nothing except that he is alone.

All this time the cat has remained on the woman's chest. Her green, blind eyes look up at him. Is she asking what is happening?

"Come," he says. "Come along. You can't do anything here. She's dead. The mistress is dead."

He lifts the cat up but her claws cling to the blanket. The blanket comes up as well and he sees the folded hands moving slightly.

"Come on," he says. "Let go now. You can't stay here."

He jerks the claws out of the blanket, puts the cat down in the kitchen, and closes the door. He has a feeling as if he is shutting himself away behind it.

Standing by the kitchen window he looks out. I'm hungry, he thinks. I haven't eaten anything since this morning. And I must shave and wash. And change my clothes.

By the bedroom door Souki is scratching the paint from the doorpost.

"Come on now," he says. "Quiet now, quiet now." He picks her up, sits down by the table, and lifts the cat onto his knees. "We can't do anything about it," he says.

For months he's been sitting alone by this table but never so

alone as now. The possibility of her presence has been removed.
A whole life, seventy-five years of contradictions, had slipped
away without his having been there, without his having been able
to do anything about it.

And tomorrow it will be me. Or you. He strokes the cat's back.
You or me. Which of us two will be the first? Tomorrow or the
day after or next week. Why not straightway? Cut everything
away at once. The rifle, at ten yards you shoot a hare to shreds.
If you put the barrel into your mouth your head bursts asunder
in bloody tatters. It takes less than a second. He puts the cat
among the plates and bowls on the table and goes to the hearth.
He takes the gun from the hook. He takes the box of cartridges
from beside the glass bell and puts it on the kitchen table. He
opens the lid, takes two cartridges out, puts one of them back.
He snaps the gun open, puts the cartridge in the chamber, and
claps the gun shut. He puts it on the chair and goes back to the
window, his hands behind his back.

Souki has jumped down from the table, comes to rub against
his corduroy trouser legs. He looks around the kitchen. I can't
leave it like this. He starts stacking the plates and bowls, shoves
the leftover bits of food together in the stewing pan.

I ought to shave and wash first.

He takes the gun from the chair and walks into the orchard.
He follows a new path among the tall grass and the stinging
nettles, as if he daren't use the old path, as if he is afraid of
meeting the familiar figure. When he reaches the woodpile he
sits down on the seat which is too low and presses his back against
the wood. He places the gun between his legs, the barrel pointing upward. I must do it properly, he thinks. This is how I must
do it. When he feels the hard steel against his palate he starts.
This is how it must be done. He puts the gun by his side and
takes out his pipe and tobacco. A few more minutes. What
would most people do if they knew they had only a few more
minutes to live? A blur comes before his eyes again. It is the
air, he thinks. It is the sun. As he strikes the match, he feels
the cat jumping on to his knees. She claws at the smoke which
he blows toward her. With the back of his hand he rubs the blur
from his eyes.

"Yes," he says, "and you? What will you do without me?" He takes the gun.

When the shot resounds against the hills, flocks of birds fly up in a panic, twittering and flapping. Souki leaps from his knees and goes after the shrieks of the injured starling. He scrambles to his feet, leaning on the gun, and watches the cat tearing the fluttering, shiny green body apart in a cloud of down and feathers. He squats beside the cat and puts his hand on her back.

"Come," he says. "We must eat something and wash and shave. And we'll have to find someone to lay her out properly. Come."

Translated by Adrienne Dixon.

JAN WOLKERS

Minister in a Straw Hat

IN the bottom part of the big olive-green baby carriage was a deep bin which could be reached by opening two flaps. You might say the baby carriage had a false bottom, considering that my parents managed to introduce a new baby into it every year. Four bottles of fizzy lemonade were laid in the bin, two of brown champagne, and two of raspberry. The hampers with sandwiches were put on top of them and the remaining space filled with rolls of fruit drops and small juicy pears. The flaps were closed, the mattress went in, then the crying baby. We were ready to depart. Swimsuits and towels weren't coming, it was Sunday, we were only allowed bare feet.

"If you have to go, do it now, you can't on the way," said father.

I shook my head and took my hands out of my pockets.

"Look at the way he's tied his shoelaces," cried Lea.

I looked down at my shoes and the laces that straggled over them like mangled grasshoppers.

"Really, to think he can't do it properly yet," sighed mother. "You're old enough now! You do it for him, Lea."

Lea knelt at my feet. I immediately clenched my toes to raise the instep because I knew she would lace them so tight that I wouldn't be able to move my feet.

"He's being a nuisance, mother," cried Lea. "Put your feet flat, and now!"

I relaxed my instep, but began to lift again very slowly. She hit my shoe with her fist and quickly made a double knot. In revenge I let a drop of spit fall on her head. It hung in her hair like a small silver ball.

"There's a spittle bug in your hair," I said, bending down to her head. "I see his green body coming through the spittle. It looks like one of the gobs that always lie on the steps around Drunken Duncan."

"You can't fool me," she replied, her mouth compressing itself, but when she stood up she ran her hand through her hair.

"You pig," she yelled, "you spat in my hair, I'll get you for this!" With her arms rigid, flailing about stiffly, she came at me. I braced myself against the wall and kicked my legs far out to keep her at a distance.

"You two keep in mind that this is the day of the Lord," said father.

"He started it, he spat on my head while I was tying his laces."

"It was a spittlebug," I objected, "I saw it."

Father walked over to Lea and looked closely at her head.

"That's human saliva," he said. He strode over to me and pulled down my arms, which were already over my face to ward off the blows. He pushed his face almost against mine. I felt his warm breath steam up my skin and avoided his eyes by fixing mine on his dark Hitler moustache.

"Look me in the face," he said hoarsely and emphatically. "Did you spit on your sister's head?"

I nodded a few times, looking at him unafraid, as though my confession had lessened the chance of punishment.

"You come with me!"

He pushed me ahead of him toward the open door. On the steps he gave me a kick in the backside. I flew onto the lawn. And I stayed there lying with my arms and legs stretched out, looking at the cloudless sky where a kestrel stood right over my head, praying.

While we were still in the village we had to walk three abreast in front of my parents.

"Just so I can keep my eye on you," said father.

I kept trying to stay behind by pulling up my checkered knee socks at the side of the road. I felt ashamed of the grand exodus and kept thinking of what the boys at school sometimes said to me: "Wow, has your father ever been busy!" Or: "When is your team playing another club?" If only we were nothing, I thought, then we could take the steam streetcar to Katwijk, like everybody else. But no, I saw the hell which would inevitably open its red, fiery gates for me after this short life. And I tried to console myself with the words of my father: "For what shall it profit a man if he shall gain the whole world and lose his own soul."

We passed the Roman Catholic church just as people were coming out.

"Look, the dirty Catholics get there pretty early," I heard my father say. "They make quite an effort for their misguided faith."

I was afraid to look for fear of seeing a certain girl among them, as very recently I had dumped an old piss pot full of cow shit on her head.

"I know a Catholic girl," said my brother in a whisper. "She's as hot as mustard. She opens up her legs without being asked. You see a bunch of hair and a red spot and you just push it in."

I didn't exactly know what he meant but pondered his words a long time all the same.

When we had passed the green bridge over the canal we turned sharp left and followed a path that ran alongside the water. It was a narrow path hollowed into the grass and the clay soil by anglers and gardeners. We had to walk one behind the other, like a jungle expedition. To the right of the path were vegetable beds and long stretches of cauliflower field. The leaf of the cauliflowers had been broken and folded inward, to protect them from the light and stop them from turning yellow. There were silver droplets on the leaves, sparkling in the sunlight.

"Hold your noses, the shit boat," called my oldest brother, who was leading.

"You'll oblige me rinsing out your mouth the first chance we get," father said to him.

The side of the boat had a blackboard nailed to it with SEWAGE COLLECTED FOR FREE chalked on it.

"That's for the cauliflower," explained father. "They use human feces for manure."

"*Bon appetit*," called my brother. "It makes you wonder how they stay white. That must be why they stink so much when you cook them. Look at that," he whispered to me, pointing at the stalks by the ground, "it's even got bits of shit paper mixed in. The minister's wife used that piece to wipe her asshole."

"Oh, do you know what Peter said, father," cried Lea.

"Hold your tongue, I don't want to hear any more from you," father called back. "And none of that dirty talk up front."

"Father heard what you just said," pestered Lea. Peter turned around.

"Old sourfaced blabbermouth," he sneered.

There was a scuffle. The line of children began to squeeze together like an accordion.

"Now it's finished up front there or I'll bang your heads together," called father angrily.

The procession moved off again. At times we had to stand aside in the grass while an angler cycled by. With the toes of our shoes wet we went on, the dew had honeycombed the grass and the crops, and a coolness rose from the earth.

"It's going to be a hot day," said father.

I felt all the boredom lying in wait for us under the sun, behind the distant misty dunes.

As we came nearer Rijnsburg, more and more rotten onions floated in the ocher-colored water between the islands of algae, which on the surface had been brushed light yellow by the sun. Occasionally a shoal of rudd darted between them with just their red fins visible.

"This is a fine spot to drop a line," said father. "You could just scoop them up here."

I even imagined hearing regret in his voice. Because it was Sunday? Near the flower auction there were so many bunches of flowers in the water that it looked like the reflection of a tropical forest. On the side of a shed hung wreaths braided from shining dark leaves.

"Life ever ending in death," said father, while he gestured sadly from the fields of flowers to the funeral wreaths. My mother sighed.

"Shall I take the baby carriage, wife?" father asked.

"No, I'm all right," she replied.

"What's the matter?" he asked.

"Nothing, nothing," she said.

"Stop, you up front," commanded father.

At the other side of the water the steam streetcar approached.

It rumbled onto the bridge. The water around the piers trembled, the mirrored image of the steam streetcar fanned out, blurred, and mingled with the reflection of sky, blue all the time. Just before the square black locomotive crossed our path it let out three shrill whistles, like a frightened animal.

"We're at least a hundred yards away," called my brother while slowly walking on.

"Stay where you are," yelled father. "Do you want an accident!" My brother stopped, disgruntled. As we crossed the rails all that remained to be seen of the streetcar was the back, a small iron balcony filled with white dresses and gay ribbons barreling into the vegetable fields amid a cloud of steam. On the other side of the rails the path became much wider and was paved with gravel, which didn't make walking any easier. We formed two lines at the right and the left where the sharp stones had been swept to the side by cyclists. The path turned away from the water. The vegetable fields at both sides were hidden from view by tall elder bushes. Overhead their tops would meet, and if you looked along the path it was like peering through a tunnel made with your hand. Below the elders grew tall stinging nettles and blackberry bushes. Only in places where there was a clearing in the wilderness and where my brother whispered, "you should see the fucking that goes on here at night," was there a glimpse of the farmland lying beyond. Flowers sometimes: carnations or gladioli. Or a heap of branches beside a tumbledown shack. Halfway along the path stood two lime kilns. Strange light gray structures with the body of a mill, a round roof with a thick stack growing out of the middle. They most closely resembled huge bottles, but could also have been built by termites. For a few hundred yards around everything was powdered with dust. The grass, the trees, the stinging nettles, even the pebbles were white. Yet when you kicked the bushes the dust didn't come off. It was embedded. The color and the sap all seemed to have gone, though the leaves weren't dead. As if the whole landscape had been laid to dry between the pages of a gigantic album. By the side of the lime kilns were mountains of shells, brought up from the beach on small two-wheeled carts by the shell-fishers. When we were past the lime kilns my brother and I had our pockets full of shells.

"Get rid of those things in your pockets," commanded father. "You'll ruin your good clothes. Those sharp things go right through the material."

"The old boy never lets you do anything," said my brother. But he, too, threw the shells away, although provocatively, slowly, one by one into the stinging nettles.

The elder bushes by the side of the pathway slowly began to make way for hawthorn, warped by the seawind. The stinging nettles were gone and the blackberries no longer grew tall but crept close along the ground. Behind the trees the dunes had now come very near. The first were green, with brisk short grass. Knolls of meadow with what looked like square patches of broken earth, or so the red brown nets laid to dry there would make it appear. Behind them came the real dunes, blue gray with marram grass and buckthorn. On our left the canal had returned and ran alongside, but far below in the depth, reminding me of the postcards that aunt Jo had sent us from Switzerland.

"They've opened the lock," called my brother as he pointed at the rust-colored water that sluggishly wheeled and swirled as if it was viscous.

"You children be careful in the sea when we get there," said father. He looked warily at the restlessly shifting water. To the left of the lock our path seemed to run up against a wall of dark blue sea. As we entered the street, solemn singing or the admonishing voice of a minister came through some of the open windows, the sound sieved by screens. The footpath had no flagstones, but was paved with tiny yellow pebbles that had short dry grass growing in between them. Sand had collected in all gutters, blown into gentle hillocks by the wind.

"Can I take my shoes off?" asked my brother. He stopped and bent down, about to untie his laces.

"Me too," cried Lea. And then the little ones suddenly grew noisy and glass curtains were pulled aside here and there to reveal a worried face over the fuchsias, watching us with suspicion.

"Keep going," ordered father. "You don't walk on the street in bare feet on a Sunday. And stop kicking up that row. You're disturbing people's sabbath."

All at once the soft rustling of the surf was there. The sky was hung with colorful kites. From behind the grass-capped tier of dunes came the sound of merry voices, so clear, that the sky seemed made of glass. We stopped at the edge of the footpath.

"Stay together when we cross," said father. "These drivers tend to fly by here at thirty miles an hour as if they're the only people in the world. Yes, it's safe now, hold one another's hand. You too, hang on to your little brother," said father to Peter.

Peter took my hand without much enthusiasm and softly said to me: "Regiment pressing on in close formation."

A couple of boys stood on the footpath, watching us as we went. They whispered something to one another and burst out laughing. Then they ran back and forth across the boulevard, flapping their arms and roaring like airplanes.

Once we had crossed over I ran ahead, up on the basalt siding. By the little harbor I stayed to watch the men fishing. They had long lines on their fishing rods and weren't using floats. When the water was still you could see the bait on the hook lying in the sand. It moved slowly to and fro. Suddenly one of the anglers pulled up a big crab. He smashed it down on the rock, dancing it on the end of his line to get it off the hook. When the creature was free it scuttled into a crevice between two blocks of basalt. The man put his rod down and walked over to pull the crab out. He sat down on his heels and took a knife from his hip pocket. It was a grafting knife with a curved tip. He cut the pincers off the crab and flicked them down the crevice with the tip of his knife. Then he cut a hole in the hard shell of the crab's back and picked out a bit of white meat. He weighed the crab down with a rock so it couldn't run away and said: "You don't kill them so they can keep their own meat fresh." He picked up his rod and stuck the piece of meat on the hook. I knelt and looked under the rock. I thought I heard tiny shrieks coming from the mouth of the crab. The arrangement of little arms moving around in there could have been inside the clockwork of a watch. His claws scratched convulsively over the basalt, his eyes on their stalks were thrust against the sandy underside of the rock. Where his pincers had been cut off, thick yellow fluid pearled out like sweat.

Where the basalt blocks ended and disappeared under the washed-up sand, my parents stood. My mother leaning over the baby carriage. The figure of my father tall beside her, overseeing the children on the ground around him taking off their shoes. Had he made a mistake in the count and not missed me yet? I approached at an angle behind his back so he wouldn't see me come and quickly sat down beside my brother.

"Where have you been all this time," asked father sternly.

"I was just looking at the fishing a minute," I replied, as I bent as far as possible over my shoes and made vain attempts to undo the laces. "They caught a crab."

"In the future you stay with us and you'll stop acting as if you don't belong."

"They burned his eyes with a cigarette. The crab's. I heard him squeak."

"Did you hear what I said?"

"Yes, father."

"Bear it in mind!"

Our shoes, tied together by the laces, socks inside them, were hung over the handle of the baby carriage. We walked south along the quiet beach. Despite the early hour quite a few people were already there. The baby carriage left a deep trail, father and mother each pulling a side of the handle. The shoes dangled between them.

"Shall we sit over there, wife," asked father, and pointed upward. "Or would you rather be in the shade of a tent."

"No, not so close to the people," she answered.

The baby carriage was laboriously pulled up to where the beach was higher and the sand whiter. The shells that lay there were bleached chalk white. Pieces of weathered wood lay around, washed up during the past winter. My brother picked up a heavy piece with rusty, crooked nails sticking out of it. He came over to walk beside me and threw his arm around my shoulder.

"This makes a beautiful sacrifice table," he said. "Just what we need. You're to catch them, you're good at it, aren't you. They used to call you Crabby, remember? Those trashy kids last year, you know who I mean."

I nodded, but I hoped that he would forget. Or lose the piece of wood. Maybe father would take it away from him when he saw the rusty nails.

"You better be careful not to cut your hands on it, that's very dangerous," I said loudly. "People have died from that, from blood poisoning."

"Throw that wood away," said father. "There are nails coming through it on all sides."

My brother squatted down and began to dig a hole with his hands.

"I'll bury it in the sand," he said. "Then no one can step in it."

When I looked back I saw that in the place where he had buried the piece of wood he had thrown up a mound of sand. He was sticking a twig in the top.

The baby carriage foundered in the soft loose sand and jerked to a standstill. The baby began to cry. My mother bent over the carriage and the baby went quiet.

"The darling," said mother. "You don't know you've got him." Using the carriage for support she let herself sink down on the sand. There she stayed, out of breath.

"Do you want to stay here," father asked her.

"It's the same as anywhere else," she answered.

My father sat down beside her. He took a short comb from his pocket and pulled it through his thick black eyebrows, then his moustache.

"Make sure you stay close," he cautioned us. "And don't go in the sea or your feet won't be dry in time for church."

"Yuck, do we have to go to church," cried my brother.

"You don't have to, you may," said my mother with pursed lips.

"Good, I may, then I won't," he said.

My father threw a somber look in his direction. My brother slowly crawled away on hands and knees toward the mound of sand. He looked around for me and beckoned with his head, but I didn't follow him.

When we came back from church, mother was still sitting in exactly the same position. But she must have moved because she had the big hamper on her lap.

"And how was the sermon," she asked.

"One of the children will tell you, then I can find out how well they listened," replied father, as he sat down beside her.

"And what was it about," mother asked me.

I pursed my lips and knit my brows.

"Well, can't you remember?"

I nodded, while my gaze followed the blue notice boards that had been placed at regular intervals behind the barbed wire, with white letters that said: ENTRY TO THE DUNES FORBID-DEN. I couldn't read the third one from where I was.

"Was it about the Old or the New Testament?" she asked encouragingly.

"Why don't you let him stew in his own juice, he's just being pigheaded," said Lea.

"Keep out of it," commanded my father in a strict voice. "Now then, what was it about?" he asked me. "Speak up."

"About God," I said dejectedly, as I dropped my head and stared at the sand.

My brother began to laugh.

"Church is always about that, stupid, about God."

"The only time he can open his mouth is when there's some-thing to eat," said father.

Mother sighed and opened the hamper.

"What would you like, a ham or a cheese sandwich?" she asked, while opening up a sandwich now and then to see what kind it was.

"Shall we close our eyes a moment first," interrupted father.

Almost guiltily she put down the bread she had been ready to hand out, and folded her fat hands over the open hamper. The sharp edge pressed into her wrists, pushing up a cushion of flesh on both sides. My brothers and sisters folded their hands too.

"It's you we're waiting for," said father with restrained impa-tience. Slowly I put my hands in one another, but very slackly, as if they were tired and I was giving them a rest. I closed my eyes only some of the way, so I could keep seeing through my eyelashes. During the prayer I cautiously looked around. The children's eyes were squeezed tight, as though protecting them from the sun. With the exception of my older brother who I suspected was also looking through his eyelashes. My father prayed out loud, just like at home. When he paused I heard the soft rumble of the breakers, as if God was answering his questions from afar. Now and then passersby halted in surprise, then walked on, turning around for another look.

"Ham for me," cried my brother immediately after the amen. Father frowned at him.

"Ham for you," said mother. "And you? Cheese. And you cheese too. And what would you like," she asked me.

"I don't care," I said sullenly.

"Here you are, one I don't care," she laughed.

I didn't feel like eating. I pulled the sandwich apart and when father wasn't looking threw the pieces to a dog with a thick neck and short, bandy legs who was hungrily watching us from a distance. I threw the bread a little shorter each time so he had to come closer and closer to get it. The slimy lobes hanging down from his lower jaw grew very sandy.

"Don't," ordered father. "Look at him, that animal is as fat as butter. We won't give bread to baker's children."

The dog kept watching me for a long time with questioning eyes, his thick head to one side, his tongue, curled like a lettuce leaf, hanging out of his mouth.

After we had finished eating, my brother and I crept on hands and knees among the tents. Suddenly I lost him, but a moment later I saw him again. He was lying in the sand behind a tent and had pulled up the canvas a little. He beckoned me and held his forefinger to his lips to warn me to keep quiet. I lay down beside him and pushed my chin into the sand so I could look into the rosy twilight inside the tent. A fat, naked woman was standing with her back toward us and her legs spread wide apart. She was running a towel back and forth between her thighs. She had such huge pink buttocks that I felt the blood run to my face. Her feet were in the legs of a sandy swimsuit. My brother lifted his head to release the hand on which he was resting his chin. He pushed his thumb against his forefinger and pressed his lips to the cushion of flesh that bulged up on his hand. Then he blew. There was the sound of a loud fart. The woman stopped moving, then let the back of the towel go, pulled it up between her legs, and studied it closely. My brother blew on his hand again, but this time he misfired and it became obvious how the sound was being produced. The woman turned and looked straight at us.

"For shame, madam, making such dirty noises," said my brother slowly and with emphasis, in pretended outrage.

He jumped up, pushing himself off on me so my head shot further into the tent. The woman looked at me alarmed and helpless as she bent her knees and clenched her legs firmly together. She tried to hide herself behind the towel, but was clasping it so tightly to her breasts that they swelled over the top, giving her a formidable aspect, like a wrestler flexing his muscles. At that moment I was kicked viciously in the side of my body. My head shot back from under the canvas.

"You fuck off or I'll kick your guts out," yelled a man with a fat, furious face. He was wearing a swim suit and one of the shoulder straps fell down, exposing a good part of his hairy chest.

"You get the hell out of here," he hissed with fury. "Or I won't be held responsible."

Slowly I crept backward in the sand, and stood up when I was at a safe distance. The man was still watching me. I cupped my hands to my mouth like a megaphone.

"Dirty rotten baboon," I yelled, and took to my heels.

My brother was walking in a shallow pool left behind between the beach and a sand bank. When I joined him I saw that he had the wood with the rusty nails and was pushing it ahead of him in the water with his foot.

"A man kicked me," I said.

"He must have belonged to that fat cow. She can count herself lucky I didn't have my air pistol with me or I would have got her right up her turds."

"He had a lot of hair right here," I said, and I pointed at my chest. But my brother didn't appear to be listening. He gazed intently into the water.

"When I see a crab you have to pick him up," he said. "You have to look for them as well of course." Suddenly he crouched over the water.

"There goes one," he yelled. "Come here!"

I recognized its dark little eyes pushing out of the sand.

"That's no crab," I said, and tried to kick up enough sand to cloud the water. But my brother slipped his foot under the crab, which started to run off at an angle, looking like a piece of sand.

"Get him," he cried, and pushed me at the water.

I caught the crab, but left my hand underwater and pretended still to be looking for him.

"He's gone. He'll be buried in the sand. They always do that when danger threatens."

As inconspicuously as possible I drew my closed hand with the crab in it out of the water and up along my leg. But before I could put the crab in my pocket, my brother grabbed my arm by the wrist and twisted it so the inside of my hand came up and showed my curved fingers around the soft yellow underside of the crab's body. I tried to wrench myself free, but in vain.

"You wanted to keep him for yourself, didn't you? But you won't get away with it. Besides, it would be a dumb thing to do, your life is at stake too. The sun is now at its highest, look, it's right over us. Something terrible will happen if we don't sacrifice soon."

Squinting my eyes I looked up.

"You see," continued my brother, "it's beginning to turn red. In a little while it'll be blood red and every living thing on earth will die." He stooped down to the water and with his other hand grasped the piece of wood, bringing it closer and closer to my hand, with the longest nail aimed at the crab.

"Spear him," he ordered.

I looked at my brother. The curls falling over his forehead were glued to his face. The sweat running down his temples formed a delta on his sandy cheeks. Was he a priest and should I obey him? I looked up at the sun making that blazing crater in the tight blue. Gradually I felt the resistance draw out of my arm. My brother forced my hand down. The nail disappeared between two of my fingers and into the tender body of the crab. I heard a soft creaking and screamed. My brother let my hand go. In piercing the carapace of the crab the end of the nail had forced itself into my palm. I was afraid to look at my hand and

let it hang down loosely. Drops of blood fell in the water where
they formed clouds and dispersed like smoke.

My brother looked anxiously at my hand.

"Please don't tell father."

I shook my head.

"I promise to give you something."

"What?" I asked, not very curious since I imagined that no
matter what he gave me it wouldn't do me much good, as I
was sure to die of blood poisoning shortly.

"You'll see when we get back home. But if you tell on me
I'll say that you look at naked women in tents. Now wash off
your hand or you'll get blood poisoning."

My brother floated the piece of wood. The crab pulsed his
legs back and forth, regularly, as if learning to swim on dry
land. Blood from the head of the nail ran down on his shield.
My brother squatted alongside and pushed the crab down the
nail. Then he gave the wood a shove and it slowly bobbed away
from us.

My father firmly held the stopper of the bottle of soda with
his palm as he pressed the metal spring outward. Low in the
bottle tiny bubbles began to rush up. He let the gas escape a
little hiss at the time. But there was still enough energy left
to make the foam run over our hands when he filled the tin
mugs we held up to him. We started slurping straight away, to
lose as little as possible. When mine was empty I held the mug
over my mouth and sucked the air out, making it hang on by
itself.

"Don't do that, it'll give you cancer," commanded father.

"You know what happened to Uncle Barend," added mother.

I wiggled my jaw and the mug fell from my mouth in the
sand.

"That was because he always swallowed hot potatoes whole,"
I objected.

"You always know better, don't you," said mother. "Your
Uncle Barend used to hang the Maggi bottle from his lip. I can
still see him. We warned him often enough, but he was just
as obstinate as you are."

"Then I'll get it too, won't I." I inspected the blue and purple spot in the palm of my hand. In the center was a dark red puncture, but no more blood came out.

"Don't scoff," said mother. "You may have to eat your words some day."

"And now you're all going to be quiet for a while so I can have a nap," said father. He took a clean diaper from the baby carriage and spread it on the sand to rest his head on. Silence reigned. If we talked at all it was in whispers. Sound coming from afar seemed to be caught by the heat and prevented from reaching us with any clarity: the voice of the surf like the raking of gravel in a neighbor's garden on Saturday afternoons, musicians in the distance hoomm . . . hoomm . . . hoomm . . . the tuba.

When I was quite sure that father was asleep, I went over and sat beside mother, and nestled my head against her plump shoulder.

"What do you want," she asked.

"Can I go catching lizards in the dunes?"

"You'll have to ask your father."

"He's asleep."

"Then you'd better wait till he wakes up."

I looked at my father. The testy set of his mouth was gone, his lips moved slightly when he breathed out. He looked content and good. If his face stayed like that after he woke up he would let me go, I thought.

"He'll sleep for another hour," I said. "If I have to wait that long it'll be too late to go."

Mother studied father as if sounding the depth of his slumber.

"I don't want it to get me in trouble with your father."

"Oh, just a little while, I'll be back in no time. I might even be back before he wakes up," I said in a conspiratorial voice.

"Who do you mean by he," rebuked mother.

"Father," I said softly.

"All right then, don't be more than an hour." I leapt to my feet and threw my arms around her neck.

"You're hurting me," she said, pushing me away. "You and your rough bony hands."

But I still managed to plant a wet kiss on her cheek, which she quickly wiped off.

"Away with you, your father will be awake in a minute."

"I need a hamper."

"What for?"

"To carry the lizards."

"Don't tell me you want to take them home," she said in alarm.

"Of course, or it's no fun at all. I'm going to set up a terrarium."

"And what about the hamper?"

"You can wash it out. Lizards spend all their time in clean sand."

"That's what you say."

"Please," I begged.

"Well, all right. The flat hamper that's under the foot of the blanket. But don't wake your little brother."

I walked to the carriage and carefully pulled the hamper from under the blanket. My little brother, his face shaded by the hood, was letting great spit bubbles come out of his mouth. Suddenly his face puckered up and his mouth opened wide. I ran away, but before I was behind the nearest tent he was crying for all he was worth. I crept on my stomach toward the corner of the tent. "The Phantom Strikes Again," I thought, while easing my head around the canvas. My father was sitting up and looked around searchingly. Mother stood by the carriage, her hand tapping the handle to make it rock. But the crying didn't let up, my mother was in trouble. She lifted the baby out of the carriage and sat down. Then she said something to father, who handed her the diaper he had been resting his head on. She settled the baby in her arms with his head by her breast, and undid the buttons at the neck of her dress. Before she was able to cover herself with the diaper, the baby's mouth had begun to search, with short jerks of his head. She made a tilting motion with her shoulder and bent forwards a little, pressing the baby tenderly to her bosom.

When the boy stood up I saw that he was much taller than I had thought. He had very long legs with dark green baggy breeches hung around them in vertical folds, that bulged over his shoes.

"Old elephant approaches," I muttered to myself.

For some time now he'd been watching me catch lizards around a potato field planted in a valley between the dunes.

"Have you caught many?" he asked, in a high, crowing voice that had to be digested before the words made sense to me and I could reply. He drew the fingers of both hands through the lank yellow blond hair that fell down behind his ears. There were dark patches of sweat under the arms of his light blue shirt.

"I've got eight. Green ones. I only catch males."

"To fry?" he asked.

I stared at him a moment in surprise.

"No, they're going into a terrarium." It seemed fairly pointless to tell him that I didn't catch females for fear their babies would be left alone, and I would have been ashamed to make such an admission in any case.

"What's a terrarium?" he asked.

"A margarine box with earth and moss. You can make a rock garden in it too."

"Then why do you just catch the males?" he asked with mistrust.

"Because they're prettier."

"Oh, I thought you wanted to eat them. With rabbits you only eat the males too. But we can fry them all the same," he proposed.

"No, I need them," I said anxiously.

"Can I have a look?"

"You can't, the hamper isn't deep enough. They'll jump out if I take the lid off." He bent down and peered through the narrow crack I had left open, as I was afraid they might die otherwise.

"I don't believe you've got eight," he pestered.

"I'm going to catch a lot more."

"Well, you're lucky to meet me, because I know a good place," he said, pointing to the next rise. "Back there, in the next valley. It's alive with them. Are you coming?"

Without waiting for my answer he turned and took off. I didn't really feel much like going with him, but didn't have the courage for a direct refusal. The more so since he seemed to have no doubt that I would follow him. He didn't even look around. I followed him, dragging my feet. His shoulders were drawn up and angled back, while his long stringy neck pushed his small head forward as if to restore the balance. I thought of inventing a reason that forced me to leave in a hurry, but I couldn't find an excuse. Simply running away wouldn't do either. The boy would have caught up with me very quickly, especially since I'd have to keep the hamper straight while I ran. At the top of the dune he halted and waited until I came up beside him.

"There it is," he said pointing down, in a voice that no longer sounded high, but husky and secretive.

It was a deep valley, completely overgrown with dense brush-wood, dead birch trees sticking out like dry bones. Most of it was in the shade. Only the birches still caught the full sunshine. Not happy light, but blanched and sickly.

This is the valley of the shadow of death, I thought, with the sickness that destroyeth in the noonday. The valley from the Bible, that father had read of only yesterday. A great oppression came over me. I directed my eyes to the surrounding dunes, but there wasn't a living soul in sight anywhere. Nothing moved. Only the sea glittered far off, between two dunes, but veiled, no longer bright. Wisps of smoke spun around the sun as if clouds were being born in terrible swirl and ferment.

"There's going to be a change in the weather," I whispered inaudibly.

"That's where we go down," said the boy, pointing at the thorny shrub where a sandy path ran down the steep descent. He let me go first and he walked so close behind me that his knees touched my backside, which gave me an uneasy feeling. The shadows gradually moved up my body. It grew chilly. When we reached the bottom he pushed me ahead of him into the thick undergrowth.

"There are no lizards here," I said, as I stopped and looked at him. "It's too cold for them. You don't find them where there's no sun, they're a coldblooded animal."

"Some of the places here get sun," he said. He avoided my eyes and looked into the undergrowth with a frown on his face. On his upperlip and his cheek just beside the ear were flossy tufts of hair. You can't tell when he's lying, I thought, he has such pale eyes.

"The whole valley is in the shade," I objected. "The sun might come here in the morning, but not in the afternoon."

"Keep walking and you'll see," he said, and pushed me on with his body.

We came to a slight clearing that actually gave the fleeting impression that sunlight reached down. The grass was dry and the color of straw. There were black patches in it where someone had lit small fires. Dry twigs on the ground snapped under our feet. Under a lean-to made of planks stood six rusty food cans.

"Sit down," he invited in a tone of voice that announced this to be his cave or secret hiding place.

I sat down and looked up the dead trunks of the birches that we had just seen from the top. They were covered with a thick meaty fungus that jutted out from the bark. Bracket fungus, I thought. I recognized it from the picture in my book on mushrooms. Suspect, it said underneath.

"I don't think we'd better stay too long," I said. "Perhaps we should go right now." I pointed at the fungus. "That's the dangerous birch killer. It kills the trees, it sucks out all the food under the bark. The leaves shrivel up. They turn yellow and fall off in the middle of summer. Then the tree dies too, because it can't get oxygen anymore. And they're also a danger to humans, that's what it says in my mushroom book. You don't want to come too close to them, and never sit under them, it says."

The boy didn't seem to be very impressed with my information. He took a stick and tried to knock a piece of fungus down.

"They've been dead a long time," he said, "they're hard." He thumped one with his stick and it gave out a hollow, woody sound. But he didn't succeed in parting the fungus from the tree. With the end of his stick he speared something black and round, lying in the center of one of the places where there'd been a fire, and held it next to my face. It was a partially charred hedgehog. The quills on its back were burnt almost down to the skin and it looked like brush that had caught fire. I pulled up my knees to keep the juice that dripped out from getting on my shoes. The boy made a brief threatening gesture at my face with it, then he changed his mind, decided to throw the animal into the bushes stick and all, and came to sit beside me.

"And over there I keep beetles and grasshoppers and worms," he said, indicating the food tins. "It's quite a job collecting them. I lock them up for two days and then I fry them."

Suddenly he opened his eyes wide and looked at me compellingly, bringing his face right up to mine. I drew my head back and stealthily closed the hamper resting beside me in the grass, that I had been protecting with my hand all this time. I could smell that he'd been eating smoked herring.

"Shall we jerk off?" he asked in a hoarse voice. "See who gets it out first."

"What?" I asked.

"Jerk off," he repeated, and made rapid up and down movements with his half-closed fist by his fly, keeping his urgent and hungry eyes on me.

I realized what he meant and it seemed that his back looked even more angular and fragile now he was sitting. He must do it eight times a day at least, I thought. He's already suffering from the spinal consumption they speak of in *Silent Sins*—a little volume at home that I had sneaked out of the bookcase and looked through.

"Don't you want to?" he asked.

"I have to go back to my parents. I had to be back in an hour." I got to my feet and held the hamper to my chest with both hands.

"It doesn't take long, or does it with you?" he asked, and unbuttoned his fly.

I slowly walked away, in a manner that might have aroused the impression I was just wandering around looking for something.

"Chicken shit," he called after me. "If you squeal on me I'll get you. I'll remember your face."

Not until I was out of the valley did I have the courage to walk faster. Halfway up the slope I looked around. He wasn't following. The valley lay entirely in shadow, not even the birch trees caught the sunlight now. It was a piece of harsh wilderness, seemingly impenetrable.

"He doesn't have the strength left to come out," I said softly. He will be as white and dry as the trees around him.

The sea was smooth as a mirror, with an occasional tremor running over it, as over the skin of a large fish. But on the beach the heat formed small whirlwinds. A scrap of paper rose up, with a funnel-shaped root of wheeling sand. Fluttered lazily down again. I ran from the top of the steep dune, down through the marram grass and stopped at the high-water mark. There I opened the lid a crack, so air could get back into the hamper, and walked in the direction of the harbor. Lying among kelp and dried-out sea lettuce were little tubes that seemed to be made of very thin glass and sand. I tried to step where they had collected. They gave a prickling sensation when they shattered under my bare soles. As if I had brand-new feet that I was using for the first time.

Was it because I recognized the bike parked against a post by the shape of the frame and the license plate in a chromium-plated frame around the handlebar, that I turned back to see who was behind the clothes draped over it? I stopped open-mouthed. There sat our minister. His closed eyes shaded by the brim of a flat round straw hat slanting down over his fore-head. The straps of his swim suit had slipped, exposing two dark brown nipples with black hair curling around them, his hands rested on his thighs with the palms turned up. I could tell from the way his thumbs stood straight up that he wasn't asleep. His tired gray eyes opened and tried to look at me, but his gaze was imprisoned by the brim of his straw hat. He opened his mouth as though he wanted to speak, his jaw dropped and trembled. I turned and ran. The lizards inside the hamper drummed along with my wild gallop. Did I hear him call, or was it the surf? I ran by the edge of the sea. The breakers tried to throw lassoes of foam around my feet, but each time I escaped them. In the distance, near the orange-and-white striped tents, the bathers flattened out as in a magic mirror, took on monstrous shapes. Torsos parted from the hips, jerked toward the sky and dissolved. Was the terror there too? Breathing hard I stopped and looked back. The post was still there, but forsaken, bleached and unreal. Could he have dressed himself in such a short time and pulled his bike up the steep slope? Or had he too been a mirage, swallowed up bike and all by the heat, ironed into the haze hanging innocently in the distance.

"He's only pretending to sleep," I heard Lea say. "Shall I give him a good shake?"

"You mind your own business," said father, "and we'll be able to have some peace."

I raised myself, my head still heavy with sleep. The stiff spikes of the dune grass were stirring, the light had changed. Just as if the whole world had been pulled into a shed. A wall of dark storm clouds stood on the horizon, the sea before it was an ominous silver mirror. The tide was at its highest, the tents had all been moved up and huddled close to one another, making the narrow strip of beach look like a fairground. Water rushed up to fill holes, melt fortresses. Voices sounded loud and hollow as if the sea and the dunes formed a sheet which made them echo.

"Look at that," said father, "the sky will be black as pitch in another five minutes. There's some really dirty weather brewing. We have to hurry. Are you ready, wife?"

"Yes," said mother. She was leaning over the carriage and tucked the blankets securely under the mattress.

"Where are my lizards," I cried, hurrying to my feet in alarm and looking all around.

"How about that, he's decided to wake up," said Lea.

"I put the hamper in the bottom of the carriage," said father.

"But did you leave it open a bit?" I asked anxiously.

"No, of course not," he answered gruffly. "What do you think?"

"But they won't be able to breathe and they'll die." I had a hard time holding back my tears.

"I'm sorry, but that's the way it's going to be. We can't risk having those things crawl all over your little brother."

"But they're not poisonous."

"Be quiet," roared father, "or you'll make me lose my temper.

And get a move on, it's you we're waiting for once again. We'll never make it home in time this way."

"Here, take him his shoes," said mother to Peter.

My brother threw my shoes in front of me in the sand and sat down beside me.

"You're stupid to go off on your own," he said. "I found a girl and had myself a . . . ." He didn't finish the sentence because father was coming our way, but he illustrated what he meant by surreptitiously sticking the end of his thumb through his looped fingers and clacking his tongue.

"You know what I mean," he said softly.

"Get on with it," said father. "And be sure to wipe the sand off your feet or you'll be walking on blisters. Let's go, son," he said to my brother, "you can help me with the carriage." Together they pulled the baby carriage toward the nearest ramp. Mother had her hand on the back of the hood but didn't look as if she was doing much pushing. My smaller brothers and sisters were lost amid the general retreat. Everywhere tents were taken down and rolled up. Far off two beach attendants, their white trousers rolled up to the knees, dragged cane beach chairs up the dune, like ants toiling with peanut shells. I quickly pulled on my socks and shoes and ran after the carriage, which stood out clearly on the fairly steep rise despite the stream of day trippers all leaving the beach by the ramp. When I reached the boulevard I looked around. The sea was black as a slate, the breakers drawing long horizontal chalk lines on it.

On the way back the weariness of a whole day at the beach settled over us. We fell so far behind father and mother that my brother could yell obscenities in shrill fishwife fashion. He also dived into the vegetable patches beside the path to return with a handful of carrots which felt lovely and cool and were far crunchier than the ones we stole off the vegetable cart at home.

"That's because they come straight out of the cold ground," said my brother. "I know a good game," he continued. "We take turns closing our eyes, and we open them when the other one says 'now.' The vegetables closest to us at that moment are the ones we eat tonight." I liked the game for a while, especially for making the long way home seem short, but I lost my taste for it when my brother let me walk into a pile of foul-smelling rabbit shit lying by the side of the path.

Malevolent yellow clouds flew over us, sweeping up other drifts of cloud to become a single gray green field pulling like a cap over the last strip of blue at the horizon. The swallows flew close by the water, without a sound.

Father and mother stopped to wait for us.

"And just what have you two been up to behind my back," said father. "Get along, walk in front of us so I can keep my eye on you." With a mouthful of chewed carrot and our cheeks sucked in, we passed.

"It's almost night," said mother. "I've never seen anything like it."

"It's not just the weather," answered father. "Don't forget we're a month past the longest day. You can tell the days are growing shorter. It'll be dead of winter before you know it."

"There you go again, father," teased Lea. "The middle of the summer and you're burying the year."

"You're still very young, my child," father said to her. "You think that life is a game, that it will never end. But it evaporates like vapor."

As we turned into our street the first drops fell, striking large dark stains on the pavement. We were the only ones still outside. Everywhere people stood at their windows.

From the sun-room I watched the storm break over our garden. Hail struck the sloping glass roof over my head and on the backsteps the hailstones bounced up and rested a moment. But farther down the garden everything turned green, as though the grass was growing up to the sky.

"It almost looks as if the end of time is nigh," said father to mother.

"We made it just before the storm," she replied.

Over the enamel dishpan in the kitchen I carefully opened the biscuit hamper. The lizards were heaped together in a corner, limp and lifeless, like wilted broad beans. My eyes filled with tears but because I clearly saw how badly I had been treated, I managed to hold them behind my eyelids. It was as though my tears acted like a magnifying glass, because I saw the scaly skins of the lizards clearer than ever before. Gingerly I picked the fragile creatures up and laid them side by side on the sink. And I looked at them while listening to the thunder-claps coming closer and closer. My mother came into the kitchen.

"What's that," she said in dismay, as she looked at the lizards.

"They're dead," I said. "Suffocated," I added accusingly.

"And you put that on my sink where I have to cut bread tomorrow morning." She bent down and took the brush and pan. With her face turned away in horror she swept the lizards into the pan, opened the garbage pail and threw them in it.

"You can't do that," I cried out in despair, "they have to be buried." She didn't reply but hummed a little tune while she put the pot with butter beans on the stove and lit the gas.

"Why don't you listen to me? They can't go in the garbage pail, they have to be buried." I stamped my feet on the ground and yelled loud enough to bring father to the kitchen.

"First you calm down," he said, as he took my arm and held it in a vicelike grip. "What's going on here?"

"Those things of his are dead," said mother. "I threw them out."

"Now you can see for yourself that there's nothing but heart-break taking those animals out of their element. From now on you stop bringing them home, understand!"

"But it's your fault," I cried. "You're the one who put them in the baby carriage with the lid on tight!"

"What," roared father, "you dare raise your voice to your parents. Your hands will grow out of the grave." He jerked me out of the kitchen and pushed me up the stairs. "Out of my sight. I don't want to see any more of you. You'll go straight to bed without your dinner. That's the end of a beautiful day by the sea for you!"

Thinking up horrible things that ought to happen to my father I walked upstairs to the attic room. There I carefully took all the rabbit and bird skulls down from the beams and packed them in a box that had a layer of shredded paper in the bottom. Then I closed the box securely and tied it up with a thin leather strap. Why I was doing this I didn't know as yet. Maybe because something terrible was going to happen that night. Or maybe because I was going to run away and never come back. Tears of self-pity began to roll from my eyes, for having nothing but this little box of poor bones. I pushed it under the bed, at the back, level with my pillow. Then I crept silently downstairs. In the kitchen I squatted beside the garbage pail. It had grown dark and the thunder shattered right over our house. Amid the tumult I heard the clatter of knives and forks on plates and the voices of my brothers and sisters. Cautiously I gripped the lid of the garbage pail and eased it up a little way with my thumbs. Did I hear rustling down there between the tea leaves and the vegetable peelings? Wasn't that the scratching of tiny claws on galvanized iron? Catching my breath I listened. Then the kitchen was struck full of light. The house seemed to reel under the blow. In the fraction of a second that the light flooded the kitchen I saw the head of my father suspended from the hook where the old shopping bag always hung, right in front of me over the garbage pail. His face was drawn in long folds that sprang from the black craters of his eye sockets and his mouth. I jumped up and fled to the stairs with the light of the dining room at my heels as the door swung open. On the stairs I didn't seem able to make any headway. I seemed to wade through a vast spider web that became more impenetrable at every step I climbed. And there, at the top of the stairs, wasn't that the specter of the minister, a grimace on the chalk white lips? Or was it the tall brittle boy from the dunes? My eyes blind with fear I entered the attic and slipped under the covers, numb, pulling the blankets over my head. Lying on my back I took off my shoes and clothes and let them fall behind the bed through a small opening in the blankets.

The thunder had stopped, as if that last tremendous crash had cooled its rage. Downstairs father was playing the harmonium. He sang along in a low warm voice. My mother was singing with him from the kitchen. Their voices met in the hall and rose upwards.

My brother didn't turn the light on. He sat down at the foot of our bed and kicked his shoes off without undoing the laces.

"Are you asleep yet?"

"What's going on?" I asked.

"The old boy is droning away at the organ. Here, I lifted a roll for you."

I had to feel around a moment before I could find his hand in the dark. Distantly the thunder still rumbled vaguely.

"They're still flushing the shithouse out there," he said.

I put the roll on the floor behind the bed without my brother noticing. The rain had stopped. The water in the gutters ran away with a gurgling sound.

"They're still alive," I said.

My brother didn't answer. He stood up and undressed. Then he pulled his pyjamas out from under the pillow.

"They're still alive," I repeated. "Mother thought they were dead, she threw them in the garbage pail. But they're still alive. Just now I heard their little feet scratch on the sides trying to get out."

My brother flung the blankets aside and slipped in beside me.

"Why haven't you got your pyjamas on?" he asked.

"I was too hot."

"You're an oddball all right. Just when the rain has cooled everything off."

"Is it possible they'd still be alive tomorrow morning?" I asked.

"Everything is possible, except nailing a fart to a board," he replied.

"What time does the garbage man come?" I asked anxiously.

"At seven o'clock. And now stop your fussing about those animals, I want to sleep."

I turned on my stomach and put my head in the crook of my arm. Tears streamed out of my eyes but I kept back any noise because of my brother. The pillow grew wet, the sand rasped my damp cheeks. There's nothing I can do, I thought, I can't help them. I'll never be able to stay awake all night. And at seven in the morning the garbage man will be here.

Translated by Greta Kilburn.

BIO-BIBLIOGRAPHIC NOTES

Remco Campert (1929, Holland)
Started off as a lyric poet, belonged to the so-called "experi-
mentals." Still a lyricist, but also a writer of short stories and
novels. Translations of his work have appeared in several languages, including English, Spanish, German, and Russian.

works include

novels	*Het leven is vurrukkulluk* (1961) *Life is Delicious*
	Liefdes schijnbewegingen (1963) *No Holds Barred*
	Het gangstermeisje (1965) *The Gangster Girl*
	Tjeempie of Liesje in luilekkerland (1968) *Tjeempie*
stories	*Eendjes voeren* (1954) *Feeding the Ducks*
	De jongen met het mes (1958) *The Boy with the Knife*
	Een ellendige nietsnut (1960) *A Miserable Good-for-nothing*
	Nacht op de kale dwerg (1964) *Night on the Bare Dwarf*
	Hoe ik mijn verjaardag vierde (1970) *How I Celebrated My Birthday*
poetry	*Vogels vliegen toch* (1951) *And yet Birds Fly*
	Het huis waarin ik woonde (1955) *The House in Which I lived*
	Hoera, Hoera (1965) *Hurrah, Hurrah*
	Mijn leven's liederen (1968) *The Songs of My Life*
	Betere tijden (1970) *Better Times*

The story "Een reisje naar Zwolle" ("A Trip to Zwolle") from the
collection *De jongen met het mes* (*The Boy with the Knife*), was
translated by Sheila Vuijsje.

Hugo Claus (1929, Flanders)
Versatile artist. Studied sculpture and drama. Spent much time

abroad. At present living in Amsterdam. His work is varied in character: poetry, novels, stories, drama, essays, monographs, screenplays. He is a translator of merit (translated, among others, Dylan Thomas). Film and stage director. His work has been published in many languages (in the United States, England, Japan, France, etc.).

works include

novels	*De Metsiers* (1950) *Sister of Earth*
	De Hondsdagen (1952) *Dog Days*
	De koele minnaar (1956) *The Cool Lover*
	De verwondering (1962) *Wonder*
	Omtrent Deedee (1963) *About Deedee*
	Schaamte (1972) *Shame*
stories	*Natuurgetrouw* (1954) *True to Nature*
	De zwarte keizer (1958) *The Black Emperor*
	Natuurgetrouwer (1969) *More True to Nature*
poetry	*Registreren* (1948) *Registrate*
	Tancredo infrasonic (1952) *Tancredo Infrasonic*
	De Oostakkerse gedichten (1955) *Poems from Oostakker*
	Een geverfde ruiter (1961) *Painted Horseman*
	Van horen zeggen (1970) *Hearsay*
	Heer Everzwijn (1970) *Sir Wild Boar*
drama	*Een bruid in de morgen* (1955) *A Bride in the Morning*
	Het lied van de moordenaar (1957) *The Murderer's Song*
	Suiker (1958) *Sugar*
	Mama, kijk zonder handen (1959) *Look Ma, No Hands*
	De dans van de reiger (1962) *The Dance of the Heron*
	Masscheroen (1968) *Masscheroen*
	Vrijdag (1969) *Friday*
	Tand om tand (1970) *A Tooth for a Tooth*
	Het leven en de werken van Leopold II (1970) *The Life and Works of Leopold II*
	Morituri (libretto) (1968) *Morituri*

screenplays   *Het mes* (1961) *The Knife*
              De vijanden (1967) *The Enemies*

The story "De zwarte keizer" ("The Black Emperor") from the collection of the same name was translated by Hans van Marle and James S. Holmes

Jef Geeraerts (1930, Flanders)
Worked as Assistant District Governor in the Congo. After the declaration of independence, back in Belgium. Deeply impressed by his experiences, he wrote several novels, strongly autobiographical in character, which aroused a great deal of controversy. His latest book was confiscated because of obscenity. Shortly afterward, however, it earned him the Belgian State Prize for Literature. At present he writes, translates, is editor of a magazine, and writes radio plays. Translations of his work have appeared in several countries, including the United States, France, and Germany.

works include
novels   *Ik ben maar een neger* (1962) *I Am Only a Negro*
          Schroot (1963) *Scrap*
          Zonder Clan (1965) *Clanless*
          Het verhaal van Matsombo (1966) *Matsombo's Story*
          Gangreen I (1968) *Gangrene I*
stories   *De Troglodieten* (1966) *The Troglodites*
          Indian Summer (1969) *Indian Summer*
drama   *De zeven doeken der schepping* (1967) *The Seven Canvases of Creation*

The story "Indian Summer" from the collection of the same name was translated by Adrienne Dixon.

Jacques Hamelink (1939, Holland)
Poet as well as prose writer. Was awarded prizes more than once, and work of his has appeared in French and German translations.

works include
novel   *Ranonkel, een soort epos* (1969) *Ranuncle, a Kind of Epic.*

stories	*Het plantaardig bewind* (1964) *The Vegetable Rule*
	Horror vacui (1966) *Horror Vacui*
	De rudimentaire mens (1968) *Rudimentary Man*
play for voices	*De betoverde bruidsnacht* (1970) *The Enchanted Wedding Night*
poetry	*De eeuwige dag* (1964) *The Eternal Day*
	Een koude onrust (1967) *A Cold Unrest*
	Oudere gronden (1969) *Older Grounds*

The story "Een opgehouden onweer" ("A Pause in the Thunder") from the collection *Het plantaardig bewind* (*The Vegetable Rule*) was translated by James Brockway.

Heere Heeresma (1932, Holland)
Worked in advertising as typographer and copywriter. Made his debut with short stories in periodicals. Published poems, novels, and short stories. Also screenplays, translations, and spy novels. His work has been translated into several languages including English, Italian, German, French, Spanish, Finnish, Rumanian, Polish and Japanese.

works include

novels	*Een dagje naar het strand* (1962) *A Day at the Beach*
	De vis (1963) *The Fish*
	Geef die mok eens door, Jet! (1968) *Pass Me That Mug, Harriet!*
	Hip hip hip voor de antikrist (1969) novel-screenplay *Three Cheers for the Anti-Christ*
	Teneinde in Dublin (1969) spy novel, *Destination Dublin*
stories	*Bevind van zaken* (1962) *According to Circumstances*
	Juweeltjes van waterverf (1965) *Little Gems in Water Color*
poetry	*Kinderkamer* (1954) *Children's Room*
screenplay	*De verloedering van de Swieps* (1967) *The Decline and Fall of the Swieps*
Television-drama	*Met z'n allen door de vloer* (1968) *A-tishoo, a-tishoo, All Fall Down*

The story "Van de dwalingen uws weegs" ("From Your Evil Ways") from *Juweeltjes van waterverf* (*Little Gems in Water Color*) was translated by James Brockway.

Anton Koolhaas (1912, Holland)
Studied sociology; journalist and theatre critic; director of the Dutch Film Academy since 1967. Author of novels, short stories, poems, plays, and film scripts (subject matter largely based on animals.) Translations of his work have appeared in German and English editions.

works include

prose   *Poging tot instinct* (1956) *Attempt at Instinct*
     Vergeet niet de leeuwen te aaien (1957) *Don't Forget to Stroke the Lions*
     Er zit geen spek in de val (1958) *There's no Bacon in the Trap*
     Gekke Witte (1959) *Dear White*
     Een gat in het plafond (1960) *A Hole in the Ceiling*
     Een schot in de lucht (1962) *A Shot in the Air*
     Weg met de vlinders (1962) *Away with the Butterflies*
     Een pak slaag (1963) *A Beating*
     Een geur van heiligheid (1964) *An Odor of Sanctity*
     De hond in het lege huis (1965) *The Dog in the Empty House*
     Vleugels voor een rat (1967) *Wings for a Rat*
     Andermans huid (1968) *Another's Skin*
     Ten koste van een hagedis (1968) *At the Cost of a Lizard*
     Mijn vader inspecteerde iedere avond de Nijl (1970) *Every Evening My Father Inspected the Nile*

drama   *Niet doen, Sneeuwwitje* (1967) *Don't Do It, Snow White*
     Noach (1969) *Noah*

The story "Een gat in het plafond" ("A Hole in the Ceiling") from the collection of that name was translated by Sheila Vuijsje.

Harry Mulisch (1927, Holland)

Successful writer of novels and short stories. He quickly rose to fame and was awarded numerous prizes. He has written a few plays; was and still is coeditor of several periodicals, one of which he started. Work of his has been translated into several languages, including English, German and French.

works include

novels	*Archibald Strohalm* (1952) *Archibald Strohalm*
	De diamant (1954) *The Diamond*
	Het zwarte licht (1956) *The Black Light*
	Het stenen bruidsbed (1959) *The Stone Bridal Bed*
	Bericht aan de rattenkoning (1966) *Report to King Concatenation*
	De verteller (1970) *The Narrator*
stories	*Chantage op het leven* (1953) *Extortion from Life*
	Het mirakel (1956) *The Miracle*
	De versierde mens (1957) *The Embellished Man*
	Wenken voor de jongste dag (1967) essays and a one-act play, *What to Do on Doomsday*
drama	*De Knop* (1960) *The Bud*
	Tanchelijn (1960) *Tanchelyn*
	Oedipus (1972) *Oedipus*

The story "De sprong der paarden en de zoete zee" ("The Horses' Jump and the Fresh Sea") from *De versierde mens* (*The Embellished Man*) was translated by Adrienne Dixon.

Hugo Raes (1929, Flanders)

Teacher, writes for several periodicals. At first a lyric poet, now chiefly prose writer. His books, several of which have been awarded prizes, created a great stir. Some of his work has been translated into German.

works include

novels	*De vadsige koningen* (1961) *The Indolent Kings*
	Hemel en dier (1964) *Heaven and Animal*
	Een faun met kille horentjes (1966) *A Faun with Chilly Horns*

De lotgevallen (1968) *The Adventures*

Reizigers in de anti-tijd (1970) *Travellers in Anti-Time*

stories *Links van de helikopterlijn* (1957) *Left of the Helicopter Line*

Een tijdelijk monument (1962) *A Temporary Monument*

Bankroet van een charmeur (1967) *Bankruptcy of a Charmer*

poetry *Jagen en gejaagd worden* (1954) *Hunting and Being Hunted*

Afro-europees (1957) *Afro-European*

The story "Explosie" ("Explosion") from *Een tijdelijk monument* (*A Temporary Monument*) was translated by R. B. Powell.

Gerard Kornelis van het Reve (1923, Holland)
His first (and only) novel is already a classic. The argument about the nature and the interpretation of his work continues. Especially in more recent years he has taken religion, homosexuality, and death as his subjects, and his work is considered highly controversial. After some court cases because of alleged blasphemy, he received the State Prize for Dutch literature. Work of his has been translated into several languages including French, German and English.

works include

novel *De avonden* (1947) *The Evenings*

novelle *De ondergang van de familie Boslowits* (1950) *Decline and Fall of the Boslowits Family*

Werther Nieland (1952) *Werther Nieland*

stories *The Acrobat and Other Stories* (1956) written in English

Tien vrolijke verhalen (1961) *Ten Gay Tales*

Op weg naar het einde (1963) *Travel Letters, The Road Toward the End*

Nader tot U (1966) literary letters and poems, *Nearer to Thee.*

Taal der liefde (1972) *Language of Love*

The novella "De ondergang van de familie Boslowits" ("Decline and Fall of the Boslowits Family") was translated by James S. Holmes.

Ward Ruyslinck (1929, Flanders)

Published several collections of poems but concentrates mainly on prose now. Some ten prose works of his have been published, ranging from novels and stories to radio plays. Especially his later work is often satirical. He is a civil servant, working in a museum. He has received a number of prizes and awards for his prose. Work of his has been translated into several languages, including German and English.

works include

novels	*De ontaarde slapers* (1957) *The Deadbeats*
	Wierook en tranen (1958) *Incense and Tears*
	Het dal van Hinnom (1961) *The Valley of Hinnom*
	Het reservaat (1964) *The Reserve*
	Golden Ophelia (1966) *Golden Ophelia*
	Het ledikant van Lady Cant (1968) *Lady Cant's Bedstead*
	De Karakoliers (1969) *The Caracolians*
stories	*De madonna met de buil* (1958) *The Madonna with the Lump*
	De stille zomer (1962) *The Quiet Summer*
	De paardevleeseters (1965) *The Horsemeat Eaters,* including the radio play *The Corridor*

The story "De madonna met de buil" ("The Madonna with the Lump") from the collection of the same name was translated by Adrienne Dixon.

Jos Vandeloo (1925, Flanders)

Previously a mining expert in the Ruhr. Later, studied Dutch and French literature. At present working in journalism and publishing. His work, which is of great variety, received several literary awards. His novel *Het gevaar, (The Danger)* has been translated into several languages. Poems of his have been published in English, Spanish, and other anthologies.

works include

novels	*Het gevaar* (1960) *The Danger*
	De vijand (1962) *The Enemy*
	Het huis der onbekenden (1963) *A House Full of Strangers*
	De coladrinkers (1968) *The Cola Drinkers*
stories	*De muur* (1958) *The Wall*
	De croton (1963) *The Croton and Other Stories*
	Een mannetje uit Polen (1965) *A Little Man from Poland*
	De 10 minuten van Stanislao Olo (1969) *The 10 Minutes of Stanislao Olo*
poetry	*Speelse parade* (1955) *Playful Parade*
	Woorden met doofstommen (1957) *Words with Deaf Mutes*
	Copernicus of de bloemen van het geluk (1961) *Copernicus or the Flowers of Happiness*
	Zeng (1962) *Zeng*
drama	*De week van de kapiteins* (1969) *The Week of the Captains*

The story "De dag van de dode god" ("The Day of the Dead God") from *Een Mannetje uit Polen* (*A Little Man from Poland*) was translated by Adrienne Dixon.

Herman Vos (1928, Flanders)
Spent some time in Argentina, where he held a wide variety of jobs. At present journalist in Belgium.

works include

novelle	*De zonen van Pepe Gimenez* (1960) *The Sons of Pepe Gimenez*
	Een man kwam van de Cerro (1961) *A Man Came from the Cerro*
	Het ultieme salvo (1964) *The Ultimate Salvo*
	Variaties in het zand (1970) *Variations in the Sand*
novel	*Ik ben de maraboe* (1969) *I am the Marabou*

The novella "De zonen van Pepe Gimenez" ("The Sons of Pepe Gimenez") was translated by Adrienne Dixon.

Dirk de Witte (1934-1970, Flanders)

Teacher of Germanic languages. Published in literary periodicals. He was obsessed by the theme of suicide, which recurs time and again in his work.

works include

novel	*De vlucht naar Mytilene* (1965) *The Flight to Mytilene*
stories	*Het glazen huis geluk* (1965) *The Glass House Happiness*
	De formule van Lorentz (1969) *The Formula of Lorentz*

The story "Een blinde kat" ("A Blind Cat") from *De formule van Lorentz* (*The Formula of Lorentz*) was translated by Adrienne Dixon.

Jan Wolkers (1925, Holland)

Painter and sculptor (pupil of Zadkine). Made his debut as a writer at the age of 35. After this debut, which caused both indignation and great admiration, Wolkers earned a prominent place for himself in Dutch literature. Much of his prose has autobiographical overtones. Translations of his work have appeared in England, the United States, Sweden, and Germany. Several of his short stories have been published in foreign periodicals and anthologies.

works include

novels	*Kort Amerikaans* (1962) *Crewcut*
	Een roos van vlees (1963) *Rose of Flesh*
	Terug naar Oegstgeest (1965) *Oegstgeest Revisited*
	Horrible Tango (1967) *The Horrible Tango*
	Turks Fruit (1969) *Turkish Delight*
stories	*Serpentina's petticoat* (1961) *Serpentina's Petticoat*
	Gesponnen suiker (1963) *Candy Floss*
	De hond met de blauwe tong (1964) *The Dog with the Blue Tongue*
drama	*Wegens sterfgeval gesloten* (1963) *Closed Due to Bereavement*
	De Babel (1963) *Babel*

miscellanea

> *Werkkleding* (1971) *Overalls*
> *Groeten van Rottumerplaat* (1972) *Greetings from Rottumerplaat*

The story "Dominee met strooien hoed" ("Minister in a Straw Hat") from *Gesponnen Suiker (Candy Floss)* was translated by Greta Kilburn.